I0617812

a
miki starr
novel

also by miki starr

Well Runs Dry

Broken Promises

Blueprints

The Miki Starr Story Book
How to Write a Love Story

PSYCHO
(A Miki Starr Short)

Olivia
Rebirth of the Anointed

The Skinny Girl's Guide: to Channeling the Fat Girl Inside

Resplendent Thoughts
Muzik for the Soul

ZellaDora

a fictitious memoir

A REIGNSTORM PUBLISHING

MINNEAPOLIS MINNESOTA

The sale of this book without its cover is unauthorized. If you purchased this book without a cover, you should be aware that it was reported to the publisher as "unsold and destroyed." Neither the author nor the publisher has received payment for the sale of this "stripped book."

This novel is a work of fiction. Names, characters, places, and incidents either are the product of the author's imagination or are used fictitiously. Any resemblance to actual persons, living or dead, events, or locales is entirely coincidental.

PUBLISHED BY REIGNSTORM PUBLISHING
Minneapolis, Minnesota

Copyright © 2008 by Shawn Michelle Johnson

ISBN: 0-9721246-3-2

All rights reserved, including the right to reproduce this book or portions thereof in any form whatsoever without the prior written permission of the both the copyright owner and the above publisher of this book.

Printed in the United States of America

Book design by Starr Eclectic Concepts

www.mikistarr.com

Reprinted 2015

"There is no passion to be found playing small — in settling for a life that is less than the one you are capable of living."

-Nelson Mandela

ZellaDora

a fictitious memoir

Prélude

Those were the sounds which defined my existence.

The rhythm of life. That pounding, smacking, contact of sweaty flesh upon sweaty flesh. The hissing and moaning and beautiful profanity that was the theme music of my days of youth. Others may have thought it retched... a child subjected to such sonnets, but they knew nothing of beauty.

In those sounds – love. In that cadence – music. So long as that undeniable pleasure of my parents existed, my mother's wails and demands upon my father's continence, assured that we'd be a happy family for many years to come.

My mother never shielded her tone. I was never certain whether her openness was based upon her intentions all along or rather an inability to contain the carnal affinity which my father aroused in her. Either way, I was raised on their vibrations. Fed it like a hearty bowl of grain on a cold winter morning. Their prose awakened my soul most everyday (oft times more frequent than once) and brought a smile to my face and glint to my eyes.

I missed those sounds when I went away to college and had to rather settle on incarnate poetry of my own. There were several with whom I shared my bed, and although every experience was rich and fulfilling, bold and beautiful, never once had I matched the ethereal lilt of my parents.

I smeared away the tears that trailed the side of my face as my eyes remained deadlocked on the ceiling. I swallowed hard and smiled a bit though my soul was heavy and emotion was creeping slowly, threatening to take hold of my being and pull me inside.

The apartments were small and the walls like paper. They'd only recently moved into the unit next door, maybe it'd been three weeks... possibly less but I couldn't recall. They made love often. I knew this because their bedroom was on the other side of mine. When I could, I listened and with eyes closed experienced the joy he must have afflicted upon her body. He was an aggressive lover. I could tell by the solos on the wall. I guess she liked it rough.

But tonight...

Tonight was different. Something happened earlier. There were muffled voices which carried across the room. A coherent word or two speckled about was not enough to decipher the scenario. I'd fallen asleep. I couldn't recall when.

Thump.

Thump.

Thump.

The sound was steady, vastly different from the normal *th-wap*, *th-wap*, *th-wap* that typically struck in uncertain rhythm. My lids were heavy, and though initially I was unaware as to what had wakened me, the gentle taps against the wall behind my bed soon clued me in. I was suddenly fully awake for I recognized the rhythm. It was familiar and a feeling not unlike panic though much more positive by definition overcame me. I searched for the remote and switched my television off. I must've fallen asleep to its tenor.

Thump.

Thump.

Thump.

Something was missing, somehow the scenario incomplete.

Frantically I searched the room. The window! Unnecessary ambience. Without haste, I moved across the room and pulled the frame down swift and firm. I returned to my temporary resting spot, on my back, eyes to the ceiling, breath on inhale... and out easy and as hushed as possible.

I listened carefully.

Her prose came to me. Muffled moans and staggered breath becoming louder as he stroked deeper. She called out, and I imagined his flesh beneath her nails. I'd never met them; I hadn't seen her as far as I was aware. So I only imagined... imagined her face brown like my own. Her mane thick and course with sweat like hers was, like my mother's was, the morning after. Her legs luscious and firm and wrapped around his waist, locking him there and insisting by their mere presence that he go deeper, further within.

I envisioned his face brown like my father's. His back strong and masculine, muscles flexing as he stroked. Sweat dripping from his brow... to her... further connecting the two.

I fantasized that they were them. That my neighbors were them. That they were my parents. My parents before she died. Before my mother fell ill and died, leaving my father alone and helpless. In my mind, in that moment, I was twelve, one of the last few years those sounds existed in my household and that impetuous call to God above was that of my mother.

I was pleased though my pleasure birthed no physical arousal. To do so would be utterly incongruous for in my mental these were the sounds of God and Earth, my own personal God and Earth eternally blessed Mother and Father.

It'd been nearly a year, the time that I'd been gone from Jacob and Zahrah's nest, since I'd ceased mourning the loss of Zahrah... my matriarch. My mother. I hadn't released her but rather only stopped. Simply stopped. No closure, no moving on. It was now my time to purge. I sensed it creeping, its presence hovering above me, breathing down my neck. I listened to her who was now Zahrah and his grunts which had become Jacob's promises to love and cherish her for all of her days...a promise he kept and continued even in her passing.

They were beside me now. I could smell her ambrosial scent and hear her weeps and moans and sighs. I could feel her mane, thick and coarse yet feathery soft; sweep the side of my face.

"Jacob," she whispered. *"Oh Jacob... I love you."*

I listened to every syllable, noun, pronoun, every adjective and verb. The thumping from behind the wall had ceased and was replaced by the thumping of my heart. My body shook as hers vibrated. It shook, and my palms locked across my abdomen as her legs locked around his waist. A painful wail escaped my frame as a guttural moan escaped her lips. My eyes closed tight in a failed attempt to dam the salty flow as her eyes widened to connect with his as she reached her apex and I, mine.

"Oh Jacob!" she cried.

"Mommy!" I wailed.

The thumping from behind had ceased long ago. My heart's pounding continued as I sat upright with a start. Frantically I sought their presence, but I was alone. I felt my bed around me... it was cold. The room was dark and silent. My forehead fell against my palm, and I shook my head from one side to the other and back. I reached to scratch the back of my scalp; my lioness mane had come undone. I inhaled deeply then slowly pushed from the size bed fit for a Queen, fit for me, Zella Dora Robeson. Named by my mother. Zella for my maternal great-grandmother and Dora for my aunt who passed only months prior to my birth. My surname evidently inherited from being a descendent of the late actor, athlete, and *'faiseur de tout'* Paul Robeson.

I staggered across the hardwood floor of my one room apartment to the bathroom. I shielded my just-brown eyes with the embedded golden embers from the light as I flicked the switch up. Stiff with layers of old paint, I offered more effort than one should have for such a simple task. I stood before the mirror, removing my hand from my face. I looked at my reflection looking back at me. My face was drenched from tears. I studied my features and saw hers staring back.

I chuckled. I sniffed and chuckled.

I sniffed and smiled and chuckled.

It was over and I knew it. I loved her in life, and I knew she'd be with me in death every time I passed a mirror or spoke a word. Every time I laughed or flashed a smile, she was there.

My matriarch.

My mother.

And now after six long years, I could move on. I was ready.

1Chapitre Un

The telephone ringing vibrated inside my mind.

In moments like this, I wished that I'd taken the Illinois Bell sales assistant up on the offer to add voicemail to my phone plan. For an additional couple bucks per month, I'd be able to ride this out for maybe one… two rings longer before I could roll over, snuggle my head deeper into my pillow and return to a peaceful slumber. But I hadn't. No, I decided it wasn't worth dipping into my monthly Starbucks stipend for someone to verbalize what standard Caller ID would digitize. Too bad I didn't have that either.

I thought I could wait it out. Eventually they'd have to hang up; it couldn't possibly be someone important. I owned a cell phone. It wasn't anything fancy, an outdated Nokia that took up an excess amount of space in my bag. It was one of those pay-as-you-go plans. Its purpose was to keep me available to my dad. I needed for him to reach me whenever, wherever. If it were him, the Basie tune I downloaded would be pleasantly lulling me into consciousness rather than the pesky ring-ring-ring of my landline. For a fleeting moment, I thought it could be Ayinde or Darwin, but they, too, knew the best method of reaching me in an emergency.

The ringing persisted. I buried my face deep in my pillows and let out a fierce growl. My fingers somehow managed to find their way through my tangled locs of hair to massage my scalp. I sent a silent prayer for peace. It'd been a long night, and the last thing I wanted was to desert my current position.

But… the ringing persisted.

"Alright, alright, alright!" I rose from my bed, pillow in hand as though keeping that object near my side didn't make it so. As though holding on to a part of my slumber could somehow keep me in that state.

"This better be good," I grumbled as I sat upright, slamming my bare feet to the wood floor. I stood and crept across my studio apartment to the recliner chair, the one my dad had for years until Mommy, on the twentieth anniversary of their union, bought him the one he presently watches his shows in.

I sat and stared at the phone, an old thing with a rotary dial. For how old it was, I was in awe that it found the energy to screech so loudly. I stared down at the ringing phone sitting there on the cute little oak table I'd found at Goodwill a few months earlier.

"Robeson residence," I spoke in my most business-like manner, more than prepared to tell the person on the other end of the line as professionally as possible to *"f'k off"*. However there was no immediate response to my greeting. "Hello? Robeson residence."

Now my face was becoming warm. I was prepared to hang up and in a state of pisstivity, return to my bed when a small voice came through.

"He's seeing someone else."

The voice was so small, so distant, I couldn't make out who it belonged to. "Excuse me?"

"I don't know what I'm going to do."

"Ayinde?"

"He's killing me, destroying me from the inside out."

"Ayinde, is that you? What are you saying? Is this about Marcus?"

"Zella."

"Yes?"

Silence.

I waited but there were no words following, only the sound of heartbreak. I was fully awake now; there'd be no more slumber on this day, not before long past the time where the sun would sink below the Earth. I gave another moment for her to offer up something more. She did not.

"Ayinde!"

"Huh?"

I tugged my hair in frustration. "What's going on? Where's Marcus?"

"He left."

"What do you mean he left? You two broke up... again?"

"No."

More silence.

"Ayinde!"

"Huh?"

I tossed my head back, blinking my eyes at the ceiling, counting backwards from three. I had a sudden and incredible urge to relieve my bladder. I took the phone by its handle, the receiver cradled in the crook of my neck. The telephone cord was a hundred-footer, long enough that my old rotary could act as an awkward portable. I carried it across the room to the bathroom. I pushed my panties to my ankles and sat before I spoke again.

My tone was soft when I addressed my friend. "Ayinde, have you been drinking?"

Her tone was innocent when she replied, "Yes."

"Baby, what time is it?"

"I don't know, maybe eight."

I let the phone slip from my ear but caught it before it could fall.

I took in a fresh batch of oxygen and withheld any desire to curse. Replacing the phone to my ear, I spoke, "Hold on."

I stood, wiped, and flushed, then carried the phone to my bed. "Yinde, are you still there?"

"Uh huh."

I opened the drawer of the table at my bedside and sifted through. I really needed a drag. I found the Ziploc bag in the back with four joints left inside. I pulled one out, lit it, and sucked long and hard.

"Did you and Marcus get into a fight this morning?" I asked while managing to hold the smoke in my mouth, allowing it to slowly leak into my lungs.

"No, he went to work. He *said* he was going to work."

"So how did you decide he was cheating?"

"I didn't decide it, Zella!"

I let out an exasperated sigh. "Fine, how do you *know* he's cheating?"

"Evidence. What do you think? I found evidence. You don't believe me."

Oh, I believed her. "I'm not saying that I don't believe you."

"You think I'm making it up. Everyone's not so perfect like you."

"I didn't say -. Okay, Yinde, how much have you had to drink?"

"I'm not drunk."

I picked up my watch and checked the time; it was 7:48 am. Doesn't make one much value sobriety either, but I knew Ayinde was fragile and when dealing with her one had to form their sentences carefully.

"Sweetie, what have you been drinking?"

"Vodka."

My eyes grew large as saucers but I shook it off. "Straight?"

"Not at first."

"I'm coming over, okay?"

"Okay."

She hung up before I could make another utterance. I sat, my eyes on the receiver, my joint burning between my fingers. I hung up the phone and took another hit.

AYINDE DOMONIQUE PHELAN

Ayinde was one of my closest friends. I knew a lot of people but had only a couple friends. She was four years my junior and regarded me as more of a big sister. I was honored to be that to her.

Yinde was a freaking blast to be around; she was funny and outgoing, unique and spontaneous. But she was troubled, deeply so. She was an experiment gone too far. The daughter of a White mother who had an extramarital affair with a Black man ten years into her marriage and two Caucasian children later. The step-daughter of a White man who despite all his efforts could never seem to escape the reality that her brown skin tone was a constant reminder of his wife's infidelity. The young sibling of the two White children who didn't understand how to dismiss what her flesh tone and kinky hair represented to the family, not to mention the stigma resulting from being the kids with the *"whore mother and nigger sister."*

Granddaughter of established racists who could never quite seem to remember her name but rather referred to her as *"the brown one."* A young woman with no identity, no culture, no love, no home. No self esteem. The only blood tie she had was her baby brother Josiah, born five years after the melee. The only Phelan family member with enough courage to love her as she was. Unfortunately, his love alone wasn't enough.

At sixteen, she escaped her lily White neighborhood and landed on her father's doorstep where she spent one tumultuous year trying hard to fit in with her new, colorful surroundings and a father that drank too much, while doing her best to escape his incestuous advances. He was shot and killed in a bar brawl over a five dollar bet. She never mourned his death.

A month later, she legally became Ayinde, the name of her father's sister, an aunt she'd heard about but hadn't ever met. She never told me her birth name. She'll never tell anyone.

She'd been with Marcus for two years. In that time, he's gotten one woman pregnant (abortion), left her twice, and cheated on countless occasions. He's no good for her, he keeps her buried, but he tells her he loves her because he knows that is what she craves. No one can convince her to leave him because she loves him, or at least she thinks she does, and chooses to believe that he feels the same way. It scares me when these things occur. My friend is a wounded animal, starved for attention and negative is how it best resonates with her.

I sat the phone along the bedside and again rose to my feet. She'd drink herself into a coma if I didn't stop her, all so that Marcus would come to her bedside and hold her hand. So he'd promise to be there for her and swear to her that an act such as this would never happen again. She wouldn't want him to say he was sorry. She needed him to show it. Demonstrative love. My fear was that someday Marcus would decide he was over her antics and leave her to die. This struggled against my hope that he would someday leave her once and for all.

I had to pull myself together as quickly as possible; she'd already been drinking for at least an hour as far as I knew. I took a final puff on my herb before I put it out in my ashtray. I jumped from the bed, slamming my naked feet onto the faux oak, moving pointedly to the bathroom. There was no time to be thorough. Instead I adjusted the running water in my sink and took a towel from the cabinet behind me. I washed my face first, then cleared any remaining debris with a witch hazel soaked cotton ball. I pulled my underwear off and tossed them in the hamper. With my lathered towel, I took a swift bird bath or as my aunt used to call it, a hooker bath.

My cell phone cried out from the other room.

Oh now what? I thought to myself.

Quickly, I pat myself dry and rushed to my phone to see if it was Ayinde calling again. It was Darwin.

"Good morning."

"Hey, what's up, D?" I grabbed a fresh pair of undies from the drawer and performing a balancing act, held onto my phone and pulled the fabric over my buttocks.

"Nothing, chillin'."

"Are you at work?"

"Of course, but I just got the strangest call a minute ago."

"Ayinde?"

"I guess you've already talked to her."

"A few minutes ago." I took this call as my cue to move faster. I held the phone between my ear and shoulder as I tried to dance into a pair of jeans. I listened to Darwin as I fumbled through my small closet for a thick enough hoodie and a pair of worn gym shoes. "Hey, what's the temp outside?"

"Uhm, it's kinda cool this morning. Probably low fifties right now, not too bad."

I nodded at the sweatshirt I'd picked out, good choice.

Darwin continued, "So what's going on with her? Did Marcus do something? She wasn't clear, she kinda just rambled on."

"Oh, she's drunk."

"She's drunk?" Darwin's voice raised with astonishment.

"Oh yeah. Drunk." I ran to the bathroom and spread toothpaste across my brush. "See wez Wakus is cheday."

"She said what was that?"

I quickly spit and rinsed. "My bad. She says Marcus is cheating. Says she has evidence, I don't know. I'm on my way over there."

"So she's drunk. From what?"

"Vodka."

There was a pause. I could hear and translate the hemming and hawing coming from Darwin's side of the conversation. "What's…

Zella, it's barely after eight in the morning."

"I know."

Darwin sighed dramatically. "Well alright, keep me posted okay."

"I will. Hey, I know you gotta get back to work, so I'll make it quick. I wanna go back to school."

"Wow. So when did this life changing decision come about?" Darwin asked, a smile in his voice.

"Last night. I can't explain it to you, but… something happened. Something miraculous and freeing, and I think I'm finally ready to get back to living my own life." I stood for a moment at my doorway, keys in hand, forgetting about Ayinde and her psycho-drama and for a moment, just a selfish moment, focused on me.

"Are you thinking about leaving us and going back to London?" he asked fearfully.

"No," I reassured. "You know I can't leave my dad. But I do think I'll go up to Northwest and check out the campus."

"Hey, good for you. You know I'm proud of you, Z."

"I know. Means a lot." I snapped back to reality. "I gotta go."

"Okay, later."

I grabbed a book for the short train ride and rushed out of the door.

There was a Starbucks on the corner a block away from Ayinde's apartment. I was in a hurry. I knew she needed me, but more importantly, I knew that I'd be unable to function or be any bit of understanding had I arrived without the benefit of my morning caffeine fix. And she'd been drinking all morning; a little caffeine might be just what she needed to offset the effects alcohol may have had on her.

I could hear a loud commotion as I neared Ayinde's door. The sounds of shattering glass traveled into the hallway. Panicked, I moved my legs faster and fiercely worked the key in the lock and let myself in.

"Ayinde!" I gasped as I entered the apartment. The place was a mess. Magazines, photos, clothes, and various other items were strewn about. Menswear covered the quaint sofa. Feathers covered nearly everything in the living space. Ayinde stood wild-eyed in the middle of the kitchenette holding a glass high above her head. My jaw hinges unlatched in my amazement. I could hardly believe what I was witnessing. Carefully, I sat the drinks on top of a speaker. When I opened my mouth to address her, I was surprisingly calm.

"Yinde, put the glass down."

She glared at me but did not move. I glanced at the nearly empty Vodka bottle sitting on the counter and wondered how full it'd been when she began her binge that morning. Before I could look away, I spotted a bottle of Rum on the counter behind her, top off and at least a glass and a half shy. I returned my focus to her.

"Ayinde. Ayinde, put the got-damned glass down."

"Aargh," she screamed, slamming the glass onto the floor in front of her.

I charged at her, balancing my way around the many busted shards of glass. I grabbed her tight, using the force of all my weight to push her away from the row of dishes she'd prepared to destroy. Her back slammed hard against the refrigerator. She was a slight bigger girl than me, but I was determined not to lose the upper hand as she struggled hard against me. I pushed against her repeatedly until she finally allowed her muscles to begin to relax.

Calmness crawled slowly but steadily into her eyes, and her face went from anger to sadness. Tears welled up as she crumbled into my arms. I fell to my knees with my friend in my possession, rocking her, consoling for what I didn't really have a clue. I noticed the trail of blood running down her leg.

"Oh, Yinde," I lamented. "Let me clean this up."

"Leave it."

"You can't just leave it; you don't know how deep it is. What if it needs stitches?"

She pulled forcefully from my grasp and struggled to her feet.

"What, are you deaf? I said leave it."

"Fine. Leave it. But what's Marcus going to think when he comes home and sees your leg, sees his house?"

"Hopefully, he'll feel how I feel."

I raised my body from the floor. "But what did he do?"

Seemingly excited for the opportunity to share her discovery, Ayinde's eyes lit up as she moved across the room to Marcus' workspace which seemed to be the only spot in at least this section of the apartment left unscathed. His laptop sat open on the desk. I was taken aback by the rotation of photos of Marcus and Ayinde that transitioned in and out as his screensaver.

"I'll show you."

I moved cautiously toward the computer as she jiggled the mouse and struggled to position the cursor to highlight a block of text. It was a previously sent message from an online networking account. I read softly, audible but barely.

"Damn, that new pic you put up is hot. You should email me some personal ones. When you coming to the city?" My eyes rolled the back of my head. *This* was the "evidence" that had me out of my comfy bed way too early?

"He's so stupid," Ayinde spoke. Not to me specifically, sort of thoughtlessly. "He forgot to log out. Stupid."

I stood up straight and turned to face her, my hand on my hip and my expression stern. "Yinde, you have to clean this mess before Marcus gets home." I scratched my neck uncomfortably as I glanced about.

"She's not even pretty you know. I looked at her profile. She's not even prettier than me."

"I'm sure. You have to clean this. I'll help you, but you have to clean this."

"Zella, you're not listening"

My fists clenched involuntarily. Not because I wanted to hit her, not that she maybe didn't deserve it in this moment, but out of frustration for being caught up in this. That all too familiar feeling of defeat was creeping up, frustrating me further. I didn't know what to tell her. It was a sin to suggest she leave, him but what else was there to say under such circumstances?

I exhaled patiently. "I'm gonna head over and check out the Northwest campus. You wanna go?"

Ayinde stared at me silently, her expression refusing to give way to her feelings toward me in that moment. Abruptly, she turned and grabbed a handbag and her house keys. She was already dressed, likely in what she'd worn to work the night before. She walked out the door. I grabbed our drinks and followed her lead.

The walk to the el stop was a quiet one. We walked arm in arm, less as a display of our fondness and undying affinity toward one another but more as a requirement for keeping her steady on her feet. She'd been drinking for years, even worked as a bartender four nights a week; her tolerance was high, so these occasional missteps reinforced my suspicions that she'd overdone it.

I glanced at Ayinde in the cool spring sunlight. She was one of the most beautiful women I'd ever met with her honey complexion and deep set brown eyes. Her curls were a much finer texture than my own and hung at least eight inches lower. There were pink streaks throughout the front; a month ago they were orange. The tiny stud diamond in her nose glistened in the sun. The tattoo that traveled from her forearm, across her shoulder, and ended at the base of the right side of her neck was my design.

No one knew exactly what it was, not even me. It was born in a dream, one where I was spending quality time having an inaudible conversation with my mother. It was on a wall that was behind her. For that reason it was important to me. It was abstract, but Ayinde found it beautiful enough when she saw the canvas I'd painted it on, to have it permanently adorn her person.

She sipped her coffee and likely hoped that Marcus would stay with her. I finished mine off and prayed that he'd finally go despite secretly fearing for her life if he did ultimately decide to move on.

They'd met two years ago at one of the bars she worked and had a one night stand that had yet to end. Ayinde was looking for love, and she was sure she'd found it in Marcus. I don't know what he was in it for outside of an apparent great lay.

"What's with Northwest?" Ayinde asked, breaking me free from my thoughts.

"I'm going back to school," I answered while cursing silently as I watched the train pass above us.

Ayinde stopped. "Why?"

"What sort of question is that? Don't you think it's time? I've been out of school for six years because of my parents. My dad is my dad, and my mommy isn't coming back. I gotta try to move on with my life."

"I can't believe you're involving me in this." Ayinde snatched away and turned back toward her apartment. I stood, in awe, frozen as I watched her walk away from me. I shook it off and ran after her.

"Ayinde, stop!" I demanded.

She obliged and turned abruptly toward me. "What do you want?"

"Stop it, okay? You just stop it. Every time I mention school, you spaz. What's up with that? What is so bad about me finishing my education?"

"You know."

"No, I don't know, but let me tell you what I do know. What I know is I work in a print shop to supplement the minimal insurance payments I get."

"So what are you trying to say?" she asked defensively.

"I'm not trying to say anything and you know it. Nothing other than it isn't for me, it isn't how I saw my life, and now *I* want to reclaim my life. You still have some good years ahead of you, but *I'm* almost thirty, and I want something more from this world."

"You're trying to leave me."

"What?"

"If you go back and finish your program, what do you think you'll do? Your little job won't be enough, your little apartment on Greenleaf won't be enough. Why would your little undereducated, underachieving friend be enough?"

"I can't believe this."

My words were directed at myself. Not knowing what to do, my hand went to my mouth, squeezing it then letting go. I stepped forward, then back, hands on hips then back down as I paced. I walked a few steps to the bus stop and took a seat on the bench beside an older gentleman who was trying hard to pretend he wasn't paying attention. Ayinde coolly moved one of her hands to her mouth and placed a black painted fingernail between her teeth and chewed, a nervous habit which resulted in the absence of nails.

I rested my forearms on my thighs, leaning forward, ringing my hands in pure frustration. I was nearing the end of my rope, and at this point, it was taking all of my inner strength to pull myself back up.

"Ayinde, I will not leave you."

"You say that now."

"You are my friend, the presence or absence of a degree does not dictate my relationships. Can you understand that?"

Ayinde was silent. Her eyes glistened, but she held her head back, refusing to allow the approaching water to create a trail. I looked away from her and into the streets. I watched students heading to classes at their respective schools and felt a pang of envy. The bus finally arrived. The old man offered me a reassuring look before climbing on board. I half-smiled in response.

I looked back at my friend, "You think if I finish school, I'll return to London."

Ayinde nodded.

And you'll be left virtually alone, I thought. "Are you hungry?"

Ayinde shook her head and smirked. "Tired."

"C'mon, my little princess. We'll go to my house and get some rest. I'm not going to leave you. I'm here for you, okay?" She tried to look away from me, but I turned her face toward mine. "Okay?"

She nodded in response.

2 Chapitre Deux

I left Ayinde sleeping soundly in my apartment.

I hopped the train for the third time that day and returned to her place, hoping to beat Marcus home. I wasn't sure what time he'd be expected to arrive; it always seemed to vary.

When we'd arrived at my house, Ayinde allowed me to clean the crusted blood from her wound. It wasn't too bad, only a scratch. Her body had already begun the process of hemostasis. It was nothing some peroxide and gauze couldn't handle. She insisted that she did not want to clean the apartment before Marcus saw it, but I knew it was the liquor speaking. With sleep would come sobriety and then there'd be reality and regret to face up to.

I rang the bell, but there was no response. I let myself into the front gate and then the building and climbed the stairs. I listened carefully as I approached the door. I tapped lightly. Still no answer, so I used my key to gain access. The mess was everywhere. I'd sort of hoped that maybe I'd remembered it wrong… that it wasn't as bad as I thought. It was and I didn't know where to begin. I decided the most dangerous area was best. I grabbed a broom and began sweeping the shards across the kitchen floor.

With the help of the espresso shots in the cappuccino I picked up while en route back, I managed to restore order to my girlfriend's residence. The last chore remaining was to put Marcus' clothes away.

"What the hell are you doing?"

I jumped so hard I nearly bumped my head on the clothes rack. I dropped the jeans I was placing on a hanger. I swore to myself before turning to face Marcus. I was certain I'd make it without crossing paths with him.

"What are you doing with my clothes?" he asked angrily.

"Shit, I'd hoped to be gone before you got home," I said, picking the jeans up from the floor.

"Gone before I got home? What are you doing in my house anyway?" He stepped forward and snatched the jeans from my hand. "And messing around in my closet. Where's Snaps?"

"She's at my house." I walked past Marcus and out of the bedroom. I moved to get my bag and keys from the counter, but he cut me off. "Okay, look, damn it. I'm not trying to be in the middle of some mess."

"Half my clothes are on the floor, and I walk in on you standing in my closet holding my pants in your hands and you *don't* wanna be in the middle?"

I threw my hands up in defeat. "Look, man, I don't wanna be here. Yinde thinks you're cheating. *She* threw your clothes everywhere along with a few other choice items. *I* was trying to be a decent friend to her and clean it up before you got home."

Marcus seemed to accept this answer and backed away from me. I let out a ragged sigh and grabbed my bag and keys.

"Why does she think I'm cheating?" he asked this as soon as I wrapped my hand around the doorknob.

"Why don't you ask her?"

"Bitch, I'm asking you."

"F'k you."

"Let's go then. That's all I been asking you to do for the past two damn years."

Disgusted, I turned the knob and exited the premises. Marcus stepped into the hall after me.

"Keys, Zella!"

In my mind, I turned and chucked them at his head, watched the blood drip down the bridge of his nose. But in reality - "They're Yinde's," I said without looking back.

"Yeah right."

I moved quickly down the stairs and out of the building. I despised Marcus.

The advertisement in the Reader for the newly released independent film gave it four stars. I had to see it, the story of an older gentleman rediscovering his love for his wife after having had an affair with a much younger woman. I'd been sitting at a table outside of the Heartland waiting for Darwin and Ayinde to arrive, passing the time by chit-chatting with Penelope, the fascinatingly androgynous waitress who always managed to serve my table.

I expected the pair at any moment. We had time; the movie didn't start for another two and a half hours, and the ride downtown shouldn't have taken more than forty minutes. I stood to leave; Penelope signaled he'd be with me in a moment. I leaned against the rail and took in the floral scent of the warm evening air.

"So you're going to check it out?" he asked in that high pitched masculine voice that men who wished they were women spoke in, while clearing the minimal dishes I'd used from the table and handing me my small bill.

"Yeah, yeah, I'm going to check it out. It sounds interesting."

"Okay, well hey make sure you let me know how it is and if I should go see it. I hear it's awesome."

"I certainly will. I'll see ya."

"Enjoy."

I entered the General Store to pay my tab. There was a short line already. I picked trinkets from the display table idly as I waited. I glanced at the woman in front of me. She was patiently waiting her turn, reading to pass the time. Being the avid reader I am, I was always curious as to what others found engaging.

"Excuse me," I interrupted.

She looked over at me. I was momentarily stunned by her exotic beauty. She was striking. Her skin was as deep and dark as a Godiva chocolate bar. Her large coal eyes were round and innocent in appearance. She was several inches taller than me with elegant and delicate features. Her wooly hair was cornrowed in three thick braids that dangled near the middle of her back.

"Yes, may I help you?" she asked in slightly accented English reminiscent of the dialect of the residents of my former neighborhood in the United Kingdom. I hadn't realized until that moment that I'd been staring.

"I – I'm so sorry to interrupt. I was just curious about what you're reading."

"Oh, it's *A Prayer for Owen Meany* by John Irving." She was up. Momentarily she diverted her attention as she counted out change for Melody the cashier.

I became consumed with excitement. "Are you kidding me? I've been trying forever to find a copy of that book. It was one of my mother's favorites. I thought it was out of print."

"So you've heard of it." Her eyes lit as she spoke. "Impressive. Yes, yes, it has been out of print for quite some time."

"So how'd you get your hands on it?"

She turned back to address Melody. "Thank you," she said as she took her receipt. We stepped aside allowing another patron to be waited on.

"My mum found it for me. She has a gift of sorts. She manages to find all sorts of rare, out-of-print literary works. You should stop by my shop someday." She reached into her purse and pulled a bulky pocketbook forth. After hurriedly scanning the interior, she handed me a simple white business card that advertised her business: Lola's

Books. The contact read, Olufemilola Sahlemariam-Brown. "We're not located too terribly far from here, just in Wrigleyville. A short walk off the Addison stop."

I smiled. "Thanks, I just may take you up on that. I'm Zella by the way."

"Very pleased to make your acquaintance, Zella, I'm Lola." She took my extended hand in hers and shook firmly. "Well, Zella, maybe I'll see you around."

"Maybe."

She tossed her bag on her shoulder as I headed back to the counter to pay. I produced a five-dollar bill and handed it over.

"What's up, Mel? How's business today?"

"Business is business as usual. My God Z, that woman was gorgeous, don't you think? You think she's a model?"

I shrugged. "Possibly."

"Like that Naomi Campbell."

I thought she was much more beautiful than Naomi. She was a bookstore owner, not a model. But she could have been in a former life.

I looked toward the door in time to see Ayinde coming through followed by Darwin. I thanked Mel and joined my friends.

The film was touching. Being a sometime aspiring screenwriter with little talent in that arena, I take great pleasure in and am very appreciative of the independent film. I like to study them and use them as guides and research for my own writing. Thus the three of us made an appearance at the Gene Siskel Theater a couple times a month.

Darwin had gotten the news earlier in the day that he was being promoted. In celebration he decided to take us girls to dinner after the film. After some back and forth, we agreed on Uno's as the prime celebratory location.

We walked the distance to the restaurant despite Darwin's

objections and insistence on catching a cab. Hell, he was among the ranks of the hundreds of thousands of residents who took to the road everyday, his legs weren't really equipped for this sort of activity. But we could all use the workout. Besides that, I love downtown Chicago, and I especially love it after dark. The sights and the sounds, the people, all gave me inspiration for the things I'd write and the images I'd paint. The scent of it got hold of my spirit and I became one with this beautiful live postcard entrenched with art and culture as much as divided by socioeconomic status and segregation. I had my way.

The place was bustling when we arrived. It was a complete surprise for us to have been seated in fewer than twenty minutes. We sat in a booth with Ayinde at my left and Darwin across from us. I was so happy for my friend; he deserved all of his success.

"I ran into Margot the other day, did I tell you?" Darwin asked.

I could feel Ayinde tense and roll her eyes without looking her way. "No, where'd you see her?"

"At Starbucks on Clark."

I laughed. "Figures."

"She was with Shane. They're together again? I'm confused."

I looked away into the distance when I answered. "Yeah, they're trying to work it out." *Another beautiful person settling*, I thought.

"She says you're painting her."

"You're painting her fat ass?" Ayinde asked with contempt. "Are you sure you have enough paint?"

I ignored her comment. "Yeah, I am."

A waiter interrupted us, and Darwin placed our pizza order. "You don't seem thrilled about it."

"Oh, I love the idea of painting her. Despite the opinion of *some*, I think she makes a beautiful subject. But it isn't for her... the painting, it's for Shane. A birthday gift."

I looked at my nails and picked nothing from them.

Ayinde asked, "So why are you painting her if her reason bothers you so much?"

There was a hint of something in her tone, something personal. I didn't answer. I wasn't sure why I was doing it. I needed the money of course. But from a standpoint of principles, I didn't know if it was the right choice to make. But to deny a client service because I objected to the purpose of the assignment, being a gift to a man who'd raised his hands to her and demanded her value as a woman be submitted to him on several occasions, may not have been my place either.

As though reading my thoughts, Darwin added on cue, "You can't judge her decision. He's still her husband... Jake's dad."

"I know, I know. I just hate seeing women settle. I refuse to ever settle."

"Well, everyone isn't like you," Ayinde said defensively.

"I'm aware."

"You can just stop it with the subtleties, Z."

"What are you talking about?" I asked sarcastically.

"You two, please do not start. You two have been bickering more and more lately. You're giving me a damned headache. Now I brought you here to continue our good time and celebrate with my girls."

"Not to sound ungrateful," I began, "but why'd you bring us anyway? Where's Miko? Shouldn't you be celebrating with her?"

Darwin looked away nervously. He scratched his scalp which I was so sure wasn't itching.

"You didn't," Ayinde exclaimed. When Darwin's eyes instantly moved to the floor, Ayinde and I both threw our hands in the air and fell back into the bench. All I could do was laugh. Ayinde allowed her head to fall to my shoulder as she shook it side to side.

"C'mon guys, you gotta understand," Darwin said.

"What? Understand what? I understand you're ridiculous. What was wrong with this one?" I asked.

"See, Z, you be trippin'."

"Me? What?"

Darwin's single dimple showed through as he smiled shyly. The waiter soon placed the extra-large deep dish pizza on the table before us. A basket of deep golden fried wings were set beside it. Since we insisted there was nothing else needed, our waiter disappeared into the crowd.

For a while we were silenced by the delicious taste of the famous Chicago delicacies. Ayinde broke the monotony, speaking through a mouthful of food.

"C'mon, D. Talk."

"Alright, okay. But you're just gonna say I'm trippin'."

"You are trippin'," I said pointing a wing in his direction. "You might as well give us the specifics."

"Her toenails are too long."

I dropped my wing on the plate and sat frozen for a second. I turned to face Ayinde who was already looking at me. Simultaneously the two of us doubled over in uncontrollable laughter. We leaned into one another, laughing so hard tears streamed from our eyes. We struggled to regain our composure.

"Toenails?" Ayinde blurted. "You are *not* serious."

"Y'all are being unfair."

"We're being unfair?" I asked amazed. "You broke up with a chick over toenails. Are you hearing yourself? C'mon, that chic was hot."

"I know."

"And she had her own car, crib, and a good job."

"Check, check, double check," Ayinde tacked on.

"I know," Darwin stressed.

"I can't believe you opened up the door to let another dude get with her over some toenails. Ever heard of a nail clipper?" I asked. "You're sabotaging again."

"I am not. Dude, seriously. I mean, you should check out my leg.

Man, she'd rub her feet up and down my leg at night and at the same time playing tic tac toe with her damn toenails. And yeah, Zella, I know about clippers, but that wasn't the issue. Miko *likes* long toenails."

"Oh my goodness, you are insane," Ayinde stated as she reached for another slice of pizza.

I shook my head at Darwin. "It's always something, D. You know it."

"I know. It always *is* something." Darwin picked up a wing and fumbled with it as he spoke. "You said it yourself, Z, don't settle."

"Oh, so this is the part where you use my words against me?"

"Why not? They're befitting, aren't they?"

"As if it's applicable in a situation like this."

"You know what," Darwin began, his face serious as he looked into my eyes, "what is considered settling, is subject to the definition of the individual involved. So yes, my dear friend, to stay with Miko would have been settling by my definition."

I shook my head, accepting what I was being fed as though I had a choice, and returned to eating my dinner.

It was well past midnight when I arrived home. I tossed my keys on the ledge before ripping the elastic band from my hair and allowing it to fly free. I vigorously scratched the back of my scalp as I walked to my bed. I took a seat and yawned as I sifted through the drawer for my goodie bag. I removed the half smoked joint that was mixed in with the others. I lit it and inhaled deeply. Instantly my body relaxed and was able to unwind.

Darwin had insinuated that I was judgmental, that I held the decisions of others up to my set of standards. He didn't vocalize it directly, but he did insinuate it. So did Ayinde. I ran my tongue across my teeth. Maybe they were mad because I was wrong... or maybe they were mad because I had a point.

I let the drug dangle from my lips as I stood and shimmied

out of my jeans and socks. I sat the burning stick on the edge of the table temporarily so I could pull my sweatshirt over my head. I loved this time of day, the end of the day. Standing free from the confines of clothing in my own home, at ease from my herbal relaxation. I took the weed to my lips again and puffed as I walked to my bathroom, then ran me a shower. Leaning my back against the edge of the sink, I puffed until the remains threatened to singe my fingertips. I stepped in my shower and washed the dust and city fumes from my figure.

When I was done, I dried my body and wrapped the plush towel around my wet hair. I walked, nude, back into the main room. Thirsty, I took a bottle of water from the refrigerator, cracked it open, and turned it up walking to my bed. I stretched out on my back and looked up at the ceiling.

It was an old building that I lived in, a recycled residence. There were several unidentifiable brown spots on the ceiling and many nights I'd lie in bed awake and play connect the dots. Some nights I'd form mysterious constellations or reproductions of infamous pieces of art. Other nights my visions were much simpler. Frequently I could form the structure of my mother's face. That was my vision on this night. Follow the trail from point A until the image was realized.

A soft *thud* shook me from my trance, my vision dissipated. It was them, they were at it again. Most every night they found their way to one. Before my experience a few nights back I hadn't minded, but with each soft blow to our mutual wall, I was buried deeper and deeper beneath a blanket of emotion. I would tune them out... I would try.

Thud.

Thud.

Thud.

My nipples hardened, and I became sensitive where I was previously unmotivated. I fought to resist being pulled into their world. I shook it off and focused in on the quickly fading dots on my ceiling.

Thud.

Thud.

Thud.

The contact became harder, more intense. Her voice was muffled but none-the-less audible. My hand rubbed the length of my thigh. It was unconscious, a natural inevitable reaction. I inhaled deeply and tried to ignore their sounds, their rhythm against my wall, the melody of her stifled sonance. My eyes closed tight, and the world around me was erased. All but their sounds.

I tried to sing it away. It was a song my mother would sing to me as a small child, "Frère Jacques, Frère Jacques, dormez vous? Dormez vous?"

Thud.

Thud.

Thud.

"Sonnez les matines..."

Thud!

Thud!

And then I felt it... their presence, they were again beside me. They were loving each other on the bed that lulled me to sleep at night. I couldn't see them, but I knew that they were there. I was afraid, afraid to open my eyes for fear that she and I would come face to face. Fear that this experience was real and she did again, truly exist. But I feared not opening my eyes for if I did, and she was not there, I may die... right there on the spot, from a broken heart.

I tried to sing, "Sonnez les matines..."

My voice cracked. Warm tears tickled the sides of my face as they streamed from my lowered eyelids. I longed to scream, to cry out and demand that they stop. It's over! It's done! I cannot take it anymore!

Th-wap!

Th-wap!

Th-wap!

A fire was building deep inside, and I feared that at any moment I would explode. I loved Zahrah, my mother, but I did not want to experience this any longer, didn't need it. A scream was inside, and it echoed against organs and intestines, reverberated off kidneys and tap-tapped at my lungs until no more could be handled. I needed to escape it!

Th-wap!

Th-wap!

Th-wap!

And the scream grew bigger and stronger, inflated further by each and every continued expression of love coming from the other side of that damned wall until I shot forward on my bed and set it free –

"Stoooop iiiiiiiit!"

… the sounds were no more. I hadn't noticed that they'd ended… when they ended. I was only relieved that their lovemaking on this night was relatively brief – and it was over. I looked around the room which was dark with the exception of the illumination from the street lights.

"Damn it," I spoke softly.

I felt tainted. I jumped from bed and went into the bathroom. I splashed cold water upon my face then stood, bent at the waist, resting my weight on my hands that clutched the sink's edge.

"Something's gotta give."

I grabbed an elastic band from the counter top and forced my mane into it. I went to my closet and pulled a tee-shirt and a pair of flannel pants from a drawer and covered my body. I took a seat on the bed, one foot beneath me, the other resting against the floor.

I reached for the drawer, thinking I needed another hit but paused before opening it. I turned and slid from the bed and landed on my knees. And there I said a little prayer for my friends and their troubles. And there I said a little prayer for the soul of my deceased mother and the lost soul of my living father. And there I said a little prayer for me.

3 Chapitre Trois

The sun crept slowly over the horizon.

Its rays streamed through my window — but that wasn't why I was awake.

Thud.

Thud.

Thud.

The neighbors were at it again.

"Oh *hell* no!"

I snatched my pillow and held it tightly over my head. It helped initially, but their got-damned noise managed a way through to bury itself deep within my eardrums.

"They've got to be kidding me! Do they ever take a break?"

I flung the pillow across the apartment and jumped from bed. It was done. Over. I couldn't take it anymore. I shifted the position of the sparse furnishings I had and cleared a path. I grasped the bed post, bent at the knees and pulled. It budged. I pulled again, and it budged some more. I pulled and budged and pulled and budged until my bed was as far from theirs as possible and then I pulled and budged further until it crossed to the opposite side of the unit. It was arguably in an awkward position, too close to the door, too near to the kitchenette, but I'd make it work. I had to for sanity's sake.

I stood, looking into the vacant space I'd just created and smiled. This would work. I swept the dust from the floor and moved my easel nearer to the window. The windows were taller than normal and the ledge extended out far enough that one could sit fully on it. A few pillows to coordinate with my illegally painted walls – yeah, it would work. It would be just fine.

I stared out the window through the spaces in the painted glass at the pedestrians passing by. Work was slow today. I'd printed a banner and some signage for a company that had a tradeshow coming up, but otherwise there wasn't much else going on. I'd been reworking a logo that I was designing for a friend of an acquaintance, but my eyes were killing me and needed a break from the screen. The hollow sound of the large window vibrating caused me to snap out of my trance.

I looked up in time to catch the head nod of the young Jewish b-boy as he caught the edge of his skateboard in his hand. I waved him in as he approached the door.

"Waddup, Z-Roc?" he greeted as he entered the business establishment, the graphics shop I worked at a few varied days a week. Josh was a cute cross-breed of Hip Hop clashed with skater kid. I'd met him at a freestyle battle a year prior.

"Workin'," I replied as we gave a pound, slapped palms, and ended with a nonchalant snap.

"Yeah right," he laughed. "Hardly workin' is more like it. Ay, is bossman around?"

I chuckled at the sight of him looking around nervously. "No, you're safe. He had some errands to run, but he'll be back in a little bit to take over and lock up. I gotta get out of here soon, got an appointment with Margot in a few. Doing a painting of my girl."

"Oh word?"

"Yep."

"Ay, you mind if I check somethin' on the internet? Tek 'sposed to be rockin' some joint tonight, but I ain't got the flyer."

"So how you know it's tonight?"

"Word of mouth. Everybody's checkin' for Tek ever since he snatched Wookie's title. I just forgot which spot. I know Z-Roc be down wit' e'ything Hip Hop in the Chi. Don't tell me you fallin' off."

I had to laugh at that. Because I knew so many people around the North Side of the city it was assumed I had a hand or at the very least knowledge of all that went on in the city, particularly where Hip Hop was concerned. It was humorous because I, Zella Dora Robeson, was by no means a powerhouse or Chi-town heavy hitter. I was just friendly.

"Nah, I hadn't heard, but I've been dealing with my own mess lately. Must have earplugs in. Too much going on."

"Well you and A1 should come through."

A1 being Ayinde. I shrugged at the possibility. Told him maybe... we'll see. The shop's phone rang, cutting us off. I signaled my approval to Josh, and he immediately jumped into my seat and launched Safari. I answered in my professional tone with the pre-approved greeting. It was my father calling to talk about my mother.

I should have been used to it by this point and to a degree I was, my dad calling about some funny thing my mother had done or said. And indeed she had done the things he claimed she did and said the things he said. Except, my dad couldn't or maybe wouldn't accept the reality that Mommy had done these things many, many years earlier. He insisted she was there by his side. He could see her and hear her but only by day. By night... well, by night Mom was gone, and Dad would cry himself to sleep.

This is why I'd moved out. Watching my father hold one-way conversations with my mother throughout the day and hearing my father – the patriarch of my family – cry himself to sleep at night was keeping me trapped in the constant state of mourning in which he resided. It was a place that I did not wish to be. So I stepped out, not far removed but just outside the entrance to this place. Far enough to exist yet near enough to keep him from wobbling completely over the edge and falling head first into the deep end.

This was also why I could not leave. Who would take care of him? Who would prepare his meals for the week so that all that was necessary for him to do was nuke them? Justifying this act as his way of helping my mother around the house. Who would clean and dust and make certain that he bathed at least a couple times a week? Who would wash and shop and be sure that his refrigerator was stocked with his favorite beer? I wanted to leave, to get away and start again – but how could I go?

I observed Chaz, the owner, driving past the front of the building and warned Josh he had moments. Quickly, he moved from my chair with skateboard in hand and made it to the door. He paused and turned back to me. "Sub T's tonight. Tek showcasing, Apocolypse on the wheels."

He shot me the peace sign and was out the door before I could respond. The speed at which he disappeared from the premises was laughable. Josh was a good kid, but an altercation between Josh and Chaz and Josh's famed Magic Marker had him eternally banned from the establishment.

I glanced at the clock. I had to get going if I was to make it in time to prevent Margot from being stranded outside of my building. I passed the torch to Chaz as soon as he entered the store and headed out in perfect time to catch my bus.

"Look at you, right on time!" Margot yelled to me as she approached the door to my building, glancing at her watch.

I smiled and reached for my keys. "Eh, I was trying to give you enough time to find parking. C'mon, the light this time of day is perfect."

We jogged up the three flights of steps to my apartment. I opened up and allowed her inside. Once indoors, I instructed Margot to make herself comfortable and I rushed to set up.

"Thirsty?" I asked.

"Uptight."

"Why?" I laughed, secretly guessing the answer. I glanced back in time to catch Margot pulling her shirt over her head.

"Uhhh, this," she said as she unsnapped her bra.

I shook my head and chuckled, amused. I grabbed the large canvas I'd reserved especially for her from the back of the closet. I gathered paints and brushes of various sizes, a stained rag, and a small bowl of clear water and set up.

I'd placed a few hand decorated throw pillows around the window ledge. The sun was due to set relatively soon. The lighting in my apartment at this time of day was breathtaking. It alone is partly why I agreed to do this piece for her. I'd been anxious for some time to see the beauty the shadows and the light would cast over a human subject. Margot was the perfect choice.

Margot Belinda Kimmer

I met Margot a few years back. Met her through Kat, a former friend of Ayinde. She partied with us one night, and she and I clicked. She was a clerk at a local art supply store that I began to frequent when I learned that she received a 15% discount that she was more than willing to share with me.

Margot and I had a lot in common. There was our love for the written word, our love for the arts, and our keen sense of freedom and liberation. Neither she nor I believed in labels and limitations. We didn't view the world in color, class, nor ethnicity though we weren't so naïve as to believe such social stigmas were irrelevant.

Though by definition she and I would likely both be categorized as heterosexual women, neither of us believed in sexual specifications either. Oddly this was more a moral dilemma for me than Margot given that I also believed (though to some degree) in the Bible as the Word of God, and I was taught, courtesy of my mother's lessons in ethics and morality, that God frowned upon same sex relations.

Unfortunately, the concept of free will and human nature

contradicted with this to a degree. Admittedly, I was at times bothered by my conflict but could not dismiss that love was a universal law not limited to or dictated by gender. Margot, who wholeheartedly dismissed the great book as being man's way of keeping the lesser in some eternal form of enslavement (though insisting in a belief in a higher power), was not subjected to these troubles.

There was even our openness and ability to speak to anyone, which we shared in common. Fear was an emotion we avoided altogether, whenever possible.

Where she and I differed was on the subject of relationships with the opposite sex. I hadn't been in a serious relationship since I left Gannon, my ex, behind in London. Sure, I'd met many interesting and wonderful men (and women) along the way, but I would never settle. Never settle.

Margot was of the opinion that I wasn't over Gannon. I still loved him, yes, but I'd put him to the back of my mind and buried him beneath my thoughts. I maintain that it isn't my love for my ex-beau that compels me but rather that I cannot follow her lead. She'd rather settle than run the risk of growing old alone.

So, she married Shane.

I suppose I should have tried harder to see the picture from her perspective. She'd dated Shane on and off for just under a year when apparently a pill mishap led to her pregnancy with her son Jake. Shane had been raised southern style and the "honorable" thing to do was to marry Margot though neither was really ready for such a commitment.

Shane drank and was verbally abusive. Many nights I'd sit and console her after catching him in some tawdry form of infidelity. By the time Jakey was three, Margot, who claimed to have had enough, was planning divorce proceedings. Three months later, a drunk driver blew through a stop sign, slamming into Margot's car and sending her careening into the side of a building. Margot survived, miraculously walked away without a scratch, and went on to become a very outspoken member of M.A.D.D. and every other anti-drunk driving program in existence. Jakey, who was not properly strapped in, did not make it.

For a year and a half after Jake's death, Shane was the ideal husband. They leaned on one another and that made living okay, eased Margot's survivor's guilt. But Shane's negative ways returned with a vengeance. Suddenly deciding that Margot was in fact to blame for his child's demise, Shane returned to his old ways and occasionally found cause to raise his hand to her. But now without her child, Margot feared more than ever the prospect of being alone, which is why she worked so hard at settling in her relationship with her husband who behaved more as an acquaintance.

I finished my set up and was ready to paint. I looked up at Margot who'd already positioned herself on the ledge. There was a large tree to the right of my window, not yet full of leaves, that cast an interesting shadow across her smooth white flesh. Her respectable size bosom cast shadows of their own across her full figured frame, creased perfectly in sections of her abdomen. The "beauty marks" that stretched across her stomach created a sort of abstract imagery, those permanent stains acting as a shrine to the life that had at one time been nurtured inside of her body.

She sat on my windowsill in nothing more than a pair of barely there bikini's with her shoulder resting against the frame and her legs angled and toes pointing toward me. Her expression was soft and contemplative as she gazed out across my East Roger's Park neighborhood.

Her arm was a work of art in itself. I'd always envied the fact that I had nothing to do with the beauteous creation, the intricate weave of reds and hues embedded in a black sleeve of dedication to the life and death of her Jakey. It was what this painting would be and in its concept was by no means erotic but rather symbolic. It was reflective and expressive. It was Margot Kimmer bearing her soul, shaking loose all of her external layers and allowing her most vulnerable side to be immortalized.

I took 35mm shots at varied angles to assist me in capturing the image in its true form during the time it'd take to do so. Kat had a darkroom and would develop the film for me. And then, I began the task of painting her, my friend… my own personal Suicide Girl.

I painted until we began to lose our sunlight. I wanted to work with my live subject for as long as possible, get as much intimate and accurate detail. The sound of the buzzer overpowered the jazz riffs that were setting the tone for our vibe session.

"Who could that be?" I wondered, rushing with paintbrush in hand to the intercom. "Who is it?"

"Darwin."

My eyes rounded as I hit the button to let him up. "Uhh, Mrs. Kimmer. Margot!"

"Huh? What is it?" Margot asked, snapping out of her daze.

"Darwin's coming up."

"So. What's the big deal?"

"Well, we have at least twelve minutes of light, and I hate to waste it."

"Then don't waste it. Let Darwin inside and keep on."

"You sure?"

She laughed. "Why wouldn't I be? This? Puh-lease, you think Darwin's dick is going to be uncontrollably hard over some fat White chick's tits?"

"You're not fat, Margot."

"Should I be paying you to do this? Clearly you're blind, maybe I should take my business elsewhere."

I pursed my lips and flipped her the bird. I unlocked and cracked the door and walked back to the easel. A moment later Darwin tap-tapped and walked in.

"Whoa!"

I glanced back in time to see Darwin stumble backward and redden when he entered as he tried hard to figure where his eyes should land. Margot and I both laughed at the hilarity of his plight.

"Uhm, maybe I should come back later."

"Sit," Margot commanded. "We're just about done anyhow."

"Oookay," Darwin answered, his eyebrows raised high coordinating with his restless demeanor.

I squeezed in another ten minutes before the shadows outranked the light. Darwin respectfully shielded his eyes as Margot crossed his path to gather her clothes despite her arrant comfort with her nudity.

"It's over, you prude," I teased and plopped down onto my bed and snatched my favorite drawer open. I pulled one of the fatter inhabitants forth and lit a flame beneath its ass. "I can't believe you're afraid of a damned pair of breasts. As many chicks as you date."

"I told you he didn't want to see a fat White girl," Margot reasoned.

"You're not fat! He's dated some *fat* girls before."

"I have dated some big girls. You don't rank up there," Darwin advised.

"See. There you have it." I handed off to Darwin who puff-puff-passed to Margot.

"Shit, girl, how much weed do you keep on hand?" he asked.

"Enough."

"You betta never get raided."

"Great, that's a nice thing to say."

"What did I say? Anyhow," Darwin began turning to face Margot. "First off, just to clear it up once and for all, Margot – you're not fat. Second, you're actually pretty sexy, but you're my homegirl, and I can't look at you like that."

We were momentarily silenced.

"Oh f'k that, it's the weed talking," Margot exclaimed, hitting Darwin over the head with one of my pillows.

He caught it and tucked it under his head. "You talk to Ayinde?"

he asked, slumping further down in my recliner, the product taking effect.

I responded by rolling my eyes. Yeah, I'd talked to her, but she was in a mood. The kind that said things weren't going right between Marcus and her and she'd take it out on me. "Let's just say she'd be better left alone right now."

"Her – or you?"

I looked at him and laughed. Ayinde was my friend and my biggest irritant at the same time. Ever since I'd known her, she'd allowed her mood to be dictated by the state of her relationship, and when things weren't well, unless she'd been drinking heavily, she'd rather be left alone. Then again in the beginning, she didn't have quite as much to complain about. But as the years went by and Marcus became more and more abusive to their union, the more dramatic and annoying and self-centered she became.

"You rearranged your furniture," Darwin said.

"And we've got a winner," I replied with sarcasm. "The prize for the most attention to detail goes to…"

"Ha ha, funny girl. What made you move it around? Kinda looked better the way you had it."

"Yeah, true. The sexpots next door and their all night porno sessions left me no other choice."

"What?" Margot asked moving the joint from her lips. "Are you kidding me? You can hear them?"

Margot jumped up from my bed and ran across the apartment and pressed her ear against the wall.

"Margot."

"Sshh."

"Margot." She waved me off, pretending to be aggravated by my interruptions. "Get away from there, silly! Anyway, man, I may as well be in bed with them. These walls are so thin."

"Kinky." Margot smiled a devilish grin as she trotted back my way.

"Well… why don't you do something crazy like, oh I don't know, tell them?" Darwin asked.

"Sure okay, next time his wife is moaning in my ear, I'll tap on the wall and say, yo, sleeping over here, can you f'k your wife on the other side of the house?"

Margot scooted closer to me. "You hear her moaning? Girl, you got some freaky isht going on over here. I should come by more often."

I shook my head. "Perv."

"No, smartass," Darwin began, "next time you see them, tell them. I'm sure they don't know."

I jumped from my seat and strolled over to the refrigerator for a bottle of water. "Thirsty?" I asked. They nodded. I took three bottles and grabbed a half-empty bag of Baked Lays from the cabinet and walked back. "Don't know 'em, never met them. Couldn't tell you if I've ever seen them."

"So what. Dude, just go knock on their door."

"And say what exactly?"

Margot piped up, "Say excuse me, you may not be aware of this, but we've been having a threesome for quite some time and well frankly, it's the most sex I've had in ages-" it was my turn to hit her with a pillow, but she continued anyway, "and, and, and I just thought it only fair that I know what you look like!"

"You two are nuts."

"Maybe," Darwin said, "but there's truth behind every sarcastic remark. Okay, you ain't gotta tell 'em you've been getting your twerk on listening. Just go meet them and find a way to move the conversation to how thin the walls are. Just put something on their mind. If they bring it up… well then be honest."

My eyes went from Darwin to Margot and back. My brow furrowed. "You want me to do this now?"

They said nothing further, but their silence spoke volumes. I huffed and rolled my eyes to the top of my head. I couldn't believe they were putting this pressure on me. I wasn't afraid to meet new people, but I *was* intimidated by my visions and I was afraid that a woman with the body, face, and mane of Zahrah would greet me. It was a ridiculous fear, but it was real. But this day was bound to come and I'd have to get it over with.

"I'll go, fine!"

"Now," Margot commanded.

"Okay, I'm going. Now. Geez."

I took a breath and exited the apartment. Silently, I prayed that no one was home although I knew the likelihood of that wish being granted was minimal. I'd heard someone enter the place about an hour before. I stood at the door, poised, fist in midair, ready to knock, but I was having trouble bringing myself to do it. Who lived there? Would it be someone like her?

I'm being foolish, I thought. I took another deep, cleansing breath and allowed my knuckles to rap against the door.

"Just a minute!"

A female's voice came to me from the other side. My muscles tensed – or rather locked up, and I just wanted to go home. I made myself wait. She asked who was at the door. I paused, unsure of what to say. Zella? Zella who?

"Um... your neighbor... from next door." I bit my lip and waited, listening to the sounds of the locks being released. Carefully the door eased open, revealing a pair of dark eyes that assessed me and my presence. "Hi, um, my name's Zella. I live right next door... right here."

"Hey, I know you."

The door opened fully, and I was floored. I couldn't believe it was her; this entire time it was her! Oh my...

I smiled wide, shielding my embarrassment. "The book lady."

"Yes. Lola." She extended her hand to greet me. "And you're the book connoisseur."

"Yes," I answered through a chuckle, taking her hand in mine.

"Zella."

"Well, Zella, it's a pleasure to meet you – again."

She had a smile that was infectious.

"I'm sorry to bother you-"

"No bother, please come in."

"Oh. No thanks, I can't... now. Company."

"Oh. Well, how can I help you?"

I shrugged. "Just thought it was time – well, my friends, my friends thought it was odd that I didn't... know you. Know my neighbors."

We both nodded, standing knee deep in awkward silence. I couldn't bring myself to bring up her sex life, not like this. I nodded for no other reason than to do something with myself. "Well, I should get back."

"Sure. Hey, would you like to come by tomorrow? For lunch... I mean if you're not busy. You can meet my husband, Sean."

I smiled. "Sure. Sounds good."

"Well okay. Let's say around one. Is that too late?"

"No, that's perfect." I nodded... and nodded. "Perfectly fine. See you tomorrow."

She nodded her okay, smiled, and eased her door shut. I turned back to my own place and went inside. Margot was gathering her things, preparing to depart.

"So what happened?" she asked. "They invite you to join in?"

"No. I couldn't say anything."

"Wuss. Well at least you know who they are. Maybe next time." With a wink she threw her bag on her shoulder and walked toward me. "I gotta get out of here. Shane's at home waiting. Thanks again."

We kissed one another on the cheek.

"Be safe."

Margot nodded and waved at us as she left. I slumped down

beside Darwin, resting my head on his shoulder. Thinking… just thinking about how good it was to have good friends.

The phone rang so long panic was beginning its descent upon me. If he didn't answer soon, I'd have to call my Aunt Leigh to check in, and Leigh was trying to find any plausible excuse to label my father incompetent.

"Hello," he finally answered.

"Dad, what took you so long?" I scolded.

"I was sitting with your mother; we don't seem to get much quiet time these days."

"Daddy…"

"Yes, Sweet Pea?"

"Daddy, Mom is… isn't…"

"Zella Dora, are you calling to start some trouble?" Daddy asked suspiciously.

I was hesitant to respond. "No, no, Daddy, I'm not. You just… I need you to answer my calls. I need to know you're okay. The last thing I need is to have Leigh poking around." I sat on my bed on the opposite side of that disparaging wall, safe from those invasive lascivious thoughts, with the phone to my ear removing paint from my toenails while Santana played softly in the background.

"Your mother is perfectly okay to take care of me."

I wanted to scream at him, somehow yell some sense into that bullheaded brain of his, but I knew that would not work. I rubbed a hand across my forehead in frustration.

"Fine, Daddy. I guess you're right," I answered softly.

"I have to go, your mother's calling me."

"Daddy!"

"Yes, Sweet Pea?"

I paused and closed my eyes tight to prevent the welling tears from falling. I sniffed. "You okay, Daddy? You and… are… do you need anything?"

"We're just fine, baby girl. I'll give your love to your mother."

The line went dead before I could say another word. I held the phone too long, just looking at it until the busy signal interrupted my restless thoughts.

4Chapitre Quatre

I was nervous, but I didn't know why.

It wasn't a date, only lunch with the neighbors. But still, I'd changed my clothes three times already. I knew I was being silly, but the beautiful and exotic neighbor of mine with the soft accent was rather intimidating, particularly from knowing her as intimately as I inadvertently did.

"It's just lunch," I admonished myself. "And she's not her. You saw her, it was all a hallucination."

I smoothed my hand across the long flowing peach skirt and fidgeted with the ribbed tank top I wore as I stared at my reflection in the full length mirror which hung dangerously loose on the nails on the back of my bathroom door. Something was missing. I clicked open the jewelry case that was a permanent fixture on my counter top. Inside there was a necklace adorned by a large flat piece of genuine turquoise. It once belonged to Zahrah. She wore it on the day of her tenth wedding anniversary when she married Jacob for the second time.

I looked just like her today with the two thick cornrowed braids hanging down and resting on the upper part of my back. I added a tiny pair of her earrings. That's it, I was done. The look was complete. I glanced at the dainty watch that rested beside the jewelry case on the counter top. It was a few minutes past one, I was already late.

I scratched my temple as I turned to head to and out my front door. I couldn't believe that I was still nervous. I tapped on the door and patiently waited, just sort of hoping that she'd forgotten about the invite. That she'd look at me awash with confusion and slight embarrassment and I'd be on my way. The locks clicked and the door opened.

"Zella!" Lola exclaimed.

"Hi." I was being shy. Why was I being shy? I am not shy.

"C'mon in, glad you came over. You look absolutely beautiful. I just love that skirt. Where'd you get it?"

"It was a gift from a friend… on my last birthday."

"Well, that friend of yours has wonderful taste, and the color suits you. Make yourself at home." She stepped aside, moving her arm in a sweeping motion of invitation.

"Thank you." I looked around the tiny apartment with respect and adoration, and maybe slight envy. For an artist, I hadn't bothered to get very creative with my own surroundings. My flat in Manchester had been beautifully decorated in luscious pastels and modern, rarely seen pieces of indie art. My crib in the Chi was minimalist at best.

I appreciated Lola's surroundings. Her walls were the color of a fuzzy peach, and her IKEA furnishings were a perfect accent. She'd told me when we met initially that she ran a bookstore. If I didn't know any better, I'd swear I was in it.

I saw the area that was their bedroom located exactly across from what was once mine. My eyes lingered. So this is where they loved. There sat what I ventured a guess to be a Queen-sized, four post bed, covered by a sheer canopy that hung from the ceiling. Candles were everywhere and I picked up the aromatic scent of Jasmine enticing my senses and making the visual that much more erotic.

My only complaint of her décor was the selected wall art. Cheap, cultural knock offs picked out of the selection of our local Wal-Mart or Target. There was a large, flat screen television encased inside a cherry oak entertainment center strategically located to create a division in the one room home by obstructing the view to/from the kitchen. Clearly this couple's bank account held more expendable income than my own.

"Your home is lovely," I commented.

"Thank you. Have a seat."

"Do you need any help with anything?"

"Thanks, but no, I'm perfectly fine. Lunch is about ready, and Sean should be back any moment. I sent him out to pick up something to drink."

"I feel terrible. I should have done that."

"Don't be silly." She headed into her kitchenette as I settled onto her futon feeling slightly discomforted from the guilt of not contributing. "So, Zella, where are you from?"

"I'm a local girl, born and raised here. Went to school in London for a couple years."

"Really, what school?"

"Central Saint Martins."

"Magnificent. A friend of mine attended, maybe you know her…" A key turning in the lock interrupted our conversation. "Oh, there's Sean now."

The door opened and Sean stepped inside. He was an attractive man with faint brown skin and sleepy, slightly slanted eyes. His face was rugged with the thistles of returning facial hair. He was head to head with Lola; he was an average height for a man while she was rather tall for a woman. He was fit enough though visibly soft in subtle areas. He looked slightly startled to see me. Like maybe he'd seen me around and was surprised. I didn't recognize him.

I stood and extended my hand. "Hi, I'm Zella."

"Hey there, pleased to meet you. I'm Sean, but I guess you kinda figured that," he said while shaking my hand and chuckling shyly.

Lola exited the kitchen and walked to Sean, kissing him softly on the lips while taking the very "green" shopping bag from his hand. "Thank you, honey. Isn't Zella as beautiful as I said?"

I blushed.

Sean nodded without taking his eyes off of me. "Yep, she is. Even more so."

"Alright guys," Lola called, causing her husband and I to finally break our seemingly inappropriate eye contact, "the moment of truth. Let's grub."

The lunch was quite tasty. Lettuce wraps with ginger and wild rice, steamed veggies, consumed through politically correct, getting-to-know-you talk. I eased up and calmed down. It indeed had been a hallucination, nothing more. They were not them, nothing like Zahrah and Jacob.

She was Olufemilola Sahlamariam-Brown. Daughter of an Ethiopian cardiac surgeon who mothered her, and a Nigerian father who moved the family from their home in South Africa to the U.K. when she was six, and then disappeared. Her mother, a strong and capable woman, made her way and raised the couple's five children on her own. It was only a few years ago that Lola decided to try life without the eagle eyes of her mother and older siblings. First stop, New York. Next stop, a brief stint in Arizona before settling in Illinois and enrolling in classes at Columbia.

He was Sean Tarik Brown, in Chicago by way of Seattle where he'd had a traditional upbringing until he moved himself to the Midwest looking for a change in his early twenties. He dated a dance student at Columbia 'til he met her beautiful African classmate. He was a software engineer. Together, they were saving to start a family and buy a home in the suburbs.

They were definitely not them.

We clicked. We connected easily though they still made me slightly timid. We planned to see each other again. I still didn't tell them my secret voyeuristic past. Maybe next time.

I sipped on a mug of Chai tea with soy while listening to Kat recap the events of the evening prior. She'd given a chance to blind dating. A friend of a friend. Margot tried her best to stifle her laughter as Kat cleverly described the odd mismatching skills of a questionable acquaintance. The chime of my cell phone distracted me from her story. I checked the display before accepting the call.

"I need you." The words hit my ear before I could fix my mouth to say my own greeting.

"What's wrong, Yinde?" I asked.

"What are you doing? Can you come by now?"

"I can't. I'm out with Kat and Margot. We're downtown."

The line went silent. I thought maybe she'd hung up. I called her name. There was no response, so I tried again.

"So, are you on your way?" she asked, completely disregarding what I'd just told her.

Irritated, I responded, "I said I can't right now. How about I come through later tonight? Or how about you just tell me what's up? Is everything okay?"

Margot and Kat paused their conversation and diverted their attention to me.

"This is some bullshit."

"What?" My cheeks were becoming warm, the temp adjusting as my mood shifted. "Why can't you just tell me wassup? Is it an emergency? If it is, can you at least give me a clue?"

"Margot and Kat!" Ayinde's voice increased by at least three octaves. "Why are they more important than me? You said I would always be your friend. Friends – real friends are there when you need them. You're not being a f'kin' good friend!"

I pursed my lips tightly, silently counting backwards from ten, trying desperately to calm myself. I knew Ayinde had been drinking. She became selfish, vicious, arrogant, and desperate. She was volatile and unstable, and I feared for her when she became consumed by anger and inebriation. But I was also fed up. I wondered if I were being played for a fool. Maybe I was concerned for nothing. Maybe she wanted me to worry, jump to conclusions, and assume she'd be a danger to herself. Maybe it's how she controlled me.

"Zella!" she screamed.

I disconnected the call.

"Zella, are you okay?" Kat asked, concerned.

"Yeah," I answered quietly.

Margot asked, "Should you go check on her? Do you think she'll do anything stupid?"

I didn't answer. I looked off in the distance at the cars passing by. Escape. I wished one of those vehicles belonged to me. I wished I were the person driving one. To live my life for me...

My phone rang again. I couldn't bring myself to answer.

Escape.

"I gotta go," I said absentmindedly.

"Sure, sure. Understood," Margot told me.

I stood and wrapped my surplus messenger bag around my body and grabbed my drink. I mumbled a weak apology and headed to the nearest subway entrance, disappearing in the dank, dark underground. I ran my transit card through and was awarded with access to the coveted side of the turnstile, the side that equated to virtual freedom. I jogged down the steps to the platform. I glanced around me. People were everywhere going about their business, living their lives, shopping and laughing, dating and just being. How many of their days were interrupted with the issues of friends and parents, I wondered.

Laughter rang out like music, that carefree sorta laughter. When everything is alright, undisturbed. I smiled to myself, the cynical kind. This was my life, being there for others. No room for relationships outside of the dysfunctional ones that dominated my own existence.

My train arrived, and I lost myself in the crowd venturing North and snagged a seat and nestled my head against the tainted plate glass window, tuning out everything during the length of the familiar ride.

The day was breezy, and the bright late noon sun shone down, absorbing into the shafts of my tresses. Three houses down and I arrived, pushing through the large black gate, across the walkway and up the couple steps to the front door where I used my key to let myself in.

The house was quiet when I entered. There wasn't usually much noise being made, but the silence on this occasion was eerie. I took the bag from around me and sat it on the padded bench and walked to the stairwell. Looking up I called out, "Daddy!"

There was no response. I jogged upstairs, calling out repeatedly here and there along the way. The bathroom and spare room were empty, and there was silence. My dad's door was open, but he wasn't inside. The bed was made up perfectly, too perfectly and not an item was out of place. My eyes squinted with irritation.

I turned and jogged back down the steps, passing quickly through the immaculate living room and calling out to my father along the way, observing the neat, dust free, perfectly lined framed photos.

"Daddy!" I yelled angrily.

The soft sound of a creaking door wafted through the air from the back of the house, so I turned in that direction. Slowly, I walked across the kitchen. The back door was open, swaying slightly when a strong wind blew in.

"Daddy?" I crept forward. I stopped in the doorway. My father stood still and silent at the top of the steps, staring across the yard. "Daddy."

Slowly, he turned to face me. "Hm? Oh, hello, Zella Dora."

His eyes were wet with tears. I rushed to his side and took his elbow in my palm and guided him back into the house and to his recliner in the living room.

"Are you hungry, Dad?"

He nodded quietly and returned to staring. I entered the kitchen and opened the refrigerator to find a shelf full of Tupperware. I peeked inside and found various parts of a full meal. I dished them up on a paper plate and placed it in the microwave. I guess I was appreciative at least for this. Since I'd never learned to cook like my mother, I'd settled on feeding my father store bought, pre-packaged and preserved meals. It was my belief that the additives and chemicals were contributing to his delusional state of mind, but the alternative was him going hungry. I grabbed a can of V8 for him and poured it in a tall glass over ice.

The ding of the microwave alerted me, and I removed Dad's meal and transferred it to a plate. I took a slice of white bread and placed it on top, then carried it out on a tray to him. He didn't budge when I placed the food before him.

"Daddy?"

"Hm?"

I carefully sat in my mother's chair. I knew that this was one of the rare occasions that it was okay.

"Daddy, was Auntie Leigh here today?"

"What's that, Sweet Pea?"

"Leigh, Daddy. Was she here today?"

"Yes."

I exhaled hard as I fell back into the seat. The neatness and order of everything answered my question before Daddy did. I knew she'd come by, and I was angry. My dad's sister rarely ever bothered to pay her big brother a visit, and when she did, it was solely for the purpose of not only trying to convince Daddy that his wife was no longer there by way of making him believe she'd left him, but that it was his own fault because he is crazy and should be institutionalized. Anything to try to take his home. I had power of attorney over Daddy, and she would not have her grown ass hoodlum children and grandchildren living here and destroying all that my parents worked so hard to maintain.

She did this every time. She knew how to get to him, and she'd gotten to him, gotten to him good. He drank his vegetable juice and picked over the food my aunt left behind. I realized he was a mess and guided him upstairs and laid him in bed to rest. I thought to call my Aunt and give her a piece of my mind but thought better of it. Instead, I curled up in my mother's chair, stale from the vague scent of her mixed with time and Daddy's and my tears, and fell fast asleep.

The sound of my phone greeted me as I awakened from my nap. Darwin's name displayed on the screen.

"Hey, D, wassup?" I answered, suppressing the urge to yawn.

"Hey. Where are you?"

"At my parents'."

"Is everything okay?" His voice was laced with concern.

"Yeah, pretty much. Leigh was here today."

"Shit. Is your father okay?"

"She worked him over pretty good, but I'm sure he'll be fine. He's sleeping now."

Darwin sighed. "Hate to bother you with this, especially now. I know you got enough on your plate."

I sat up in the chair. "Bother me with what? What happened?"

"Have you talked to Ayinde today?"

"Briefly, why?"

"Did she sound okay to you?"

"Dramatic as usual. Was having tea and coffee downtown with Kat and Margot, and she called. Demanded I leave and come see her. Wouldn't say what, if anything, happened. Why, did she say something to you?"

"See, I don't know. She called, but I was wrapping up a meeting, so I couldn't answer. I called her back, musta been ten minutes later maybe. No answer. She left a voicemail, but it was strange. She sounded far away or like she was talking through a pillow or something. I could hardly make anything out, but it sounded like she said something about Marcus leaving. I'm not sure."

"Damn it!" I exclaimed, pounding my fist into the arm of the chair. It was always something.

"I've been calling her for the past two hours, and she won't answer her phone. I think I'm going to go to her house... just make sure she's okay."

"Let me call you right back." I hung up before he could respond and dialed Ayinde's number. I disconnected from her voicemail and tried again. When there was still no answer, I dialed from my father's phone.

I hung up and called Darwin back. "Where are you now?" I asked as soon as he picked up.

"I'm rolling through Evanston."

"Come get me first."

"Okay, see you in a minute."

I ran upstairs to check in on my Dad. I tapped on his door. In a wispy voice, he invited me in. I eased the door open and peered into the shadowy room. The curtains were drawn. I walked carefully across the room and sat on the bed, the mattress dipped slightly beneath my weight. My father was lying on his side, that was all, just lying there. I placed a hand on his leg.

"Daddy?"

"Yes, Sweet Pea?"

"You feeling any better?"

"Oh, I'm just fine, just catching some rest here with your mother."

I swallowed hard the knot quickly forming in my throat. Daddy was back... to "normal". I could only nod my head. I stood and walked toward the door. I stood with my back to him so he wouldn't see the disappointment in my eyes and become disappointed with me.

"I'm going to leave now, Daddy. Your plate is in the microwave. Do you need anything else?"

"Oh no, Zella Dora. We'll be just fine. You go on and be with your friends."

I nodded and exited the room, closing the door behind me. I'd barely made it to the stairs when the sound of the Shirley Horn 45 came to me. Daddy and Mommy's song. I pulled myself together and jogged downstairs to wait for Darwin to arrive.

I didn't have to wait long. If it hadn't been such a potentially serious situation, I may have burst into laughter at our police dramatics. He'd barely stopped at the curb when I ran up and dove inside the car and we peeled away. But it was serious, and we needed to make sure Ayinde hadn't done anything stupid.

"Did you reach her?" Darwin asked immediately.

I shook my head no. I hadn't actually tried again. Something told me no matter how many times I dialed, she wasn't going to answer if for no other reason than spite.

Darwin and I rode the short distance in silence; he'd not even so much as turned the radio on. Several minutes later, we lucked up on a parking spot that someone was pulling out of.

Darwin leaned on the bell; however, there was no response. I noticed for the first time in the brief time we'd been together this evening, the look of concern etched across his face. I read his thoughts and shook off his apprehension.

"Maybe she's not home." Darwin sighed heavily.

I took a deep breath and used my spare key to Darwin's surprise. He'd believed I'd given the key back after the last Marcus confrontation. I didn't acknowledge his scornful look, only focused on my duty and the task at hand. I pushed open the gate and marched to the front door where my key came in handy yet again.

At the apartment, we hesitated, all the gusto I'd had only moments earlier eluded me. I approached the door cautiously, as though I were afraid it would bite.

"Well, Foxy Brown, unlock the door," Darwin whispered hoarsely.

I rolled my eyes at him and continued forward. There was the faint sound of music in the distance. I didn't know the artist, but I was aware of the genre. Emo. Marcus was a "head"; he loathed Emo. It was Ayinde.

"She's here," I stated as the sound of the electric guitar goaded me forward. I walked across the apartment to the bedroom. In the very moment I pushed the door to open, it dawned on me that I may be walking into something I shouldn't see.

"Oh my God," I gasped.

"What is it?" I heard Darwin ask, but it was needless for me to answer. I rushed inside with Darwin hot on my heels. "Oh shit." There were tears stuck in Darwin's throat; I could hear them clearly.

Ayinde was slumped on the carpeted floor against the bed. I knelt beside her and felt her neck. My breathing caught in my lungs, and for a moment, I thought I'd never breathe again. I touched and I pressed and I felt the trickle of an escapee tear trace a path over my cheek. And then I felt it, the faint beat, that subtle vibration that I desperately sought.

"Oh God, she's alive. Call 9-1-1!"

Darwin sprang into action as I fell fully to the floor, suddenly feeling weak as though I'd run an intense triathlon. I glanced around. From here... to there. Despite the music filling my eardrums, I was ironically emotionless. As I looked at Ayinde, I no longer saw her as human... flesh. I saw acrylics and oil pastels. Charcoal. She was a painting, my painting. And I call her Beautiful Tragedy. As she lay there potentially passing over, her face was magnificent, as I'd never before seen it. It seemed to glow beneath the frame of her dark hair. It appeared as though the scene was created specifically for my viewing pleasure. She was dressed in only a pair of panties and a t-shirt. It was pink and said 'Pretty'. Pretty in pink... interesting.

An empty rum bottle was at her bare feet, and she'd smoked a tree; the remnants were in an ashtray that was beside the bottle. I saw the pill bottle, but I didn't touch it. Oxycodone. I just knew it. What I didn't know was how many she'd taken. Enough so that she was dying... before my eyes she was dying.

And then I saw the knife.

"Darwin," I screamed. My heart rate jumped and I thought my heart would explode. "Darwin!"

"They're coming," Darwin exclaimed as he rushed back into the room. "What? What is it?"

I pointed to the small blade as I crept to the other side of her body, determined to confirm what the traces of blood already proved but afraid of what I would see. I carefully tilted her wrist just enough to see the cut. I turned to face Darwin, my eyes wet with the onslaught of my tears. Fear was strong in his eyes.

The sound of the buzzer caused both of us to nearly jump from our skin. The two of us scrambled to allow the paramedics inside. I hung back as Darwin guided them to the bedroom. I sat in the corner of the room with my back to the wall fighting my mortal instinct to feel guilt and blame myself for the actions of another adult.

The music continued to play… the words coming to me clearly as if speaking her thoughts:

"Now I know that I can't make you stay/

but where's your heart?/

but where's your heart?"

I ran my hands down my face, smearing the salty wetness, rubbing it into my skin. Darwin sat beside me and placed an arm around my shoulder:

"A life that's so demanding, I get so weak/

A love that's so demanding, I can't speak."

I wished somebody would turn off that got-damned music! I watched as they wheeled her out. Unable to breathe and empty inside, I couldn't move… only watch. Silently, I prayed that she wouldn't give up. Spite. She'd die out of spite.

"Awake, and afraid/

Asleep or dead…"

When I was twelve, Zahrah got the call.

Hypoglycemia, that was the diagnosis. Daddy had insisted she see a doctor because she'd been fatigued and weak a lot during that period. Mom insisted otherwise; she'd been working hard, that's all. There were a few galleries requesting to feature her work in upcoming shows. There was the small business, the restaurant that she and Daddy had just opened. And then there was me, a good child maybe… a handful definitely.

She insisted that she was only tired but out of a love of and respect for her husband, she made the appointment. Hypoglycemia is what they told her was wrong.

I sat up in the bed with my back slumped, my chin to my knees and my arms embracing my calves. My eyes were transfixed on the back of Darwin's head, watching the waves, becoming nauseated by them. He twitched once, then rubbed his nose with the back of his hand. I watched him as he crossed over into the land of the living.

His head turned slowly in the direction that I'd previously occupied; his eyelids eased open. Realizing I was missing, he glanced up, his line of vision landing on my toes, then slowly creeping up my legs and to my eyes that were staring down at him.

"How long you been up?" he asked in a strained voice.

I shrugged, "A little while."

"Couldn't sleep?"

My eyes moved from him to the window.

I felt Darwin shift, adjust, then move from the bed. I listened to the sounds his footsteps made as he walked by me and to the bathroom, closing the door behind and leaving me to return to my thoughts.

When I was twelve, four months before my thirteenth birthday, my mother got the call stating that she was hypoglycemic, and though she'd hoped for a clean bill of health, this was the most acceptable news she could have gotten, for it could have been much worse.

"Did you hear me?"

I jumped at the sound of Darwin's voice. "No... no, did you say something?"

"Yes, I asked what time you want to go to the hospital."

"Whenever you're ready. I have no plans today. Don't you have to work?"

"I have a meeting this morning at eleven. I'm going to go home and get changed and head out. I'll come for you right after the meeting."

I folded my lips in and nodded as Darwin slipped into his gym shoes. I abruptly jumped from the bed and went to the refrigerator and grabbed two bottles of water, tossing one to my friend. He stood to depart but looking at me, he sighed. He walked to me and wrapped his arm around me, pulling my body against his, my head to his chest. His free hand stroked my wild hair.

"No worries, Z, alright? No worries, no guilt. She's fine, she didn't die, and she'll recover. The authorities at the hospital will make her get the help she needs."

"Someone should tell Marcus," I spoke into his body. I stepped back. "Someone should tell Marcus so he can understand the depths of her instability and go away once and for all."

"You can't be that one."

"Someone needs to tell him to stay the f'k out of her life."

"Zella." Darwin said my name firmly. Between his thumb and forefinger, he took my chin and tilted my head so that we could make eye contact. "Ayinde will be fine. She's going to get the help she needs."

He held his gaze a moment longer to allow these "encouraging" words to sink in before he released me and grabbed his keys and made his way to the door while reminding me that he would call me when he was on his way.

I locked the door behind him then took a seat on the windowsill. Ayinde had indeed survived her rather aggressive attempt on her own life. Her wound was a surface wound; apparently even under the influence of drugs and alcohol she was conscious enough to lack the ability to dig a knife so deeply in her skin as to sever a vein.

All that she'd ingested was pumped out, and she'd been stabilized, but she hadn't yet opened her eyes. At some ungodly hour, Darwin and I thought it a good idea to get some rest. Too tired to drop me and then drive home, he opted to crash at my place.

I'd slept restlessly for a couple hours, but memories of Zahrah haunted me. Thoughts of Daddy plagued me. And tainted ponderings of Ayinde had me concerned. Besides, I wasn't used to sharing my bed.

With Darwin gone, I laid my head on my pillow, snuggled down into my covers, closed my eyes, and coaxed myself into going to sleep.

Darwin Darnell Frazier

I met Darwin the year that my mother passed, almost six years ago. At the hospital, that was our special place.

Zahrah's hypoglycemia turned out to actually be only one of many symptoms of Addison's Disease. Maybe she'd been properly diagnosed too late, maybe her prescribed medication dosage was incorrect, but seemingly, suddenly she fell extremely ill and had to be hospitalized, and I was swiftly thrust into the process of negotiating the terms of making up the exams I'd be missing.

Two weeks we lived there, Daddy and I. When we moved in, Darwin had already been residing there on and off for the better part of the past two months. It was his sister, a rare bronchial disease was killing her gradually, had been for years. In those days, I was a train wreck right beside my father. We knew we'd be lost without her, our matriarch.

Darwin was our pillar. Darwin understood our pain; he'd been there, done it and wore the tattoo on his chest. He made sure we ate and slept. He made certain we left the facility even if it was only to walk around the hospital grounds and inhale the fresh crisp winter air.

Darwin's older sister Dareese slipped away in her sleep one day before Zahrah went into cardiac arrest and died. Both of our lives were forever changed for our loss as much as for the friendship we gained.

Wynton Marsalis escorted us to the Uptown area hospital. Darwin's meeting had gone well, and his spirits were higher. He'd called ahead and spoken to the nurse on duty and been advised that Ayinde was awake but in and out of consciousness.

I should have been all smiles and high hopes as I followed Darwin's light steps from the elevator to the section of the hospital that Ayinde had been moved to. Instead, I was uncomfortable. I didn't know what to expect when we entered that room.

Darwin, with flowers in hand that he'd picked up before he came to get me, gained clearance from the redhead at the nurse's station. Together, we walked to Ayinde's room. Darwin tapped lightly before entering. I cringed as I looked at her; I'd never seen her in such a state. Her sallow skin was drained of all color, and her bloodshot eyes had dark circles beneath them. Her normally beautiful thick, curly hair was tangled and matted. She looked as though she'd been on a binge for weeks.

"How you feelin', babygirl?" Darwin asked, all smiles. "Look, I brought you something to hopefully brighten your day."

I stood to the side, watching her watching the television overhead. She didn't smirk nor smile; she refused to acknowledge our presence. Only stared at the faces and figures above.

Darwin continued to fuss over her like a doting mother hen, placing the flowers in their vase at her bedside, seemingly oblivious to the chill in the air.

"They treating my girl okay?" he asked, but there was still no response. "C'mon, Day, don't be like that. Please. I'm sorry I missed your call; you know I would've answered if I could have. I called you right back. As soon as I could, I called you right back."

Finally, Ayinde shifted her line of vision to meet Darwin's gaze. He was beaming, proud because in essence her acknowledgment said she was forgiving him. But forgiving him for what? For having something we didn't, a real job? For being a responsible American? Why must he, either of us apologize for not adjusting our lives to fit her needs?

There was my discomfort, but it wasn't discomfort at all; it was anger. It was what I suspected all along. After putting us through hell, she expected the blame for her actions to be split three ways and one was definitely not hers.

"I can't do this," the words tumbled out before I could reason with them. My body shifted toward the door, all involuntarily.

Ayinde's voice was a hoarse scream when she addressed me, "That's right. Turn your back on me again. Run to Kat and Margot. They need you more than I do."

I turned back quickly to face her, pointing an accusing finger in her direction. "You know what, you ungrateful bitch-"

I couldn't finish my thought. Darwin felt the oxygen leave the room, he saw the venom in my eyes and sensed that my poison tipped tongue was about to be released. He was on me, gripping both of my forearms tightly and carrying me out of the room, shoving me down the hall. The lovely redhead eyed us strangely as though contemplating banning our admittance to the third floor sick ward.

"I can't do this, Darwin. I don't know if I can do this," I blurted.

"Zella, now is not the time."

"When then? Darwin, when is the time? I love her, you know how much I love that girl, but I can't take the abuse of my friendship and lack of gratitude anymore."

"You knew she was troubled when you started bringing her around. Now, three years later when she needs you most, you can't handle it? She's lying in a hospital bed hooked up to an IV, stitched up and cleaned out. Zella Dora, now is not the time."

"After what we saw... what we went through last night, what she put us through-"

"She is the same Ayinde today as from day one, the same troubled, fragile little girl. And we... this here, we're all the family she's got. You want out of this relationship? Marcus wanted out, and look where she is... where she almost was. Don't do this, Zella, not now. Don't do this now."

Darwin turned away from me and headed back to the room. I didn't know what to do, I didn't know if I should follow or walk to the nearest el stop. But Darwin's truth rang in my ear; it was a warning. I loved my friend, but somehow, at some point this relationship came to exist on her terms and I was locked in whether I liked the present arrangement or not. It was dangerous for her if I left... and poisonous for me if I stayed.

I slammed the broad side of my fist against the wall and with a roll of my eyes, turned my body, and planted my back against it. I almost laughed at the irony of it – my back was indeed against the wall.

"Oh. Hi," Lola said startled when I opened my front door. She was bent low, a piece of paper in hand that I'd clearly interrupted being slipped beneath my door. I scowled at her as she straightened her posture. "I'm so sorry, I hadn't meant to... well I was just going to… here. It's an invite to – to brunch on Sunday."

I took the folded paper but didn't speak.

"Oh… okay well, I should just get – are you okay?"

I wasn't okay, and I wanted to be a mean bitch, but that was not my true nature, and Lola looked at me with such innocence and sincerity. My frown lines softened. "I'm… sorry. I just got home. My friend is in the hospital."

"I'm sorry to hear that. Is he… she…"

"She."

"Is she going to be okay?"

"She tried to kill herself."

"Oh my goodness, Zella, I'm terribly sorry."

Her hands were suddenly gripping mine. I looked down at them, then back to her eyes. "She's fine, physically anyhow. Darwin, he's our other friend, says it's a blessing actually. Now she'll get the help she needs."

For a moment, we were quiet. I didn't know what else to say, caught up in my own emotions. Lola was intimidated. What do you say behind something like that, how do you make it alright?

"Hey, thanks for the invite," I said for lack of anything better.

"Sure, sure. Hey, Sean and I are just sitting down for dinner. You're welcome to join us."

"No, I wouldn't want to intrude."

She waved me off. "No intrusion. I've got a huge pot of spaghetti and turkey balls the size of your fist. Besides, when I leave, you're not going to do anything but sulk and you know it."

I couldn't help but smile sheepishly. "You're sure?"

Lola grabbed my wrist and pulled me out of the door. "Come on."

I snatched my keys up quickly and allowed myself to be led away.

Dinner was enjoyed through mouthfuls of chatter and animated laughter, and for the time being, I'd forgotten about Ayinde's brush with death and put her to the back of my thoughts. For the moment, I was able to be a normal person again without concerns of my father ravaging me. Blood coursed through my veins, and I was reminded that I was alive.

In the presence of Sean and Lola, I was made conscious of my carnal self as well. I was shaken and confounded by the realization of this. Was it Sean with his lovely brown complexion and tired brown eyes, his careful muscle tone and the swell in his lower lip that aroused my senses? Or was it his wife? Could it have been Lola's African beauty, deep mocha melanin and lean dancer's physique that ignited my passion? Maybe it was the beauty of the memories of the love they made behind our shared wall or the conjuring of beautiful memories of my relationship with Gannon when I watched Lola and Sean interact.

Maybe that was all. Maybe it was simply what they had that released an intense stir within me. The love they shared. The beam of pride from Sean whenever his wife displayed her enviable intellect or the look of love in Lola's eyes when her man was expressing himself. The way they touched ever so gentle and the way they smiled at the mention of the other's name.

As simple and innocent as the couple's interactions, it was incredibly erotic and intoxicating, not to mention enviable. I'd loved many with great physical passion, but I'd never known such depths of genuine love of the heart.

I rose to my feet, stretching the kinks from my legs. "Thanks for a wonderful meal, but I should get going."

"Aw, you're leaving so soon?" Lola asked wide eyed.

"You guys have to work in the morning, and it's getting kinda late."

"I really — we really enjoy your company. I'm glad you came by," Sean added.

"So am I, but hey, I live right next door. Maybe I'll cook you guys dinner someday... when I learn to cook."

"It's no problem. None at all," Lola said, taking my hands into hers and looking into my eyes. Her gaze felt longer to me than what it was in reality. Nervously, I reclaimed my hands and glanced sidelong at Sean, wiggling my fingers toward them to signify my departure.

I was anxious that night as I lay in my bed which I'd moved far from the eroticism that lied on the other side of my domain. Unfortunately, I couldn't shake those memories and a part of me desired to be close again.

I couldn't help but see Sean's slim brown fingers stroking the dark flesh of Lola's breasts and stomach, down to her thighs. I shook my head aggressively; I didn't want to entertain such thoughts. Sean was handsome and his wife, phenomenal. And though I'd slept with a couple women in my college days, never would I a married one. I couldn't dare consider violating the sanctity of such a covenant, not that I believed neither Sean nor Lola would even consider me in such a way.

I breathed heavily as I felt the softness of Sean's lips pressing against my spine. I shuddered at the touch of Lola's legs on my own. My earth throbbed, and my nipples swelled against the fabric of my gown, at the feel of their warm breath against my warm and moist flesh. I inhaled sharply and sat upright in the darkness of the night. I glanced around the room. All was still. The only noise was my breathing and the low hum of the refrigerator.

"You're an idiot, Zella," I whispered to myself before I lay back down and forced myself to return to a restless slumber.

6 Chapitre Six

I'd had a difficult night's sleep.

I found it hard to recover after 6:45 am and so decided to get up. I grabbed a Patterson book that I was partway through and made my way down to Sheridan Road and up a few more blocks to the nearest coffee shop. Their caffeinated selections were just as appetizing to the buds as their mogul competition, and they were nearer to my home – not to mention cheaper.

I purchased a pre-packaged egg and cheese on a biscuit and a latte with a double shot of espresso. I went outdoors to eat, drink, and read on the corner of a busy street at a steel table beneath an oversized umbrella. It was a beautiful morning, and the breeze off Lake Michigan increased my level of relaxation. A car pulled to the light, the music loud and demanding I pay attention. It was a song by an addict about being an addict in denial. My mind instinctively went to Ayinde. I wondered how long they'd keep her in custody. I didn't know the legal ramifications behind attempted suicide and in my haste and anger hadn't bothered to inquire.

Darwin would return to visit and find out the details. I knew she needed us, but I wasn't so sure I could be a good friend and be there for her right now. I was relieved that she'd survived and very grateful to the Father above, but I was still terribly angry with her. How could she be so thoughtless, so self-centered?

I couldn't concentrate on my reading. The book was great, Patterson wasn't one to disappoint, but I couldn't keep my thoughts under my control… my mind from wandering. *Does Marcus know?* I asked myself. It wasn't that I really cared about him, but I thought he should know what his own selfishness had contributed to. Darwin warned that I shouldn't be the one to call him. He knew me well and knew that if Marcus said anything I deemed out of line or disrespectful, I'd lose my temperament and that wouldn't help.

I took my phone out of my bag and held it in my hand, flipping it over, and side to side, contemplating. I paused my movements and looked at the face of the phone. I ran my tongue across my teeth and furrowed my brow. Slowly I scrolled my address book, taking the scenic route to Marcus' name. My finger hovered above the CALL button.

I was startled out of my trance by the early a.m. ringing. It was Kat. I frowned; it was unusual for anyone besides those closest to me to call me early. I couldn't take more bad news.

"Hey Kat, is everything okay?"

"That's what I wanted to ask you. Rumor has it Ayinde's in the hospital. Is she okay? Is it related to that call you got from her yesterday?"

I temporarily took the phone from my ear. How in the hell could news have traveled so far, so fast? I shook it off. I could assume Darwin told Margot who mentioned it to Shane and from there it found it's was to Oak Park and the residence and greedy ears of Kat Ortega.

I had a reasonable thought. "Yeah, yeah she is."

"What happened? Is she gonna be alright? The rumor mill says she tried to kill herself."

I hated the f'kin' rumor mill. But the gossip queen who was still a friend of mine was rumored to have once had a tainted relationship with Marcus that she never got over, and would most assuredly get word to him if I confirmed it, if only to rub it in his face. His girlfriend, the woman he'd chosen over her was as looney as a Warner Bros. character.

"Uh no, it was an accidental O.D., not as scandalous as it seems." She didn't need to know all the intimate details.

"Hm."

I smirked. I knew Kat suspected that I was covering, but I didn't care about that as long as she speed-dialed Marcus and spilled the beans. Kat could take him away from Ayinde. I could have cared less. It could only help her in the long run.

"Was Marcus there... when she O.D.'d... accidentally?"

I stifled my sarcastic laughter. "No, he wasn't."

"So he doesn't know?"

"Probably not."

"Are you going to call him?"

"Kat, you know me and Marcus don't get down like that."

"But Z, this is kinda bigger than you and Marcus, don't you think?"

"So says you. Yinde didn't die. And she has Darwin and she has me. You think Marcus should know, then Kat, you call him."

There was a short stint of silence before Kat responded to my offer. "I just think he should know. I mean, they are still together, right?"

My cheeks were becoming warm, and it had nothing to do with the temp outdoors. "Try again, Kat. You got Marcus' number. Do whatever you think is the right thing."

"Are you going to the hospital today?" she asked slightly shifting gears. She knew I was getting annoyed.

"Sure, later on."

"Maybe I'll go with Margot."

"I don't recommend that, Katty-Girl."

"Well… I have to get to work. Don't wanna miss my bus."

"Sure thing. I'll holla at you later."

Kat ended the call without a goodbye. I knew she was thinking… pondering how she could best use this situation to her advantage.

KAT ORTEGA

Kat had been Ayinde's friend before she ever became mine. She was a beautiful woman. Small, no better than five-feet tall with skin tinted the color of red clay and short dark, feathered hair. Her deep slanted eyes screamed Asian mix, but she claimed Black American with a Blackfoot bloodline.

She tended bar a few years back with Ayinde. She came to us with Margot and a great weed connect, so we kept her around. Things were fine between Day and Kat until the rumor mill began circulating the headline that Kat had engaged in a short-lived fling with Marcus who apparently backed off when Kat claimed pregnancy. These rumors were never confirmed and by abortion, miscarriage, or secret delivery and adoption no one knows, but an infant never materialized. The possibility alone was enough for Ayinde to abandon their friendship and forever disown our Katty-Girl.

Frustrated and unfocused, I cleared my space at the table I'd been occupying and tossed the book inside my favorite bag. I needed to do something… go someplace unrelated to any of the sources of drama and aggravation in my life. I dug through the back pocket of my bag until I came across the business card I was looking for. I peeped the address, not far from the Addison el stop. I doubled back toward my apartment and hopped the train.

I'm not sure why I took my chances showing up at Lola's Bookstore; I didn't know if she'd be there or not. Maybe she started late; owners and managers alike could do such things. Chaz did it all the time.

Maybe she was even still home. I was certain I'd heard her leave earlier in the morning, but maybe it was Sean getting a late start. It didn't matter; I'd already made my way to that side of town, might as well take my chances.

My phone chimed in my pocket. I pulled it out and glanced at the face of it. It was Marcus. Good ol' trusty Kat. I rejected the call. Not a minute later, it rang again. I allowed it to continue on into voicemail; I wasn't in the mood. One final beep signaled that he'd left a message, a snarling one no doubt.

It was barely eight-thirty when I found the address. The sign on the door informed me that she wouldn't open until nine a.m. I could wait but at the risk of looking like some sort of stalker, I opted to turn back. There were errands I could knock out early, and besides, there was Margot's painting that I hadn't yet completed.

I turned back and walked in the direction of the station.

"Zella?"

I looked up from the concrete I was unconsciously studying into the exquisite facial features of Olufemilola Sahlemariam-Brown.

"Hey... Lola. Uhm, good morning." I'd come to visit her and now suddenly I was intimidated.

She continued forward with me following behind. "What are you doing way over here this early in the morning?"

"I... well I was uhm." I was searching for a reasonable lie, that's what I was doing. "I was just running some errands. A friend... of mine lives near."

Her smile was beautiful and her teeth, the whitest I'd ever seen. She nodded at my ridiculous explanation as she jiggled her key in the door's lock. I wished I could crawl inside myself and disappear.

Lola led me inside the shop and locked the door behind me. I stood and looked around. Three hundred and sixty degrees of books, old hand-me-down vintage books. There were replicas of her own bookshelves at home resting against every wall, only twice as large. The stale, slightly musty scent of an attic lingered in the air. I looked down. There were two bins beside me filled with paperbacks;

a small rectangular sign that read BARGAIN BOOKS hovered above in each one.

Lola crossed over to the counter and momentarily disappeared from sight. When she stood, she held several sticks of incense and a lighter in her hand. She lit them, placing them in holders stationed throughout the shop. I grabbed a novel out of the BARGAIN bin, one by Anne Rice, and moved over to the large window. I waited patiently, alternating between glances at the city's patrons passing by, likely on their way to earn a better living than I, and glances at the pages that I was flipping through.

"So," Lola said, startling me yet again as she headed back in my direction. "What really brings you this way?"

I smiled shyly and rubbed my fingers across the Kangol I was wearing. "I just thought... well, you I guess. I thought I'd come by your shop and check it out."

"At nine in the morning."

I nodded and glanced away.

"Is everything okay, Zella?"

I so loved her accent. I scratched the bridge of my nose out of nervousness but shook the feeling off and looked directly at her. "Not really, just a little stressed."

"About your friend?"

"About my friend, about my father... about myself."

"You want to talk about it?"

"No," I stated putting my hands up in defense. "No, that's the last thing I want to do. I guess... well, I guess I came here because you're so far removed from all of my issues that by being around you I could escape."

She smiled that beautiful toothy smile. "So you're using me."

I looked toward the dusty floor smiling and nodding my head. "Yeah, I guess I am."

"Well, it's perfectly fine."

My eyes connected to hers. Smiling but not speaking. I guess it's what writers describe as a lingering gaze. A knock at the door broke our connection, snapping me back into reality.

"I'll get it," Lola said jokingly as she headed for the door. She unlocked it and shared some private, humorous words with the woman she was allowing in. She was a young girl, maybe about Ayinde's age. "Zella, this is Patrice. She helps me out around here during the week. Patrice, Zella, my next door neighbor."

I walked toward Patrice with an extended hand, meeting her partway. "Pleased to meet you, Patrice."

"Same here. Zella. What an interesting name. Kinda sounds like a superhero. Like you should have mutant powers or something."

"Wow, thanks. Was my great-grandmother's name on my mom's side."

"Cool. Zella," she said to herself as though rationalizing it in her mind as she walked away to begin her early a.m. traditions. I suddenly felt foolish and out of place.

"Zella," Lola interrupted my thoughts, "C'mon back with me. I've got to take care of a couple things in my office."

"Actually, I think I'll head out. You guys are busy."

"Oh nonsense, I'm a wonderful multi-tasker, and Patrice will handle opening. We won't be busy with customers for another couple hours."

I considered her offer for a moment. "I shouldn't... I can't. Go ahead and handle your business. I should take care of some things myself. I'll see you back home."

"Well, alright. Hey thanks for stopping in, come by anytime. And don't forget about brunch this Sunday."

"I won't," I answered. I shoved the book back into its place in the bin.

"You don't want the book?"

"Out of cash."

"Take it." I opened my mouth to protest, but Lola walked to me, what in the moment felt closer than socially acceptable. She was a couple inches taller, so I had to angle my line of vision to see her eyes. "Zella, please stop rejecting my every suggestion. If you want the book, take it. I guarantee it will not bankrupt Sean and me."

I laughed at my own foolishness. Why did this woman make me so ridiculously shy and awkward all of a sudden? I pulled back the book I hadn't yet taken my hand off. I chuckled. Lola gently held my shoulders and leaned into me, kissing me innocently on my cheek. I thought I'd faint for lack of oxygen.

"I'll see you around the house," she said before casually turning away and disappearing into what I presumed to be her office.

I waved goodbye to Patrice.

"See you around, Zella. Was nice meeting you," she said smiling broadly.

"Why the hell you ain't tell me Snaps was in the hospital? I bet you think that shit my fault. That's why you couldn't call me? F'k you, Zella. I'm so sick of yo' ol' arrogant ass, judgmental bitch. And I know you know it's me. I would appreciate a damn call back. Let me know the details."

I tried my very best not to allow Marcus' ignorant rant to affect my mood, but my shallow breathing and clenched fist proved I was fighting a losing battle. If he was really concerned for "Snaps", as he callously referred to her based on her frequent instigated jealous fits, he could find out what hospital she was in quite easily. I despised Marcus.

I called Darwin to inquire whether or not he was going to make it to the hospital. He advised me that he had an extremely loaded day and wouldn't be able to make it until later in the evening, that he was planning to connect with Margot and they'd go together hopefully making it before visiting hours ended. Since I was already on a train headed in that direction, I gave in to what I knew was right and continued on to Edgewater.

I swallowed deeply when I arrived at the hospital. I hated

them. The sterility, the antiseptic fragrance. The hurried steps and mysterious swinging doors with signs warning that the general public was not welcome. My mother died behind one of those doors.

It was hard being there on my own without Darwin to distract me from thoughts of my mother. I hadn't seen her the day she went into cardiac arrest. I'd planned to, but I was busy. Zahrah was too strong to be taken down by something as silly as a rarely heard of disease. I knew she'd be fine for a few hours. I had finals to take when I returned to the U.K., when all of this was over. I needed to keep up my studies.

I went to the library. It was quiet there, peaceful. None of the anxiety that was present in my everyday existence resided there. I hate cell phones and what they represent and how they contribute to the destruction of society, so needless to say, at the time I didn't own one. No big deal, right? I'd told Zahrah and Jacob I would study 'til one and then come by the hospital to spend the evening. I just needed different surroundings.

Sure, I went over... didn't pack my things 'til 2:30 but so what. How could an hour and a half make a difference? Besides, it was my mother who encouraged me to take a break from the hospital in the first place. It was she who put it in my head that very morning, insisting I take some time to live a little of my life. I was being an obedient child and diligent student. I had no way of knowing that I'd arrive to an empty bed and a grieving widow, as a motherless child, forty minutes too late.

I made my way to Ayinde's floor and past the redhead from the day prior. She eyed me suspiciously before returning her attention to the paperwork she was dealing with. I carefully pushed into the room, taking a deep breath before moving in her direction. I held back in the shadows mentally prepping myself before I announced my arrival.

She looked much better today. She'd been out of bed, and it appeared she'd washed her hair and her face. She was wide awake, sitting up high in the bed, shoveling much too yellow eggs into her mouth and watching a weekday morning talk show.

She paused her fork centimeters from her mouth as her eyes shot to the left becoming aware of my presence. She didn't speak, didn't move, only stared. Her teeth eventually clamped onto the fork, pulling the food across the threshold of her mouth. She chewed, looking at me looking at her. I twisted my mouth and walked to her bed, taking a seat at the foot, looking up at the television. A commercial played, making me hungry.

"What we watching?"

"Kacey and Mitchell."

"Cool. I like Kacey Rivers. She's funny."

For awhile we watched in silence, occasionally breaking up the monotony with giggles and chuckles at Kacey's antics. Madame Redhead interrupted briefly, taking Ayinde's blood pressure and clearing away her tray. I moved from the bed when I got a dirty look and planted myself in a chair. To prove a point, I looked at Carrot Top as I took one of Ayinde's little plastic cups of apple juice, poked a straw through, and inhaled it. I was certain she rolled her eyes at me as she turned away. I aggravated her and that knowledge lifted my spirits.

She left us alone again after inviting Ayinde to let her know if she needed anything and tossing one last snarl my way. I exhaled roaring laughter when she was gone; Ayinde joined me. We wound it down, and I caught my breath.

"What exactly did you do to her?" Ayinde asked of me with a smile on her face.

"Nothing," I claimed, feigning ignorance.

Her brow raised, and her head shook. "Where's Darwin?" she asked.

"Work."

"Oh. Did he say he's going to come after?"

I nodded. Ayinde lowered her eyes and picked at her nails.

"How long are they planning to keep you?"

"Another day maybe. They're milking Judy's insurance."

I was thoroughly surprised. "Your mom is still insuring you?"

"The least she can do." Her voice dropped an octave, and she continued to pick at her nails. "Please don't be impressed. That little gesture is how she gets to keep claiming the right to say she's a good mother."

"She know?" It was my turn to sound intimidated.

"No. She'll find out. She'll try to butt in my life... play the role. Paul will be pissed and pitch a bitch about the bill and she'll back off me to keep his focus off the memory of her indiscretions as a wife and his *short cummings* as a husband."

I chuckled quietly. She glanced at me but turned away. I thought she wanted to say something, but she suppressed it. I didn't push it; she'd express herself when she was ready.

I moved forward trying to get to the heart of what I wanted to know. "You look fine, why another day?"

"Counseling." She looked pointedly at me when she said it. It was as though she were somehow finding me to be at fault, blaming me for her doctor's decision. I didn't fold. She looked away. I wanted more detail. Was she being required to continue after her release? She knew that not only did I want to know, but I hoped so and that was enough reason for her to withhold. Darwin would find out the details, and he would tell me.

She glanced awkwardly at me again. Annoyed I asked, "What, Kid, what?"

"You call Marcus?"

I sighed and fell back into the seat. "Day, you know me and Marcus don't talk."

"Under the circumstances-"

"Under the circumstances you created doesn't require me to put up with his shit."

"So what if I would have died? You wouldn't have told him?"

"But you didn't die, and I'm not getting in the middle of it. You're not using me for that."

"I'm not trying to use you, Z."

I rolled my eyes away from her.

"I'm not," she insisted, sounding very childlike.

"Then call him yourself."

She exhaled defeated. "So he doesn't even know I'm here."

I opened my mouth to speak but stumbled over my thoughts. He knew alright but he hadn't bothered to track her down. Wouldn't be hard at all. Call Margot. Call the local medical center and ask if she's there.

"I'm not sure. Maybe Margot told him."

"You told Margot?" she exclaimed in utter disbelief.

"I didn't tell Margot, but I think Darwin may have mentioned it to her."

"Damn it! Why would he feel the need-?"

"I'm sure he didn't mean any harm, Day. She loves you like we do. He probably just thought she'd want to be here for you."

Ayinde made a face like she was in pain, but she didn't fight it. Her only real issue with Margot was her closeness to me and best-friend relationship with Kat, her nemesis. She knew if Margot showed up she wouldn't shun her and deep down she'd be happy to have someone else there for her.

She looked over at me again. Her eyes were suddenly damp but there weren't any tears. "Zella?"

"Yes, Ayinde."

"Are you mad at me?"

My shoulders slumped further. "No, Ayinde, I'm not mad at you, I'm disappointed in you."

"I'm sorry, Z. I'm really sorry I put you and D through that."

"Don't be sorry. Just don't do anything that stupid again."

She nodded at me and if I didn't know better, I'd swear she meant it. Would have sworn she was really going to try harder.

Unfortunately though... I did know better and that's what scared the hell out of me.

The entire day was spent at the hospital with Ayinde.

Twice during my visit Carrot Top, who I learned was actually Nurse Dupree, came to escort Ayinde to hour-long counseling sessions from which each time she returned silent and moody. I didn't ask what was talked about, and she most certainly didn't volunteer anything.

Darwin and Margot arrived in just enough time to spend with her before visiting hours ended, which pleased Ayinde very much. She smiled more than I'd seen her smile in some time. She was like a small child, excited to have her parents back together doting over her. We ate gyros and fries from a nearby Vienna restaurant and violated the visitor's timeframe for as long as we could before Nurse Dupree ejected us.

Ayinde was expected to be released the next afternoon. Darwin and I would pick her up and take her home. Margot wanted her to stay at her house with her and Shane for a few days, an offer to which Ayinde predictably declined. She was anxious to get home to see Marcus. He hadn't visited her nor had he bothered to call. He assumed. Assumed what, that she didn't need him, I don't know. That we would be enough maybe; too bad we weren't.

Though the words went unspoken, it was expected that I'd look after Ayinde closely for awhile after she came home. No one knew if Marcus would even be around, and the guys were concerned about what she'd do if he wasn't there when she got there or if he wasn't around much.

It was not spoken but expected that I was the likeliest candidate considering she and I were closest in relationship and because we lived in close proximity and furthermore, I just didn't have as many day to day responsibilities as anyone else. What better did I have to do? But for me, at this point, it became my burden rather than my pleasure. It was an assignment I didn't want but couldn't possibly reject.

I fondled the edges of the university's catalog that had been delivered in the mail the day before as I rolled along on the short bus ride down Clark Street. I had studied it all morning and was contemplating enrolling in class in time for the fall semester.

It was the Sunday of the brunch that Lola had invited me to attend, and I was a little on edge. I felt like slapping myself. I'd spent enough time around this woman that by this point I should have been at ease around her.

I shoved the catalog back inside my bag, stood, and pulled down on the thick wire, signaling my desire to get off. A warm breeze blew beneath my sundress as the doors opened. I used my hands to keep my dress down, maintaining my privacy and stepped off the bus and into the sunlight. The café was on my right. I spotted Lola laughing with a couple other women before she noticed me.

I inhaled deeply. *Okay, Zella, don't trip. She's just the chick from next door.*

"Zella!"

I was jarred. She was standing at an outdoor table, signaling wildly as if I could have somehow missed her and her little entourage. I approached the table and tried to be confident, not come off like a silly schoolgirl in the presence of these strangers. Lola grabbed me and pulled me tightly to her and kissed me on the cheek.

"I'm thrilled you made it. I was hoping you wouldn't bail on me and leave me alone with these weirdos."

They chuckled at Lola's quip. I smirked.

"Ladies, this is Zella. Zella, this is Lauren, Janessa, and Karen. They studied dance with me at Columbia. Lauren's presently a professor of English Lit at Columbia. Janessa's a corporate attorney, and the great Mrs. Karen Buchanan is the smartest of us all; she married into loads and loads of money and has no use for a job. Gets in the way of shopping!"

Karen laughed and slapped Lola's arm with a napkin. I offered up a pleasant 'Hi, nice to meet you all' to the women and took my seat.

"Zella. Awesome name," Karen said to me. "Does it mean something?"

I shrugged. "It was my maternal great-grandmother's name. I was named in her honor."

Karen nodded and moved a few strands of shimmery golden-blonde hair behind her ear.

"So, Lola, this is the artist you keep bragging about." That was Janessa. She had a deep throaty voice with startling masculinity. I very discreetly scanned her features and wondered if the shadow from her face that thrust across her neck was concealing a larger than normal Adam's apple.

"This is her." Lola was all smiles and praise.

I raised an eyebrow. I'd certainly mentioned to Sean and Lola over lunch that I was somewhat of an underground artist, that I'd paid my rent a few times off of my work, but I hadn't yet shown her anything, I hadn't even had them over.

"She's wonderfully talented," she told them. I almost opened my mouth to say something. As though reading my thoughts, Lola pat my thigh beneath the table as if to warn me to keep quiet.

"Don't let me leave without getting your number, Zella. Lola tells us your passion is portraiture," Janessa said.

"She'd be correct."

"Excellent. I've been wanting for quite some time now to have a painting of Justice and I to hang in my foyer. Justice, that's my husband. He's an attorney as well. Let me ask you, Zella," Janessa leaned in closer as though preparing to share some deep, ominous secret, "are you opposed to painting your subjects in the nude."

"Nessa," Lola scolded.

"What? Wouldn't that be just devilish?"

"Zella, I'm so sorry," Lola laughed.

"Don't apologize." I laughed in turn. "It's all good, and no, I'm not opposed to it. Working on a nude piece for a friend of mine as we speak."

"Really?" Janessa said with a hint of mischief.

I nodded, and Lola's friends went wild with laugher. I laughed along but not exactly with them. They were like boarding school girls who just learned of the all-boys school down the road. The giggles and snickers and failed attempts at commonality proved that this was a circle of chicks that I didn't want to be included in, and I couldn't wait for the food to be served and the torture to end.

However, something unfortunate about this gathering helped to ease my nerves. It made me calm in Lola's presence and curious... quite curious. Maybe I'd missed something, maybe Lola wasn't who or how I'd pegged her to be. If she found these shallow females relatable maybe she wasn't someone I really wanted to know.

When the last morsel was consumed and Lauren, who was their resident alcoholic-in-denial, inhaled her last glass of Shiraz, the tab came and was paid and it was time to go. Thank. God.

Janessa, the most arrogant and overbearing of them all, unfortunately did not forget her vow to get my number. I didn't want to be rude or fib in front of my neighbor, so I caved and gave up the digits. Lauren also took my number though I wasn't sure why. I was just anxious to leave. For some reason Lola's presence was aggravating me. I couldn't help to think, *So, this is who she is when she's out in the real world.*

Lola and I stood together on the curb waving goodbye to Karen,

Janessa, and Lauren as they pulled away in Janessa's overpriced gas guzzler.

"Pretentious bitches." That was Lola, not me.

My body stiffened, and I was suddenly awash with confusion. I turned carefully to face Lola.

"What was that?"

She dropped her hand to her side, rolling her eyes as she turned to face me. "I cannot stand those shady bitches. Oh, Zella, please don't tell me you enjoyed them. I could read it on your face."

I was confounded. "Why... why did we just endure nearly two hours of talk of Alexander McQueen and Anna Sui and Janessa's new two-thousand dollar purse if you think they're pretentious bitches?"

"Oh that? That was for you." Lola smiled bright when she spoke. "Business, nothing more. You told me you're an artist. Nessa and Karen have been buzzing about having some portraits done. If you can get the business, why not? But they weren't simply going to consider you on my word alone. They had to meet you, to like you-"

"And feel like they were somehow contributing to society's underclass by helping out someone less privileged than they."

Lola suddenly looked like a kid with her hand caught in the cookie jar. "I hope you're not terribly offended."

"Please. Their money spends as well as anyone else's, and they have more of it to spend. I ain't that self righteous."

We laughed, and Lola looked relieved. Then it happened again. The edge was back. Shyly my eyes fell from hers to my feet, and I absentmindedly scratched my scalp gently with one finger. A breeze swept by ruffling the hair in my ponytail and bridging the gap in our conversation.

"I could use another cup of coffee," Lola said. "How about you?"

I nodded. "Yeah, I could go for another."

Together we returned to the little café and took seats at a smaller table outdoors. We giggled at being teased about our swift return to the establishment then ordered our caffeinated beverages and a pastry to share.

For awhile nothing was said though something was different. It wasn't just me trapped in moments of insecurity. Lola suddenly shrank before me. Her dark cheeks were maroon. We smiled and chuckled; clearly both had thoughts we wanted to share but were intimidated.

Our order was delivered and we both anxiously sipped our drink, grateful for having something to occupy us. I pinched a piece of the crumb cake and nibbled on it trying to think of something to say.

"Zella, may I ask you a question?"

I paused mid-chew and my eyebrows rose slightly. "Um, yeah, of course."

The tip of her tongue rested outside of her lip in that manner of contemplation. She hemmed a bit before she finally addressed the issue. "Can you hear us?"

"I'm sorry. I don't think I know what you mean."

She dropped her head and laughed before she spoke again. "Sean and I. Can you hear us at… at night? Y'know when…"

"Aha." I nodded slowly with recognition, then more vigorously to answer. "Not so much anymore though."

"Oh my."

"Well, once upon a time my bed was directly on the other side of your bed-"

"Oh my gosh!" Lola's hands shot to her face, covering her mouth and her heeled feet danced along the pavement. "You had to move your bed?"

I only raised my brow and sipped my drink.

"Zella! I'm so, so sorry about that. You should have just tapped on the wall and yelled at us or something. Uhh, hello you freaks! Would you mind backing up a bit? Something."

"Well once I did scream for you two to stop it."

"That's what that was all about? Oh, I'm so embarrassed. I remember that night. I heard you that night, and I just assumed you were speaking to someone in your apartment or on the phone. I actually thought it was rude and was waiting for you to cry out again so I could knock on your wall. Oh how dare me."

I laughed heavily and felt my uneasiness finally washing away. With my dirty little secret exposed, it was easier to relax in Lola's presence. I could feel the cool sweetness of relief washing over me from head to foot and was happy to be able to chat and not feel that intrusive heat on the back of my neck. She invited me to redo my previous furniture setup, even offered a hand. She would have Sean pull the bed from the wall giving us the privacy we both deserved. I wasn't yet sure if I'd take her up on the offer. Her bed would be off of our mutual wall, but we'd still be in the same vicinity, and she could be – ahem, rather loud and invasive.

Despite having seen her, I wasn't sure if it was enough to cease the visions if I were to still hear her up close. Or worse, having been in the presence of the attractive couple, new visions may possibly occur.

Lola placed her hand on top of mine, encouraging me to focus on her and what she was about to say. "Zella, please don't be put off by me, but I must say this. Sean thinks – well both Sean and I find you to be absolutely beautiful. Stunning. Is that weird… for me to say?"

I knew I was blushing. My cheeks must have been warm to the touch. "Uh, no it's not weird. Thanks. Thank you. Wow."

"We just… find you to be so amazing, and it isn't your beauty alone, it's just you. Your personality. Everything about you. I don't believe I've ever met another woman quite like you."

Her eyes were locked on mine and her thumb running across the back of my hand. A chill shot through me. I didn't really know what she was trying to say or if she was saying anything more than the words that came from her mouth.

She was the attractive one. *She* was the stunning one. *She* was something I'd never before experienced, and Sean was an extension of that. I'd been with them intimately. In some ways I'd experienced this couple and here she was, the elegant and delicate wife filling me up with her compliments. And I, I didn't know if it even meant anything. And I didn't even know why I cared.

Lola took her hand back slowly, teasing my flesh and I tensed until we were completely separated. She said, "I should go now. It's getting late, and I've got a few errands to run before heading home."

We stood and gathered our personal belongings. Lola insisted on covering our drinks despite my protests. After all, she'd already paid for my meal. She promised that I could return the favor next time.

We were headed in opposite directions.

"Thanks again for the meal and the coffee... and the potential clients."

Lola smiled at me, silently looking as though there was something intense running through her mind. She leaned forward and kissed me gently on my cheek. "Thank you for coming. I'll see you later."

We parted ways. My hand unconsciously moved to my cheek, and I fought off the urge to smile.

Count Basie rang in my head, louder and louder. For a moment I labeled it to be merely the background music to a dream I was having. My eyelids fluttered, and the fog in my mind began to dissipate. I jumped with a start. I paused for the briefest of moments waiting for confirmation of my reality. When the tune picked up again, I scrambled to my feet and in the darkness, followed the sound to the iridescent glow.

I hurried to accept the call.

"Daddy? Dad!"

"Oh my Zella, oh my!"

"Daddy, what's wrong?"

My father's voice went away from the phone. I could hear him speak, incoherent ramblings, and I could hear thumps and bumping in the background, but he didn't acknowledge me. Fear was creeping up my spine, and the pits of my arms were suddenly damp.

"Daddy," I called to him, steadying my voice as best as possible. "Dad answer me please, you're scaring me."

"Oh, Sweet Pea, I can't find her, I can't find her! Oh dear Jesus where could she have gone?"

The tears were already building without need of any further explanation. My voice cracked when I spoke. "What is it, Daddy, who's gone?"

"Your mother, I can't find your mother. Oh Lord, sweet Jesus. Father God, help me."

I moved the phone from my ear and held it low with both hands covering the receiver just in case I cried out in emotional pain. My eyes rolled to the heavens, and my tears spilt forward in huge, heavy drops. I had to steady my breathing, had to remain calm in order to calm him. I took in a lung full of oxygen and placed the phone to my ear again.

"Daddy, listen to me."

"I gotta call the police, what if somethin' happened to her."

"Daddy, I need for you to please listen to me, okay?"

"Sweet Pea, I'm fixin' to call the police. I'm scared what coulda happened-"

"Daddy, no!" I closed my lids tightly. The salt was causing them to sting. "Daddy, listen. Don't call the police, okay? Don't call anyone else. I want you to go to your room and wait for me. Okay, can you do that for me? Please."

"Sweet Pea, I'm worried for your mother's safety."

I was already stepping into a pair of shorts as I spoke. My gaze was set longingly on my dresser drawer, and I craved its contents.

"I know, Dad, I know. I'll find-" I swallowed the lump in my throat. "I'll find her. Okay, I'm on my way."

"You gotta help me, baby. Please hurry, you gotta help me."

He was crying now. His voice was thick with tears and in that moment, I hated myself for having moved away. What was I thinking trying to have a life of my own? My dad needed me now, more than maybe he'd ever needed me before and the best I could tell him was wait.

Fully dressed, I grabbed my bag and keys and rushed to the door. "I'm going to help you Daddy, I promise. Somehow I'm going to help you."

I rushed from the building and into the dark streets. I hadn't bothered to check the time until this moment. It was 2:15 a.m. What was he doing up so late?

Fortunately I'd been considerate enough not to move too far away. The house I grew up in was only seven blocks from the building that I'd presently lived in. I headed in the direction of the Lake. It was late and though we lived in a relatively quiet section of the city, it wasn't always the safest, and I wanted to go the route of traveling by street and headlight. I wasn't in top notch shape, I hadn't run much since high school, but somehow I managed to run the majority of the distance to my father's home.

All of the lights were on when I approached. I paused before crossing the gate, took a second to get a grip on myself, then rushed through and to the door. I let myself inside and ran breathlessly into the main room.

"Daddy, where are you?" I called.

He was wild eyed when he rushed from the kitchen dressed in the new flannel pajamas that I'd bought for him. My breathing was labored, and my mouth was dry. This was foreign territory, a new low. For years, despite being in a delusional zone most of the time, he was calm and consolable. The worst were the occasions he seemed to come out of the fog and realize his wife wasn't there. The worst case scenario was that he'd cry himself to sleep.

And there of course were the times that Leigh would tell him that his wife had left him. I suppose it was her twisted way of sparing him the pain of the reality of his wife being dead. It hurt him no less. But this? He was a wreck, his hands trembled, and his eyes were bloodshot from his tears. And he was looking to me, his daughter, his Sweet Pea to find his darling Zahrah and make it all right again.

Then, suddenly it hit me. Like taking a steel bat to the midsection, the truth and the possibility that accompanied it hit me. And I wondered if maybe I was doing my father an injustice by trying to keep him in his own home rather than having him institutionalized as my aunt would like.

I watched him - my mind going a million miles per minute -talking to me… pleading. But I hadn't heard a word he said. It just didn't register, and it didn't matter. He wanted me to find a dead woman. What the hell was wrong with him? And I promised to come do it.

What the hell was wrong with me?

"Daddy. Daddy!" I grabbed his forearms firmly and looked deeply into his eyes. "I need you to listen to me… okay? Calm down and listen to me, please."

"Sweet Pea, Sweet Pea, you gotta help me," he protested trying to squirm away as I led him to his recliner.

"Daddy, sit down. Please… sit and listen to me. I need you to listen to me."

Reluctantly he sat. His eyes on me, innocent and childlike and filled with insurmountable fear. I knelt before him, holding his hands in mine.

"Zella Dora, what is it?" He was becoming angry and getting flustered with me. This was important, my mother, his wife was missing, and I wanted him to sit and talk.

I swallowed hard, tilting my head back slightly in an attempt to ward off more tears. "Daddy, listen to me carefully. Mom is gone."

"Well I know that, that's why I need you to help me find her."

"Dad, you're not hearing me. Mom is gone. She's gone. She's not – she's not coming back." I felt as though I'd suffocate. Saying these things to my father made me feel what I'd felt on that very day it happened. Strength was fleeting, but I pushed through. I took a deep breath. "Mom is dead."

My voice had become a whisper, but he'd heard me nonetheless. He sat still, staring down at me. I assumed, processing somehow what he'd just been told. Suddenly he snatched his hands from mine and stood.

"I'm calling the police. If you won't help me, maybe they will."

"No, you can't do that Daddy! Mom isn't coming back. Do you hear me? She's not coming back, she's dead! Dead! And she's been dead for six years! Do you get that? What is wrong with you? You can't bring her back, I can't bring her back nor can the got-damned police!"

I'd snapped. Lost it. I was breathing harshly through my nostrils, my face was hot. There was no more reasoning, accepting his need to believe that she was still with him. At least not in the moment when he'd spiraled so far as to be willing to file a missing person's report on a dead woman.

He stood still with the phone in his palm. He didn't dial, just stood, focused on me. I charged across the room to a shelf where there was a stack of photo albums. There was one that I'd put together years earlier in honor of her memory. I opened it and flipped through pages until I found the obituary.

I charged toward my father with the book opened, the page on full display. "Look at it, Daddy. Look at it!"

With his free hand, he slowly reached toward it… reached to touch it, touch her. "Cookie," he gasped. The phone fell from his grasp, and he turned abruptly away and disappeared up the steps.

A feeling washed over me as though I'd had some outer body experience, and my soul was returning. I clutched my stomach and fell back against the wall. Mournfully I watched the empty steps that he'd ascended. A shiver ran through me. Sluggish and filled with emotion, I replaced the album and slowly made my way to the stairwell. My legs were heavy as I climbed. I stopped outside of my father's door, my fist poised in midair in preparation to knock, but halted when the sound of my dear father's heaving sobs came to me.

I began to hyperventilate. I struggled for breath as I was being strangled to death by tears of my own. I tried again to will myself to knock, but I couldn't connect. I pulled my phone out of the pocket of the hooded sweatshirt I wore. After several rings, Darwin picked up.

"Zella? What time is it?"

I tried my best to respond, but I couldn't steady myself enough to find my voice.

"Z, what happened?" He was awake now, I could hear it.

"I'm... I apo... apologize... I..." I tried to speak between gulping air.

"Calm down, baby girl. First of all, where are you? Are you home?"

"No... no. I'm at Daddy's."

"Did something happen to Mr. Robeson?"

"No. Y-yes... kinda." Slowly I was regaining control of my breathing and myself.

"Where is he?"

"In his... his room."

"Is he hurt?"

"No."

"Okay, I want you to take a deep breath. Try to relax and tell me exactly what happened."

I obliged. I inhaled... and exhaled. Inhaled... and exhaled. Then explained that my dad was losing it or had completely lost it and how he was now in his room crying over his deceased wife, and I was too shook up to help him. I was failing him, both of them, Dad and Mom.

Darwin's voice was firm and rational when he addressed me. "Zella Dora, go back upstairs and sit outside your father's door. If you can't find the strength to go in, sit there and be mindful. Just in case... well, he's really hurt right now, so just be on guard. I'm on my way. I'll be there as fast as I can."

I nodded a fervent yes that he couldn't see. When he hung up, I did as instructed. From Dad's room, there were no sounds other than his bass-filled woes.

It took Darwin close to twenty minutes to arrive from his 35th Street apartment. I nearly fell down the steps running to let him in. I hadn't been this happy to see him in a very long time. I grabbed him, held him tightly, and he held me in return, digging his fingers deep into my hair and pressing pleasantly into my scalp.

Holding me against him, he led me to the living room and sat me in my mother's chair. I sat staring across the room blankly while he went upstairs to tend to my father and clean up the mess I'd made. I couldn't help but to think how I didn't know what I was doing and maybe Aunt Leigh was right after all. But I just couldn't bring myself to have my father locked away like some... some crazy person having strangers be responsible for his care.

Jacob Louis and Zahrah Felice Robeson

Zahrah was only thirteen when she met a handsome young teenage boy named Jacob. He was new to Memphis, had moved from Mississippi with his family and into the small downstairs apartment. The two didn't quite get along with one another. Zahrah was a quiet girl who spent much of her time reading books, painting portraits and still life, or taking the piano lessons that my grandmother required of her and her three sisters.

She had a bit of a crush on then sixteen-year-old Jacob which she kept quiet about. He quickly fit in with his new surroundings and earned the reputation of being somewhat of a ladies man. He had a mutual crush on Zahrah, but alas, she was young and distant, and was always mean to him, so he turned it around on her. He began dating Zahrah's big sister Dora. Not as sassy as Zahrah but just as pretty and more developed.

After high school, Jacob immediately enlisted into the Air Force.

Legend says a near death experience taught him the value of life and the penalty of wasted opportunities. He sent a letter back to Memphis addressed to a young Ms. Zahrah Cooper. Dora was angry and my mother highly offended. Jacob was not deterred.

With every leave that allowed him an opportunity to come home to Tennessee, he sought out his true love. With every quiet moment, he professed his feelings for her through letters that either remained unopened or ignored. And though she rejected him every time, unbeknownst to her she was falling in love.

In 1968, Zahrah was out of high school, working as a sales girl at a local retail shop, and helping her sisters care for her ailing mother. She was also, at the time, warding off accepting an engagement to her then boyfriend Denny Williams, a close friend of Jacob.

In 1968, after having been injured in Vietnam, Jacob was discharged and free to return to Memphis. His first stop, the brownstone on Lester Street where he sat on the stoop, patiently waiting for Zahrah to come home from work. As soon as he saw her, he knelt before her, professed his undying love and devotion and asked for her hand in marriage. She said yes. One year later (and with Dora's blessing) they were married at their home church before a modest gathering of friends and family. The next day he swept her away to begin a new life in Chicago, Illinois. Eleven years later – they had me.

Darwin returned to the living room and took a seat on the sofa. He sank into it with one arm resting across the back, the other on the arm.

"How's he doing?" I asked timidly.

"He's sleep now. He's… okay. 'Bout as well as one would expect. I wouldn't recommend leaving him tonight though."

I shook my head no and sniffed. I looked down at my hands as I played with my fingernails. Darwin patted the space beside him.

"Come here."

I rose to my feet and dragged my body to where he sat. I

snuggled my body firmly against his and laid my head on his chest. I closed my eyes and savored the feel of his fingers against my scalp.

"I yelled at him," I spoke softly. "I yelled at him that his wife is dead. How could I have done that?"

"It's okay," Darwin whispered. "Everything's going to be okay."

I didn't bother to wipe away the warm tears that ran down my face from my closed lids. I just laid there feeling safe in Darwin's protective arms and drifted off to sleep.

Darwin was gone when I awoke.

I'd slept through the night on the sofa. At some time during the night, Darwin had left me there resting soundly. I pushed back the throw blanket that he'd laid across me and sat up on my elbow, rubbing the crust from my eyes. Sun rays streamed through the window and laid a bright pattern across the carpeted floor. I slid my hand into my pocket, reaching for my phone, but it wasn't there.

I leaned over the edge of the couch and felt around. My fingers grazed the tip of a piece of paper. I yawned strongly as I picked it up to read. It was a note left by Darwin saying that he'd come for me by late afternoon so we could go and pick Ayinde up from the hospital. He instructed me to call him if I needed him for anything.

I sat the paper beside me and picked up my cell phone to check the time. It was the latest I'd slept in days. I sat upright completely and eased my feet to the floor. I rubbed my eyes again and scanned my immediate surroundings. I wondered if my dad was better or if today would be a repeat performance of what happened during the wee hours of the morning. I prayed not.

My concerns were soon addressed. The stairs creaked slightly as he walked down. I turned sideways on the sofa, pulling my knees up and looking back in his direction. He was dressed fully in a gray stripped button down shirt and slacks with house slippers. His eyes met mine. He looked tired, as though he hadn't gotten much sleep. He likely had not. I was afraid to speak for fear he'd be angry with me. I'd yelled at him. Yelled that his wife was dead.

I only watched him.

"Well good morning, Sweet Pea," he said in a gruff tone. "A pleasant surprise for an old man."

I smiled. "Good morning, Daddy."

"Why you sleep on the sofa? Your room is always available to you, you know that."

"I know, Daddy. I just fell asleep down here, hadn't meant to."

I didn't know what else I should say, what I shouldn't say… so I waited for him to make the next move.

"I'm just going to gone on in here and fix up a pot of coffee for me and your mother."

I actually smiled at that. I breathed a twisted sigh of relief. He was by untraditional standards, okay.

"Are you hungry, Dad? I can fix you up some eggs, toast, and bacon."

He smiled warmly at me. "Sounds good, baby. You gonna join me?"

"Of course, Daddy. How could I possibly resist having breakfast with such a handsome young man?"

"Awww, gone now with that. I know I'm an ol' goat."

I approached my father and looped my arm through his and walked arm and arm with him into the kitchen. He was back to his old ways and for at least this moment in time, it was a pleasure.

Ayinde's release had been scheduled, but her doctor wanted her to submit to one final in-patient evaluation before she walked. She'd been prescribed on-going treatment at the hospital for the following two weeks minimum. She was warned about a repeat occurrence. There were no longer any laws in place in the state of Illinois making attempted suicide illegal, but there certainly were alternatives. This demand did not sit well with Ayinde. I didn't believe that it was because she wanted to try to kill herself again... I believe she just wanted the option.

Darwin and I waited patiently in her room for her return so that we could finally wrap things up and leave. Darwin sat quietly in the chair, playing around with a small teddy bear he'd purchased for her as a gift. I was stretched out in her bed, flipping through basic cable stations.

I propped one flip flopped foot on top of the other and glared at my toes. "I so need a pedi."

"What's that?" Darwin asked.

"I said I need to get a pedi... pedicure. Can't have crusty toes or God forbid long toenails, you might stop seeing me," I joked, peeking back at him.

Darwin snatched a pillow from beneath my head and swatted me with it. I laughed and dodged but couldn't avoid being slammed.

"Nice one, Z. You're a funny, funny girl."

"I know right!"

"Ha. Ha." Sarcastic laughter. "Did you call and check in on Pops?"

"Yeah. He's... well, back to uh... normal."

"Cool." He played around a bit more with the bear before addressing me again. "Ay, wassup with your neighbors? You ever tell 'em about... you know?"

I bolted upright in the bed. "I didn't tell you, did I?"

"Tell me what?"

"So I go to brunch with Lola-"

"Lola?"

"The wife."

"Ah, the hot African."

"Yes, the hot African. Anyway, I hook up with her and some of her girlfriends… former dance mates, degreed, and pedigreed. She was trying to hook me up with one or two for clients."

"Aw word, that's dope."

"True indeed. So we hook up… an uppity bunch. We eat, they leave, and it's just the two of us. So she says to me, ahem, hold on, let me get the accent right." I pretended to clear my head and capture my chi to prepare for my brilliant acting. "She says, *Zella, I've been meaning to tell you that Sean and I find you very attractive. You're beautiful with a great personality, and on and on.*"

Darwin is all eyes and ears and probably a bit turned on at the thought of a woman doting over me.

"Oh word? So you about to hook up with the neighbor's wife, huh?" Darwin fell back into the chair, twirling the bear and grinning from ear to ear.

"Of course not, perv."

"You said she's hot."

My cheeks warmed up, and I knew I must have been turning beet red. "She's hot, so."

"She's hot, and you're blushing."

"I'm not blushing." I tried to sound as serious as possible.

"Yeah, you are. Zella, are you into this chick?" Darwin shot up in the seat again and leaned toward me.

I tried to avoid his eyes when I responded. "No. No, I am not." Why did I feel as though I was trying to convince myself more than convince my friend? "I think she's attractive, but that's it. I mean, she's smart… and has that great accent. But she's my neighbor – my married neighbor. My very married neighbor."

"Hot damn, you're interested in the freak Queen from next door."

"I think her husband is hot, too. Does that make me interested in him, too?"

Darwin raised an eyebrow, smirked, and relaxed back into the seat. I contemplated his words for a moment. No. No, it was a foolish notion. Of course I found her to be attractive, who wouldn't? But Sean was also attractive. Were he not married, and I'd met him, he'd definitely have an opportunity.

I waved Darwin off, dismissing his accusation as merely a ridiculous notion.

"Don't go breaking up a marriage. You ain't been laid since Dred Scott was down south killing crackers. She look at you sideways and you liable to attack."

My response was the ever-cherished middle finger.

The door to the room opened, and I braced myself for the solemnity that typically accompanied Ayinde whenever she returned from one of her dreaded counseling sessions. I was pleasantly surprised to see the smile on her face and light in her eyes when she entered.

"Good to see the gangs all here," she said. "Let's ride!"

I glanced at Darwin who glanced at me. We shrugged in unison. I pushed myself from the bed with a grunt. Darwin stood and went to Ayinde, arms wide, and pulled her into a warm embrace. He whispered some private words into her ear which made her smile and blush, and I found myself, in that moment wishing that I could see her in that state all of the time.

Marcus had yet to call Ayinde, but she was surprisingly accepting of it. He hadn't called me since the rude message the other day, and I hadn't bothered to return his call. On the drive to the hospital, I'd confided to Darwin my fear regarding taking her home. She seemed to be able to adjust to life without Marcus when she was away from him long enough, but what would she do, how would she react when she returned home and had to face him? I supposed that was Margot's fear when she offered the spare bedroom that Ayinde declined.

As far as I was aware, she hadn't tried calling him either. Her rationale... what made her tick wasn't apparent to me, to any of us, but we were aware that it was *something* and that something had G.

Marcus Walker written all over it.

The lively chatter in the vehicle died down the nearer we got to Ayinde's block. I observed every car on both sides of the street as we approached the building, looking for the one belonging to Marcus. I didn't see it, but that didn't mean that he wasn't there. It just meant his car was not parked on the street in front of the house. Parking in her Uptown neighborhood could be scarce particularly after work hours ended and everyone had begun arriving home. He could have been located on any number of surrounding side streets.

As Darwin slowed and began the process of looking for a place to settle his vehicle into, the air in the car suddenly became relatively thick. Ayinde, who'd previously been all joy and laughter, was now very serious.

"You don't have to park the car," she insisted.

"I'd like to walk you up," Darwin informed her rather dismissively. It didn't take any particular level or abilities in discernment to recognize it wasn't a fear that some paroled criminal lay in wait, lurking in the shadows beneath the stairwell just waiting for a beautiful young woman like Ayinde to carelessly wander through. It was the brotherly love that commanded he look the man he felt bared some brunt of the responsibility in this situation in the eye, and assure him that he'd be even more a protector of her now than before she cut sideways as opposed to lengthwise down her wrist.

"I'm perfectly capable of walking myself to the door."

"I understand that, but-"

"Darwin. You don't need to come up with me. I'm fine. Neither do you, Zella."

My head jerked slightly and my eyes opened wider in surprise, but I didn't respond. Little did she know, I had absolutely no intent on offering up the Zella Dora Robeson escort service. I was less interested than a little bit to potentially run into Marcus because I knew I'd likely lash out. I'd probably call him a punk muthaf'kr and then there'd be trouble, potentially sending Ayinde to the hospital all over again.

Darwin sighed but relented. "Aiight. Call me if you need me."

Ayinde's mood 360'd. She'd gotten her way and was bubbly and bright eyed again. "Thanks," she said leaning in to kiss Darwin on the cheek.

I climbed out of the backseat of the car so that I could claim rights to the abandoned passenger seat. Ayinde grabbed me and held me in a tight embrace. I squeezed gently in return.

"I love you, Kid," I told her and pecked her on the cheek. "If you need anything, call one of us."

She nodded and turned, bouncing and smiling, toward her gate. Darwin and I watched until she was safe inside, then he pulled away and took me home.

Middle of the night phone calls were beginning to become a staple of my existence. The effect they'd previously had on me was lessening with each random call. It was the house phone this time. I held my breath as I reached for it, exhaling only to issue a greeting.

"Hi, Z. Did I wake you?"

"Ayinde? Yeah, you did, but it's okay. What's wrong?"

She paused for a moment, like she was deciding whether or not involving me was a good idea. "I'm uh... I'm kinda scared, Z."

"Scared of what, baby?"

"Marcus wasn't here when I got home. I called him... told him I was home. He said he was at his family's in Blue Island and would maybe come home, but he didn't, and I'm scared here alone. I keep hearing noises. I can't sleep."

I suddenly felt like my mother. I'd gone through a phase sometime around age six where I was afraid of the dollhouse that sat in my bedroom. I swore I heard voices and saw Smurfs bouncing around my dollhouse at night when the lights were off. I'd dig deep for the courage to jump from my bed and run to my parents' door. My mother would come out and console me and convince me that I was safe.

I scratched my scalp and stood and walked to the kitchen. I was suddenly thirsty and needed a bottle of water. "Did you try turning the television on? When I was a kid and scared of the dark, my mom would sometimes let me sleep on the couch and turn on the television so I didn't feel like I was alone."

She seemed to contemplate this for a moment. "Can you come over?"

"Day…" I whined.

"I can't be alone right now, Zella, please. I know I can't and I don't want to start thinking bad thoughts or do anything stupid."

My forehead crashed against the kitchen counter, my hair spreading across, covering most of it. Dear God, why me?

She continued, "I know it's late. I'm sorry, but you said to call you if I needed you, and I need you."

I peered over at the microwave, it was shortly past midnight. "Okay, okay."

"I'm so sorry, Zella. I'm sorry."

She sounded as though she may have been crying. I closed my eyes tight and suppressed the urge to scream.

"It's okay. It's alright, I'm coming."

I disconnected the call but didn't budge immediately. I felt like I was being *Punk'd*, had to be. Desperate calls all hours of the day? That wasn't the norm, that wasn't my life, but certainly it'd become that.

They'd all teased me, all of my friends. At some point they had some cynical remark to share with me. This insane life I led, being there for everyone but myself prevented any real romance from occurring over the past years. Thanks to being at the beck and call of nearly everyone close to me, I hadn't been in a relationship since I'd left Gannon Kerrion Crichton behind in London.

I was never big on relationships, but I'd met Gan during my second year at St. Martins, and we connected immediately. He was something special, and he was beautiful. Skin the color of a fading summer tan, reddish-brown hair which he kept cut low and gelled back, green eyes, and that rustic beard he loved so much. That rustic beard that would scratch my cheeks when we made love. That rustic beard that I'd scratch my nails across as we stared into each other's eyes.

His mother, a striking blonde who appeared to be ten years younger than her actual age, loved me and couldn't resist the idea of planning Gannon's and my wedding and naming our future children. Unfortunately for her, or unfortunately for us, though Gan and I loved one another dearly, we'd no intention on going to that next level. I hadn't realized just how deeply I felt for him until I had to break it to him by phone that my mom had died, and I would not be returning to the Queen's country. My roomies SaraBeth and Eliza would handle my affairs.

It was a very cordial, very business-like dismissal of our affair on my end. But there was no time and room to mourn our loss when I was mourning something much greater. I had to bury him and move on. And now here I was in the good ol' U.S., having at times been teased for not having enough romantic affairs and I ask – with all the drama that others had added to my life, where does one find the time?

The trip to Ayinde's wasn't long, but it was exhausting. I struggled against the urge to succumb to the rhythmic movements of the train and slip into the darkness and dreams, for fear of missing my stop. I sorta dragged along. Pulled myself forward and onto the platform nearest her house and down the steps, into the street. The warmth of the season brought the Uptown residents out of hibernation. I staggered by in my pj's and a barber's jacket looking very much like I belonged with the throngs of the mentally challenged patients that roamed the area on a regular basis.

I made my way to Ayinde's block and building. I waited patiently to be buzzed up. The door was ajar when I arrived outside of her darkened apartment. I eased it open and stepped inside, locking up behind me. I was surrounded by silence. Blanketed in both darkness and silence. Darkness and silence and that eerie presence of mourning. I walked to the bedroom and peered inside. I stood there in the doorway observing my little friend, the one I frequently referred to as The Kid. She looked tiny as she sat on her bed beside the window staring out at nothing. Or, maybe staring out at hope. Hope that she'd catch a glimpse of Marcus walking up the sidewalk... coming home to her as he said he would.

I entered the room and walked to the bed. She was aware of my presence, but she didn't move, just continued staring. I sat on the bed beside her and watched her watching the section of the city that she called home... the section that was visible to her. Her eyes glistened, and I couldn't tell if she'd actually been crying or whether she was merely on the verge of it.

I sat with my back against the wall, one foot to the floor, the other in front of me. I lowered my head and gently created imaginary drawings across my ankle.

"So did he call?" I asked in a voice that was nearly a whisper.

I looked up in time to see her shaking her head no. I placed my hand softly against her exposed thigh and looked into her face.

"C'mon and get some sleep," I said. "You need your rest."

She didn't fight me. She allowed me to take her hand in mine and pull her up from her place on the bed. I pulled her comforter back, allowing her to crawl beneath first and I followed. Ayinde moved her body back until hers was snuggled against mine. I embraced her in my arms, burying my chin into her ringlets. With both hands, she held my arm firmly in place.

"Z, what's the matter with me? Am I crazy?" she asked, her voice hushed.

"No, Kid, you're not crazy. You're no crazier than the rest of us."

"Well that's not saying much."

She chuckled. It was a joke. Relieved, I smiled. If she could joke, she'd be alright.

"Funny, funny girl."

She snuggled deeper into me and gripped me tighter. I felt a warm wetness spill onto my arm and slip forward.

"Thanks, Z," she whispered.

I kissed her head through the bushel of hair that belonged to her. "You're welcome, Kid."

Chapitre Neuf

I awoke to unfamiliar surroundings.

My eyes fluttered open and began to adjust to the lack of familiarity. Given that Ayinde lived in an apartment where Marcus was the lease holder, I certainly did not sleep over often. As a matter of fact, there was only one other occasion that I had even attempted to stay the night. It was a couple years back when the two had only just moved in and before I came to despise Marcus.

It was on that very occasion that my strong negative feelings toward him manifested. They'd only been dating for a couple of months and though at that point nothing was confirmed, I had my suspicions about him.

GAVIN MARCUS WALKER

Ayinde met Marcus at a popular hole-in-the-wall Hip Hop joint that she'd been a cocktail waitress at. It was her responsibility to show up. He was a regular.

She and I agreed he was handsome. Very much so, with a sepia skin tone, round warm brown eyes, and low waves that were soft to the touch. His teeth were even and white and all features in place.

He stood a decent height, just under six feet with solid pecs and biceps and abs you could bounce yourself off of. Not only did he possess great looks, he had a pretty good job managing an upscale men's boutique in the posh area of Bucktown. Mix in his flirtatious nature and great mouthpiece and you've got all the fixings for a stereotypical playa.

Dots connected, and Ayinde and Marcus became a couple.

Try as I might, I could not avoid passing judgments or making assumptions regarding Marcus' lifestyle and intentions with my friend, but I managed, in the beginning at least, to keep my thoughts to myself. In the beginning, we were quite the three-plus-one-some (Darwin tagged along whenever he was free).

We'd gone out one night. Sub T's maybe, or The Blue Note. I'd drank too much that night. I no longer consume alcohol, but back in the days, I certainly did, and I'd surpassed what my system was capable of sustaining. I couldn't make it home alone. Marcus and Ayinde were closer, so I stuck with them.

Exhausted and drunk, Ayinde collapsed in bed minutes after walking through the door, defining the concept of falling fast asleep. I, on the other hand, decided to try and patch myself up and avoid waking up with a killer hangover in the morning by eating bread and guzzling water. The hope? One would absorb... the other would flush.

Wired and unable to find sleep even when I tried, I stayed awake, sitting on the sofa, Marcus and I chitchatting away until he decided that somehow (unbeknownst to me) I'd waved him into home and he leaned in to kiss me.

Drunk, my reflexes didn't work so well and though my arm and open palm went up immediately to halt him, I wasn't fast enough to stop him from reaching his target. I was disgusted, angry, and annoyed, all made worse by his own obvious dismay. His own disbelief that I would turn him down when I "clearly" wanted it, have been wanting it since we met and now that there was nothing but opportunity between us, I chose to front on him by playing the goody-goody role. And even worse, to add insult to injury, I vowed to tell Ayinde first chance I got. Marcus put me out, Darwin had to come pick me up, and Ayinde slept through the whole damned thing.

I followed through with my threat, told her what happened while Marcus stood by to bear witness. I guess it could be said that he and I had a draw. Ayinde pretended to have heard nothing that I said. She continued her friendship with me and continued her relationship with him though immediately thereafter began her crazy antics and clear distrust. Marcus and I have despised each other ever since.

I slowly gained recognition of my surroundings and realized exactly where I was at. I shifted my body and turned around only to come face to hair with Ayinde. A strand tickled my nose; I crinkled my forehead and fanned her hair away. A light snore escaped her and came to me.

I turned back and swung my legs over the edge of the bed and landed on my feet. The soft carpeting felt good between my toes. I stood and walked from the bedroom and across the short hallway to the couple's bathroom. I looked around. It needed a good once over. It was obvious that Marcus had been gone for days. He was the neat one.

I picked the damp blue bath towel that was bundled from the floor and shook it out. I hung it over the shower bar, allowing it an opportunity to dry. I put the cap back on the toothpaste and placed it in her cabinet. I found a previously used rag and a can of Comet beneath the sink. I cleared away dried toothpaste, long hair strands, and conspicuous orange spots which I reasoned was likely drops of Jazzing or Manic Panic, whatever she was using these days.

My bladder soon reminded me why I'd come into the bathroom in the first place. I found the relief I so sought, I washed my hands and walked back to the bedroom. Ayinde sat partway upright, massaging the back of her scalp and looking up toward the window.

"Hey Kid," I spoke in a low voice. Didn't want to shock her senses so fresh from dreamland.

She turned to face me, a hint of sadness mixed with comfort in her eyes. "Good morning. Thanks for staying with me last night. I know you really didn't want to come out here so late."

"Eh." I twisted my open palm side to side as I approached and stretched my body out on the bed beside her.

"So what's on your agenda today?"

"Well..." I paused, measuring my words. I turned on my side and rested my cheek on my open palm; the other hand I allowed to tangle in the ends of Ayinde's hair, looping a loose curl around my finger. "It's my intention to try heading up to Northwest again."

I glanced at her face, waiting for her to react. She smiled softly and nodded.

"I can go with you if you like."

My eyebrow arched. "Are you sure?"

She nodded. "Yeah, I can support you in this, right? You're always here, always there. Wherever I need you to be my friend, you're there. If going back and getting that degree is such a big deal to you, then I shouldn't stand in the way of it." She looked into my face, made contact with my eyes. "I just don't want you to leave me, that's all. I'm broken, Z. I know I am, and I wanna be fixed, but I can't do it alone."

I'd never been prouder of Ayinde than I was in that very moment. I blinked a few pleased tears away. "I know, baby girl, and I thank you for deciding to stand by me. But you know Darwin is here for you too."

"I know. I love Darwin... and you. I love both of you so much. You're both so good to me, better than I deserve."

I took it all in. Stroked her hair and took it all in. As devastating as it is to have a friend who tries to take their own life, this may have turned out to be the very best thing to happen to her, that and Marcus' disappearance. I suddenly felt closer to Ayinde than ever before, more committed. Maybe she could be saved. Saved, fixed, and healed.

Then... reality set in. This self reflection and sudden new

perspective was mostly attributed to Marcus' absence and here we were, relaxing and soul searching in an apartment that had his name on the lease. He was subject to return at any moment.

"C'mon. Hit the shower. Let's get up to the school before you change your mind. I'll just borrow something from your closet."

She laughed at me. "Girl, like your narrow behind can fit my clothes."

"They're a little baggy. Hey, that's what belts are for."

"Help yourself," she said as she scooted out of bed.

I couldn't wait to get home to my place after Ayinde's and my venture to Admissions at Northwest University. I am a lover of color. Oranges and peaches, golds and various rainbow shades complimented the warm brown of my skin tone. Ayinde, unsurprisingly was a dark girl. Black dominated her wardrobe. Typically her only splashes of color came from whatever dye job that front section of hair sported that week.

It was springtime, and though it was a particularly cool day, I still felt more in tune with the season if I wore splashes of the season's color palette. At the very least variants of her favorite shade.

Unless the unforeseen occurred, I'd likely begin classes at NW in the fall. We'd work out the kinks, deal with the finances, transfer of credits, classes, all over the coming months. Soon I'd be amongst the throngs of the higher educated coming one step closer to the coveted master's that I'd always desired and had every intention on earning. Hell, maybe I'd keep on going toward my Ph.D.

I was ecstatic.

Ayinde lit one of my joints and slipped into a state of complete tranquility. I removed her gear and slipped into a pair of well worn gray sweats that got stuck beneath my feet when I walked, and a fresh white tank top with the word LONDON spelled out in blood red fabric letters. She passed the stick my way as I dialed Darwin's cell number.

"Hey, what's up, Z?" he greeted.

"Yooo."

"Aw snap, you over there getting lifted."

My eyes swelled as I allowed the smoke to escape from my mouth. "What? How you know what I'm up to?"

"I know you, woman. What I tell you about blazing by your lonesome?"

"Said it was rude and meant less for you."

Darwin laughed. "Wassup, girl?"

"First off, I ain't blazing dolo. The Kid's here with me."

"Oh really? How's she feeling today?"

"Better than you can even imagine. Aren't you off soon?" I handed off to Ayinde and walked to the kitchen to grab two bottles of water from the refrigerator.

"In about an hour. TGIF. I need a break."

"Why don't you come through? Let's do something. Go somewhere. Hit up a spot."

"I'm down man. Find out what's popping off tonight and we can do the damn thing."

"Cool. Let me call my boy Josh and see what's on the agenda. I'll know something by the time you get here."

"See you soon."

I disconnected and collapsed on the bed next to Ayinde, reaching to take my turn as I dialed Josh's number. As suspected, he had a schedule of events which he happily shared with me after first teasing me for having apparently gotten old and out of the loop.

I knew which of the choices I was given held the most appeal for Darwin and me, but I also knew Ayinde wasn't very big into Hip Hop music. It wasn't a culture she'd grown up in as we had. I settled on a House set, something we could all appreciate.

"Hey Z?"

"Yeah?"

"You mind if I stay here with you for a couple days?"

My thoughts flashed back to the long twisted strands of hair in the sink and tub and for a moment I was frozen. But then I recalled her words from earlier in the day and how good she was adjusting while being apart from her lover.

"Yeah... yeah Day, sure."

She nodded and turned my television on. In the perfect mindset, I got up and prepped my trade tools and worked toward the goal of finishing up Margot's painting.

She wanted to go back.

We were on our way out, on our way to a little off the map joint on the North West side of town. We were zoning, it was the weekend, and good DJ'd music in the company of strangers was our long lost friend.

We were amped up and ready to step in the name of love, but Ayinde insisted that we first take her by her place to gather a few days worth of clothing and her toiletries. I knew she'd need to go home and gather some of her belongings, but I sort of hoped to wait until a time where we could somehow be certain that Marcus was not there when we were.

She hadn't spoken to him, he hadn't been home for days, and I had a sneaking suspicion this trip at this most random time was more about the potential of bumping into her beau than anything else. I fought against it, saying we could do it tomorrow, but she resisted my reasoning. I could tell, too, that Darwin was reluctant, but how could we possibly justify rejecting her?

And so, our driver accepted her will as his own and drove from my place to her Uptown neighborhood. I kept my eyes peeled for Marcus' car, like I always did when we rolled through this way, and my chemically altered brain worked overload for some believable way out in the event that I spotted it. I breathed a sigh of relief when I realized the chances of his being tucked away inside, sipping warming bottled beer and picking up chicks on the net was slim to negative one.

Darwin was just about to double park and have us run inside when a space opened up at the end of the block. We walked in silence, Darwin a few steps ahead and slightly annoyed by the unplanned detour and demands of servitude. He wanted to be in and out, he wanted to get this over with. He'd worked hard all week, and all he really wanted was a drink and a two-step. Maybe he'd even run into one of his ex's... one he was still on good terms with (which incredibly was most of them) and have a little weekend love jones. Even better, maybe he'd meet someone new and could give me the keys to his whip and catch a ride home with Ms. New Booty.

I quickened my steps and caught up to him. I placed my hand on his lower back, rubbing gently in a circular motion. I could feel some of the tension seeping from his pores, deflating him. Ayinde chose to ignore the obvious, every bit of the spoiled brat daughter or baby sis, and moved quickly ahead to unlock the doors.

Inside it appeared that nothing had been disturbed since we'd left. The glass I'd drank water from that morning still sat on the counter top. The jacket Day'd changed her mind about wearing at the last moment still lay across their small sofa. Darwin moved it over and took a seat. I stood with my back against the island. Ayinde retreated to her room.

"Miko might show up," Darwin said in a voice that could've easily been directed at himself.

I snapped into consciousness. "Oh really? She told you that?"

"Her sister. She works with me. Said she and Miko heard it was going down... that the DJ is ill, and if she can get a sitter for the shorty, they plan to come through."

"Miko or the sister?"

"Sister."

I nodded. "How you feel about possibly seeing her?"

He smiled shyly, pausing before he answered. "I miss her. Miss her and her son."

I smiled back.

The sound of a key working the lock jarred me. Both Darwin's and my spine straightened immediately. We looked to each other, then toward the bedroom, then back to the door. That's where our two sets of eyes were when Marcus walked through the front door.

"Aw hell naw. F'k y'all niggas doin' up in my crib?"

"Nice to see you, too," I replied, chock full of dripping sarcasm.

Marcus tossed his house keys on his desk. "What y'all doin' here?"

Darwin intervened before I could utter another provocation. "We're waiting for Ayinde. We'll be gone in another minute or so."

"Where the hell y'all think y'all takin' Snaps this late?"

I stepped away from the wall, moving a hair nearer to him; the feel of ghetto bitch began to work its way through my veins. I felt Darwin's energy urging me to stand down. I pretended to be oblivious.

"She's coming out with us and then she's going to stay at my crib for a couple days."

He laughed. "She ain't stayin' nowhere but right here where she belongs."

"You been gone for at least a week, didn't bother to come to the hospital-"

"I'm home now."

"-didn't bother to call to check on her."

"I'm checking on her now."

"Too little, too late, dawg. She freakin' needed you, and you was off wherever the hell doin' whateva the hell, leaving us to care for her."

"What is it, Zella? You jealous?"

"Jealous? What the hell I got to be jealous of?"

"You want my girl? Wish she was yours?"

I rolled my eyes with disgust. "My, that's a dumb ass thing to say. Oh. I'm sorry, Marcus, was that meant to be clever?"

"Is that it, Z, touch a nerve? You know now that I think about it, I ain't seen you wit' a nigga since I known you. You trying to get up in *my* girl's panties, is that it? Munch on her carpet?"

"Interesting concept and observation. Maybe she'd like that since your slow witted ass ain't sticking by long enough to handle it."

As if on cue, we stepped closer to one another. Just as I raised a finger to point in Marcus' face and continue my jabs at his manhood, Darwin was in front of me.

"Aiight, aiight, y'all good. That's enough. Zella, reel in the tantrum. Marcus, just back up from her, man."

Marcus' attention went from me to Darwin. "It's all good, D, I know you gotta protect your little girlfriend. You trying to get in them draws and here she is steady sniffing around between Day's sweet thighs."

"C'mon now, Marcus. Shit. Drop it." Darwin was flustered. He was slow to anger; he was a rather even tempered guy, been that way as long as I'd known him. He was better at keeping his emotions under his control, not as easily pushed as I. "Ayinde is standing right there. She's still fragile, she just got out the damned hospital yesterday. I know y'all don't like each other, but can you just back up off Zella right now?"

I glanced back. Ayinde stood at the mouth of the living room, her travel bag in hand. Was certain she'd been standing there for awhile but she had yet to say a word.

"I'll back up if that bitch back up off me."

My head snapped back into position, and my finger pointed at his head. "You know what, that's the last bitch I'm gone be to you."

"Bitch, f'k you."

I reacted… didn't plot it or plan it, didn't even feel it come on and neither did Darwin lest he would've tried to stop me. Not Marcus for I'm sure he figured my greatest retaliation would be more keen wordplay and besides, he likely determined I didn't have the balls. But he didn't scare me, not at all. I despised him, and I'd warned him about disrespecting me repeatedly by calling me out of my name.

There was a sting when my palm connected to Marcus' cheek. It happened so fast. I'd hardly realized what I'd done until he was moving angrily toward me, aggressively and with malice. I'd slapped the shit out of him, that's what I'd done, and I didn't flinch or think twice about it. F'k Marcus.

Marcus came at me, shouting obscenities and very willing to strike a blow of his own in return. Adrenaline was coursing through me, adrenaline fueled by a subconscious fear. I'd hit a man more than twice my size, a man who cared not about fighting a woman if he felt that she deserved it, a man that had been scorned by me, and yet I was trying as I might to push past Darwin and handle mine as best I could. I had my keys in my pocket, and I'd whip 'em out and stab that bitch in the juggler if I had to.

"Darwin, get the f'k out my way," Marcus commanded, spittle spraying from his lips.

"Hell nah! You crazy as hell if you think I'm 'bout to let you hit a woman, especially this woman."

"Step aside, dawg."

"Ain't happenin'."

Marcus' fists were clenched, and there was a wild look in his eyes. I'd clearly lost my senses, had to. I stood at attention, clenched fists of my own. Jaws tight. Eyes locked. Sights set. Had taken boxing lessons with Gannon back in the day. Hoped it was like riding a bike and those skills would come rushing back when I needed them most.

Suddenly, Marcus made a move forward, his nose inches from Darwin's; a finger to D's temple. "Move the f'k out my way. Don't make me tell it to you again."

"Muthaf'ka, you done lost yo' got-damn mind! You better back yo' ass outta my damned face." Darwin's hands pressed into Marcus' chest, shoving him back hard, sending him flying and stumbling toward the door. Immediately, he recovered and was steady on his feet once again, back in Darwin's face, his fist aimed at his jaw. The missed blow caused Marcus to swing around, allowing Darwin to dip low and grapple him by his midsection.

"Stop it," Ayinde screamed. But tempers and temperatures had risen. It was well past the point of reason. Darwin was trying to slam Marcus, the two struggling for control in the tight space and I, I was somewhere off to the side trying to weasel my way in to get a blow without receiving one.

"Stop fighting!"

She screamed it, loud and piercing, and I paused, but I didn't want to try to break it up, didn't want it to break up. Marcus was strong, but Darwin was no punk, and there was a chance that my homeboy could take the asshole down.

Ayinde was behind me… in the kitchen on the opposite side of the island. I never saw her move there, but I heard that final scream for peace. It overlapped the sound of Marcus crashing into the desk hard, sending his laptop sliding, centimeters away from falling. And when I looked, I saw the blade pressed against the vein and aimed in the proper direction.

It took a wasted moment for me to find my voice, but I pulled it together, located it, and shrieked, "Stop! Ayinde's got a knife!"

Darwin stopped, and Marcus sucker punched him in the jaw, sending him reeling and helpless. Venom was in Darwin's eyes, was a look I'd never seen on him before. He massaged his jaw and glared at Marcus, then to Ayinde. He pressed his hand to the wall and guided himself up.

Marcus stood victoriously, taunting Darwin with his eyes, seemingly unconcerned that his girl was threatening to end her life by slitting her wrist right there in his kitchen. So badly I wanted to snatch that knife from her hand and jab it through his skull.

I faced Ayinde. "What are you doing?"

"I asked them to stop it."

"Day, what the hell are you doing? Put the knife down."

"I asked them to stop it," she screamed at me.

Darwin charged across the room to her. His voice was deep and powerful when he spoke. "Ayinde, put that got-damned knife down right now."

Ayinde's heart skipped a beat at his words and his tone. I knew this because I saw the flinch and the fear when it jumped into her eyes... and because it had jumped into mine, too. During the course of our friendship, Darwin had been brotherly, he'd been stern, but he'd never shown anger.

Ayinde jerked a bit but was obedient and sat the knife on the counter. Darwin snatched it up immediately, returning it to the butchers block.

"Now get your shit and let's go."

"She ain't goin' nowhere, D, I told you. That little tussle ain't shake nothin' 'round here," Marcus stated.

I couldn't bring myself to look his way. I stood fuming... heated and I could not turn back to look his way. If I'd had a gun I would've turned back and shot that son of a bitch point blank in his left testicle. Oh, how I despised Marcus!

Darwin ignored the statement, kept his eyes deadlocked on the side of Ayinde's head who was looking straight ahead. With Darwin's warm breath flowing against her, she divided her time between looking at Marcus and looking at me... then eventually looking at nothing or no one.

Darwin's sore jaw clenched when he spoke. "Ayinde. Get your shit and let's go. Now."

Her brims began to flood. She responded, "I'm going to stay here."

Her voice was a hoarse whisper. Darwin's eyes were slits.

"You for real?" She nodded to him. "Stay yo' ass here then. But don't call me. When shit hit the fan, don't call me. When this coward muthaf'kr walk out on you again, don't call me."

I forgot about my anger and disdain for Marcus. In that moment, all I could hear was the sound of Darwin's heart crumbling inside his chest. Ayinde opened her mouth to say something. Likely an apology as was typical, but Darwin silenced her.

"Don't say it! Don't you f'kn dare say it. Don't say sh... just don't say nothin' else."

Darwin charged to the door. He barked for me to follow. I moved my feet immediately, looking toward Ayinde in agony and disappointment. Silently pleading, willing her to not fail this time. To make a statement, show us that we're more important than Marcus. Pick up the bag and follow us to the car. But somehow, I knew it would never happen. I glared back at Marcus who sat coolly upon his sofa, sitting there as though nothing had transpired.

"Yeah, bitch, take you and that pussy nigga out my crib."

I took the insult. Not because I'd wanted to but because Ayinde had silenced us. That one irrational action had lessened our vigor... thrown baking powder on our flames.

I turned and headed out the door. Darwin turned and came back, addressing Marcus from his doorway. Offering every bit of a challenge with his words. "If anything happens to her, I will kill you."

Marcus was settled back... calm, relaxed. Vulnerable and carefree... arms outstretched across the back of the sofa. "F'k ya, ol' corporate bitch ass, just keep it movin' homie."

"I ain't always wore neckties and cufflinks, homie. Like I said, if *anything* happens to Ayinde... I *will* kill you."

There was suddenly a different vibe in the air, and for the briefest of moments I saw something like fear... recognition. Darwin's point was made and from the looks of things, received. I backed out the way so that Darwin could turn, and we could depart, leaving Ayinde to deal with her own mess for maybe the first time ever in this dysfunction of a relationship.

10 Chapitre Dix

We rode in silence.

Darwin hadn't said anything to me since leaving Marcus and Ayinde's apartment. I was too intimidated to do anything...say anything. Three times he'd pounded his fist against the steering wheel. I'd flinched and without realizing when, become teary eyed.

Bam!

Bam!

Bam!

He did it again.

I looked away and out of my window and discreetly flicked the tears from my eyes. I glanced in the direction of Ayinde's building and wondered what was going on inside.

I felt Darwin's fingertips softly press against the flesh of my arm before grasping me and sliding his hand down and into mine. I turned to face him.

"I'm sorry, Z. I'm sorry you had to see that side of me. I shoulda tried harder to hold it together."

"You didn't have a choice. He provoked the hell out of you."

He nodded and took his hand back.

"What the hell is wrong wit' her, Z? I try so hard – we try so hard to be that family she didn't have, and she just spits in our face every time. Every time she chooses that punk nigga over us, she spits in our face."

I agreed but in silence. The question asked was rhetorical. He hadn't actually expected I'd have the answer. If I did, we could have solved the problem by now.

He continued, "Nothing I do for her is good enough, Z. I thought, girls and women who gave their womanhood over to these sorry ass cats did it 'cause they didn't have positive male figures in their life. Daddy went A.W.O.L. or was iggin' they moms 'cause he was sticking his hand up her Barbie Doll gown at night.

"For Ayinde… I'm her friend, I'm her brother, I'm that positive male figure, but she spits in my face. She spits in my f'kn face and chooses this punk over me."

I couldn't find any words… no consolation. I felt it, what he was going through, felt it. Or could I? Ayinde had made decisions that at times hurt and disappointed me, but at the end of the day, I knew I was enough for her. For what she needed in a female, I was enough. I was mother, sister, best friend – I was enough. She'd never put another woman – any woman, over me.

But Darwin… he'd been there for her continuously, repeatedly. Were it not for his commitment to her, she'd very possibly be dead. He'd visited her in the hospital and brought her flowers and stuffed animals and food. He'd done these things because he loved her. Not out of any self-serving desire, hadn't wanted anything from her other than what he felt he deserved. To be loved in return… to be respected as a man and a friend and considered above all other guys who would not love her the way he did.

Darwin would always lose. There was no explanation, no rhyme or reason. Darwin would always be second to Marcus, Marcus or any other guy that may come along and take his place while she was in this mind state. He'd always take a backseat whether he thought he should or not. Darwin would never be enough.

And why?

Because Darwin was the good guy. Because Darwin was the one who brought flowers and teddy bears. Because he was the one who'd come running when she called. And Marcus was the one who'd swoop into that little place that Darwin had made neat and new and treat her like shit. No rhyme. No reason.

Darwin abruptly snapped back to consciousness and turned the key in the ignition and pulled from the parking spot. It was a safe bet the House set was off. His possibly seeing Miko was over. I didn't question it. My mood was shot, and I thought it rather safe to say his was, too. He turned back and returned me to Roger's Park.

"Why don't you come up? I got a couple movies I haven't watched yet that I need to either return tomorrow or pay a fee. Horror flicks. *The Ghost of Frankenstein* and *Bowery at Midnight.*"

Darwin forced a smile for me. "A night of Bela, huh? Thanks but no. I'm gonna go home. Been a rough coupla days. I think I'm gonna turn in."

"Okay, well if you change your mind…"

Darwin nodded that he understood. I reached for the door handle, began to exit stage right when he caught my arm and stopped me.

"Zella, wait. You know when Marcus made that comment… that rather crude comment about me wanting you for myself?"

Slowly, I sank back into his plush seat, bracing myself for what may come next.

"He wasn't… he wasn't completely wrong. I love you, Z… have for awhile now. Don't know why I'm telling you this… now. I know it's kinda heavy, and you're dealing with so much. It's just that Day put that knife to her wrist… did it twice. She could have died and that reality makes me think of our mortality. I don't want this to change us… I don't want anything more from you than you're ready – willing to give. You can even file this somewhere deep in the TMI file, I don't really care. I just… wanted you to know."

We watched each other for a moment. I tried to digest all that he'd said and understand what affect this revelation would have on our relationship. I looked at Darwin, I mean really looked at him maybe for the first time. He was beautiful. Fair-skinned with a clean face that housed a set of almond shaped gray eyes. It was amusing how his strong features contrasted with the eyes genetics blessed him with. He was 6'2" tall with a slim yet toned build. He'd been a runner in college, a track star actually and ran most every day since. It'd done his body well.

Darwin broke contact... looked straight ahead. He was releasing me. Wasn't looking for a response, some profession of mutual affection or explanation as to why we couldn't be or why he shouldn't have spoken his true feelings.

I knew him enough to know when no words were needed nor wanted, but I just had to say *something*. I opened my mouth to speak, but Darwin raised his hand in protest, cutting me off before a solitary word could escape. He knew me enough to know what I'd say. I lowered my eyes and exited the car. I'd barely closed the door before Darwin pulled away, not waiting long enough to watch me get through my front gate and door as he normally would.

I closed my eyes and took a breath, hoping that in that action a miracle would occur, and I'd open my eyes and realize it'd all been just a dream. Maybe I'd smoked too much weed. I'd open my eyes and I'd be lying on my back on my bed with Ayinde at my side and Darwin in the recliner across from us. We'd never seen Marcus... the fight never ensued. I had no clue that Darwin was in love with me.

I opened my eyes.

I was standing on the curb... alone, in front of my residence, seeing nothing more than the empty lanes beneath the viaduct.

I swallowed my emotion and turned toward home. I opened the gate and passed through, taking my time across the walkway. I staggered upstairs and to my apartment and went inside. I stood upright and held my head high, tried to pretend nothing was wrong. It'd be fine, no big deal. This was just something that happened. In a couple days, everyone would have cooled off and calmed down and we'd all be fine.

I tossed my keys on the counter and grabbed a cold bottled water and cracked it open. I gulped it halfway down then sat the bottle on the countertop. I glanced over at my drawer. My high was low and buried. I walked to the nightstand and reached for the drawer and withdrew from my stash. I was running low, would have to make a phone call in the morning.

I picked up the VHS tape that sat on top of the television. It was *Bowery at Midnight*, an old horror flick dated back to 1942 starring my beloved Bela Lugosi. In this one, he played a soup kitchen operator and professor of criminology who lets a gang of criminals use his facility 'til things get out of hand. When Bela kills one, he turns into a zombie in the cellar of the soup kitchen. I'd seen it once before but never high.

I had a thought. I first lit my joint, taking a couple deep drags before putting the flame out and retiring it for the time being to my ashtray. With the tape in hand, I quickly walked from my apartment to my neighbors place and tapped on the door. She was home. She asked that I announce myself.

"It's Zella."

I waited while the locks were undone and the door was opened. She was gorgeous. She stood before me, smiling that infectious smile… her coarse hair shining and pulled back tightly. She wore a beautiful African gown that beheld a colorful pattern on a gold backdrop and hung to her ankles, hugging her frame perfectly along the way. I glanced at the French-tipped toes peeking from beneath before looking back up to her eyes.

I was intruding… clearly I'd come at a bad time. The apartment was dark except for the light of several candles. The scent of vanilla wafted into the hallway. I imagined Sean lying naked or stripped down to a pair of boxer briefs in a queen-sized bed of roses, waiting for his beautiful wife. A chill ran through me.

I shook away the fantasies and opened my mouth to apologize and excuse myself. She grabbed my wrist and pulled me inside.

"Zella! Hello darling, what a pleasant surprise! I didn't hear you come home."

I stood slightly off balance, thrown by her excitement at my presence. I'd overdone it on the fantasy. Sean was seated on the sofa watching something on their large screen television. Unfortunately, he was fully dressed in a gray t-shirt and basketball shorts.

"Hey, Zell, what's going on?"

I hated to be called Zell, but I'd take it from him. I was quickly reduced to shy and awkward.

"Guys. Hey, my bad. I see you're trying to have a romantic evening-"

She cut me off. "Romantic evening? My no! Just watching a bit of late night tele, that's all. Care to join us?"

"I don't wanna-"

"Zella! Now I've spoken to you about this before. How many times do I have to explain that you're never intruding?"

Sean spoke, "It's the candles, babe, the candles and the fruity smells."

"It's vanilla, Sean, and it's not a fruit."

"Whatever it is, Zell, don't worry about it. She does this every night."

Lola nodded and mouthed the words *I do*. I flipped the tape around in my hand for a moment, trying to quickly decide on what I wanted to do. Go home, blaze a tree, and watch *Midnight* alone or sit fanning flames that were igniting within me between this sexy ass man and his exotic wife. I should go.

Lola looped her arm through mine and led me to the sofa, sitting me down beside her husband. "You're staying, have a seat. Sean, if she tries to leave, hold her down." She laughed as she walked to the kitchenette. "Zella, would you like a glass of wine? It's a Riesling. Sweet."

"Sure, I can go for a glass." I know I said I wasn't a drinker anymore, but I was nervous, and I didn't think it appropriate to say, *Yo, I'll be right back. Just gonna run next door and grab my rolled up narcotics. Want some?* "I'm sorry I knocked on your door so late. I hadn't thought – shoulda thought about it."

Sean took the tape from my hand. "It's ten past eleven on a Friday. What you think, we're some old farts who eat the early bird specials and retire by nine?"

Lola handed a filled wineglass to me. "So what's that you've brought us? Hopefully better than this crap we're watching. Pay all this money for a ridiculous amount of channels, yet there's still nothing on T.V."

Sean waved the cassette at Lola, smiling. "Bela Lugosi and on VHS!"

"What do you know about Bela?" I asked him.

"Better question, what do *you* know about Bela?"

"VHS?" Lola exclaimed. "Oh God, have you and my husband been speaking behind my back? Sean loves, hear me – loves watching movies on VHS tape. I keep trying to modernize him and here you come thrusting him straight back into the 80's."

"Because movies were so much better pre-modern technology," Sean boasted.

I sipped my Riesling. "Ah, a man after my own heart. I couldn't agree more. I swear I was born too late. I mos def shoulda been an adult in the 1980's."

"A young adult," Sean added. "I try to tell Lola. She don't understand."

"Most don't."

"I tell her, today's music is whack. The best music is from the 80's and that goes for most everything. Hip Hop... White Folks-"

"Are you kidding me? I love 80's White Folk!"

Confusion read on Lola's face. "And... what exactly *is* 80's White Folk?"

I answered, "It's a movement of music that was recorded by White's in the 1980's that was Pop by definition but had great crossover appeal. Remember the Thompson Twins? A... E... A, E,

I, O, U... U... -"

"- and sometimes Y!" Sean and I sang in unison.

Lola stood and frowned playfully. "Zella, may I have your apartment keys, please? Clearly the two of you are much better off without me."

Sean took Lola's fingers and led her forward. He grabbed her hand, pulling her onto his lap, nuzzling her neck. "Don't go, babe, you know three's always better than two."

"So you always tell me."

A stab of envy shot through me. I loved what they had, wished there was room enough in my life for it. Darwin wanted to be that to me, fill that void. Wanted to be my special love and I his. But we'd come together under the wrong circumstances. That couldn't be for us. We were already so much more than friends, we were family. He was a brother to me, had been for six years.

Over those years, he'd never once professed to love me. Over those years, I'd seen him in and out of relationships. Over those years, he heard about my flings and affairs. He'd protected me, looked out for, and helped me out with my father. He'd become my big brother, and I loved him for six years as such. There was no way that I'd be willing to jeopardize our relationship now.

Lola giggled, pushing away playfully. She took my borrowed tape from her husband's hand and walked to their television. I'd noticed the couple owned a VCR the last time I'd visited their place which is what compelled me to bring the tape by. I snuggled into the corner of the sofa, feeling more at ease now that the wine was taking effect. Lola grabbed the bottle, setting it at our feet.

As the movie began, their 1080i being reduced to black and white, Lola snuggled firmly into her husband's side looking every bit of a woman crazy in love. I smiled at them as I observed Sean's finger gently stroking his wife's temple. I opted to reject jealousy and just be thrilled to bear witness to this young Black couple in love.

I sat reticent on my windowsill amongst and snuggling firmly one of my colorful throw pillows, gazing out into the early a.m. The sun was burning away the night, creating a wonderful swirl of orange and pink in the Midwestern sky.

I felt a volt of electricity shoot through me and past my womb, landing like an arrow in my heart as I reflected. I felt the heat of her breath on my neck... his strong hands kneading my flesh. Her wooly hair made soft from mango butter and fruit juice derivatives... his lips and kisses made soft on contact.

It began with several glasses of Riesling during a 1942 Bela Lugosi film. Enough to relax the nerves, warp the senses, and loosen the tongue. It started with a question.

Lola: *Zella, have you ever kissed a girl?*

I had kissed girls before, a couple. One girl in particular I'd kissed very frequently prior to my relationship and sharing exclusive kissing rights with Gannon. I shared this information openly and willingly. She confided that though she'd never kissed a woman, she was curious... had been for some time.

She asked: *Zella... would you mind... y'know? Kissing me?*

She giggled when she said it. Giggled like a naughty school girl. I felt myself blush. She watched me, didn't take her eyes off me as she waited for my reply. I looked to Sean, waiting for an objection or at least a look of contempt. She was his wife. Not some girlfriend or merely some chick he liked, but his wife. The one he'd made a commitment to... shared a covenant with. He blushed – but he didn't object. She was happy, smiling, cheesing from ear to ear and watching me in pure anticipation.

She was absolutely beautiful.

She wanted to kiss a girl. She wanted to kiss me.

I shrugged and with my wine induced buzz, slid across the couch, stopping close in front of her... my hand immediately gripping firmly the back of her head and my lips pressed against hers. I bit down on her bottom lip gently... then firmer, sucking it into my mouth and tickling it with my tongue. My nipples pressed against my shirt, and my fingers massaged the back of her scalp as I listened to her sigh and moan like I was sucking on more than her lip. I nibbled out that sweet Riesling flavor.

I released her and kissed her lips one last time before backing away. My shoulders dropped as my tension floated from my body. We'd both gotten our way. She'd kissed a girl… and I'd kissed her.

She collapsed backward, her head landing on Sean's lap. She was smiling and glowing, eyes lit, a look of ethereal bliss upon her face. She whispered her pleasure to him, *I kissed a girl!*

I laughed. Sean smiled down proudly at her and stroked the side of her face.

We should ask her, Lola said to Sean.

Sean objected, adamantly objected. *We can't ask her something like that.*

Why not? She asked.

Because, Lola, it's inappropriate, he answered.

Can't be more inappropriate than me asking her to kiss me.

I listened to the two of them carrying on a conversation where I was the focal point, as if I were not there. My curiosity had been piqued. Greatly. And I wanted to know. For as nervous as this back and forth was making me, it was a nervous excitement.

Lola said, *I'm going to ask her.*

Sean resisted objecting. I felt his need for an answer to the mysterious question rising. I wanted to know, but I was afraid to encourage. Lola propped herself up on her elbows and looked to me.

Have you ever had a… she giggled. *A ménage à trois?*

I stopped breathing momentarily. My eyes widened and that curious feeling formed a question mark on my face. I pulled myself together as best and as fast as I could.

Well… uhm, as a matter of fact, I have… once – twice. I have twice. Once in college. Again after my mom died. In mourning, trying to escape my pain. Don't remember much about it. Who with… how it happened.

Only know it happened because I called my friend Darwin… he picked me up… cleaned me up. Dumbest, scariest thing I've ever done.

Lola was stroking my hand as I poured out my darkest secret. She was rubbing my hand and loving me through it, in spite of it.

Lola said, *I'm so sorry, Zella.*

I shrugged. It'd happened. Too much laced smoking and way too much drinking. I'd been tested every four months for two years following, praising God that nothing negative ever showed up in my bloodstream.

Sean wants a threesome.

My eyes bulged, and I blinked a few times. Sean's eyes brightened, but he still did not object.

Lola continued, *He's joked about it a number of times… ever since before we were married, except he wasn't joking-*

It was just a joke, babe. They were just jokes, Zell.

They weren't jokes… are not jokes.

Sean dropped his defense. Lola continued her shielded request.

He's never done it… never had one. Every man wants to do it, don't they? I never wanted to. I've always been curious to kiss a girl, but I've never been particularly interested in them. I thought he was just a perv to be perfectly honest. Told him, the only way I'd ever even consider such a thing… she'd have to be really something special. I mean really special. Not only would she have to be incredibly beautiful, she'd have to have great sense of humor… make me laugh. She'd have to be smart, make me think. She'd have to be creative.

She would have to turn me on as much as turn him on. I could not possibly believe that such a woman existed… could possibly have such an affect on me. And then… you knocked on our door.

I wanted to ask for a sip of water, anything that could possibly drown out the effect the 13% alcohol was having on my mind and my loins. I balanced myself… took another sip of warm wine, peering at Lola over the rim of the glass. Riesling made Lola bold, and boldness produced by Lola's Riesling made Sean shrink into the background. Waiting. Hoping for a positive response but not wanting to be caught in the crossfire in case my response was a negative one.

I was speechless. Lola was brazen.

They were married. She could care less.

She leaned over to me and took my glass away, sat it on the floor. She gripped my neck this time. This time gave me her tongue. I'd avoided sharing that with her before. It wasn't her tongue to share... wasn't mine to take. But she gave it to me, and her husband didn't object.

I sat on my windowsill, my eyelids heavy, listening to the soft thud... thud... that erupted from behind the wall next door. Not bothered by it. Not seeing ghosts or feeling the presence of spirits that weren't really there. Recalling the look of ecstasy on Lola's face as my tongue traced the chocolate coated trail between her delicious b-cup breasts. Recalling the sting of Sean's bite on the side of my neck. I hadn't actually had sex with either of them, just made their foreplay better.

Lola hadn't wanted me to leave.

I laid between them in their Queen-sized bed. Sean snoring quiet Z's. Lola holding me like a baby doll... her favorite possession. Stroking the loose hairs crowning my head. Speaking strings of accented words that my faraway mind was unable to process.

She'd asked me an unheard question, prodded me for a response. I didn't know what she'd asked, didn't ask that she repeat it. I sat upright. I had to go, needed to be out of their marriage bed. Lola didn't want me to leave... pleaded for me to stay. I couldn't. She followed me to the door naked and smelling sweetly of sex, with her husband's juices still sticky between her thighs. She tried to convince me to stay, spoke in hushed tones so not to awaken her life partner.

She blocked me from exiting, asked that I kiss her. If I had to leave, please kiss her goodnight before I go. And I did. I kissed her deep... I kissed her with passion. I sucked away her very life force then offered it back to her. I kissed her and left her torn between wanting me and catching her breath.

I staggered from my windowsill, eyelids heavy and collapsed onto my bed. I'd gotten what I'd pretended that I hadn't wanted... had my way with a married Ethiopian-slash-Nigerian mix and her handsome husband. Touched her intimately. Kissed her in erogenous places that she hadn't realized existed. Allowed his hands to roam a body with curves different than that of his wife... massage breasts slightly larger than his wife's. I'd had my way and given them what they wanted.

So why did I feel like crap?

They were the sounds of my present existence.

The *tap*, *tap*, *tap* against my bedroom wall was intended to reach out to me, awaken me from slumber if I were sleeping. If I were awake… encourage me to rise from the comfort of my bed.

Tap.

Tap.

Tap.

I lay on my back in bed staring up at the small brown spots on the ceiling, trying to connect the dots while ignoring the beckoning raps for my attention. There was too much on my mind. Thoughts, questions and concerns all merged together, swelling my cells, expanding my brain and causing it to beat relentlessly inside my head.

I repeated the process of raking my nails through my hair and across the front of my scalp.

It was a Sunday morning, and the sun hadn't yet fully risen into the sky. I lay on my back with my head sunk into the pillow, juggling my emotions. I laid there trying to relax my mind, battling between feeling greatly flattered and an intense frustration.

A frustration brought about as a result of the present state of my relationship with my best friends. Ayinde hadn't yet returned any of my many phone calls. I'd given her a week after Darwin fought her boyfriend. A week to calm down and decide she wanted to see us. But she didn't call me. Not one time during that week did she bother to call me.

Initially I wasn't bothered by it, was actually rather pleased. Ayinde was drama – too much drama. She'd stood back and taken what Marcus had dished. Stayed behind. Chosen him over us... Darwin and I. She faulted us for the fight. Didn't have to verbalize it, her choice told us all we needed to know.

And besides, Darwin and I had our own aftermath to cope with without her issues adding to that headache.

Why had he done it? Confess his love for me... what was I to do with that information? How did he expect me to process it? He'd told me to let it go... told me to file it under TMI, too much information, but that wasn't possible. That confession altered the dynamics of our relationship and would continue to do so no matter how we tried to ignore it.

He was already being weird. When I'd called him the day after he professed his undying love, he was short with me. Not attitude per se... quick. To the point. Talk to ya later. Our traditional playful banter not present.

Awkward.

Uncomfortable.

We'd never before this point had timid conversation. From the time we met 'til that point things had always flowed between he and I. But now...

Now...

I hadn't yet educated him about my budding love affair with the neighbors. Not that I didn't want to. I knew if I told him he'd see me through it... be my moral compass. He'd likely confirm my already rather sound suspicions that what I was engaging in was wrong. Tell me sleeping with a married couple whether I went all the way with them or not was unethical. He'd probably talk me out of continuing it with the threat of some posthumous spiritual penalty.

But Darwin had just confessed a love for me and no matter that he'd advised I file those words under TMI, something like common sense told me it wasn't the time.

I lay in bed... laid on my back in a fog. My thoughts shifted back to Ayinde. During our relationship, she'd been my girl, my little sis. She'd been like a daughter and ultimately and in many ways, my responsibility for so many years that I suddenly felt an emptiness without her presence.

But I'd called. Swallowed my pride. Gotten over myself and made the first step. Reached out to her. Wanted to at least be sure that she was okay. No answer. I left a message from which there was no response.

I refused to care. I fought hard to continue not to care. I was certain that she was fine. Didn't believe she'd actually done anything stupid... made any further attempts on her life. It didn't make any sense that she would. Ayinde didn't do these things because she wanted to kill herself. I wouldn't believe that Ayinde actually wanted to die. The girl only wanted attention, and I knew by her lack of communication that she'd *not* done anything foolish.

I knew what she was actually doing. She was working us over but in a different way, trying to get attention in a different form. She was making a contradictory statement. She wanted to prove that she didn't need Darwin or me by forcing us to focus our attention on her... which she needed very much.

It was a twisted psychological game she was playing, and for as much as I did not want to be sucked into and become a pawn in it, I knew I didn't have very much of a choice. Because at the end of the day, she was my friend and I loved her and I didn't have a choice – and she was counting on that.

I tried avoiding thoughts of her. I'd ignored her presence while walking along the lakefront. Ignored thoughts of her as I sat sipping a chai latte at my neighborhood café. Pushed her presence from the forefront of my mind and replaced her with Grisham's fictitious character Rudy Baylor from his novel *The Rainmaker*.

I lay on my back in my bed, staring at the dots on the ceiling with tension inside my head, trying to push thoughts of her away - and failing miserably.

I sat upright. Yawned and swung my feet over the bed's edge to the floor. The room was brightening at a slow but steady pace. I opened my drawer. I really needed to ease the pounding inside my head. The best way to achieve that would be to relax my thoughts.

I took the smallest joint I could find. It was early. I just needed enough of a hit to soothe my mind. I put it between my lips and lit the end. I took a deep and extended inhale... held it for a moment, appreciating the feel of the smoke swirling about inside my mouth before exhaling some of my frustrations.

My eyes landed on the telephone. I bit down on my lip in contemplation. I put the joint to my lips once again, taking my final drag before squeezing the tip with my fingers to extinguish its heat.

I gripped the base of the bulky device and carried it with me as I eased back fully into the bed. I sat with my back to the wall and the phone balanced on my knees, struggling with myself.

I lifted the receiver and put it to my ear, holding it against my shoulder. I dialed Ayinde's cell number... patiently awaiting her recorded voice to greet me.

"Hello?" Her voice came through groggy and low.

I was caught off guard. I hadn't expected an answer. I didn't know what to say. "H-hey."

"Who is this?"

"It's me, Zella."

"Zella? What time is it?"

She hadn't known it was me. She answered without checking the caller ID. She'd answered reflexively. I'd effectively snuck up on her.

"I'm not sure. I guess I woke you."

"Mmhm... worked a double last night. That chick Vickie didn't show again."

The polite thing to do in a situation like this was of course to offer her the opportunity to return to slumber and call me back later except I knew she wouldn't call. Not only that, she'd be much more cautious about answering her phone the next time around.

"I didn't mean to wake you, but I've been worried about you. What's going on, why haven't you returned my calls?"

She sighed and I could hear her shifting around. "It's just not a good time for me."

"Well I'd tell you to call me back later, but you probably won't do it."

"I don't..." she yawned then continued, "...I don't want to talk. It's not a good time for me."

"What don't you want to talk about?"

"Look, Z, I know where this is headed. Just stop calling me, alright."

Bitch! I thought to myself, but I kept that word contained to my thoughts only. I didn't want to make matters worse and push her further away. "What do you mean, stop calling you? I haven't heard from you in... in forever it feels like. Last time I saw you we were bringing you home with stitches in your wrist-"

"I know, I know."

"- and now you're ignoring my phone calls and all you have to say to me is, stop calling you? You don't have to worry about me calling you anymore. Your wish is granted. I am so through with you, this bull is just too ridiculous." I was becoming emotional... my voice elevating.

"Z! C'mon. Please! Just stop it... for now. Please." She was begging me. There was no anger or malice in her voice... no aggression. "Don't be like that. Don't be through, just be patient. I'll call you when I'm ready to talk. Okay? Please?"

I paused. Had so much to say to her... so many questions to ask but thought better of it. I'd heard her voice and heard the longing in it. She missed me. Wanted to see me but for reasons not my place to know she couldn't. Not now.

I asked one last question. "Day, just tell me if you're okay."

She gave one final response. "I'm fine, Z, I promise you. I'll call you when I'm ready. I promise."

Then, she hung up.

There was another tap against my wall, jarring me and preventing my thought process and assessment of the brief conversation I'd just had.

One tap... only once this time. I'd raised my voice when I was speaking to Ayinde; maybe Lola overheard me and knew I was awake.

I wondered if her husband knew she was beckoning me. I almost tapped out a response – almost. I wanted to... at least my body did.

I leaned over and sat the phone on the floor. I turned over and lay down on my stomach and looked ahead at the wall. Stared at it. Wondered what she was doing on the other side of it. Wondered if she was lying there hopeful and frisky. Wondered if she was nudging her husband... rubbing her small perky breasts against his back, trying to rouse him. I licked my lips as I watched the wall, wondering if... hoping maybe she was watching her wall, too.

I reached toward the wall, but I couldn't bring myself to rap my fist against it. They were married. Involving me in their love life couldn't be okay. It had to be wrong. I dropped my arm to the bed and my face to the pillow.

I'd become a staple in their intimacy though I'd never actually had sex with either of them. I made their sex better. Touched. Kissed. Caressed. But never did I have sex with Lola and Sean. Not once had I removed my boy shorts while I was in their bed.

I jumped from my bed and grabbed my robe. I rushed across the apartment to my door... but stopped.

"Shit," I whispered.

I loved touching Lola's body. Loved the softness of her skin... how it felt against my lips. I loved the feel of her fingers tangled in my hair. I craved the feeling of our legs intertwined as she reached back to grasp and grip hold of the slats of the headboard, writhing in pleasure as my mouth consumed her and my hand grazed across her flesh. I was warmed by the fresh memory of Sean's eyes on my body as my eyes roamed the length of his wife.

She was my one great pleasure. She was my physical art. I touched her and stroked her in the same manner in which my brush maneuvered the canvas.

But she was married.

I respected the sanctity of marriage. Before my mother died, my parents had a wonderful marriage and even in death they somehow managed to be happy and committed.

But... I hadn't gone behind anyone's back. They brought me into their bed. Didn't just extend an invite, they insisted. So how could it be wrong?

How could it possibly be wrong?

How could it...

...be wrong?

"Screw it."

I grabbed my key ring and undid the locks. I closed the door behind and walked to my neighbor's place. I hesitated a moment... then moved my fist forward to tap. The locks were undone and the door opened immediately.

Lola smiled shyly as she peered at me from the other side of the door.

"You heard me knocking, didn't you?"

"Maybe."

"So what took you so long?"

Lola reached out and took my hand in hers and guided me inside.

I ripped the packaging away from the Hungry Man meal of fried chicken and mashed potatoes and placed it in the microwave. I set the time and then walked from the kitchen to the living room where a basket of dark clothes awaited me.

I was visiting my Dad. Was taking care of the odds and ends around the house. I'd gone grocery shopping earlier and stopped in a discount retail shop to pick up a couple packs of new socks. I'd tried to convince him to join me. He, of course, declined my request. He always denied my request. Since his wife died, he rarely left the house.

Occasionally, on a good day, I could convince him to go for a walk with me. We'd done so on this day... gone for a stroll around the block, but he would not venture any further.

I glanced at the clock to check the time. I suppressed my emotions. Darwin often came by after work on the days that I spent at my Dad's, keeping me company. Many times he and Daddy would play chess or we'd all find a good mystery show or watch whatever sport was in season. I'd spoken to him earlier in the day. He said he'd be by after work, but he had yet to arrive.

I took the basket and balanced it on my hip, carrying it downstairs to the basement. I took the whites and tossed them in the dryer. Loaded the soiled darks into the washer and started the load.

This was another place my Dad wouldn't venture to.

Our family's basement had been Zahrah's art studio. She'd spent a great many hours there creating. From six to eight in the evening most every weeknight and unscheduled four hour blocks on the weekend, my mom would be locked away in her studio hard at work.

Throughout my childhood, I'd frequently join her. She'd set a bowl of fruit on the table or create a scene with my favorite dolls and stuffed animals and challenge me to paint it. At the time it seemed impossible. How could I imitate such a setup using a pallet of goopy colors? How could I ever hope to be anywhere near as brilliant as she?

Eventually I found my own voice... found my style. Found that

I could create beautiful imagery with paint and brush. I also realized I wasn't exactly wrong either. I hadn't been as great as my mother was, and I didn't expect I ever would be.

She was my American idol.

When she died, I spent the first three months following in our basement trying to become her…and hating myself for being unable to do so.

It was my new friend Darwin who helped me to see beyond my rather limited expectations. He helped me understand that I was great in my own right. No, I wouldn't be my mother, and I shouldn't strive to be her. She was wonderfully talented, but Zahrah was uniquely Zahrah. I had a responsibility to honor her by being exactly who I was.

Uniquely Zella Dora.

I sat the basket on top of the washer and returned to the main level. I went directly to the kitchen and retrieved Dad's meal. I transferred it to a dish and tossed a slice of enriched bread on top. I poured a glass of pop over ice, then carried the food to him, placing it on his TV tray.

Dad sat in his recliner watching a contestant attempt to spin the wheel to win a large fortune and trying to solve the puzzle himself.

"Thank you, Sweet Pea. Looks good."

"You're welcome, Daddy. Let me know if you need anything else."

"Well ain't you gonna eat?"

"Yes sir, but I want to finish straightening things up so you… so you… guys won't have to."

My father grabbed my hand and squeezed. "You're such a good girl, you know that?"

"So you keep telling me," I giggled.

He released me and returned his attention to the puzzle. I returned to the kitchen.

I washed the few dishes in the sink. Swept the floor… wiped

down the countertops. I wasn't as good as my Aunt Leigh "the domestic goddess," but I did my thing.

I finished the chores. Had a Hungry Man for me but wasn't quite ready for that meal yet. I climbed onto a barstool beside the small table that sat in the middle of the kitchen. I slapped the rag I held repeatedly against the faux wood as I stared out of the window into the distance.

I jumped up. Walked to the window and retrieved my phone from the ledge. No missed calls. I walked to the other side of the kitchen and lifted the receiver from the phone hanging on the wall and dialed Darwin's number. He greeted me after two quick rings.

"Hey you."

"Hey lady, what's up? You still at Dad's?"

"Yep. Just fed him. He's in there watching his game shows. I've got a load going."

"Did you get him to go out with you today?"

"Some. He wouldn't leave the area no matter how I pushed. I did get him to go for a walk though. Did like three blocks before he was ready to go back. I was proud of him."

"That's dope."

"Yeah… it is. An improvement." There was a pause in the conversation. I continued, "So umm… you still at work?"

"Uhh, no. I just got home."

I nodded knowingly. My fingers followed the path through the coils in the phone cord. I began twisting it… wrapping it around my digit. "Thought you were coming through here. What happened?"

I listened to him breathe… deciphered the hemming and hawing on the other end of the line. "I… yeah, I didn't think it was a good idea."

"Why not?" I hated myself for asking, immediately after the whiny question escaped my lips.

"I just got a load on my mind right now."

"Is this because you… y'know, said what you said?" I asked tentatively.

"I told you it wasn't a big deal. I don't even know why I said it."

"You sure? I'm saying, D, I don't want that to break us apart. You're my best friend, and I don't know what I'd do without you."

"Z, Z, told you, TMI file. Okay? We're good. My mind is just bogged down with a lot of things."

"Well, tell me about it. You know you can talk to me about anything. You know it's therapeutic to get things off your chest."

We were quiet again. I didn't believe him. Wanted to… but I just didn't.

Darwin sighed. "I don't really want to talk about it… not now. I just kinda need some time. Time to sort things out…make decisions. Y'know, I gotta deal with my own crap. I'll talk to you about it when I'm ready. I just need you to give me some time right now. Just give me some room… please."

My eyes watered. Instantly watered. I wasn't a weak woman, didn't break easily, but emotion just overcame me. I leaned my head back to avert the flow.

"You need time, huh."

"Yeah, I just… I just need some time."

"So you're on with Ayinde, huh?"

"What? I don't know what that means."

I leaned into the doorjamb, scraping my nail across the white paint. "She, too, instructed me to give her time."

"Aw, you finally talked to Day? When?"

"Yesterday morning."

"She alright?"

"Yeah, I wouldn't really know. Like you, she needs time. She doesn't want me to call her anymore. She said she'll call me when she's ready."

Darwin was quiet. "Yo, Z, look. I'm sorry. I mean, I'm not really saying you can't call me, I'm just saying I need a little reclusion. I just need a few days to sort things out. Can you just give me that?"

"Yeah, sure." I exhaled. "If that's what you need… time, I'll give you time."

"Thanks. I'm not — I'm not pushing you away. Hey, tell Pops Robeson I said what up. I'll holler at you later on, alright?"

"Yeah… yeah alright."

Darwin disconnected before I could. I held the receiver… dropped it down and held it to my lips.

Tapped.

Sighed.

Resignation swept over my frame. My arms fell to my sides. I summoned the strength to put the phone back in its cradle, then walked to the back door. I unlocked it and stepped out into the evening sun. I dragged my heavy spirits across the porch and took a seat on the swing, trying my best to not think about Darwin's needs or Ayinde.

12 *Chapitre Douze*

I worked on the finishing touches of a portrait.

Janessa, the dancer friend that Lola hooked me up with, had commissioned me to do two paintings for her. One, of her and her husband Justice that she would hang in her foyer for the world to see and envy. The second, a large narcissistic beauty portrait that she would hang over their bed. She'd chickened out on the nudity, opting instead to wear a soft pink teddy. I was working to finish up the public one. She was in a hurry. I didn't mind, she paid very well.

I glanced at Lola. She was stretched across my bed reading a dated book by a brilliant author. She pretended to not pay any attention to me, but I'd felt her eyes. Felt the holes they burned on the side of my head. But when I looked her way, she was suddenly reading with a fierce intensity... in a land far away from here.

I grinned as I averted my attention back to the swatches and swirls of colors on my canvas. I'd done a damn good job on this one if I said so myself. I was proud. Pleased and proud.

I moved my eyes to Lola again. I was too fast for her this time... or she was just too slow. Our gazes locked. Mine coming from behind the colorful canvas with my brush in hand continuing its strategized strokes. Hers, from over the top of a dusty book.

"Why do you keep sneaking peaks at me?" I asked her lightheartedly.

"The better question is why you persist on stealing glances at me."

"You're flirting."

"How am I flirting?" She laughed mischievously. I shook my head and returned my focus to the task before me.

Lola had begun spending much of her time with me. Watching me paint, watching Bela, listening to Rahsaan Patterson... and getting too close. She was certainly being flirty. She'd been flirting with me... opening the door for some one-on-one time for a few weeks. I didn't clock many hours at Chaz's shop to begin with, fewer now that I was earning a decent living off the additional income from working my passion and Lola's leads. Since I was home so often and during Sean's work hours, Lola found an ample amount of excuses to leave work early and Patrice in charge. Oh the benefits of ownership.

I glanced at her again. This time she didn't try to hide. She looked directly at me. Intense eyes. No smile.

"What?" I chuckled. "Why you staring at me like that?"

"Why don't you leave that bloody painting alone?"

"Can't do that, L. Have to finish it. Janessa's stressing me. You know your girl."

"You're being rude, Zella. You have company."

"You knew I was working on this when you came here," I said imitating her sing-song voice.

"I don't care about Janessa and her over-the-top demands. She'll get her painting when she gets her painting. If she bitches about it, I'll deal with her."

"Well, I would agree 'cept I do care about Janessa's money paying my rent next month and putting food in my fridge."

"I'll buy your food."

"Then who's gonna pay my rent?"

Lola stood and walked toward me. She approached but continued past and to the kitchenette. "Are you thirsty, love?"

"Parched."

She returned to me with a bottle of water that she'd already courteously cracked open for me. She stood near as I continued to work. Her goal was to distract me. She was in heat and that warmth was to spread to me. I guzzled my H2O and hoped to cool down.

"Why do you insist on ignoring me?" Lola whined, sulking toward my bed.

"Not ignoring you."

"Zella. Zella!" She paused and reflected for a moment. "Answer me one question. Why haven't you yet made love to me?"

My eyes bulged, and I nearly spit water out and onto Janessa's painting. With the back of my hand, I smeared the wetness away. I sat the large brush inside a cup of tinted water and collapsed in Daddy's recliner.

"Get to the point, why don't you," I said sarcastically.

Lola sat up on the bed facing me, a bottle of water in one hand, resting on her elbows and waiting for a plausible response from me. I wasn't sure how to answer her, for I wasn't so sure as to what my position on the matter was.

The times I'd joined Sean and Lola in their bed, I opted to remove all but my underwear. That first time, she'd grabbed me by the back of my head and shoved her tongue deep inside my mouth sending shock waves through my system. I was slow to fully reciprocate. This was my neighbor. This was my neighbor's wife. This was the hot African beauty I'd pretended to not be interested in. And well... this was a woman.

She hadn't been my first woman, no. My sexual preference was by far for men, and I did not seek out attractive girls to play with, wasn't how I generally got down, but sometimes it happened. The first girl it happened with was Nanette Bridges. It was the early 90's, so we called her Nannie B.

She was the most fascinating person I'd met and absolutely gorgeous. A short girl with a tall personality and Belizean blood. Soft caramel swirl skin. Smooth. Like the flesh of an infant child. Light hazel-brown eyes that glistened in the sun. Two tone brown hair that nearly reached her elbows that she kept in a simple ponytail. When I was around she'd let me braid it.

We were sixteen years old. She lived in a large two-story house at the end of Aunt Leigh's block with her mom, six brothers, and a man that she called Uncle. In the time that I'd known her, Uncle had changed faces somewhere around four times. I didn't know what a lesbian was before I met Nannie B. I'd heard of them... was of course familiar with the concept of homosexuality, but it held no real meaning for me.

Nan and I were at her house. She'd just copped a sack, and I was charged with the responsibility of rolling the blunt. Her way of helping me to improve. Never knew when your weed rolling skills were going to be put to the test, and Nan made certain I'd be prepared.

She told me she was a lesbian, confessed to only liking girls while I gutted the Philly. I asked her how she knew. She shrugged, said she just did. I asked why? She was a girl. Shouldn't girls like boys? Wasn't that the law of nature? I licked the paper... closed it. Ran a flame beneath 'til it dried. She took the finished blunt from my fingers. Held it up... inspected it. Told me I'd done a good job. I beamed like a proud student. She put it to her lips. I lit it for her.

I asked again, asked why she liked girls... how it could be possible. Her eyes glazed over for a moment. I thought it may have meant something but then decided maybe it was just the onset of a high. A sec later she said to me: *If God wanted me to like boys, he wouldn't have put me in a family with six of 'em.*

I laughed.

She did not.

She wanted to know if it bothered me that she was gay... if it made me uncomfortable. I shrugged that time, I could care less. That night brother number four found us in the family's basement, a fresh blunt to my lips and Nan's face buried deep between my thighs.

Our affair lasted about three months. Since she lived out in "the wild hundreds" and I lived up North, it was nearly impossible for us to have any time together. She started kissing between another girl's thighs and I, having had the experience, returned to bat for my original team only occasionally being lured to the other side for a game.

And now I'd been seduced by the sensuality and sexuality that the other team possessed. I'd been enticed by more feminine prowess. This one wasn't a slightly butch lesbian who'd been around the block a few times and could get whoever she wanted. Wasn't a sexually bored bi-girl who was just looking for a change of pace and a little fun.

This one was a lioness who was playing with fire and determined to be completely ignited. It began as a kiss and had opened the flood gates of desire to so much more. If a consensual ménage wasn't defined as adultery, what she was asking of me now certainly had to be.

"You've made love to a girl before. Haven't you?" Lola asked.

"Haven't I?"

"Made love to a girl before, silly."

I nodded and sipped more water. "I have."

"Many times?"

She was excited. Sitting up on my bed, coal eyes bright. Legs crossed at the ankles and shaking from her nervous exhilaration.

"I've been with a couple."

"Who was the first?"

"Nanette Bridges."

"How old were you at the time?"

"Sixteen."

"Sixteen?"

"Sixteen."

"Really?"

"Really. Sixteen."

"Was she pretty?"

"Beautiful."

"More beautiful than me?" She posed when she asked that question. I laughed loudly.

"No. No she wasn't, silly."

"Are you just saying that?"

"She was different from you… definitely. She was not more beautiful."

"And where is she now?"

"Jail."

"Oh." Her smile evaporated.

A year after Nannie B had taken my… er, uhm… virginity, she went on a rampage and shot her second and third eldest brothers, the ones that'd been raping her for years without the slightest bit of remorse, without anyone knowing. One was paralyzed from the waist down. The other died at the hospital days later. Her mother testified against her, refusing to believe that her boys could have done such a thing. She had no remorse about helping to send her daughter to jail for the rest of her life.

When her verdict was read and at her sentencing, Nan didn't cry. She accepted the fate she was given, and in the courtroom as she was being led away, she looked back, taking advantage of the last time she'd probably ever see her mother… and with no remorse, flipped her the bird. Or so rumor had it.

"I'm serious, Zella, why won't you make love to me?" Lola whined. "Come here please, come lay beside me. I won't try anything, I promise."

"That's why your fingers are crossed?"

Lola blushed.

I stood from the recliner and walked to where she sat back

on my bed. I semi-reluctantly took a seat beside her. Immediately, her hand landed against my thigh. Low but purposefully. My eyes chastised. Hers mocked.

"C'mon, Zella." Her voice was deep and throaty.

Her hand began a slow ascension up my thigh, but my hand blocked her.

"Lola... Lola..." I swallowed hard the lump in my throat as her hand began to force mine to give way. "L!"

"What, Zella, what? Why the hell do you insist on continuing to fight this? I know you want me, you must. Love my body. The things you do..." She gulped air, and for a moment, her eyes glazed over before coming back. "Incredible. You touch me in ways and places Sean couldn't possibly know how to. Only a woman could know."

"What happened to your just wanting a kiss... a ménage to appease Sean?"

"I didn't know it could be like this. So sensual and beautiful, and... and magnificent. You're like a drug. Better than any drug. Every time I have you, I want more. Every time you reject me, you destroy a little part of me."

"Isn't that just a bit melodramatic?"

She shrugged. I reached into my ashtray and pulled the half-smoked fatty. I needed to clear my head. Eyes focused intently, Lola took it from my fingers and put it to her lips. She reached for my lighter. I snatched it away.

"L, c'mon. What are you doing? You don't even get high."

"If I did, would it turn you on?"

"Not anymore than you already do."

She took the lighter back. She held the flame to the tip, and she inhaled as she'd seen me do many times. She choked, hard. Coughed and struggled to catch her breath. I took the L and patted her back. Her eyes watered and turned red. Looking at her like that... looking at her attempt to impress me moments after having tried to seduce me, it did something to me.

She took deep cleansing breaths. She was fine. I put the joint to my lips and moved a stray piece of hair behind my ear before I stood and walked away. I had a responsibility. I wasn't going to help her alter the dynamics of her existence. I walked away.

"Zella, why are you walking away from me?"

"L, c'mon. I like you, I really do. I like you a lot. But Sean loves you, and I'm not gonna let you do this."

"Do what?"

"Do this! Smoke my weed. F'k me behind his back!"

She stood from the bed. "*You're* not going to allow *me* to do this. What are you, my mother? I'm doing what I want to do and let us not forget whose idea this was to begin with."

"Sean didn't ask for this, you did!"

"I gave Sean what he wanted, and he loved every bit of it. Never once did he try and stop it."

I sank slowly back into the seat. "I just don't think his consent included this."

"Zella. Love. He is my husband. Why don't you let me worry about what his consent does or does not include?"

I sighed and closed my eyes, my elbow on my thigh and my fingers massaging my temple. When my eyes opened, there she was, sitting on her knees on the floor before me.

Her hand grazed the side of my face.

"There, there, Zella. I appreciate your concern for Sean's and my marriage but we'll be fine. It's you and I that I'm thinking about."

"This is adul…"

I wasn't able to complete my sentence. Her lips were on mine, stealing my breath away. My rationale and righteousness were buried beneath layers someplace deep within my subconscious. What remained of my herb burned between my fingertips. Lola eased back and took it from me. She pulled on it a couple times, hit it like a pro, then put out its flame and proceeded to work on the pilot beneath mine. We kissed sweet serenades as her fingers played their way up my bare thighs like ebony and ivory were attached.

Then, there was a knock at the door.

"Don't answer it," she whispered into my mouth. "Pretend you aren't here."

"I can't. I'm expecting someone," I whispered my response.

"Well, they can come back later."

"L…" I gasped as her hand gripped the wet folds of flesh between my thighs. "L, stop it… stop."

Breathlessly, I grabbed her shoulders and pulled her back. There was a knock again then Margot's muffled voice insisting that she knew I was inside and to hurry because she had to pee.

I mouthed the word "sorry" before jumping to my feet and rushing to the door, trying desperately to conceal my relief. Margot brushed past me, apologizing as she rushed inside and directly to the bathroom. Kat laughed as she approached me, pulling me close for an embrace and kiss on the cheek as was customary with us.

"Hey sexy. Cute dress," she stated as she entered.

"Thanks," I answered in a low tone. I closed and locked the door, hesitating before turning back around.

"Hi," I heard Kat say to Lola. "I'm Kat, a friend of Z's."

I turned in time to see Lola reached out to limply accept Kat's hand. Her previously melodic voice was suddenly monotone. "Lola. Pleased to meet you."

She dropped Kat's hand quickly, like it was contaminated. Kat glanced at me. I discreetly shook my head. Lola gathered her belongings. Margot stepped from the bathroom, shaking her damp hands dry. She looked at Lola who was suddenly in a big hurry.

"Hello. I'm Margot."

Lola glanced her way. "Hey."

She moved fast across the floor in my direction near the door.

She glared at me. If looks could kill.

I searched for something to say. "You can... stop by..."

"No I don't think so. I'll talk to you later. Enjoy your company."

She unlocked and opened the door and stalked out turning right toward the staircase rather than left toward her apartment.

Slowly I closed the door, wondering what exactly I'd gotten myself into.

I stood outside the building. Stood beside a medium size U-Haul truck that had Margot sort of blocked in. It was a hot summer day. I loved the feel of the warmth of the sun wrapping itself around my skin. I felt the vitamin D seeping into my pores and enriching my melanin. Days like this, I craved Harold's Chicken and grape pop and remembered my childhood. Days like this, I missed Zahrah and Jacob.

I laughed as I deciphered the four letter words that Margot mouthed as Kat pounded her fists against the dashboard in hysteria. Margot finally managed to maneuver her vehicle. She double beeped as she drove away with Shane's portrait gift wrapped in brown paper in the back seat.

Tomorrow was Shane's birthday, the day she'd been waiting on... planning for. The day all my effort amounted to. I brushed away the twinge of irritation that was beginning to creep up on me. It was her decision. She decided to love him. He'd fathered her child. I'd done my part... done my job. I had the check drawn off the Bank of America account to prove it.

I wanted to call Darwin and vent but I remembered that I'd promised him time. He and Ayinde needed time and for some ridiculous reason I'd agreed to honor that.

I turned to head back inside the building alone. Margot and Kat spent at least two hours at my place after Lola left, and I still hadn't heard her return. I could venture a guess, but honestly I had no clue where she'd disappeared to. She had her cell, I could've called her. I couldn't bring myself to.

I felt a pillowy softness connect with my arm. Thinking of Lola had me distracted... walking into things or rather people. I jumped and stepped aside. Apologized.

"Oh it's okay, baby," the feminine voice attached to the person I'd nearly mowed down in the door entrance told me. "Zella, right? 3B?"

I paused and looked up nervously. "Yes?"

"Oh, hi honey. Such a pleasure to finally meet you."

I shook the hand that was thrust at me, completely awash with confusion. "And you would be?"

She giggled like a small child, and a look of embarrassment swept across her face. "Sorry. I'm Ms. Theadore Thompson. Miss... Theadore Thompson."

"Oh hi. Mr. Thompson's wife."

"Oh. No, no, you don't listen very well, do ya, child?"

I blushed.

"I am *Miss* Theadore Thompson. Miss? We're divorced. Jackass and I are divorced. See that's what I call him. You call him *Mister* Thompson I call him, no-good-cheatin'-jackass-who-can't-budget-for-shit."

I tried not to laugh as hard as I wanted to and only approved the release of a small chuckle. I didn't know the appropriate response to ex-husband bashing so all I said was, "Oh."

There was thunderous laughter from her and her plum cheeks turned round and rosy while her massive bosom jiggled.

"Oh, don't tell me you ain't never heard an old bitter divorcee bash her trash husband before? In this day and age when don't no one stay together? I guess you one of the lucky ones. Your parents ain't divorced?"

"My dad's a widow."

"See, Thea, there you go with that big ol' mouth of yourn. Listen, never mind me. See these feet I'm standing on here. Ain't bit mo' than a size five. God knew what he was doin' when he gave me small feet. Knew they would spend mo' time in my mouth than on the ground!"

I laughed at that. Laughed hard. *Miss* Theodore Thompson put a plump hand to my cheek. "There ya go, chile. Got such a beautiful smile. Ooh and such pretty white teeth." She looked at me like that for a short while... her hand on my cheek, smiling at me. "Oh well, I had better get to getting. Got a couple mo' things in this truck I need to haul upstairs."

"The U-Haul?" I asked. She nodded. "Do you need me to help?"

"Oh, honey, that would be just wonderful if you did. Oh, but I can't ask you that. You ain't too busy, are you?"

I chuckled. "No, ma'am."

"'Cause I can handle things myself. Gregory – that's the jackass you call *Mister* Thompson –never would accept that I could be independent and handle things on my own. Best believe that jackass believe it now!"

She walked from the doorway, began charging down the walkway. Signaled for me to follow. I helped her finish unloading. Just bags mostly. A couple boxes and a 13" television. Her big items, furnishings were already inside. Told me those things had been officially moved in the other day. Her nephew and Greg's – I mean, "The Jackass'", two boys had moved her in. I was unaware of the change in tenancy. I must have been clocked in at Chaz's that day.

I didn't really understand the point of this second trip and truck rental, alone and without the help of the children. She explained something to me about the things coming from the basement of her former home and being private. I decided to just let it be and help. Wasn't really my business anyway. Apparently her daughter didn't understand either. After a small battle regarding it, it seemed Ria, her daughter and only biological child, rented the truck and told her mother to call when she was done so that she could come get it and turn it in.

We finished in at least a third of the time it'd taken her alone. When we were done, I began to leave. She stopped me.

"You have to leave so soon? C'mon, let me fix you up a mug of tea. Least I can do. My way of saying thank you." She turned and walked away, talked to me from the kitchen. "I got some new tea, too. Plum monkey. Try it with me."

She had such a contagious personality. I couldn't resist her. "Yeah, sure *Miss* Thompson. I don't think I'm too busy for tea."

"Oh chile, now just because I'm gone be your new landlady don't mean you got to go being so formal." She paused for a contemplative minute. "Well except for maybe on rent day. Chile, I ain't nobody's friend on rent day. But after money change hands, we can pick right back off where we left off at. You can just call me Thea." She paused and thought about it for a moment.

"Well, nah, wait a minute. You 'bout half my age, and I ain't a bit mo' interested in trying to pretend I'm some young thing. Them days been gone. Besides, when I pop off my bra and this voluptuous bosom drop down to my knees like sandbags, I don't really think I can fool nobody no way. Miss Thea. You can just call me Miss Thea."

I smiled. Cheesed actually and laughed. "It would be my pleasure to have tea with you, Miss Thea."

"Well that's alright now. Go on and have a seat. A small thing, ain't you? Cook much?"

"Not really. No good at it."

"Aw Lawd. Ms. Thea here now. Gone have to fatten you up. Got a boyfriend?"

I blushed and shook my head no. She only pursed her lips and shook her head at me.

I sat in a chair at a small round table by the window. A very dated one. Had to be the same table she'd fed her daughter at when she was a toddler back in the early 1970's.

Ms. Thea was going to be my new landlady because she'd been awarded the building as part of her settlement agreement with my former landlord, Mr. "Jackass" Thompson.

I'd never before had the pleasure of having met her though

she'd visited the building a couple times to introduce herself before the transition. I was out on those occasions. She'd met Sean and Lola. Managed to do it twice. Thought they were a lovely couple. Reminded her of how she and Mr. Thompson used to be back when they met and married, back when little Ria was just two and didn't know what it meant that her biological father had disappeared and this man, who already had children of his own, had stepped in to claim her as his.

She'd recognized me strictly based on Lola's description. Now that she'd met me, thought I reminded her of her grandchild... Ria's daughter Delaney. Was crazy about Delaney because she was nothing like her "uptight, over-educated, over-achieving, power broker mother." I asked Delaney's age. Ms. Thea smiled and looked away, changed the subject to tea. I didn't have much input. I was a known coffee girl, but I did enjoy the conversation and the plum monkey nonetheless. Enjoyed it so much so that I gave my word that we'd do it again as brunch the following Sunday.

I licked my lips as my eyes stayed locked on Lola's mouth.

The cool silver smoke from the burning roach created a path from Lola's lips and into the atmosphere. I hadn't brought my vice into Sean's home willingly. Lola stole it from my ashtray. It was one I'd had a small influence from shortly before she knocked on my door three days after she'd walked out of it in what seemed to be a small fit of jealousy.

Three days went by without having spoken to Lola. There was quiet on the opposite side of my wall for as long as there was silence between she and I. I was unsure how to translate her behavior, but I was rather relieved to be taken out of the equation. Not that I wasn't missing her like crazy, especially when I heard her coming and going.

The first time I detected her in the hallway, my heart caught in my throat. I was busy reading a VC Andrews novel. I was on the chapter where Alice was showing Craig the attic. I couldn't concentrate. I read the words but didn't comprehend.

She stood in the hall for likely longer than was necessary... likely contemplating knocking on my door. Probably holding her breath in perfect sync with mine. I exhaled seconds before I heard the click of the Brown's door. As much as it pained me to think it, I hoped that whatever had set Lola off to begin with convinced her that our three-way affair could not continue as it had.

It hadn't.

It was day three... the evening of day three and once again I sat in the middle of Sean and Lola's pillow-top amongst ruffled sheets and tossed pillows. Observing them. Observing the changes within them. Two months. Two months later and here I was observing major changes in them... this couple that shared a love that I'd envied.

Lola leaned toward me, interrupting my train of thought. I glanced away from the spans of space in which I'd been unconsciously staring at and into the reality that I was presently in.

"Shotgun," she whispered to me, giggling.

"Excuse me."

"Shotgun." She was smiling at me. Smiling broadly.

I glanced at Sean. He was laid on his back, eyes closed. But he wasn't asleep. My eyes returned to hers. I looked over her face. She smiled brightly.

"Exactly how long *have* you been doing this?"

She laughed softly and eased her hand across my cheek. "Just a couple days, love."

"And you're offering me a shotgun."

She nodded. Smiling... still smiling and staring at me. Sexy and beautiful. "Come. We're almost out. Hurry, please, I'd like for this thing to not burn off my fingerprints here."

"How do you even know what a shotgun is?"

"Love."

"L."

She huffed and pouted. "Saw it in a film last night. It looked sexy... then I thought about you."

I glanced at Sean again. He was still on his back, still nude beneath the sheet that was pulled up just past his pelvis. Quiet. Not moving but not asleep. Definitely not asleep.

My eyes returned to Lola's.

"I have to go," I whispered.

"Why? Come on, Zella, just open your mouth. Let me try it."

I stared at her, contemplating whether or not to give into her whim. A three day old weed head offering me a shotgun.

"Babe, what are you doing?" Sean said.

We, Lola and I, turned at the same time. We looked to where Sean was still lying. He hadn't moved, continued to lie on his back beneath the sheet with his arm stretched over his face and concealing his eyes.

"Trying to have a little fun, love," Lola answered.

"Why are you smoking anything at all?"

"It isn't a big deal, Sean."

Finally he moved, quickly. Flung his arm from his face and eased up. "It *is* a big deal, Lo. It's a drug. No offense, Zell."

"None taken."

Lola rolled her eyes and returned her silly, cute grin to me. She bit down on her bottom lip staring lustily at me before speaking. "Zella's smoked for years and she's beautiful and intelligent and sexy... it hasn't ruined her."

I blushed.

Sean twisted and rested his weight on his elbow... looking up at me. He took my foot in his hand and began to massage it. "No. It hasn't."

Our eyes locked. The way he looked at me... made me blush again.

"Shit!" Lola cried out, jumping and dropping the roach onto the bed. She scrambled for it, finding and hurrying to put out its heat, placing it on the small round table at their bedside.

Sean's fingers kneaded my flesh, deeper and harder. His eyes didn't leave my face. I watched him watching me, his eyes refusing to look away. I was afraid to blink; afraid I'd miss out somehow if I broke contact.

Without disconnecting his stare from me, his head eased lower, and his mouth wrapped around my toes. I gasped quietly as he took me into his mouth. I'd lost track of Lola. I felt her presence... knew she was watching and even sensed a change in her energy, but I couldn't look away from her husband's beautiful face.

"Why do you do it, Zella?" His eyes eased closed as he tasted me, enjoyed the flavor that my toes apparently transmitted.

I swallowed hard, and my voice escaped as a hoarse whisper, "Why do I do what?"

"Drugs."

"I don't do drugs plural... I do *a* drug."

"Why do you do *any* drug?"

I moaned a little and fought to keep watching him... to not close my eyes. His hand caressed my calf. "I don't... mmm... I don't know. I like... it. Like... how it makes... me feel."

"Mmhm. How about me? Do you like how I'm making you feel?"

I'd dismissed Lola, forgot she existed. No longer knew where she was in the room. She could have been right beside me or she could have been gone from the apartment. I didn't know. Wasn't aware. Didn't care. I only saw Sean. Only felt his breath and the warmth of his mouth as he took turns suckling my toes and massaging my feet. Only felt the shooting electricity coursing through me, causing the dam within to break sending wetness shooting down to my already sticky and moist panties.

My back arched and my lids hung low. Without considering my actions, I allowed my hands to roam my body... squeezing my breasts and teasing my hard nipples.

"Yes," I answered, allowing my eyes to close and my head to fall away. "That feels great."

"My wife... she wants to impress you."

My eyelids fluttered open... slowly, and my head turned to the side. I found Lola sitting there only a few inches away, glaring at Sean. Smile gone and speechless.

My body stiffened, and my sexual high began to decrease. Reality was settling in. I thought... thought she was angry and jealous that her husband was showing another woman the attention that should have been reserved for her. But that wasn't it. She glanced at me... caught me looking at her, and immediately I knew that wasn't it. Her expression softened when she looked at me.

She eased across the bed, lifting her leg and swinging it around, she straddled me. She slowly rocked back and forth, rubbing her body against mine. Her mouth opened wide then closed around my neck, her teeth sinking into my flesh. Sean continued loving my feet with his mouth as Lola's hand gripped and caressed my breasts while she nibbled and sucked my neck with great passion.

I fought my erotic emotions. Fought hard. I moaned and sighed as my breasts heaved. I swore quietly both as an expression of carnal pleasure as much as out of moral conflict. I battled against myself, within myself. Wanted to allow myself to slip away. Be had. Be taken right there. Both genders. At once or in turn. Wanted to give them what they desired. Allow Sean inside of my body. To thrust deep within and feel my tightness gripping him as he swelled between my walls.

Allow Lola to stroke me. To taste me, lick me until I came and clear liquid flowed from that spot deep within me. That part that I couldn't reach or point out but knew by its vibrations that it wasn't a myth, it truly existed.

I was getting lost... swept away. My nails clawed against Lola's back as her teeth sank into me and her hand pushed down the side of my panties. My body volunteered assistance. My hips lifted from the bed and a chill rushed over me as Lola's fingers grazed the top of my southern hemi as a result of her attempt to continue undressing me. I swore passionately. I would let her do it. I'd let her do me and I would do her... and then I'd have my way with Sean.

"F'k me, Zella," she whispered fiercely in my ear. "F'k me and make me feel like I've never felt before."

My breath caught in my throat, and my eyes opened. I looked to Sean. He was pleasuring me but mentally he was no longer focused on me. His eyes were on his wife's back... watching her grind against me and tug my underpants further down. He watched her and that intensely aggressive look that had just moments earlier been in his wife's eyes when she watched his interaction with me, was now in his.

It wasn't what it was meant to be.

It wasn't what I wanted it to be.

This was no longer the loving couple that I'd found so enviable.

In that moment, I began to fully understand what it was. She wanted me over him. He wanted me so as to make her jealous and bring her back to him.

It had become twisted.

The wages of sin...

"I have to go," I stated quietly, pulling my foot away from Sean's grasp and moving Lola's hands from my undergarments.

"Don't be silly," Lola whispered while still kissing and biting and reaching toward what she wanted once again. "Now hand me your knickers and let's play a little game."

"No, Lola, seriously."

"Zella. You can't be −"

"Lola, stop. I have to go."

Lola ceased her kisses and fondling and sat upright on me, no longer smiling.

"You're for real."

"Yeah, I'm serious. You gotta get up."

She stopped kissing me and fondling me, but she didn't get up. She sat... straddling me and glaring down as I glared up. Sean mumbled for Lola to "Come on" and tried gently to remove her, but she twisted hard and removed herself from his grasp.

"Zella, why do you have to go?" Her eyes were pleading.

My head shook side to side. Thoughts were racing through my mind. I glanced at Sean, saw the desperation and confusion etched across his face. Our eyes met. I communicated my non-verbal conflicted emotions and from what I could tell, he understood.

"Get up," I told Lola.

"No. First tell me why."

"Get up."

"No, Zella! Tell me why!"

"Because it's wrong!" I grabbed her by her waist and managed to remove her from me. She didn't fight me as she'd done her husband.

I stood from the bed and pulled my underpants back up to my waist. I found my bra, t-shirt, and shorts and began to dress, ignoring Lola who stood beside me wrapped in a sheet pleading with me to answer a question much deeper than the one she was actually asking.

I sighed and tried hard to avoid looking into her face… couldn't look into her beautiful face and those beautiful coal-colored eyes. I averted my attention. My eyes landed on Sean's back. He sat quietly on the edge of the bed with his back to us and his head low while his wife remained oblivious.

She continued pleading.

I continued in my efforts to stop her. "L. L!"

"Yes, love?"

"Look at your husband."

"What about him? He's fine."

"No, he's not!" I wouldn't look directly at her. I refused to make eye contact. If I did, I would have melted beneath her gaze. "L, this isn't cool anymore."

She laughed uncomfortably. "Love, Sean and I are fine. I've told you that."

"Sean's not fine, Lola."

"Rubbish! He'll be fine."

"Are you hearing yourself?"

The sound of footsteps and then a door slamming rocked the apartment. Sean had closed himself off in the bathroom. Lola jumped from being startled but didn't otherwise budge. I finally faced her. She was pissing me the f'k off.

I pulled my shirt completely over my head and glared at her. "Either you're blind, dumb, or you just don't give a shit, but *this* isn't working. Not any longer. You're standing here throwing your pussy at me while your husband is locked away in the bathroom! I didn't sign up for this."

"Zella, don't…"

"Lola, no. Go tend to your husband." She grabbed my wrist, but I snatched away. "Let me go. Please. Just let me go."

Her hands dropped away. I turned and stalked from the apartment and walked next door to mine. I closed the door softly behind me and pressed my forehead against its frame. I thought of my parent's marriage. Heard their laughter. Saw their smiles, the way they would look at one another. I turned and stood with my back to the door and my eyes closed tight. A tear trailed. For the briefest of moments, I felt Zahrah's presence beside me.

Laughter and the sounds of sex emanated from my childhood home. Embedded in each and every crack, crease, and pore of our place. I respected the sanctity of marriage, truly I did. I'd f'ked up… we'd f'ked up. This… what we'd done was hard to resist. For me, Lola was hard to resist.

In the beginning, I'd envied their love. When it was over, when they were done love making, they touched. We'd talk and they'd touch. I'd take more pleasure in watching them flirt and fondle, cuddle and snuggle up against one another than in what we'd actually just done. But it changed. Someday, one day along the line things switched a bit, and soon Lola spent our moments after sex snuggled to me and stroking my hair while Sean indulged in his obsession for fondling my feet.

I pounded my fist once against the door and stepped away. I laughed a little, couldn't help myself. I was crazy. Crazy for the accented African. The handsome northwestern American with the sexy lips. I was also a hypocrite. I laughed at myself. I needed a smoke. I needed a drink. I needed some fresh air.

I grabbed my phone and walked to my closet and dropped down beside it. I sat on the hard floor and reached inside, pulling boxes of shoes forward, lifting each top and peaking inside. As I did so, I dialed Darwin's number.

I hadn't realized how nervous I'd be. There hadn't been much conversation between him and me since he poured his heart out to me. When we did speak, on the occasions that he'd call me to ask about my father or find out whether I knew how Ayinde was doing, the conversations were rather strained and awkward. Our most recent conversation consisted of him requesting I give him time and I'd agreed. Foolishly, I had agreed.

This phone call… this reneged on our deal. But maybe… maybe if we fixed our relationship, I could escape my adulterous one.

I held my breath as I held the phone to my ear listening to the ringing of his phone while I held up a hot pink heel I'd taken out to contemplate. Darwin was my friend… he was family. Had been for six years. There was no other option. I didn't have time. We had to fix this.

He answered, "'Sup, Zella."

"Hey, D. What umm… what are you doing?"

"Not much. Just rented a movie. Is everything okay?"

"Yeah, why? Something's gotta be wrong for me to call? I mean, I know you said you needed… time, but you did say you weren't forbidding me to call."

"No, no, it's fine. But uhh… what's up?"

I twirled the shoe in my hand then balanced the heel on my finger.

"Don't… you… wanna go out?"

There was silence from his end. I imagined him looking away and sucking his teeth.

"I'm tired, Z."

"C'mon, D. Haven't seen you in forever. You can't keep avoiding me."

"Zella…"

"Darwin. You just got paid. It's Friday night. Party at the Abbey Pub jumpin'."

He laughed, and it sounded oh so sweet to my eardrums. His voice crackled when he spoke. He didn't want to tell me no, but he hadn't said yes.

"Z, I…"

"They're having a freestyle battle. Guess who's in it."

"Naw, naw. Not who I think."

"Rikers."

"Hell naw. Didn't that fool get boo'd off the stage last time? At The Note?"

"Can't fault the man for having resilience."

Darwin laughed heartily. In that moment, it was almost like old times — almost. But I wasn't so naïve to believe that we'd miraculously picked up where we left off… that suddenly we were healed.

"Naw, I suppose I can't." He exhaled heavily. "Aiight girl, how long you need?"

"I can take the train, D. I don't want to take you out of your way."

"Stop it. How long?"

I smiled childlike. "An hour tops."

"See you then."

We disconnected, and I couldn't stop grinning. I'd missed him so. My best effin' friend.

The bass from the music the DJ was spinning lured us to the door. I skipped along in the hot pink heels I'd finally had an opportunity to rock, with my arm looped through Darwin's and my head resting on his forearm. I felt good in his embrace. Loved his touch. Felt like home.

My boy Josh was standing outside the club as we approached, passing slick and colorful flyers into the hands of the patrons who'd had enough for one evening and were heading to some place other than this. He hugged me close and whispered his appreciation of my body dressed in a denim mini that hugged the contours of my hips perfectly.

I tossed my head back in laughter and smacked his arm. I reminded him that he was merely a kid. He reminded me that age was just a number and he could show me how much he was *not* a kid if I would dare give him a shot.

I scolded him with a look.

He laughed and pretended it was all a joke.

I knew better but let him off the hook.

He reached back and held the door open for me and I stepped inside, and Josh and Darwin exchanged courteous niceties as men do. I walked ahead to the cashier and hurried to pay the tab for the entrance for two before Darwin had an opportunity to protest. It was my idea to come out to this place; therefore, I should have been fiscally responsible.

I stepped aside and waited for Darwin to catch up to me. We intermingled with the crowd. Lovers of real Hip Hop, its music and culture. Not the watered down crap the generation succeeding us was being raised on.

"You know you're a jerk, right? You know that, right?" he said loudly to me so as to be heard over the music.

I laughed. "Almost done with a painting so I'll be getting a nice fat check. Consider this my celebration. My treat."

"Word? Who'd you do a piece for?"

"This chick named Janessa. You don't know her. A friend of my neighbor. One of the pretentious broads she went to Columbia with."

"That's tight. Well, congratulations, Sweet Pea!"

Smiling, I punched him playfully in his arm for referring to me publicly by my childhood nickname.

We continued forward, deeper into the thick of the crowd. Body heat rising up all around. It was a nice place with a cool crowd that had grouped together in the middle of the dance floor as soon as the stage action began; giving the appearance of being more crowded than it was in actuality. The vast majority of spectators clumped together, oohing and aahing and rocking their bodies while nodding their heads to the sounds of the DJ cutting in the background, playing a popular beat to accompany the tall lanky White cat who tried his very best to control the mic – but wasn't quite getting it. His opponent stood off to the side… a female, holding her mic and moving her upper body backwards and forth while mentally preparing her rebuttal.

I loved this. This was me. A perfect bullet point definition of Zella Dora. There weren't many women in the crowd, the males outnumbered us at least five-to-one. And the ones that were there, I would have ventured a guess that at least seventy-five percent were there out of obligation… not really all that interested in what was going on yet entertained nonetheless.

This was something else that Darwin and I had that no one could take away from us. It was that positive thing that we had in common and over the years we'd done events like this frequently. Freestyle battles. Break battles. Beat battles. Underground shows featuring local MC's. Graf art showcases. Many nights we'd sit around my place or his with our invisible friend Mary Jane embracing us, wisecracking, snacking and listening to Hip Hop classics.

The female won the round sending up whoopin' shouts of girl power throughout the crowd, self included. Darwin and I looked at one another as Rikers took to the stage. I could only laugh at

Darwin's expression. His eyes went back to the performance in progress and mine managed to connect for the second time that evening with a good looking brown skinned guy a few steps away. He smiled, his gaze going from my eyes to the side of Darwin's head then back to me. Discreetly I shook my head no. His smile broadened and I was pretty certain my cheeks blushed. For awhile we flirted… with our eyes, from a distance.

"You would think this guy would learn!"

I'd heard Darwin say the words, but they didn't immediately register. "Huh?"

Quickly, I took my sights from my new interest and to Darwin's face. Darwin looked from me and into the direction I'd been smiling in just a sec earlier, then back to me.

"Never mind."

"What did you say?"

"Ay, I'm going to go to the bathroom."

"Darwin!"

He walked away not acknowledging any further utterances from me. I almost suspected that something was wrong, but the feeling that someone was invading my three-feet of personal space interrupted my assessment and turned me around.

"Thought he'd never leave," he said. "That ain't ya man, right?"

"Nah, just a close friend of mine. Like a brother."

"Word."

I smiled. So did he. He was handsome. Tall and dark with full lips, an ideal nose, and perfectly shaped bald head. He extended his hand and introduced himself to me and I to him. He was fit, and I couldn't help myself; I had to fondle his strong arms, bare from him wearing a short sleeved Polo shirt.

We'd seemed to have forgotten the battle that we'd paid to see. We were spending more of our time fact sharing with one another over the heavy bass lines than engaging in and reacting to the clever wordplay being displayed on the stage several feet before us.

He wondered if I was new to the scene.

Told him no, been a B-girl for as long as I could recall... since I'd seen *Beat Street* with Aunt Leighs' eldest at the dollar show when I was just a kid.

Said he hadn't seen me around.

Told him I hadn't been around in the past six months or so.

Said he liked my pumps.

Told him thanks, I liked them, too (wink).

He gave me his number. Was gonna get back to his boys... the people he'd come with.

I kept mine secret. Wouldn't have to wait on his call that way. Control was all mine.

He asked that I promise to call.

I played coy. Said I'd think about it. Smiled and waved. Turned away. Went to find where Darwin had disappeared to. Felt Brown Skin's eyes watching me as I searched for an opening in the crowd and made my exit.

I stopped and stood in the area near the bar, steps from the door, looking around. Darwin had excused himself to the men's room at least fifteen minutes prior. Unless he was having plumbing problems, logic said he should have already been done.

I glanced up and spotted him watching the events from a chair on the second level. Agitation breezed by me, but I allowed it to continue forth. Didn't bother to catch it. I made my way to the stairwell and walked up and over to where he sat. I found an empty chair and pulled up beside him. He sat with his arms resting on the railing, drink in hand and gaze intense and expressionless.

"What you drinking?" I asked over the music.

"Coke." He stretched the drink out in my direction without looking to me.

I held up my hand and gently pushed it away as if to say *No thanks*.

I sensed something was up, but I was hesitant to deal with it. I sat quietly beside him, trying as I might to ignore the eight-hundred pound gorilla that'd just walked into the club.

"Let me know when you're ready to go," he said suddenly, still not looking my way.

Startled, my head jerked back. "Are *you* ready to go?"

"I'm ready whenever you're ready."

I leaned back in my seat and looked away, recounting the events of the very brief evening. Trying hard to calculate what went wrong.

I turned back and leaned closer to his ear. "What's the matter with you?"

"Nothing. I'm cool."

"And you were good when we walked up in here, so what made your status drop down a notch?"

"I said I'm cool, Z. When you're ready to dip, let me know."

"C'mon, D, stop playing me like I'm brand new."

Finally, he turned to face me. "I'm ready to go. You done pimpin'?" It was a label, not an accusation.

I glared at him. He glared in return, showed no trepidation whatsoever. I sucked my teeth and stood and moved for the stairwell. He was left behind, taking his time. Moving awfully slowly for someone in a hurry to leave. I waited at the bottom of the steps for him to catch up. He silently moved down the stairs and passed by me. Continued forward as though I weren't even there. My breaths became heavier and more labored. I caught up to him and passed by, stopping just beyond the doors outside.

Darwin, on the other hand, didn't stop. Saw me, but didn't stop. Told me he'd go get the car and meet me in the front of the club. Guised it as his doing me a favor by keeping me from needing to do too much more walking in my pretty shoes. I grabbed his arm. Approached him like a scorned girlfriend who'd just busted her man hollerin' at another chick.

"What are you mad about?" I asked.

His voice was eerily calm when he replied, "Not mad."

"Yes, you are. You must have forgotten who you're talking to."

"Can we go, Zella?"

"Sure can, just as soon as you tell me what got your draws in a bunch."

"Shit, Zella! Ain't shit! I just wanna go home, is that too damn much to ask? It's late. I'm tired. Should've never brought my ass out to this bullshit anyway. Miko at the crib -"

"Miko?"

" – shoulda followed my first mind. Trying to be there for you -"

"Be there for me?"

"I don't have time for this shit anymore. I'll be thirty-six years old this year. I'm too damned old to be playing these games."

"Hold on!" My body was warm, my entire body from temple to toes. I was heated. This was my best friend for years. How could he dare play me out like this? "Just hold on one got-damn minute! I didn't make you go anywhere. I asked you true indeed, but you didn't have to come. Coulda told me you had company, that's first off. Second, don't try to front on me like now all of a sudden you're Mister effin maturity entertaining your silly little friend -"

"I didn't say that, Z. Don't start with the melodramatics."

"Then what you sayin', D? Cause if I recall just a couple months back, you were down with a house set out West. What, you just grew the f'k up over the balance of the Spring season? Or maybe it's that since your little confession you've decided that you can't bear to see me take an interest in a guy other than you."

"Never known you to be so full of yourself."

"What happened to file it away in TMI? I did that... did what you asked and now we hardly speak, and it's awkward at best when we do 'cause you decided to get all Dr. Phil and share your emotions."

Darwin looked like a wounded puppy. Tried hard to conceal his emotions... protect his ego. He shook his head. Looked like he left his body. Wasn't really speaking to me anymore. Speaking his mind. Talking around me.

"Doesn't really matter. It's my fault. You're right, it's my fault. Should've known. I'm too much of a nice guy to ever be taken seriously. Nice guys are always the friend. Never leave the friend zone. I'm not a thug... not hard enough."

"What the hell are you talking about? I am not that chick. You *know* I am not that chick." I shook my head, tugged at my hair. "You just shouldn't have told me. You're supposed to be like my brother... like family. I just wish you'd have never told me."

Darwin looked at me... stared into my eyes. "Yeah... I wish I hadn't either."

We looked at one another for a moment. I wouldn't budge... couldn't. He couldn't take it back. Couldn't make it go away or pretend it hadn't happened. So where'd that leave us? Hopefully in a condition we could recover from but for now –

"Going to get the car. Wait here."

I sulked into the shadows, hoping to not be recognized as he began the three-block trek down the street to get the car.

The little red teapot sat on top of a colorful oven mitt.

Hot water brewed inside. In the basket that sat firmly in place at the top, reddish-purple leaves steeped. Plum Monkey. We'd tried it for the very first time together the day I met Ms. Thea and helped her finish moving into her place on the second floor.

I stood in her kitchen in front of the counter slicing a lemon. I found a small pink bowl and placed my handiwork inside. I pulled two teacups forth and located their matching plates. I sifted through a drawer finding a long slender spoon with a dip.

As I carried the teapot and paraphernalia to the round kitchen table, Ms. Thea mixed the fruit slices she'd hand cut on a serving dish.

Peaches.

Apples.

Cantaloupe.

Strawberries.

Honeydew.

All of those fresh summer fruits covered the dish. She took the half of the lemon I had not used and squeezed a bit over the fruit then sprinkled it with a pinch of pumpkin spice. A large bowl of green and red grapes already occupied space on the table which sat by a window overlooking the courtyard.

This had become our unofficial Sunday tradition. Ms. Thea, my fifty-two year old newly divorced landlady, had somehow become my new best friend. Ayinde was still refusing to take my phone calls and in all honesty, I hadn't bothered calling her as much as I had immediately following all that'd gone down. I took it as a well deserved break. I had plenty enough new stresses in my world, didn't need any from her to add to the top of that pile. If she was around, my Jenga tower would surely collapse.

I hoped that she was okay although I had a sneaking suspicion that she wasn't. But I wouldn't dwell on that, couldn't dwell on that. We were all adults, and at some point, one has to finally say enough is enough and grow the hell up. She had to do that on her own. Couldn't be expected to reach that breaking point that would either destroy her completely or allow her to rise like a Phoenix from smoldering ashes if Darwin or I were constantly hanging around with proverbial needle and thread and mending her heart.

I had to let her be.

Allow her to be broken.

And in the absence of Ayinde and Darwin, Ms. Thea had become my new best friend because my old ones egos wouldn't allow them to have me active in their lives.

Two weeks had gone by with no word from Darwin. No casual concern for how I was doing. No what once had been an obligatory phone call to see how my father was doing. No call born of curiosity to see if I'd heard anything from Ayinde.

He'd driven me home and then drove himself away from me. We'd left the club without witnessing the conclusion of the freestyle battle I'd paid for us to see all because I'd flirted with a handsome stranger in front of him. He wouldn't admit it. In the interest of manhood, he'd withhold that information, wouldn't ever confirm it, but I knew better.

Miko had been at his house, or so he said. He'd left Miko alone at his home waiting because I'd called on him and then I'd gone and made eyes with a handsome brown skinned stranger who I hadn't bothered to call, for he represented the possible demise of my very best friendship.

And then there was Lola. I avoided running into her in the hallway that we shared, and she managed to maintain her distance from me.

The night where everything that could go wrong did go wrong and Darwin drove me home in dead silence, dropping me at my gate and peeling away without any closure, Lola tapped on my wall.

One tap.

She was awake… or awakened when I got home. Must have heard my door. Contemplated… maybe. Or maybe was giving me time to get settled in. As soon as I laid my head on my pillow, there she was. Hovering. Longing on the opposite side of the wall. Craving me as my walls clenched tight in my craving for her. Smelling her scent that was long gone… washed away only a couple hours earlier. She was probably smelling my scent that was still fresh in their bedding.

One tap.

She issued one tap that jarred me, aroused me, sent my hand involuntarily into the space between my thighs, squeezing tightly, refusing to succumb to the desires of my loins.

One solitary tap.

Had I been anywhere but there, I'd have missed it. I wondered where her husband was when she attempted to beckon me. Was he there beside her, encouraging her to try again or was he somewhere deep, deep in the land of dreams. Was he still holed up in their bathroom working hard to save face and determine how he felt about this thing we had going on, this thing that was slowly pulling his wife away from him and into the intimate embrace of another? Maybe he'd left her alone and she wanted me to come fill that void while he was away.

Had she tapped twice I may have gone to her.

But she didn't.

And because I couldn't talk to Lola and because Ayinde and Darwin was absent from my life, the woman who'd be collecting a check from me once a month had become my new best friend and Sunday brunch buddy. A woman old enough to have mothered me. A woman named Theadore, named after her father who'd died in a war, only spelled different. A father she'd never known but always imagined what he'd be like.

A quick-witted woman with one biological daughter whose nerves she loved to stand on for the sheer pleasure of it and because she decided it was her right as a parent to do so.

A short robust woman with breasts much larger than any other part of her figure. A bright skinned, green eyed woman who's straight dark hair stopped at her waistline.

A Creole woman from a small Louisiana town outside Nawlins who, when she was a beautifully exotic sixteen-year-old mother of one, met a handsome stranger who was passing through her town named Gregory Thompson, who'd swept her off her tiny little feet. A stranger who she followed all around the South during the conclusion of dangerous times before making him her husband after landing in Chicago, one year later.

Now, here she was after thirty-five years of marriage, alone and kept company by a woman young enough to be friends with her only child and a renewed cigarette habit.

No wonder she called him Jackass.

Delaney was all I couldn't understand.

Delaney was Ms. Thea's only blood related grandchild, Ria's daughter. There were photos of her everywhere from various points in life. From a sweet little red faced infant with shiny dark hair to a beautiful young girl with large brown eyes and skin a shade darker than her Nana's.

The photo I determined to be the most recent was one taken at school as memorabilia for that academic year. She smiled bright.

Her two front teeth noticeably larger than the others nearby. The chipmunk stage which indicated she had more teeth to lose. Her long brown hair extended beyond the frame of the shot.

She was clearly her grandmother's pride and joy. Besides images, Ms. Thea's apartment was filled with trinkets... gifts Delaney had given and art she'd created exclusively for the grandmother who loved her so.

I wasn't sure of Delaney's age, but judging by her school picture, I ventured a guess of eleven or twelve. I was aware that reading and art was a passion of hers, Ms. Thea had let those facts slip out in the midst of conversation in response to my revelation of my own passions.

Ms. Thea wouldn't otherwise reveal anything further about Delaney. And if I asked any specific questions, she would only smile as her eyes glazed over... then change the subject.

Ms. Thea sat the fruit tray on the table as I returned to the kitchen to grab the plate of salmon cakes and Ms. Thea's homemade plum sauce. Together the two of us finished setting up. I took a seat and began preparing myself a cup of tea and sat two cakes on a plate with sauce on top, fruit selections on the side.

Ms. Thea raised the window a little higher. Her cigarette pack sat on the sill with the lighter snuggled firmly beneath the plastic. Dressed in a lovely yellow dress that looked nice against her skin tone, she sat in her seat and prepared a dish of her own.

"Will I get to meet your daughter today?" I asked frowning at my Plum Monkey that needed more honey.

She shook her head no.

"Thought you said she was coming by today."

"Had a fight this morning."

"What about?" The question slipped out before I could catch it. It wasn't my place to ask.

She answered, "Oh the usual. She wants me to go to church with her. Says I need it. Hmpf. I ain't got time to be goin' to pray to nobody's Jesus that ain't done nothin' for me 'sides get on my damned nerves for the past three years."

"You didn't say that to her."

"Why didn't I?"

"Ms. Thea, come on. You didn't say that."

"Eh, in so many words I right guess I did. She shouldn't be so damn sensitive, shouldn't take it personal. Don't hardly concern her. This is between me, the Messiah and his Daddy. She should just stay out of it. Don't hardly concern her."

I chuckled. "You just can't go dissin' people's spiritual beliefs, Ms. Thea and not expect some backlash."

"You a Christian?"

"I suppose by definition."

"By definition? Nah, what's that supposed to mean, chile? Are you a Christian? Yes or no?"

"Well I believe in Christ... was raised to. Still do. But I don't like labels. I recognize Christ, but I don't need some religious title to validate that belief."

"Hmpf. Well I believe in him, too. Believe he can be just as ornery as some men I know. That bother you?"

"Well no but what *I* believe above all else is that we're all entitled to our own beliefs. Now your daughter-"

Ms. Thea waved me off and sipped her Plum Monkey. Lemon slices added. No honey. No sugar.

"Let me tell you something about my daughter. She hates when I call her Ria. But I named her Maria Denise and any variation of that I have every right to use. She hates that I divorced her Jackass of a father, but he cheated on me and has been taking care of not one but two children behind my back for the past ten years. Ten years! Fool had some sort of mid-life crisis, and when he found out his old ass sperm still swam, thought he'd double check and make sure it wasn't a fluke.

"Yet my daughter is mad at me for leaving her precious can-do-no-wrong daddy all alone. Ain't my fault the child he had the kids by – and she was a child when she got pregnant with that first little boy – ain't my fault that little pretty young thang ain't won't nothin' more from my husband than his guaranteed financial support, but my child is angry at me.

"So this thing with God is just one mo' thang for her to be angry at me about. Don't make me no never mind, that's just how most daughters are. Always gotta find some way to blame Momma for all life's little issues. But not granddaughters though. Never granddaughters."

Ms. Thea smiled and that glazed over look returned. I opened my mouth to question her about her granddaughter but immediately closed it around a piece of salmon cake instead.

I tried to process Ms. Thea's statement that her daughter held her accountable for the demise of her parent's relationship. According to Ms. Thea, Mr. Thompson had had that affair for no better reason than she began gaining and retaining more weight in her forties and a sexy young thing with all her curves still in the right places and less than half his age was batting her lashes.

Ms. Thea had learned about the relationship very early on and was assured that it had ended. Ten years later, when their household was affected by hard economic times and Mr. Thompson missed one child support payment too many, the mistress of his past came back to haunt the couple's present. Didn't see how a daughter could possibly blame a mother for that.

We ate, making small talk and sipping tea until our bellies were satisfied. We each leaned back in our respective chairs and placed the heels of our bare feet on the windowsill, hers crossed at the ankles.

Ms. Thea reached for her pack of Kool Lights. She pulled the yellow lighter from behind the plastic and sat it on the table before tapping the pack against the palm of her hand and pulling her stress reliever forward. She placed it between her lips and lit, puffed hard a couple times before blowing the dirty smoke out of the window. She enjoyed her drag. Was visibly relaxed by it, elevated to a peaceful existence. All her concerns for her daughter Ria, or Maria as she preferred to be call, and her jackass husband dissipated in a cloud of cancerous smoke.

"So let me ask you something," Ms. Thea began, "how well do you know Lola Brown?"

The question caught me completely off guard. I coughed, choked on nothing, glanced away trying to conceal the look one developed when you're caught with your hand in the cookie jar.

"I don't – I don't... I mean, she's my neighbor so we... know what neighbor's should know."

Ms. Thea turned to face me. Her eyes were stern, and I wondered if my expression and gibberish of an answer had betrayed me. Ms. Thea smirked, returning her eyes to the window and her vice to her lips. I exhaled finally, realizing that I'd been holding my breath.

"Umm, why do you ask?"

"Lovely couple... the Brown's. Sean Brown, now that's a fine young thing. If I wasn't so old and he wasn't so married, I'd have to teach him a thing or two."

I smiled uncomfortably and scratched the pit of my arm that was suddenly tingling.

Ms. Thea turned to face me again. "And that wife of his, Lola... sure is beautiful. Exotic thing. What is she, from one of those islands down by Miami?"

I worked hard to keep my emotions neutral as I answered. "No, she's African. Umm... born in Nigeria, but her mom's Ethi... opian." I wondered if I was saying too much. Was I being natural? How much information would I divulge if I weren't intimately connected to her?

"So that's what that accent is."

"K-kinda. Africa... meets England."

She nodded at me, smiling. Her gaze lingered. My guilty conscious forced me to break first. She finally looked away, blowing smoke and tapping gray ashes into her black ashtray.

"Lovely couple. Shame if anything should come between them.

Or anyone."

I nodded in agreement and acknowledgment. Wouldn't look at her, refused to though I sensed she was watching me again. I wondered how she knew... or if she knew. I didn't ask. Such a question would ultimately serve to confirm what it was so clear she suspected.

My body warmed and the pits of my arms were tingling again. It felt as though the walls were closing in on me. I wanted to be out of there, but if I rushed out suddenly I'd look guilty.

I didn't care. I stood to gather my things.

"I-I... my dad. I gotta go check on him."

"Is he okay? Your father?"

"Yeah... I mean, I just gotta... y'know, make sure. He's alone. No woman to take care of him... except me."

Ms. Thea smiled and nodded. "Maybe I'll get to meet him someday. If he's as handsome as his daughter is pretty, maybe we can work something out."

She winked at me then smashed her cigarette out. I tried to smile. She stood and walked me to the door, thanking me for the company.

"You're welcome. Anytime."

We hugged close and promised to do it again before I walked from her door with a full belly and a renewed sense of guilt for my previous actions.

I left Ms. Thea's and headed in the direction of my father's home a few hours earlier than I'd anticipated. I had to get away. Somehow my landlady had suspected there was something extra neighborly about Lola and me. How, I couldn't understand.

Technically I wasn't guilty of anything, not any longer at least, so there really was nothing to be ashamed of. But for some reason, I still was.

It'd been two weeks since I'd caressed my neighbor's flesh and sucked on her neck while she sighed my name more often than the name of her husband.

It'd been two weeks since my hands roamed about her dark skin, squeezing her small breasts and massaging the thickness that was her clitoris as she eased up and down on her man.

Had been two weeks since the last time I'd grabbed her by her coarse hair, yanking her head back so I could sink my teeth into her neck while hubby's tongue caressed and penned his name on his property.

Two weeks since I'd pressed her against her wall, my bare breasts to her bare back, my breath on her neck, my fingers collecting her sweet sticky cream and feeding it to her husband.

Technically by this point all of my sins should have been forgiven. Yet I still remained filled with guilt, maybe because I still yearned for our passion and those late night tap-taps against our "bedroom" wall.

The black Deville was parked in the driveway causing a surge of bittersweet emotions to clash within me. That car had once resided in the spot that it was presently occupying. Used to before Mom lost her life and Dad lost his mind. Once it became apparent that my father wouldn't be driving himself anywhere, anytime soon, I caved and sold his beloved vehicle to my Aunt Leigh.

I'd opted not to keep it for myself. Too painful. Would constantly expect to see my father driving away or pulling up in it. Would always desire to see my mother sitting in the passenger seat. Sold it to my aunt with the stipulation that she care for it as well as my father had. It'd been in his possession for twenty years and when I sold it, it was still like new. From the looks of it, she'd kept up her end of the bargain.

I was pleased by that.

Her presence here, however, was another emotion all together.

I unlocked the door and went inside. Noises that hadn't been a mainstay in the home for years existed. The scent of fried chicken, a crispy kind that would put KFC, Popeye's, and all those other poultry franchises to shame, wafted through the air. Two female voices took turns speaking. One belonging to my aunt, I tried to make out the other.

I entered the living room. All was clean, spotless actually. The only mess being the two oversized purses on the sofa. I wondered where my father was. I headed for the kitchen. I saw my cousin Peaches before she saw me. She sat on the stool flipping through a magazine and popping gum while she talked to her mother. It was a pleasant surprise. I hadn't seen Peaches much since she'd moved to Minneapolis a few years earlier.

Aunt Leigh was placing a large breast she'd just pulled from the hot oil on a tray when I entered the kitchen.

"Hey, Sweet Pea." Her eyes brightened when she saw me.

Peaches glanced up. She smiled and jumped quickly from her stool and ran to me with arms wide. I suppressed my irritation and suspicion of her mother and accepted and shared love.

"Sweet Pea! Girl! How you doin'?" she asked stepping back from me, smiling, then hugging me again.

"Pretty good, how about you?"

"I'm great. I ain't seen't you in like forever! What it been, like two years?" She squeezed me tightly again and kissed my cheek before finally letting me go.

"Yep, sure was. Aunt Betsey's ninetieth," I answered.

She looked me over. "Girl, look at choo! Still so pretty. Look just like yo' mama. Don't she, Ma? Look jus' like Auntie Cookie, don't she?"

"Mmhm," Aunt Leigh affirmed and continued putting chicken parts in a paper towel lined tray.

"What choo into these days, Sweet Pea? Still paintin'?"

I smiled at my aunt's eldest. "Yeah. I do some work at a print shop, but I've been getting more and more portraiture work lately. Trying to make a steady living with the talent that God gave out, and Mom passed on."

"For real? That is so good. I am so proud of you."

"Thanks." I blushed.

"For real, I am. Always have been. You was my baby when you was little, wasn't she, Ma?"

"Shole was," Aunt Leigh answered.

"Told you. You was so smart and so pretty. Had them pretty brown eyes and that long pretty hair. And thick! Ooh wee! Pressin' dat junk out! I used to ask Auntie Cookie all the time why she don't put a perm in that mess. Auntie ain't believe in that though. Only a handful of Black folk that can get away with being natural, an' y'all was part of that little club."

"I tried to get a relaxer once. Tried to trick Niecy's cousin into doing it for me," I confessed.

"Niecy who? That stayed next door, Niecy?"

"Mmhm. I was like ten I think, and I lied and told her my mom asked that she do it. She had everything all ready and whipped up. I mean, that crap was all slathered on her comb and everything and Niecy came running across the house in slow motion like, *noooooool!*"

Peaches and my aunt fell into laughter at my story.

"Cookie like'da kilt you had that girl put that lye in yo' head," my aunt said.

Peaches added, "Sweet Pea *and* ol' girl!"

We laughed heartily.

"I see yo' hair still jus' as thick and pretty and natural as yo' mama's was. 'Member, Mama, how I used to pretend she was my baby?"

"Mmhm, now you got plenty nuff of them rugrats o' ya own."

"Aww, hush now, old lady."

Aunt Leigh pretended to threaten her daughter with the oily tongs she held in her hand. She rolled her eyes to me. Sitting the tongs across the chicken, she said, "Come on over and give yo'

Auntie some sugar."

I hugged my Aunt, her thick arms squeezing me tight.

She stepped back, took a top off a pot and stirred. "Sweet Pea, you gone stay an' eat wit' us, ain't you?"

"Smells so good, how can I say no?" I winked at Peaches who smiled at me.

"Don't be gassin' up her ego."

I laughed. "Auntie, where's Daddy?"

She pointed to the back door. "Right out there, sitting with the kids."

I walked outdoors and saw my father sitting in a chair in the middle of the yard, three small children running around him. A boy and two girls, one of which appeared to have only just learned to walk. I waved to the children as I approached my dad.

"Daddy?" I said cautiously.

He turned at the sound of my voice. "Sweet Pea. You come by to visit this old man?"

I bent down and kissed his cheek. "Yes, Daddy. Is everything okay? How you feeling?"

"Oh, I'm just wonderful, Zella Dora. Just enjoyin' these youngsters that your cousin Peaches brang by to see me. Ain't they just precious? Make me wish me and your momma woulda had more. Oh but your momma had so much trouble when she had you... almost lost her life, we ain't wanna take no chances. It was okay though, we had our little Sweet Pea. You looked just like a little sweet pea. You was so tiny and ain't hardly ever shed a tear. You had so much love in you, I reckon we didn't need no more than you no way."

Daddy held my hand as he spoke, but his eyes were on Peaches' children.

I smiled... hesitated a moment. "Daddy, where's Mo – where's Mommy now?" I held my breath.

"Upstairs resting. She had a rough day. Wasn't feeling too good.

Maybe her sugar's low."

I swallowed hard and pretended nothing he said surprised me. "Did you tell Auntie?"

"Well, naw, I didn't. She didn't ask."

"Okay. Everything else okay? You need anything?"

"Just a plate of my sister's good cooking."

I smiled and kissed his cheek again. "Coming right up."

I waved goodbye to the children and walked back across the yard and inside the house. It appeared that the lunch was ready. Aunt Leigh was spreading butter across slices of bread while Peaches stirred sugar into a pitcher of Kool-Aid.

I leaned against the table... chose my words carefully.

"Hey Auntie, thanks for cooking for him... for Daddy. He misses having home-cooked meals."

"Well he *is* my little brother, Sweet Pea."

"I know, I know. It's just... I wish... well you know I'd like for you to call me and tell me when you're coming by."

She paused and sat the knife on the counter top. "He *is* my brother, Sweet Pea."

"I know, I know, but he's my dad."

Aunt Leigh returned to the task of buttering bread. "Been my brother much longer than he been yo' daddy."

"That's not really the point, Auntie."

"Watch yo' mouth now, little girl. You ain't neva too old to have to show me respect."

"Sorry, I don't mean any disrespect, Auntie, but come on, you know how I feel. He's my responsibility, not yours. When you come here... say the things you say... when you leave, it's on me to handle things."

"Sweet Pea, if you were handling things we wouldn't be in this mess...wouldn't have to constantly fight this losing battle."

She looked at me.

I looked at her.

Peaches said, "Y'all know what, this sounds personal. I'mma go check on the kids. Make sure they ain't drivin' Unc cra... zy." She gave an apologetic look then rushed from the house.

"Auntie, I'm by no means trying to fight you. I love you, and I respect you, but this doesn't really concern you."

She slammed the butter knife and placed her hand on her hip. "How you figure? That is my little brother out there, sittin' 'round here thankin' his wife ain't dead. What he thank, Zella Dora, Zahrah out buyin' some milk? What she been stuck in traffic for six years? This is jus' gettin' – no, it done been got ridiculous, and I'm sorry, but I'm gone have to put an end to this."

"What do you mean? What are you talking about? Put an end to what?"

She looked away for a moment then back to me. She started to speak but hesitated. Panic struck me, but I didn't know why. My voice raised an octave when I spoke.

"Put an end to what?"

"We're takin' you to court, Sweet Pea."

"Taking me to court for what?"

"Jacob is sick Sweet Pea–"

"Taking me to court for what? Who the hell is *we*?"

"Me, Darren, Phyllis, and Sybil. Your aunts and uncle. We're takin' you to court to get Power of Attorney transferred over to us. We need Jacob to get some help. I'm sorry, Sweet Pea, this ain't jus' about you, this is about our brother."

"Really, Auntie? Really? Or is this about you getting this house to move Chantal, her jailbird husband, and your bad ass grandkids into? 'Cause you know, that's what I think this is about!"

"Now, Sweet Pea, you know–"

"I'll tell you what I know, Auntie. I know I've been taking care of my father the best I can since my mother died. I know if you take him away from here, we will lose him. We *will* lose him! And you're willing to take that chance?"

"I have to do what's best for him, Sweet Pea."

My breathing was heavy. I nearly choked on my tears. My lashes splashed against the water building up in the brims of my eyes.

"Do what you gotta do, Auntie!"

"Sweet Pea, don't walk out when I'm talkin' to you!"

"Do whatever the hell you gotta do!"

I charged from the kitchen, tuning my Aunt's words out, ignoring her cries for me to come back and discuss this matter like a mature adult. Treating her as though she were a stranger on the street as I felt she was treating me. I moved across the house and out of the front door, slamming it hard behind me.

I sat in my bed that night. Sat in the dark, feeling more alone than ever before. My back was against the wall, ankles crossed, chin to my knees. Tears streaming. I'd tried praying. Like I did when I was a little girl whenever I was sad. Zahrah would tell me to pray. She'd said that God would hear me, and he'd answer those prayers. So I did as my mother would have had me do were she still alive. Unfortunately, it didn't make me feel any better. It didn't feel like anyone was listening, not even God.

They were going to fight me. My aunts and my uncle. My own family was going to fight me for the right to have their brother committed... to have my dad institutionalized. As though that would help. I believed he'd held on for as long as he had, for as well as he had for being in his home near my mother's presence, with his daughter nearby.

Putting him in a home? That could only serve to make him sink further.

Now was not the time to not have your best friends by your side. I needed them. Needed someone to talk to... a shoulder to cry on.

It couldn't be Lola.

Couldn't be Margot.

Couldn't be Ms. Thea.

They didn't know about Daddy's affliction, nor did they need to know. Ayinde wouldn't answer my call if I tried.

Darwin...

Darwin...

I took a breath. Inhaled deep.

Grabbed my phone and dialed his number. I waited... listening to it ring, that and the drumbeat of my aching heart. I needed to know that if they proceeded with this, that they couldn't win. I needed for someone to assure me that I had absolutely nothing to worry about – even if it weren't true.

The phone rang so many times I began preparing mentally the message I wanted to leave behind.

"Hello," Darwin finally answered hesitantly.

I strained to keep the tears from choking me as I spoke. "Hey, Darwin, can you talk?"

"I'm a little busy right now."

"I'm sorry, I just need to talk to someone. I don't mean to bother you, I just don't know who else to turn to."

"Sorry, Z, but I-"

"Darwin I know you're mad at me, but can we please put that off to the side right now? Please. I'm pleading for a stay of execution. Please. I just found out today that my family is going to try to take Power of Attorney over my dad. You know what that means if they do that. Aunt Leigh's spearheading it. She'll put him in a home, take his home, and let her grandkids destroy it like they did hers. And Daddy... who knows what will become of my daddy."

There was silence from his end. This was the part where he was supposed to sympathize. Say he was sorry to hear it, follow up with some encouraging words. Flex a little anger of his own. But for a moment there was only silence.

"I'm sorry to hear that, but what do you want me to do? Tell you it'll be alright? Tell you that they're wrong?"

I was dumbfounded. "Well... yeah!"

"Can't do that, Z. You tried it your way for six years. Maybe your aunt is right. Your way hasn't worked. Let someone else give helping him a shot."

"I don't believe this. I really don't believe this. You know locking him up will push him over the edge, why are you saying these things? Just because I won't be with you... cause I flirted with some guy, you're trying to hurt me?"

"Get over yourself, Zella Dora. Everything ain't about you. Look, I'm sorry I couldn't say what it is you wanted me to say, and I'm sorry that your aunt is putting you in this position, really I am. But if it helps Mr. Robeson in the long run, it's worth every bit of pain you're feeling right now. If you're waiting for me to say what you want to hear, you're just going be waiting. Now I have to go. Miko's waiting for me."

"Miko. Again with Miko. Not that long ago, you couldn't get over her scratchy ass toenails, and now all of a sudden you can't seem to get enough of her!"

"You about finished? We got reservations, and I'm not trying to be late."

"Quite finished."

Darwin hung up.

I tried to calm myself... breathed deeply. Placed the receiver in its cradle. Stood and walked to the kitchen, grabbed an ice cold bottled water from the fridge. I sipped slowly, staring out into the darkness. It was too much to bear, more than I could handle at one time.

Ayinde.

Darwin.

And now Daddy.

I slid to the tiled floor in the kitchen; the open water bottle falling at my side. Tucking myself into a ball, I rocked back and forth as the tears that had been stuck inside of me, gushed forward sending waves of convulsions throughout my body.

I rocked and longed for my mother.

I rocked and wished she were there to hold me close and make everything alright.

Broken shards… bits of glass… that was my life.

I'd swept them up… clumped them together, but I hadn't yet figured the best way to glue them back and make them whole again. Still, I hadn't trashed them either.

I was still Zella Dora Robeson, Zahrah's child.

True, I was short two best friends and that hurt my heart to no end, but I was still Zella Dora Robeson, Jacob's daughter.

Yes, my aunts and uncles were busy strategizing a way to take my father from me, but when it was all said and done, still I was Zella Dora Robeson, and I was not a quitter.

I'd figure it out. One way. Someway, somehow. I would figure something out.

I had dinner scheduled with Margot. She'd been crying to me again, complaining about her relationship with Shane. It had been important to me to be a good friend, all my life it had been my priority. I had been the best to Ayinde, wonderful to Darwin as much as he'd been wonderful to me. And Margot. I'd maintained "shoulder availability" as she stumbled through life in a relationship with a man who wasn't respecting her.

But now... now I had my own worries, my own concerns, and no one to hold my hand through it. I didn't need this. I didn't need anyone else's burdens to add to my own and carry on my slumped shoulders, but my personality and my need to be a good friend trumped all else.

She'd cried on the phone.

I'd cried on and off in my apartment for the better part of the past three days.

She needed me... Margot needed a friend.

I needed to take my mind off what I was facing – at least for a little while.

So when Margot asked me to meet her for a quick dinner and wine at Leona's, I accepted. Reluctantly, but nonetheless accepted.

I walked out of my apartment, felt the contrasting stickiness of the hallway, opposite of the intense evening coolness on the inside. I'd pressed my hair straight earlier in the day, leaving it to hang long and caress my shoulders. I was fearful that if I didn't get out of the building quickly, I'd be instantly reverted back to my Black Power-esque natural.

I headed toward the stairwell but stopped short at the top, frozen in place. We were eye to eye. I'd managed to go without seeing either of them unannounced the entire time we'd resided here together, and now here we were.

Lola stopped where she was, looking up at me. She opened her mouth... seemed she was trying to speak, but just as quickly her mouth closed. Same for me. There were words there, I wanted to release them... wanted to share with her what it was I was thinking, how I'd missed her, but none would escape.

Wasn't all about our sexuality. She was intelligent and funny. A great conversationalist. Pleasant to be around. When she wasn't trying to find a way up under my dress, she was a wonderful companion.

I missed her and would have loved to have her back in my life, but I didn't believe we were ready for strictly friendship.

We eyed one another until I glanced away shyly.

"You look amazing today. I love what you've done with your hair," she spoke in a soft voice.

Slowly I turned back to face her. "Thank you."

"Hadn't realized it was so long. You didn't put a chemical in it, have you?"

"Oh no... no. Just a hot comb. Needed to see something different in the mirror for a change."

"Oh thank goodness. Too many Black Americans ...or maybe Blacks in general want to run from their roots, no pun intended. Anyhow, I've admired the pride you've taken in being yourself... how you've celebrated your ethnicity through your crowning glory."

I chuckled. "You're just on a role today with the hair puns, huh? I wouldn't give me too much credit. Plenty times I've considered copping a Bantu. But I've found this to be a great way of honoring my er, roots as you say, part of which being my mother who didn't believe in altering anything about the beauties that God had given us."

She nodded. "Your mother sounds like she was a wise woman."

"She was. Very much so."

She nodded again. Words were there. Unspoken words which she seemed to debate sharing. I suppressed my own thoughts and began to move forward.

"Well... I should get going. Don't want to be late."

"Oh. W-where are you going?"

"Dinner... with a friend."

She bit her bottom lip and looked at me, but she didn't move. In my mind, I was screaming at her, demanding she move the hell out of my way so that I could run and hide my feelings. Didn't have to see her. See how her rich deep melanin skin flowed flawlessly down her frame. I needed to leave so that I wouldn't have to see her doe eyes gazing through me... penetrating my soul.

She wouldn't move.

Watched me, watching her. She stood... two steps down and just out of reach wearing a white cotton tank top and a pair of casual beige capri's, her thick locs caressing her strong shoulders. I fought my animal urge to move my fingers through her hair. Fought the desire to feel that abrasion against my flesh. Fought against my wanting to suck her bottom lip into my mouth and graze my tongue across it. To put my lips to her ear and whisper my inquiry of when her sexy husband would be home.

"Zella!"

"Huh?" I snapped out of my fantasy.

"I said that I... I said that I miss you."

My eyes lowered. "I miss you, too, but you know..."

"I know. I know what you're trying to do but... and I respect... I..." She took a deep breath and laughed softly and shook her head. "I'm rambling."

"A bit."

"Go on. You're going to be late. Go."

I nodded.

I started down the steps. She didn't walk up, stayed there two steps from the top. Only turned, put her back to the wall forcing me to ease my body past hers... feel her heat. I held my breath.

When I reached the next step she grabbed my wrist. "I really miss you, Zella. Miss your friendship. Miss everything about you. I hope I didn't – hope we didn't blow it."

I smiled and eased my hand away. I continued forward, leaving my guiltiest pleasure and naughtiest desire behind.

When I was ten years old, a couple moved into the neighborhood about three houses down. A biracial couple. Black man. White woman. Two small mixed race children, younger than I was at the time.

The woman, I recall, was very attractive. She was a tall slender woman. Very beautiful, should have been a model. Her brown hair was always shiny.

And long.

Beautiful.

I knew her by her hair. She'd come by to talk to my mother, seeking advice, and she'd let me brush her shiny hair.

I enjoyed her kids. One boy. One girl. One year apart in age. Pretty kids with soft brown complexions, bright eyes and curly, sandy brown hair. I took to them right away, and they enjoyed spending time with me at my house.

The longer they were our neighbors, the fewer casual visits the woman made. I would tend to her pretty children while their mother disappeared with mine, speaking through stifled tears and in muffled tones behind closed doors.

I'd seen him at times, the husband. Seen him yelling at the woman with the shiny brown hair. In the street. In front of children, theirs and everyone else's on the block. Ms. Thea thought Mr. Thompson was a jackass. But *he* was a jackass, the husband of the woman with the shiny brown hair.

He was a jackass who never once spoke to me despite knowing exactly who I was, or maybe because of it.

He was a jackass who threatened my mother with his eyes, causing Daddy to be on guard at all times, ready to handle him.

She was a beautiful woman with such pretty and shiny, long brown hair and I could remember wondering why she would put up with the disrespect. Any man would want her. Black or White. Any ethnicity. It made no sense to my young mind.

At some point she ceased coming to see my mother. Just stopped completely. No explanation, no nothing. I could remember my mother's concern and hearing Dad talk her out of showing up on that lady's porch. Said it would likely only make matters worse. What matters, I didn't know. And what defined worse, I had no idea.

I don't know if my mother ever knocked on that lady's door.

What I do know is the lady disappeared for awhile and when we finally saw her again, she didn't look anywhere as pretty as she had when she first moved into our neighborhood. There was a bruise near her eye and though she tried her best to conceal it, I could see a tooth was missing. Although it'd only been a couple months since we'd last seen her, she looked aged. And she was distant... very distant. Almost pretended to not know us.

Her long, brown, pretty and shiny hair was no more. Cut short and looked dirty. It no longer shined. That was the first time my mother explained the concept of self-esteem and settling for less.

I would watch my parents after that. Really observe them from that day forward. How Dad would treat Mom. How he'd hold open doors, pull out chairs. How he held her and kissed her cheek. The gentility in his voice when he told her he loved her.

And the sounds.

The sounds of love making that'd been present for my entire youth took on new meaning.

Mommy married her big sister's ex-boyfriend, but she hadn't settled. Neither would I.

Margot, no matter what her argument and what evidence she presented, Margot did.

Margot had sat on my windowsill in the early Spring, naked except for the racy red undies that clung to her thick white hips while I captured her essence on canvas in a myriad of colors. This was done for Shane. This was all done to please her husband. She'd paid me five-hundred dollars to do this, to show him that she loved him in this very special way.

He loved it.

She told me that he loved it. On the day of his birthday when she revealed it to him, she said he was happy. Loved it and held her close, loving her all night as his way of saying thank you. But now, just weeks later, he was back to wearing his true colors. A wolf wearing sheep's clothing, who'd come home drunk, liquored up and smelling of another woman's personal scent. Come home yelling and throwing things, labeling her *'the bitch that killed his son'*.

She cried over pizza, cried more after the second glass of wine kicked in. Cried and asked me for advice that she didn't really want... that she wouldn't actually heed. Cried over spilt milk but at some point one has to accept that you are the one that knocked the damned carton over.

Cried in the passenger's seat as I drove us in her car back to my place. I wanted to grab her shoulders... shake her up. Remind her that she was a beautiful woman deserving of respect. Convince her there was someone out there for her, there was someone better for her. She didn't have to settle for Shane. She'd married him because she was having his child. She didn't have his child anymore... so why stay in the marriage?

But I couldn't ask her that.

I had just unlocked the door and let Margot inside when I heard The Brown's door slowly creak open. My heart was in my throat. I didn't know if it was Sean or Lola, but I didn't think I could take seeing a Brown twice in one day.

I continued forward being very conscientious not to look to my right. I paused involuntarily. Took my time crossing the threshold. I guess I kinda hoped... but then I heard the click of the door closing.

I let it go and stepped inside.

Margot had moved quickly. Had dipped into my stash, grabbed one of its medicinal residents and was flaming up. Had managed all of that before I was able to lock the door behind me.

She inhaled deep, exhaling out of my raised window sending evidence of our indiscretion into my courtyard. I grabbed two water bottles and walked to Margot, taking the joint from her outstretched fingertips and replacing it with purified H_2O.

"Why do I keep putting up this shit, Z? What is wrong with me?" A rhetorical question no doubt.

I shrugged and pulled the breath of the herb into my lungs. I tuned her out as she continued whining pointlessly then handed the spliff back. I walked to Daddy's recliner and collapsed into it. Let her moan and complain as my mind drifted to Aunt Leigh's promise to me.

A knock at the door jarred me from my private thoughts. I stood and walked to answer. Margot didn't miss a beat in her venting. My eyes rolled discreetly to the back of my head. I leaned into the door and peeked out.

"Damn it," I whispered. I waited. Weighed my options. I couldn't very well pretend I wasn't there. It must have been she who'd opened the door as soon as I got home.

I undid the locks and opened my door. Lola stood staring shyly. She'd pulled her locs back tightly into a bun and changed into a pair of blue sweats and a white collegiate tee.

"Wassup, L?"

"Zella. I'm so sorry to bother you. Please... may I speak with your for just a moment?"

"Sure, what's going?"

She gazed at me. Smiled sadly. "You do look quite beautiful this evening. Your hair... it really is lovely in that manner."

I returned her bashful smile. "Thanks again."

"Can I... speak with you inside? I promise I'll behave. I only want to talk."

"I have company. Margot's inside. You're very welcome to come in, but I get the feeling this is a private matter."

"Does she know?"

"No, no." I shook my head. "No one knows. No one but the parties involved."

"Oh. Good." She looked at her fingers then to me. She took a step closer but maintained a fair distance. She glanced nervously toward the staircase then back and locked on my eyes. "I *really* miss you, Zella. I know I told you this earlier, but I really miss you. Everything. I miss every aspect of you. I miss talking to you. I miss sharing with you. I miss watching you paint.

"I miss… I miss kissing you. I do. I miss touching you, every bit of you. I miss it. I tried to not think of you. For two weeks! You have to admit I've been good. Haven't tapped on your wall once."

I nodded and chuckled. "Well once."

She laughed. "Okay once. Forgive me for that, but I've really tried, Zella. Things just aren't the same without you. Sean and my intimacy… it isn't complete without you."

"Lola…"

"Wait please… just hear me out. Sean and I…" She again, glanced at the stairwell then back to me. "Sean and I… we fight. Not about you but… about what… we're frustrated I guess. You completed our circle. Made us a trinity, and without you there, in everyway it's like we're incomplete."

She took my hand in hers… held it. Stepped closer. Close enough that I could feel her breath… smell peppermint. Blood rushed to my head, and a volt of electricity shot through my body. I wanted badly to wrap my hand around her slender neck and push her against the wall behind her. Put my lips to hers and absorb her peppermint flavor into my tongue.

But I didn't. I maintained my will power.

"This is why I have to stay out of it, Lola. This is why it's so important for me to stay away."

"Zella-"

"L, listen, I have to go. Margot needs me right now." I slipped my hand away.

"But I need you too. I need you, Zella."

I smiled regretfully. "Take a number."

She whispered my name. It was only my name, but in it she was begging me. Turning herself over to me if I would have her… and pleading for me to accept her. I couldn't comprehend it no more than I could understand why she affected me so. My knees weakened, and my legs were like jelly, but I kept forward into my home, vowing that I would not involve myself with my neighbor's wife any longer.

I stood outside Ms. Thea's door the day after Lola had stood outside of mine calling to me with every fiber of her being. Needing my companionship and longing for the feel of my flesh meshed between theirs... or maybe more so just hers.

I knocked again, hoping she'd answer. I needed someone to talk to... anyone about anything. Well anything other than the things that I really needed to talk about. Like my father. Like Lola and the things I'd done with Lola and her husband.

Ayinde wouldn't answer my calls. Still wouldn't answer my calls. I'd tried just that morning.

Darwin...

Darwin...

He was probably with Miko and besides, he'd pissed me the hell off not to mention the fact he was just being a flat out ass.

Margot only wanted to moan about Shane and if she said one more thing about that scrawny little no good piece of nothing motherfu... sigh... I couldn't talk to her. Just could not.

And Kat. That gossipy broad would have my business all over the Chicagoland area before I even hung up the phone.

I knocked again.

Waited.

Listened.

Ear to the door.

No answer. Ms. Thea wasn't home.

I flicked a tear of frustration from beneath my eye and turned to walk toward the stairwell. I felt terribly alone... for the first time since the day my mother's spirit left this Earth. I didn't know what to do, where to go, no one to turn to. No one I could be one-hundred percent honest with.

Didn't know what I'd done to deserve everything in my world

taking a dive. Or had I done anything at all. Urban legend dictated that things happened in three's. Ayinde, Darwin, and Daddy. Could that have been my three?

Hey, I'd had a good run for awhile. Maybe it was just my time, I was overdue. But how did Lola and Sean factor in? Or did they?

I exhaled as much negative energy as I could and exited the building. It was a blistering hot day. Good thing I'd had the forethought to pull my temporarily straightened hair back into a ponytail; it was a sure bet that my freshly straightened ends were bound to frazzle.

A walk was maybe what I needed.

Maybe a walk would do me justice.

Sweat out my stress.

I reached for the knob on the heavy black gate as I contemplated walking the distance to the nearest Starbucks.

"Well this has to be a record." An accented voice said.

I glanced up into Lola's eyes. A feeling of relief washed over me, and I smiled at her.

"Yeah, has to be." I chuckled.

We stood in silence, looking at one another. Hopeful silence. Not awkward, contemplative. I touched my hair unconsciously. Looked away then back to her.

"Soo…" she began, "you're off to enjoy this blistering day?"

I nodded. "Yeah, I suppose. Starbucks has a mint chocolate frappuccino screaming my name."

More smiles and contemplation.

"Zella, I'd just like to say that I am really sorry to have put you in an uncomfortable position."

"You don't have to-"

"No, no. I'd like to apologize. Really. It'd be smashing if we could begin again. I mean, we are neighbors after all. Sean and I aren't going anywhere anytime soon, and I hope we haven't run you out of the building."

I laughed. "No, you haven't. Good rent for the space. I'm not going anywhere right now."

This time she laughed. "Come to dinner tonight, Zella, please. I'm making fish. Whiting. Some veggies on the side. Some brown rice. I promise it'll be delicious."

"Lola, I-"

"Don't say no, Zella. Please. Just think about it. At least think about it. No pressure. My word. Just good food and good conversation. Maybe a movie. I'm sure there's a Bela you've been dying to see. Tell me the title and I'll pick it up."

"Lola," I whined her name, wanting to say no but feeling as though I was running out of steam and logical reasons not to agree. Instead I said, "I will think about it."

"Marvelous. That's all I ask."

The heavy gate swung open, releasing a small brood of antsy children into the street followed by a tired looking young woman who couldn't have been much older than twenty-five. She waved a weighted hello before yelling at the eldest child to take hold of the younger one.

"You ready for all that?" I asked Lola.

Her eyes lit up as they followed the family down the block. "Terribly so."

I gave her another brief moment to fantasize before I cut into her private thoughts. "So uhm, I'm gonna make tracks toward that frap. I'll check you out... later. Maybe."

"Please do. I hope you do. See you later... maybe. Seven p.m. in case you decide to come."

We moved awkwardly around each other and away from each other. Lola, behind the black gate and I, beyond it. I glanced back, couldn't resist. Saw her looking back at me, catching me looking at her. Deep brown cheeks darkening, she turned away before I could.

Humidity didn't evaporate with the setting of the sun. It lingered. That moist, warm, sticky thickness blanketing the air. I'd managed to keep myself occupied throughout the day. Spent time at the park, spent time near the water... stayed away from my residence, my temptation and my most self-piteous thoughts.

I'd gotten a call from Kat while I was out, sitting inside the Barnes and Noble in Evanston. Wanted me to join her and Margot and a friend of theirs for a girl's night out. A men-ain't-shit-but-dogs-and-pimps night. There were two rules on such nights, do not talk about the no good man you left at home and blow off all the sex-on-the-brain brothas that step to you throughout the night no matter how good they look. The odds of enforcing such goals after an unspecified amount of alcohol filled one's system, however, were slim to none.

I wasn't trying to dwell on my problems... and I sure as hell wasn't trying to hear about theirs.

It was about a quarter past seven when I made it back to my block. Five minutes later, I still had not walked in. Dinner at the Brown's would have already begun, and Lola would be anticipating my knock at the door. Only I didn't think I should knock. She assured me it would be friendly... like the early days before too much Riesling loosened her tongue, but I wasn't so sure I could believe that. Not just yet.

If I went to my place, she'd hear me and maybe she'd knock on my door. Wouldn't take much coercion on her part if that happened.

I took my chances and entered the courtyard. If she was near her window, she'd see me. I ventured a guess that she was sitting on her sofa in front of her television, near the door keeping an ear out rather than an eye.

I took to the steps once inside the building, landed on the second floor. I held my breath as I approached Ms. Thea's door, hoping that she'd be home this time. I exhaled when I heard her shuffling around inside. Her movements became louder as she got closer. Abruptly all went quiet as her eye covered the peephole.

"That you, Zella?" She called from the other side of the door.

"Yes, Ms. Thea. It's me."

I stood patiently as she unlocked the door, relieved that I wouldn't have to take my chances on the third floor. The door opened, and she stepped aside, allowing me in.

"Couldn't keep away from me, huh?" She laughed and so did I. "So what's wrong?"

I paused in my tracks. She locked the door then walked over and hugged me.

"What makes you think something's wrong?"

"Well let me think. It's about seven at night in the middle of the week. You're half my age. You wouldn't just pop in here if nothing wasn't wrong. So either you broke something up there and you're hear to sweet talk me into fixing it or... you're hiding out."

I contemplated... then answered, "Hiding."

"So are we dealing with it or ignoring it?"

"Ignoring it, please," I begged.

"Fine by me, but you know until you deal with it, you're just going to keep hiding out."

I nodded my understanding. "I know, but I just need to hide for a little bit longer."

"Well, ignoring we shall do. Gone 'head make yourself comfortable. You hungry? Thirsty?"

"I'm fine."

"Well if you change your mind, you know where the kitchen is."

Ms. Thea took her seat in front of the window and propped her feet up on the windowsill. I sat at the table across from her propping mine up as well.

"I came by earlier, but you weren't here."

"Oh you're *really* desperate to hide, aren't you?"

"Eh."

"Went to church today," Ms. Thea said, lifting her lit cigarette out of the ashtray.

My feet slipped back to the floor, and I flung around in my seat. I faced her, my eyes large and round, and a smile emerging from my lips.

"You went to church today?" I asked. She nodded. "What happened to your not needing to be bothered with Jesus and his daddy?"

Ms. Thea hunched her shoulders. "Well, Ria called me up and invited me. Said she finally understood my anger and frustration with those two and that what we really needed was what every dysfunctional relationship needed."

"And what's that?"

"Counseling. And what better place to do it than in the house of the Lord. It's free, you know he's available, and we ain't gotta set no damned appointments."

I laughed hard and turned my body back toward the window. The visual of God, Jesus, and Ms. Thea sitting around in plush leather chairs in front of a big desk, telling their version of their story to Sigmund Freud popped in my mind sending waves of chuckles through me.

"But wait, isn't today Wednesday? Who goes to church on Wednesday?"

She blew smoke out the window then looked to me with curious eyes. "Didn't you tell me you were a Christian?"

"I said I believe in Christ."

"Don't believers in Christ generally go to church?"

"I went when I was a kid, when my mom was alive, but we went on Sunday, not Wednesday."

"Well…" she rolled her eyes up playfully, "there is a Wednesday service and many people attend. My daughter being one of those people."

I paused… bit my lip before I asked my question. "Did your granddaughter go with?"

Ms. Thea sorta jerked a bit. She smiled at me. Picked up her cigarette and inhaled it. Sad eyes. Blew smoke but forgot to face the window. Sat in silence for a moment. Then her demeanor slowly changed back.

"Going to church Sunday. Maybe you should consider going back. Might help you stop hiding... might help you deal."

I could go to church. I wasn't anti-church. Would go if I felt the urge, but I didn't want to talk about damn church. What I wanted to know was what was up with her granddaughter. What was up with Delaney.

"Ms. Thea."

"They say you can always come back, don't matter what wrong you did, you can always come back."

"Ms. Thea, answer me."

"God is supposed to forgive you, all you gotta do is ask. That's what they talked about today. Well, ain't that real nice and arrogant of Him. But what about how He's wronged us. They didn't address the fact that maybe He should get off His high horse and apologize to us for the wrong He's done to us...ask us for forgiveness."

"Ms. Thea!"

"What gal, what?"

"Delaney. Your granddaughter. Why won't you talk about her?"

"You know you got a lot of nerve, little girl-"

"Does she exist? Did something happen to her? Why won't you talk about her?"

Ms. Thea slammed her palm hard against the table, so hard I jumped in my seat. Hard enough to cease my flow of questions. She stood, pointed her fingers at me... the ones that held her cigarette between them.

"Now you listen to me. Ain't none of yo' got-damned business 'bout my grandchild. You hear me? It ain't yo' business, and I don't want to talk about this again, else you gonna have to find you someplace else to hide at, you understand me? Do you understand me?"

My voice was hardly a whisper, "Yes, ma'am. I'm sorry."

She continued standing and pointing... glaring at me. I'd been wrong for prying, but I couldn't imagine that my questions alone were enough to cause such a reaction.

"I'm sorry," I repeated.

"Never mind being sorry, just don't do it again."

"Yes, ma'am."

She put the remaining bit of cigarette to her lips and took the final drag. This time she remembered to exhale facing the window. She flicked the butt out to land in the courtyard she was responsible for maintaining.

"I'm done smoking these things. Ain't doin' nothing but killing me softly. May I suggest you quit, too."

I became immediately defensive. "But I don't... s-smoke..."

She eyed me then turned and walked to her bathroom. Having been reprimanded and in essence busted, I turned away and buried my shame-filled face in the palms of my hands.

My aunt Dora Cooper dated my dad before Zahrah did.

Dora was the first born and only child for three years until my grandparents decided to expand their family tree and had another girl. Typically a child that has been a sole heir for more than a couple years is jealous of the new sibling, spiteful, and I've even witnessed some behavior that was downright mean.

Legend says, Dora was not that way.

They say Dora was thrilled to have a baby sister, that she loved her. Mom told me that Dora was more of the mother of the home than Gram C was.

My grandmother was a maid and spent much of her time away from the home trying to earn enough to support the family after my grandfather had taken ill. He'd been knocked off his feet by his sickness by the time the youngest girl, Claudia, was six. It was at that time that ten-year-old Dora stepped up, assuring her little sisters ate breakfast and got to school on time. Made certain that they had lunch and dinner and ate all of their vegetables.

Dora helped them with homework assignments and protected

them on the streets from older, stronger children. She combed their hair in the morning and got them into their pj's and off to bed at night.

Jacob was the last man Dora dated. When his affections turned to Zahrah, Dora turned all of her attention to caring for their ailing mother (by then my grandfather had already passed on).

During the first nine years of my parents' marriage, Dora lived with and cared for Gram C. Zahrah offered on many occasions to talk to Jacob about returning to Memphis, and Auntie Claudia over the years was more than willing to move her family back from Oklahoma City, but Dora insisted they stay put.

At the end of the ninth year, Gram C passed on. Zahrah and Jacob told me that they'd been concerned about Auntie Dora. She'd never married, she had no children. They worried about how she'd fare living alone with no one to care for after having spent a lifetime caring for others.

Auntie Dora spent one relatively peaceful year caring for no one but herself before a cancer, that no one knew she had until it was too late, spread throughout her body and sent her home to be with her parents about seven months before I was born. I was given the second name Dora in her honor.

My mother always told me how I was like my aunt in so many ways. I didn't know if I was like her because of her name or in spite of it. Either way, I've always been proud to carry it.

Tuesdays, Thursdays, and Saturdays were the days I generally preferred to clock hours at Chaz's print shop. The rest of the days of the week were mine to do with as I pleased. Janessa had referred me to two of her friends so that free time would be filled very quickly.

Today was a Thursday, a very busy Thursday. Chaz wasn't able to slip away and run his own personal errands. His heavy clientele on that day forced him to stick around and assist me with working some equipment.

I was thrilled to see the end of the workday. Was ready to go home and shut down my brain. Get lost in swirls of color and fragrances of paint additives.

It had been a frustrating day.

My cousin had called earlier, my Aunt Sybil's son. He wanted to know if I were aware of what my relatives were up to and if so, find out how I was holding up under that pressure. Told him I knew... was fully aware; Aunt Leigh had warned me. Or rather threatened me. But had I known they'd found an attorney that would take the case? That, I had not known.

I had a migraine.

The shop closed promptly at six. I waved a limp goodbye to Chaz, strapped my army green bag around my body, and hustled out the door leaving him to be sure everything was locked up and put away.

I moved toward the nearest bus stop, tuning out the sounds of the city. The cars passing by. The pedestrians and their chatter. The sound of my name being called.

I slowed my stride and furrowed my brow. Opened my ears and listened carefully. Engines roared by and people at a nearby café chatted but no one called my name.

I continued forward, restarting the process of shutting everything down when I heard it again, this time much closer.

"Zella!"

I whipped around, not believing my ears. Saw Lola. Saw her running to catch up with me. Like a stalker. I wondered what she was doing there. Couldn't imagine she had any business by my job. It was possible... I didn't work too terribly far from home. It was highly possible but not very probable.

She was almost to me. "Zella, wait up!"

"What are you doing over here?"

"I have to talk to you."

She was in front of me now, locs pulled back into a ponytail that continued to sway from her having run down the block after me. Yellow top that popped against her dark skin tone, short skirt revealing beautifully toned legs that extended forever.

My anger slipped down a couple notches when she looked into my eyes, but I couldn't shake the look of irritation that was etched across my face.

"Zella, please wait. I have to talk to you."

"Here on the streets? You know where I live, Lola."

"You're always avoiding me lately."

"So fine, talk."

"Come on, I'll drive you home. We can speak in the car."

"The car? Since when do you take the car?"

"Since today. I dropped Sean at work this morning. I needed the car to run errands."

I stepped back. I was suspicious of her motives. "So this is a pre-meditated stalking."

"Oh f'k, Zella, get off it. No one's stalking you. I really was running errands, and I was passing by this way, and I saw you leaving the shop."

"You just happened to be coming past my job at the very moment I got off work?"

"Yes, I happened to be passing by your job at the very moment you got off of work. I'm double parked. Please. Just talk to me... fifteen minutes. That's about as long as it'll take me to get you home."

I stood there for a moment looking at her. I had a migraine. I was tired... too tired for battle. I gave up. In that moment I gave in and gave up running. Why hide? If I did, she'd be there. Until I found my escape or she packed her things and left, she'd be there. He'd be there. Right next door, right beside me. Why concern myself with protecting their relationship when she wasn't concerned. He must've known that she was pursuing me, yet he wasn't concerned. So why was I?

She was my neighbor. A woman that I liked and had been

forging a pretty good relationship with before we crossed the line led by the trail of a Riesling. She merely wanted to talk. My aunts and my uncle were trying to take my father away from me. I didn't have time to worry about the Brown's and the state of their union.

I nodded and agreed.

She waved me in and I swiftly followed her back down the block in the direction from which I'd come. Sean and Lola's quaint brick red 4-door was indeed double parked outside of my shop. Her hazards blinking, serving as notice to oncoming traffic that they'd need to find their way around her little inconvenience.

She rushed to her side and jumped behind the wheel as I eased into the passenger's seat, tossing my bag into the back. Much to the relief of the driver behind her that was having difficulty trying to get around, Lola pulled away.

We rode in silence for a couple blocks. The sound of Sade's voice softly wafted through her speakers. She'd insisted she wanted to talk; however, she had yet to utter a word since we climbed into her vehicle.

My head pounded more. I wanted an Aleve, Tylenol, Bayer, all those name brand pharmaceuticals at once. We were stopped at a red light listening to the beauteous Brit express to some unknown recipient how the pair didn't share an ordinary love.

I decided to harbor my frustrations for a little bit longer. I was hers for about the next twelve minutes. This was her opportunity to express herself. If we rolled onto Greenleaf and parked the car, her time was up.

Lola flipped on her blinker and pulled onto a tight side street with a dead end that saw little action. There were more than a couple gaps in parking, and she pulled into a space, placing the car in park, and shutting the engine off.

"What are you doing?" I asked. "Where are we going?"

"No where just yet."

"So why are we parked here?"

"So we can talk."

I sighed. Closed my eyes and gently scratched my eyebrow with my thumbnail. My aunts and uncle were trying to take my dad. I had a migraine. Aleve. I needed Aleve. She wanted to talk to me on a side street too far from my home and my medicine cabinet... about what?

"You said you'd take me home."

"I will. But first I'd like to talk... while I have the opportunity."

"What are we talking about, L?"

"Are you mad at me?"

"Why would I be mad at you?"

"Dunno, you tell me. You're sure acting as though you're mad at me."

I battled with my emotions... my frustrated emotions. "I'm not mad at you, Lola."

"So then why all the attitude?"

"I have a lot going on with me right now. You show up unannounced insisting you need to talk... offering me a ride home. And now here were are, but you're not talking. Haven't given any indication of what you need to talk to me about. And I just wanna go home, I'm tired."

We were quiet again. Across the seat from one another, only a gear shift away but felt as though we were an ocean apart. Lola sat upright in her seat, hands on steering wheel, staring straight ahead. I slumped into the door, gazing out the window and willing my mind to go blank.

"Zella."

"Yes?"

"I have feelings for you. You know that right... that I have feelings for you."

The statement lingered in the air. She hadn't looked my way nor had I broken my staring match with oblivion, but that information floated in the air between her and me. It took a moment to acknowledge her confession, absorb, and process it.

I replied without turning her way. "Feelings like how? You're a married woman. What kind of feelings could you possibly have for me?"

She shifted, turned toward me. "I-don't-know feelings. Strong feelings. Not feelings like, I-think-I'm-in-love feelings and I'm-gonna-divorce-my-husband-to-be-with-you feelings. Feelings like... when I see you or hear your voice, my stomach does cartwheels. Feelings like, I think about you all the time. Feelings like, when I'm with you I don't want you to leave and when you're gone, I miss you so much.

"How do you expect I explain that? I can't explain that. I never wanted to be with a girl in all my life. I'm not gay... not a freakin' lesbian and yet I have these sorts of feelings for another woman. How is that even possible? How would you like for me to explain those feelings?

"But I know something. I know that you feel what I feel, Zella. You're only running because you're afraid you'll destroy what Sean and I have, but you won't. And actually it's causing more harm, your being away than your being nearby."

I faced her. Free of animosity. Free of tension. Open. Seeing her. Hearing her. Allowing myself to feel. Giving up. Giving in. Resigning my will. I was tired, too tired to fight.

She continued to speak. "I know... I know. You're a woman. I'm a married woman. I don't know, I just can't explain it... can't help what I feel. When I asked that you kiss me I had no clue that it would lead to this. No idea I'd feel for you what I feel, but I can't help it, and I can't make it go away. I can only deal with it.

"I'm not asking you for anything, Zella. Not asking that you join us in bed again. Not asking you to be the third party in our union. Just asking for an opportunity for us to be friends again. I'm sorry I put you in an uncomfortable position. Sorry I ignored your feelings. Sorry that I've been so overwhelming. I am terribly sorry for it all.

"For as much as I'd love for you to join us once again... as much as I'd love for you to make love to me just once, that isn't what I'm asking of you. I am only asking for a second chance at friendship. I want you in my life – need you in my life, and if I can't have you one way, I will certainly take you the other."

She took a deep breath. Exhaled... then smiled at me. She'd said a mouthful and she knew it.

We sat facing each other, looking at one another. During her speech we'd managed to position ourselves slightly nearer to one another.

I'd listened to what she had to say... heard every word of it. Pushed aside all of my self-righteousness and preconceived notions and truly paid attention. She wasn't asking me for anything more than my friendship.

Friendship.

All of that was just to say that she wanted me in her life again if only as a friend. All she wanted was everything that I needed right then.

My hand moved.

I hadn't told it to.

Moved and placed itself softly against Lola's cheek, grazed it for a moment before moving up. Moving to the side of her head, toward the back of it. My fingers gripping the back of her head... becoming lost in her hair. Gripped the back of her head and pushing her face closer to mine as I moved mine toward her.

Our lips met.

For the first time in weeks, our lips touched. For the first time in weeks I felt alive.

I eased back... looked into her eyes. Saw the relief and the desire. Longing. I could hear her breathing, hear its weight increase. My eyelids slipped down as I leaned forward... kissed her again.

Added more passion.

Ran my tongue across her bottom lip then bit down, sucking it into my mouth. Moving slowly. Savoring the taste of her.

My hand moved slowly. Upwards. Deeper into her infinite valley of locs. Fingers wrapping around ropes of hair at the base. Holding them. Tugging them as I felt her tongue entering my mouth, seeking out mine.

Entangled.

Caressing.

Hers dancing slowly and sweetly with mine.

A Tango. Venetian Waltz.

I felt her fingers graze my flesh, sending electric chills through me. My skin began to heat, warm beneath her touch. Her fingers moved up my arm lightly to my shoulder... moved down grazing across my breast. My nipples swelled instantly, reacting to her touch.

I wanted her.

I wanted her right then and more than ever before. Wasn't concerned about her marriage, her relationship with her husband. Wasn't concerned about who she desired more. Didn't care at all. All I cared about was feeling her heat against my skin.

Her tongue intertwined with mine.

Tasting her. Absorbing her.

The feel of her fingers digging into my scalp. Wanted her mouth wrapped around my breast, inhaling my nipple... biting down.

She grabbed my hair, held a firm grip and pried me away — but not too far.

Her voice was a soft whisper when she spoke, "What are we doing?"

"Making up."

"What happened to friendship?"

"We're friends. Good friends."

I kissed her again. Kissed her harder. Mouth open. Closing. Sucking her in. Moving her out. Teasing her tongue with mine.

She pulled back again.

"I love this, you know I love this."

"So why do you keep stopping me?"

I leaned forward to kiss her again. "Wait, wait." She stopped me.

I dropped my head. Shook it in frustration. "What, what? I thought... thought you wanted..."

"I do, I do. I just... just don't want you to do anything you'll regret. Can't risk losing you again."

I glanced up at her. "You won't."

"But how do you know?"

"You about done?"

"Well, yes, it's just that-"

"Shut up."

"- just that you're important to me and-"

I laughed. "What part of shut up don't you understand?"

I inched forward, reaching between her legs and beneath her seat.

"I just don't want to lose you."

I was stretched across her lap. Reaching beneath her chair trying to find the bar, the lever or whatever tool would push the seat back as far as it could go.

"You said that already. Are you done now?"

She looked down at me. Smiling. Looking happy. "Yes. I am."

"A little help here."

She reached for the lever, sliding the seat backward until it stopped moving. Then grabbing another lever, she leaned back, reclining as far as she could go.

I eased from my seat, over the gearshift. Easing myself between Lola's body and the steering wheel with as much grace as possible. Laughing along the way, though at what I didn't know. Maybe laughing at myself for being so damned weak. Either way I was happy... we were happy.

Both happy.

Happiness. My long lost friend.

I stretched my body across hers. Laid there. Stroking her locs. Looking into her eyes. Our faces inches apart. Feeling her breath against me. Her hand went to my face. My eyes closed, and I nuzzled against her palm. Tuned out everything. The world around us. The pain and problems I was facing. Tuned everything out.

Nothing mattered but the moment.

Nothing mattered but what was happening in the moment.

I kissed her lips… and nothing mattered…

I bit her lip… but the moment…

We kissed. With power and passion. Kissed like it was our very first time. Like two people in love. Or, two people searching for something that we hadn't realized was missing.

Gripping each other's hair, trying to pull ourselves deeper into one another. Getting lost in the other. Becoming one. Two halves becoming whole.

More passion.

Intense.

Lips smacking. Spit swapping. Heavy breathing. Long sighing.

I moved southward. Kissed her chin. Down to her neck. Bit down… hard. Just hard enough. Made her squirm and her back arch. My hand squeezing her breast. Owning it. Claiming it. Teasing her nipple through the thin material.

Her body moving erotically beneath me.

Grinding.

Groping me. Pulling me firmly against her. Moving as best we could in the confined space.

My hand moving down, beneath her shirt, pushing it up, my fingers brushing against the lace bra.

"I missed you, Zella." She breathed her words against me. "Missed you so much. I want to taste you, Zella. Please. Want to know what a woman tastes like… want to know what you taste like."

"Shh," I said placing my mouth over hers, forcing her into submission while my hand pushed the material of her bra away. I squeezed the soft flesh. My thumb grazed her erect nipples.

Sucked her breath away slowly… then offered it back.

I wanted her naked. Wanted to be naked with her. On a feather down comforter. In a bed of roses with the scent of jasmine and lavender surrounding us. The light of candles dancing on our flesh. Aromatic oils and potpourri.

Instead we were in a vehicle… a hot car with the windows open partway. Parked by the curbside on a dead end street in the early evening summer light where any passerby could look inside and see, but I didn't care. Clearly she didn't either.

I moved down, bumped the steering wheel. The horn blew quick and loud. She and I laughed. I adjusted. Took my hand, moved up her thigh… beneath her skirt. Found her heat. Moved my fingers there. Her panties were wet. Sopping. She wanted me in a terrible way.

I grabbed the edge of them and tugged downward. Her hips raising slightly, helping me out. Encouraging me to continue. Moved them awkwardly until they landed around her ankles.

She was now naked from the waist down. Panting and craving me rather loudly. For a moment I was self-conscious. The windows were half down. The back ones were tinted, but Illinois state law prohibited tinting on the front two. We were exposed. Any passerby could hear her craving.

Lola grabbed my face between her fingers, interrupted my thoughts and stripped me from my potential fears. Ripped me from reality back into her sexual fantasyland. She pulled my face to hers. Kissed me aggressively. With vigor.

Her head fell back and she sighed. My face moved downward again. Pushed her shirt up. Small breasts exposed. My mouth hovered above. Closer. Pulling away. Moving nearer… nearly tasting. Pulling back.

My hand traveled the length of her body, landed between her

thighs. Massaged the soft flesh. Teasing her on both ends. Driving her mad. Arousing. Hovering her erogenous zones.

She was breathing heavily. Panting actually. "Zella... Zella please... touch me. Touch... me please."

I obliged.

Sucked her nipple into my mouth. Loved it. Licked and nibbled as my fingers crept deeper and deeper between her thighs, rubbing the folds of flesh sticky from desire.

Suckling and massaging. Pulling.

Pressing firmly. Driving her wild.

She moaned my name over and over. Squirming. Fighting her instincts only because a mother with her child... a perv or an impressionable youth could be passing by at that very moment.

I felt her body. Felt her passion run down my hand. Felt her absorb me... consume me. I looked at her face. Removed my mouth, raised my head and watched her as I stroked that urgency beneath her waist... beneath her skirt.

Her eyes were closed.

Face tensed.

Ugly... beautifully ugly.

Mumbling profanity. Accented words of pleasure. Some words I couldn't understand. Possibly a foreign language.

On edge.

Pre-orgasmic writhing.

Her voice became louder. Her cries became hoarse. Broken.

She cursed. Swore at me in English. Swore at me in a language that didn't sound like English. Demanding I press harder... go faster... don't stop.

"Don't stop... don't stop... don't... Zella... please."

I watched her. As I fondled her, I watched her tense and relax. Eyes wide... eyes closed tight. Observed her reaction when I eased pressured... slowed my movements. When I sped up... pressed harder. When my intensity wavered.

Her cries became louder. Inconsolable. Water escaped her right eye… ran down the side of her face.

I smiled at her, laughed actually.

"Hush up, you're too loud."

"Oh f'k you… Zell… Zella!"

I kissed her in random reachable places. Sporadically. She struggled to talk. Struggled on the edge of an orgasm that I wouldn't allow her to have. Struggled to control her pleasure to prevent our being jailed for indecent exposure.

"F'k Zella, let me cum already before… someone calls the… bloody police!" She growled.

I obliged. Let her culminate her pleasure. Felt the height of her joy on my hand. Felt it drain from her long, lean frame. Watched her ugliness turn lovely once again. Watched her chase her breath then finally… catch it.

Witnessed the emergence of that naughty smile spreading wide, teeth showing.

I took my damp fingers… took them to her mouth. Let her taste her own womanhood. She sucked my fingers clean. I kissed her mouth. Used my tongue to search out that essence.

"That was… that was wonderful. My first girl on… girl orgasm. Does this mean I'm no… longer a same sex… virgin?"

I laughed. "That's a taste. More to it than that, but that's a taste."

"I want to taste you, Zella. I need it."

I chuckled. "Slow down."

"I don't want to slow down. I want you. Want to keep going… keep going."

"You're trippin'."

I eased back to my seat. Leaving her sticky and out of breath, reclined with her arm across her face.

"Not tripping. I want more of you."

"You might wanna get us out of here. I'm sure someone heard your loud behind."

"I don't give a shit. Besides if they did it's your fault. Are you hearing me, Zella?"

"I hear you, L."

She moved her arm and looked at me. I smirked at her. Feeling naughty. Feeling dirty. Making a beautiful married accented woman cum in a car during daylight hours had me riled up... feeling adventurous.

Rebellious.

I asked, "When do you have to pick your husband up from work?"

"In two hours."

"Then you'd better drive fast."

She licked her lips. Sat up. Tried to adjust her bra. Pulled her shirt down while starting the car. Adjusted her seat then pulled off.

Fled the scene of our crime.

17 *Chapitre Dix - Sept*

We held hands like lovers as she drove.

We giggled like silly school girls as she sought out a parking space in our neighborhood.

Sean generally worked incredibly long hours. This day wasn't any different than many other days. It was already just about seven, leaving us with an hour of alone time before she'd have to head to his job to pick him up.

Searching for parking was wasting time. She was squeezing my hand in anxiety.

"L, maybe we should just wait."

"No, no. Let me just turn up here. We didn't try over here yet."

"Lola, sweetie, look at the time."

"Plenty of time."

"Don't want you to be late."

"He can wait." She turned another corner. Her eyes lit and she pulled her hand from mine... began pointing. "See! See! What'd I tell you!"

My eyes rolled back, and I laughed.

Lola parked the car. Moving quickly, she turned the engine off, pulled the keys out, opened the door. She'd started down the block – then stopped abruptly. I laughed as I watched her return to the car from which I hadn't yet moved. She rushed to my side, looked in at me.

"Zella!"

"Yes, dear." I struggled to hold back my laughter.

"What are you waiting for? Get out the bloody freaking car!" She looked as though she were about to explode. "Stop laughing at me. Come on."

I fought to control my chuckles as she struggled to conceal hers. She grabbed my hand and pulled me along, practically dragging me the three block distance to the building. Time was running out, and she was determined to have her way before that happened.

My self-consciousness kicked in right about the moment we entered our courtyard. I wondered where Ms. Thea was. She'd seemed to suspect something. I wasn't sure at all how, and I didn't want to risk confirming anything. I tried to be discreet in the event that Ms. Thea was sitting in the window sipping Plum Monkey and craving a Kool.

I fought against my desire to look up, kept my face concealed. Kept my head low and struggled to maintain an amiable distance from Lola, which she was making quite a challenge. It seemed forever before we entered the building and made it to the third floor. I unlocked the door and allowed her inside. She walked directly to my drawer as I locked us in.

"Um, what in heaven's name is this all about?" she asked in awe.

I feigned ignorance. "Why, whatever do you mean?"

She pointed to the open drawer. "This? The gum factory you have in here."

"Oh. Yeah, that. I stopped smoking."

"What do you mean you stopped smoking?"

"I... quit. Dropped the habit."

"Just like that?"

"Well no, not just like that hence all the gum."

I walked to the drawer and began fondling the packs with my fingers, trying to mentally will them into packs of little fatty's.

"What made you turn over the new leaf?"

"Lola, we've got what, forty minutes or so. Do you really want to spend that time talking about my habits?"

"Oh, God no!"

"I didn't think so."

I pushed the drawer closed and approached her. Kissed her. Fingers tangled deep within the jungle of hair. Aggressive. Dominant. The way I presumed she wanted me to be. Pushed her backward without breaking our lip lock. Led her toward the bathroom... beyond the door. Pushed her fully inside before I released her.

Her eyes lit with excitement. "The shower?"

I nodded... mischief lighting mine. She sat on the toilet top watching...and waiting as I reached in and turned on the water. Adjusted the temp. Turning the knob back and forth until it was shooting out at the desired degrees.

I'd be with her in the shower. She had to leave to pick Sean up from work in less than an hour. Didn't want her to be stuck with my scent on questionable places, encouraging suspicions. She'd arrive freshly washed, smelling sweetly of mango and pomegranate.

And so I crossed the line.

The car I could be forgiven of. The act of sin... that indiscretion was one of those things that truly *just happened*. She showed up outside my work unannounced. She showed up and confessed a desire for no more than friendship, and I looked into her eyes and lost my sensibilities.

I couldn't be blamed for that. It wasn't my fault. I was a lonely girl, missing my two dearest friends. I was a sad girl with no mother to confide in and without a father to look up to. I was an angry girl with no family to trust.

And here was this doe-eyed woman needing me for reasons beyond her ability to properly explain... needing me during a time that I was oh, so needy. How could one expect that I could possess a will strong enough to reject her?

But this... crossed a line.

There was no turning back. No simple Hail Mary or prayer of repentance. No simple apology that would clean my slate and make me innocent.

There was a line... and I'd crossed it.

This wasn't just happening, this was pre-meditated. I accepted my role and shirked my responsibility.

The shower was the perfect temp. It was ready. Like Lola, it was ready.

I caught myself... looked at Lola.

"Hey, L, you sure... you sure you want this? Sean's a great guy."

Lola stood. Her expression turned serious. She walked to me... kissed my lips softly, then stepped back. Without taking her eyes off of me, she reached for the bottom edge of my tee-shirt. Raised it over my head, then tossed it to the floor.

She undid the buckle of the belt I wore to hold my shorts in place. Pulled it out. Dropped it. Unsnapped. Unzipped. Slipped my cargo shorts down to land at my feet.

I stood on my bathroom rug in a black lace demi-bra and boy cut panties. Lola's expression didn't change. Quickly, she pulled her top away... dropped her bottoms.

We stood before one another in our undergarments. Me, suddenly feeling shy. Those old feelings returning with a vengeance. She, looking the part. I wanted to ask the question again, ask if she was sure, but I couldn't bring myself to say anything.

Lola took a deep breath, swallowed her fears, reached back and unhooked her bra... covered her small breasts with her hands. I was every bit self-conscious as though I hadn't seen them before. I followed her lead and set my breasts, two sizes larger, free.

She smiled shyly. Removed her hands, exposed those two erogenous zones then, slipped her thumbs into the top sides of her underwear and eased them away. I, then, did the same.

Godiva chocolate.

In that moment, all I could think about was Godiva chocolate.

She stepped into the tub... stepped behind that earth tone curtain and I followed. We cemented our position. There was no turning back. That act... that act completely changed the dynamics of our relationship, and there was no turning back.

And she had her way with me. In the limited time we had to be together, Lola had her way with me. In an uncomfortable position in a tight tub, with my backside pressed against cold porcelain and my leg firmly planted over her right shoulder, she had her wildest fantasy come true.

I stretched and yawned, scratched my eyes as I slowly entered the realm of the living. I sat upright in my bed, the sheet covering me to my knees. I picked the corners of my eyes clean, then tried adjusting them to the light.

Judging by the brightness outdoors, I ventured a guess that it was rather late in the morning. I reached around for my cell phone but was unable to find it.

I shuddered. Something was off about the day... something I was supposed to remember but could not.

I stretched across the bed and turned the television on, keeping the volume low. The round table of hostesses playing live through my monitor let me know it was some time past ten.

I pulled my sheet up, covering my bare breasts. I glanced backwards at my wall. Lola hadn't beckoned me. The only tap-tap against it had been late the night before when it was apparent the couples love making had been so vigorous it caused the bed to slide. Hadn't heard that tap... that insistent tap created by passionate love making in a while. I swallowed hard.

As I looked back at the wall, a feeling began to bubble in my gut. Anger? Jealousy? Couldn't be jealousy. Shook that emotion away, returning my attention to the television and the opinionated discussion. Half listening. Trying not to think about the happenings of the day before. Trying not to remember the feel of Lola's tongue stroking my most precious parts.

She was nervous at first... jittery. I thought she'd come to her senses before I could cum. Thought she'd remember she was a married heterosexual woman. Thought she'd remember that I too was a woman, the one that enjoyed the exploration of sexuality... not her. But ultimately those things mattered not. In the end, she loved me below like she'd done it all of her sexual life.

My legs shook violently, and I'd fought to keep myself balanced on the tub's edge. It became increasingly difficult not to slide away as she pressed my button harder, flicking her tongue back and forth, sending waves of vibrations throughout my body. My voice was a shrill cry, rocking the very foundation of the building we were engaging in... or so it felt.

She definitely did not make it out in time to pick up Sean when she was supposed to. The first concrete sign that what we were doing was wrong was her call to him on her way out saying she was on her way, claiming that she'd fallen asleep. Said she was sorry for that.

If that lie was offensive to me, I was obligated to ignore it... pretend it didn't matter and that it was true.

She made love to her husband that night just like the old days. Just like she used to. With vigor and passion, sending their bed to thump furiously against our shared well. Taunting me almost.

I ran my tongue across my teeth and snatched my drawer open. Gum. Nothing but gum.

Winterfresh.

Peppermint.

Citrus fruit.

Raspberry mint.

I rolled my eyes. I grabbed two spearmint pieces and ripped away the wrappers, shoving them inside my mouth.

I frowned. Something was definitely off.

My phone chimed. It was the alarm.

I picked it up and read the reminder. I took a deep breath... dropped my head.

"Man." I sucked my teeth.

I scrolled to Darwin's name in the address book and pushed the button to dial the number. I didn't know if he'd answer or not, but it didn't matter. Not this time, not on this day. All twisted emotions, negativity, and anger had to be pushed aside.

It was the anniversary of Darwese's birth, Darwin's deceased older sister.

If he didn't answer, it was less likely to be out of any malice toward me but rather a result of his sullen emotions regarding the loss of his sister. It'd been six years, but he hadn't yet moved on enough to be able to lead his normal everyday activities on that special day.

Every year on her birthday, he took the day off work (if it landed on a weekday) and spent his morning in prayer and solitude. By early noon, he arrived at his mother's home where they participated in their ritual of visiting Darwese's gravesite, then returning home for a celebration of her life equipped with her favorite foods and music and a special gift that was bestowed upon her young son and daughter in her honor.

The phone rang repeatedly, eventually dropping me into his voicemail. I left a message... my crinkly morning voice singing an off-key rendition of *Happy Birthday* to his sister. It was an important day to him, and I knew he'd appreciate it.

I rose from bed, relieved that I'd resolved my conundrum – or, rather it resolved itself – but still fighting my confliction regarding Lola Brown.

I wrapped the sheet loosely around my nude body and shuffled to the kitchen, desperately in need of a bottle of cold water.

I stood behind the counter with my arms folded, holding the sheet in place and sipping the water... watching the wall.

"Don't be this way," I warned myself, sitting the bottle on the counter and shuffling to the bathroom to find relief.

I sat on the toilet, staring now at the tub but trying not to. I sat longer than necessary trying not to reflect or care about the events that had recently occurred. And even more so, I tried to not think about or care about what she'd done when she returned home with her husband.

The sound of my phone ringing removed me from my thoughts. I finished up quickly and moved swiftly to the main room and grabbed it. I answered without paying attention to the caller.

"Hello."

"Good morning, honey."

My eyes closed and my body warmed. The muscles between my thighs tensed. I blushed and smiled involuntarily. She sang those words, and chills ran through me.

"Hey, L."

"How terrible is it that I'm missing you already?"

My smiled dropped out for a moment. *You weren't missing me last night when you were doing your husband only a couple hours after you did me*, I thought. I shook away the mounting envy.

"It's not terrible. Actually I think it's kinda sweet."

"What are you doing today?"

"Painting. I got another assignment."

"How exciting! Another of Janessa's connects?"

"Yeah, a woman from her firm. See why it was so important that I finish her work on time?"

"Yeah, yeah. Good for you and Janessa."

I smiled at her effort at jealousy. I took my time walking back to the bed. I sat on the edge, holding the phone with one hand and picking at the fabric wrapped around me with the other. I bit my lip... searching for something to say.

"So... how is your morning so far?" I asked.

"Eh, could be better. Wish I could get out of here and come and watch you paint."

"Well, why don't you?"

"Well, because of Patrice. She called in sick today. Third time in two weeks. I swear the girl is pregnant, but she denies it."

"Oh well, that sucks. I mean, unless she wants to be pregnant."

"She has a good guy."

"So do you." The words just slipped out. I wished I could have taken them back the moment I realized I'd said them.

"Yeah, well, now I've got the best of both worlds."

There was an odd tone in her voice... a bit distant. I hoped I hadn't upset her.

"I umm... I... can't wait to have some time with you again."

"Maybe we can plan something for tomorrow."

I'd hoped to be with her that night, possibly with her and Sean together... like old times. But I didn't ask. I wouldn't ask. I'd never before invited myself into their bedroom, and I wouldn't now. Besides, something told me she wouldn't want to share me anyhow.

"Sure thing, just let me know.

"I definitely will. I have a customer. I'll call you later, love."

We ended our conversation. I sat with the phone in my hand a bit longer... fighting a smile – and losing.

Carlos Santana. Something about listening to his music while painting brought my colors to life. It gave them a spirit. The reds bled just a little bit deeper. The yellow shone a little bit brighter. The blues, just a little bit wetter.

I played a variety of music when I worked. Miles. Coltrane. Sergio Mendes. Mark deClive Lowe. But somehow I always found my way home to Santana. I'd get lost in his riffs and create worlds from the inside out.

I was creating a magnificent piece for a woman named Deana Dennison. She was not only a partner at the firm Lola's dancer friend worked at, she was a true art buff herself. She knew what she wanted, and she knew her artists and styles. She was a challenge to create for and that challenge was such a pleasure.

The buzzing of my doorbell interrupted my flow.

"Damn it. Who in the hell could this be?" I wasn't expecting company.

I moved my brush from the canvas and squeezed my eyes tight, wishing the intruder away. But the buzzer sounded again. No such luck. In great irritation, I willed my bare feet to move toward the intercom.

"Who is it?" I barked.

"Darwin."

"Darwin?" I mumbled in awe. I snapped myself out of my daze and hurried to buzz him in. I unlocked the door and stepped back. I was fidgety… nervous like a divorcee on her first date post marriage. Or, a teenage girl on the night she's planned to lose her virginity. I hadn't seen my friend in weeks… had barely spoken to him and now he was suddenly at my residence unannounced. I hoped nothing was wrong.

I twirled the paintbrush between my fingers and ran my nails across my scalp. I stood tapping my foot… and waiting.

Darwin knocked as he pushed my door open slowly. The feeling… seeing him there in my doorway, that feeling was indescribable. A sense of relief. A sense of gratitude. A feeling of warmth. An urge to cry.

Darwin peered at me from the other side of the door.

"Hi."

"Hi."

"Can I come in?"

"Of course."

He entered my domain. Gently closed the door behind him. Everything was amplified. The click of the door closing. The sound of my breathing. The sound of my beating heart. He stood near the door... looking at me. Hands in pockets... looking at me. Looking... looking... looking damn good.

"Come here."

I moved from my position. The brush dropped from my hand as I moved swiftly across the room and into his arms. He embraced me. I felt his muscles tense as he squeezed just a little bit harder. I squeezed back, the side of my face pressed to his chest and my tears creating a wet spot on his white t-shirt.

His hand moved up my back. Moved up to my head. His fingers dug a path through my hair, which was pulled up into a haphazard bun on top of my head, and kneaded my scalp. I sniffed... tried not to leak much on his crisp, clean shirt.

I eased out of his grip. I stepped back, looking at him through bleary eyes into his.

"Hey," I said laughing nervously.

"Hey, beautiful. I've missed you."

I smacked his arm playfully. "Oh my God, don't stay away from me for so long ever again!"

"I won't, I won't." He laughed, pulling his body into a defensive position. Darwin walked past me and to the easel... took in the swirls of colors. Viewed the image of the exquisite blond, nude and stretched across the length of cotton. "This is freaking dope, Z! Amazing. What is this for?"

I blushed. "It's for the blond. She's a co-worker of a client of mine who commissioned me to do this piece for her."

"Wow. This is bomb, sis, for real. This is the best I've ever seen you do. She must be paying you a grip for this."

I winked and smiled. "She's paying a pretty sweet amount."

I walked to my bed and took a seat. Grabbed a stick of gum from my stash, then reached over and turned the CD player's volume down. Darwin sat down in the recliner. He looked at me... smiling. Made me blush harder.

"Got your message. Thank you. I appreciated it. A little out of tune, but nevertheless it meant the world to me."

"You're welcome." I glanced at the time. "It's kinda early. Celebration over already?"

"Uhh... no. We didn't do it this year."

"Really? Any particular reason?"

Darwin sighed heavily. He sucked his teeth... glanced at the ceiling, likely trying to avert a flow of tears. "Umm... it's been six years. Mom and I thought – agreed, it was about time to move on. Ranesha and Davion... they have to be allowed an opportunity to grow into fully functioning members of society, and we just thought by not... letting go of their mother – allowing them to let go of their mother, we were maybe hindering them. We've probably been doing them a disservice by pretending that... Dar isn't..."

I shook my head vigorously. I understood. They didn't want Dar's children to suffer what Daddy was suffering through. Made sense.

Darwin sniffed and flicked a tear from beneath this eye. "So umm..." Darwin continued, "I didn't come here to drag you down with me. I just needed to talk to you. Face to face."

My ears perked up. "What about?"

"Well for starters, my being a jackass."

I laughed. "You're not a jackass!" Darwin nodded. "Okay, maybe yeah, maybe just a little bit."

He leaned forward in the seat, elbows resting on his knees, fingers intertwined. "Z, I'm sorry. I'm so sorry. You were right, we're family. For all these years, I've never pushed to be more, so why now should I expect you to trip over your feet and fall into my arms? Just silly I guess… lonely maybe. I'm rolling up on forty and I've a great career that I love but no wife… no kids. Not even a damned dog."

I scrunched my forehead. "You want kids?"

"Hell yeah I want kids. I want a team of 'em!"

"More power to you, bro."

"You want kids, too, Z. Don't you? Someday?"

I shrugged. "Someday maybe. One or two, definitely not a team."

Darwin laughed. "Ay, D love the kids, what can I say? Anyway… I was trippin'. I'm sorry. You were right, I was jealous, and I guess I was just a little salty. For all we been through and for what we mean to each other, I guess I just expected you would feel the same. How arrogant of *me*.

"I know I told you to store it in TMI and I tripped, but I mean it now. Put it in TMI, sealed file, locked drawer, toss the key. You won't hear about it again. I just want my friend back. Nothing is worth losing something as solid as what we have."

To my surprise, I felt sort of let down, but that feeling was suppressed beneath the extreme joy I had from having my best friend back in my life.

"Aww, baby." I stood and walked to where he sat with my arms outstretched. He reached for me, pulling me down onto his lap. We hugged again.

I was home…

I was home…

He leaned back. I sat there on his lap, his arms around my waist, my arms around his neck. He rocked side to side.

"I have some news for you," he said.

"Good news I hope."

"Great news."

Darwin's fingers moved gently up and down my arm, reminding me how much I missed his touch.

"What is it?"

"I'm getting married."

I felt my heart stop. For a moment, I forgot how to breathe.

"You're doing what?" There was anger in my tone. I hadn't meant for there to be, but there it was, anger.

Darwin stopped rocking. "Married. I'm getting married."

I sat upright... removed my arms from his neck. Freed myself from his embrace. "To who?"

Darwin eyed me suspiciously. "To Miko."

"Miko," I repeated. I stood from his lap and walked to the kitchen. I was suddenly dehydrated.

"Okay, this is the part where you're supposed to say 'Congratulations Darwin. I'm happy for you Darwin.'"

"Why are you marrying Miko? You barely know her."

"What's this about, Z? What, do you have something against Miko?"

"No."

"So what then?"

"I'm just saying, you hardly know her. I mean, you dated for like, what, two months before you broke up with her over her toenails. You've only been back together for a couple months."

"And your point?"

"I'm just saying."

"No, you're not saying anything. What are you trying to say?"

"I don't... I don't think you should do it."

Darwin looked at me. He folded his lips in and nodded. He stood up. "You don't want me. You don't want anyone else to have me."

"It isn't like that, D."

"Oh no? Tell me what it's like, Zella Dora." There was an uncomfortable silence. I didn't know what to tell him. I didn't want him to marry Miko… the idea bothered me, but I didn't know why. He'd confessed his emotions about me to me, and I didn't want him but… the thought of him loving another woman with as much vigor or even more passion than he loved me was unsettling.

"I just think you should know her better."

"Well, if it helps to ease your insecurities about it at all, she'd like to be engaged for a year before we go making anything official. That should be enough to alleviate any concerns you may have."

It wasn't.

"Yeah, sure… that's great. Plenty time. Congrats."

We looked at each other until my conscious forced me to look away.

Darwin broke the silence. "Hey, I'm gonna get up on out of here. Miko and I are taking little Tarik to the zoo, soo…"

"Oh yeah. Yeah… that's important."

"Yeah, it is. I'll call you later," he said as he walked to the door.

"Okay." I joined him.

"Thanks again… for thinking of me."

I nodded, fighting back an onslaught of tears. Darwin kissed my forehead then exited my apartment. I closed and locked up behind him.

Marriage?

Taking little Tarik to the zoo?

It felt as though a thousand tiny knives were stabbing my insides, and I had no clue why. Darwin was family. For six years… family. Just family. Like a brother. And it was perverse for sisters to hook up with their brothers, so there was no way he and I could hook up – except… well… we weren't really related.

18 *Chapitre Dix-Huit*

I loved Margot's place.

I absolutely loved it. One wouldn't be mistaken if they accused me of a small amount of envy either. A vintage loft style apartment in Pilsen with large windows and loads of light. Vaulted ceilings, cherry wood floors, and way more square feet than two people could handle.

She owned her place... inherited it from an aunt that she was close with her entire life. The aunt, Sylvia, knew she was going to die soon. The usual suspect, an aggressive cancer that spread because it wasn't detected in time.

She'd changed her will just a week and a half prior to passing, leaving the lavish fully furnished loft to her niece and great nephew Jake along with a third of her savings and a trust Jake would never benefit from.

I was rather suspicious that a big part of the reason Shane stayed in his marriage to Margot was the security of the home and the decent-sized inheritance his bride possessed. Not nearly enough that she could quit her job as a call center supervisor to become a professional shopper, but enough that Shane could slack off on his work ethics and know that the bills would still be paid.

The painting I'd done for her was beautiful in its position on the wall above the couple's bed, illuminated by the track lighting that had been installed. Made me damn proud.

"Hmpf. Look, Mom, I'm giving you a run for your money these days," I whispered quietly as I adored it.

I stretched my body out across the bed, picked up the remote, and began absentmindedly flipping through hundreds of channels while Margot changed outfits for the third time that evening.

I rolled my eyes while listening to her shifting about inside the walk-in closet, tugging and zipping. Doing a bunch of unnecessary preparations.

"Do I look okay?" She stepped into the doorway and posed for me. A black pencil skirt with a red tunic. She bent forward, checking herself out. With a finger, she moved her bobbed jet black hair behind her ear and awaited my response. I thought she was cute though very much overdressed.

"What are you doing?" I asked.

"What do you mean?"

"Margot, honey, we're going to a movie."

"Correction. We're going to a film festival."

"We're going to watch independent films, not star in them."

"I've gained weight," she said almost to herself. Her hands moved to her waistline. She rubbed across the material, feeling for expanded fat pockets. "Last time I wore this it wasn't so tight."

"Oh my word, here we go."

"Seriously, Zella, as if I weren't already fat enough."

I sat up in the bed. "I'm not going to lie to you, yes, you have gained weight, but it's nothing significant. If you would stop stressing, you'd stop eating so much, and you'd knock it right back off."

She exhaled a frustrated growl and smacked her thick thighs.

"I'm changing."

"Freakin'-A man." I turned back to face the television. I yelled, "Put the pedal pushers back on!"

We were going downtown to the summer indie festival, going to check out some good – and some not so good – independent films. My annual ritual. Margot had never before gone with me. It was generally something Darwin and I, and occasionally Ayinde, did together. But Day was being distant, and Darwin was skipping out this year to do something that Miko had requested of him a couple weeks prior.

The mere thought pissed me off. We did this every year. That sorta made it a tradition. And in my eyes, I felt that tradition trumped new girlfriend. Except he was calling the new girlfriend his fiancée and apparently fiancée trumps old friend... even one's of the *best* variety.

I didn't know why this thing with Darwin irked me so. I should have been happy for him... thrilled actually. Isn't that one of the expected duties of the best friend?

He'd confessed to loving me, and I had rejected him because as I saw it, we were family, and we couldn't threaten the purity of that by becoming lovers.

He'd come back and not exactly retracted that confession but come to understand my perspective and accept my belief and decision as his own. He'd chosen to settle for friendship and work toward our return to the former completely platonic state we'd lived in for so many years. He'd decided to move on with his life and try having a future with his most recent ex Miko.

So why the hell was I so bothered?

I liked Miko once upon a time. I'd hoped that they fixed things the night before the fight with Marcus occurred. But now the mere mention of her name sent venom shooting through my veins.

And Darwin... I couldn't shake thoughts of him. He was showing up in my dreams and when he did, he was barely dressed – or rarely dressed.

For a moment, I thought that maybe it meant something... maybe I really did have some sub-conscious desire for him. But then I'd snap back into reality and recognize the ridiculousness of that notion.

He was actually talking about getting married. It was probably all just a deep-seeded fear of losing him once he connected himself to another woman.

"That was Kat!" Margot yelled from the closet.

"Huh?"

She poked her head out. "That was Katty-Girl on my phone. She said she'll be here in like fifteen minutes. Her brother's friend is dropping her off."

"Cool. Well, are you almost ready? I hate being late."

"Yeah, yeah, nerd girl. I know, I know. Just gonna brush my hair back and brush my teeth."

She disappeared again.

"Did you settle on something to wear?"

"Yeah! The black pedal pushers!"

I smirked and chuckled.

I reached over and picked up the framed photo that sat on her nightstand. Jake and Margot. A close-up shot of their faces pressed together. Jake's piercing blue eyes made me smile and almost water up.

Shortly thereafter, Margot flipped the lights off and joined me in the bedroom when she was done. She sat on the bed beside me. Picked up a bottle of lotion and began lathering her legs. I handed her the photo so she could return it to its former position. Her eyes lingered before focusing again on what she was doing.

"That's my buddy," she said.

I rubbed my hand comfortingly across her back. We'd all experienced great loss in our lives. My mother. Margot's son. Darwin's sister. Ayinde... to a degree her entire family. Maybe that was what brought us together, what bonded us.

Margot turned to face me. "So what's weighing on your mind?"

I was jolted with surprise. "Nothing, why you ask?"

"I don't know. Your vibe tonight is off. Your energy... something doesn't feel right."

The corners of my lips turned down. "I guess my energy *is* off. I sort of have a bit of a troubled mind."

"So... spill it."

I eyed Margot. Contemplated. Debated whether or not I wanted to share. I could trust her, but if I were planning to spill the beans, I needed to do so in fifteen minutes or less. Had to do it before Kat arrived.

"Okay I'll tell you, but you cannot tell Kat."

"I won't, I swear."

"I'm serious, Margot. I don't want her in my business like that."

"Z, c'mon. Have I given you any reason to believe that you can't trust me?"

"No, you haven't and let's keep it that way."

She gave me a knowing look.

"Fine... okay." I took a deep cleansing breath, then exhaled heavily. "I'm kinda having an affair."

"An affair? What do you mean you're having an affair? With who?"

I paused. "My neighbor."

Confusion passed over Margot's face. "Who? Which neighbor? Who's on your floor besides that old broad that lives down the hall that never leaves her apartment?"

"The ones next door. Directly to the left."

That confusion stalled for a moment then her eyes widened as the cloud lifted. "Not the freak-nasty neighbors that you used to listen to?" I nodded. "Oh. My. God. You're screwing your neighbor's husband?"

"Not exactly."

"Not exactly, what do you mea – Zella Dora! You are not!" I nodded again. Margot jumped from the bed. "You're screwing your neighbor's wife!"

"Well we're girls, but I suppose you can call it that."

Margot's mouth dropped open as she eased down slowly onto the foot of the bed. "You've got to be shitting me. You dirty girl, you're screwing your neighbor's wife. No f'king way!"

I smacked Margot's hand. "Don't be so crass."

"You're kidding me, right? You're having an affair with your damned neighbor's wife, and I'm being crass."

"Touché."

"Since when do you care about foul language anyway?"

"I don't know. Trying to be better I guess."

"I guess. Anyway, how in the fu – how in the *world* did that happen?"

I confessed. The tipsy kiss. The naughty threesome. The messy breakup. The daytime passion on the side street of a residential neighborhood.

Margot slid from the bed, landed with a soft thud onto the wood floor. She looked up at me in sheer awe and amazement, damn near admiration. I smiled… felt a little lighter, a little freer having gotten that secret off my chest.

"So let me get this straight. You were screwing around with both of them as a couple, but your conscious got to you and you ended it. And now you're just chipping with the wife and as far as you know, the husband has no idea."

"Right."

"Why you little hussy! I had no clue your life was this f'kin' exciting! O.M.G., I am so jealous! Oh, I need a hit. I was gonna wait 'til Kat showed her ass here, but she's taking too long."

Margot pulled an ace and a lighter from her purse and set flame to it.

"But isn't it wrong?" I asked.

"Hell no, she's the late one."

I waved her off. "No genius, what I'm doing with a married woman. Isn't it wrong?"

She coughed a bit and blinked, looked like her eyes were burning. "Hell no. He already consented. Clearly the thought of her with another woman turns him on. I doubt he'd give a shit. Probably just makes their sex life better."

She reached to pass to me.

Inside I was hyperventilating. This was my test... my first test and I hadn't considered how I'd handle it. On the outside, I remained calm and confident as I said, "No thanks."

She continued holding the drug toward me. "What, next you're gonna tell me you don't get high anymore."

"Well, as a matter of fact..."

"Oh get the hell out of here. Not Ms. Weedhead of the Millennium. Since when?"

"Few weeks actually. But if you got some gum in that vortex you call a purse, I'll take it."

The buzzer sounded and Margot stood. "Funny girl," she joked as she exited the room and walked the length of the hall to the intercom to allow Kat inside.

I followed. "Oh yeah, and Darwin told me he loves me."

Margot pressed her finger against the button. "And that's news because?"

"What do you mean? Are you saying it's *not* news?"

"Woman, please, everybody knows Darwin's crazy in love with you... well everyone except you apparently."

"Are you kidding me?"

Margot opened the door as Kat approached.

"Katty-Girl, does it amaze you to know Darwin's in love with Zella?"

"How do you mean?" she asked.

"Is this news to you?"

Kat laughed and looked to me. "I guess you finally caught on, huh?"

"He finally told her."

Kat rolled her eyes and shook her head. She took the spliff from Margot's fingers. "Well, they say sometimes the smartest people can be so dumb."

"Bite me," I said to her.

Margot added, "And the award for oblivious person of the year goes to."

"Funny, funny girl."

"Oh, and when you're done pass that back my way. Ms. In-the-dark here apparently doesn't smoke any longer."

"What?" Kat said amazed. "You're messing with me now, right? But you know what, Z, I'm proud of you. That's an honorable thing you're doing."

I smiled. "Girl, please. You're only saying that 'cause it means more for you."

"Can't knock the hustle."

I laughed as I turned to gather my things so that the three of us could finally head out the door.

I had Margot drop me at Dad's house. It was rather late at night, but I just needed to see his face. Wanted to hear his voice and hold his hand. One of the films was about a father's relationship with his daughter. They were close until he became afflicted with Alzheimer's and began to slowly forget who she was.

In the end, as she stood by his bedside watching as Death led him away, he managed to grab her hand and squeeze. It was as though in that final breath of life he knew her once again.

And then... he was gone.

I sent Margot to drop Kat at home. I could walk home when I was ready. It was a refreshing night, and a walk would do me good. And I had a fresh tube of mace on my keychain in the event that I picked up any unwanted company.

I let myself in. The house was dark with the exception of a blue overcast light from the television.

"Daddy?" I called softly being careful not to startle him. "Hey, Dad."

He stirred in his seat and shifted until he'd made eye contact with me.

"Sweet Pea. Hey, Baby Girl," he said in a tired voice, smiling. I kissed his forehead. "What you doing here so late?"

"Better question, what are you doing up so late?"

"Oh, couldn't fall asleep. Tried to go to bed earlier with your mother, but she... she wasn't... I just couldn't..."

"It's okay, Daddy. Sometimes... y'know, you just gotta take a little time for yourself. It's okay to do that."

I held his hand in one of mine and stroked the back of it with my other.

"You coming from someplace with Darwin?"

"Nah, not this time. He's got a new... he's got a new girlfriend that he's spending his time with."

"Is that right?"

"Fiancée actually. He uhm, he asked her to marry him."

Dad looked up at me. "Really now? How do you feel about that?"

I made a myriad of faces while searching for a better way to say, "I feel fine about it."

He smiled at me awhile before speaking again. "You know, it's okay to not be okay, Sweet Pea. I understand you're friends, and you want to be supportive. You're a good friend, and Darwin's a great kid. It'd warm this old man's heart to see you together."

I frowned. "Daddy, D's like a brother to me, how could we cross that line?"

Dad pulled his hand away and chuckled as he faced the TV. Was he laughing at me? "Oh, my Sweet Pea. You ain't related to that boy. Like a brother, ain't a brother."

"I know that, but..." I waved my open palm toward Mom's chair, "may I?"

He looked to me and then the chair. He hesitated, then nodded. "Go on."

I sat and continued my explanation. "My point is this, relationships are work, and if we fail at it, we can run the risk of damaging our friendship. I don't want to risk that. You don't get that many true friends in life. I can't afford to play that game."

"You do have a point there; however, friendship is the best foundation any relationship can have. And you're right, Sweet Pea, you could pursue something with Darwin and it not work out... not be meant to be, but if you really love one another, and the two of you are true friends, you *can* work it out."

My head drooped, and my eyes watered for multiple reasons. First and foremost, there was the realization that I was actually having a father-daughter heart-to-heart. I'd not had that in... in years. There were still issues there. Daybreak would find him longing for Mom again, resolving the issue of her death by just believing she were there, but in that moment in time, it really felt as though I had my Dad again.

I was also hearing my father dismiss my fears of moving from friendship to intimate relationship as being foolish and paranoid. And there was the realization that if – *if* he was right, I'd already messed up and pushed Darwin into the arms of another woman.

"So my sister wants to take over responsibility for me," Dad said, interrupting my thoughts.

My head jerked. "You know about that?"

His eyes remained locked on the television screen. He sighed.

"Yeah. I know."

"Don't worry, Daddy, I plan to fight. They are not getting you out of here, no way."

"Sweet Pea, Sweet Pea… it's okay."

"No, it isn't okay, Daddy. They wanna – she wants to lock you up."

"It's alright. Maybe… well, maybe I do need help."

"Dad, what are you saying?"

He turned to face me. "You're a young woman. A beautiful, intelligent, and talented young woman with such a bright future ahead of you, and you're sacrificing yourself, sacrificing your joy for me. For an old man."

My eyelashes splashed wetness. "I don't care."

"But I do. Let them do what they feel they need to do. Free you up. Let you go back to London. Fall in love. Maybe… just maybe, make me and your mother grandparents."

I slid from the recliner and across the floor to where my Daddy sat. I wrapped my arms around his leg and hugged tight. This wasn't him… wasn't my father of the past six years. I'd missed this Jacob. It wasn't until that moment, that long awaited conversation where my father spoke as though he were truly present for the first time in years, that I realized how much.

This solidified my belief that there was hope.

I wouldn't argue with him. I'd give him the last word. I'd allow him to believe that I'd honor such a ridiculous request. If he pushed, I'd reject him, but for the moment, I'd relish it… tattoo it on my brain… affix it to my memory in case I never had it again.

Dad massaged my scalp, same as he had when I was a child… same as Darwin liked to do, and tears of joy drenched my face.

We sat there for awhile… tangled together and watching a news network, quietly.

Dad groaned, "Alright, Sweet Pea, these old eyes can't take much more. I'm going to bed. You're sleeping here, aren't you?"

I stretched and yawned. "No. Can't. Early appointment. A client is coming by to pick up a painting."

"Sweet Pea, it's late. I don't want you walking this time of night."

"I'll be fine, Dad. If it makes you feel any better, I'll walk over to the el and take the train down there."

"Zella Dora."

"Daddy, I have to. Can't risk not getting home on time."

The truth of the matter was I couldn't risk waking up to the Daddy of yesterday should the Daddy of today not be present tomorrow.

He stood.

I stood.

We faced one another.

"Baby Girl, be careful. Please. You got your pepper spray?"

I held up my key ring and smiled. Dad grabbed me and pulled me into his arms... held me oh so tight. Held me like he hadn't seen me in awhile... like he hadn't seen me in six years.

He pulled back and moved toward the stairs.

"Okay, I'm headed to bed. If you won't change your mind, be very careful."

"Yes, Dad. I love you, Daddy."

He paused... one foot on the bottom step. "I love you, too, Zella Dora."

Daddy walked up the steps as I watched. When he was out of sight and I heard his door click, I turned off the television and headed out the front door, locking it behind me.

Despite telling my Dad I'd hop the train, I walked the distance home. It gave me a chance to think and clear my head. And, at least I'd stay on a lit street rather than exiting the train beneath the shadow of a viaduct and walking the empty path two blocks alone.

My mind insisted on dwelling on Darwin and the things my father had said. I didn't want to ponder it… couldn't afford to. I'd rejected him with vigor. How could I come back and say, *my bad, I changed my mind. Leave your fiancée and let's hook up.*

I couldn't. I just simply could not.

I paused steps from the big black gate and my heart caught in my throat. A figure sat slumped in the shadows. On the ground… against the gate.

I felt my hands become clammy as I approached cautiously, straining my eyes to get a clearer look. There was no movement, and I feared the worst. I felt for my phone, was poised to dial CPD. Then, just as suddenly, my heart began to accelerate. I squinted and moved forward, faster.

"Ayinde?" I whispered. "Holy shit!"

I rushed toward the figure that I was almost positive I recognized. Hurried closer and dropped hard to the ground onto my knees. I lifted her head and it rolled from my fingers. It was indeed Ayinde. I panicked.

"Ayinde!" I cried out as I searched for a pulse point. "Day!"

"Hm?"

Her head rolled slightly as my fingers landed against her neck. I exhaled a cleansing breath; she was alive. I grabbed her hands and turned her palms up to check her wrists. Clean.

I gently slapped her cheeks. "Ayinde. Ayinde, wake up."

"Hm?"

"Day, wake up."

She raised her head and looked at me. "Zella? Zella, is that you?"

"Yes, Kid, it's me." I carefully pushed her hair from her eyes. "What happened to you? Why are you out her asleep? What in the world is going on?"

She came to life. Slowly but steadily until it seemed she'd never been passed out to begin with. Tears flooded her eyes, and she grabbed me. Threw herself at me actually, and wound her arms tightly around my neck.

"Zella... Zella... he left... he left me, Zella. He said, I have to go. Thirty days. He left. He said I only get thirty days. *Don't be there when I get back, bitch. I'm done with you.*"

She continued to ramble and squeeze me tight. I pried her away, but she continued explaining that Marcus had dumped her yet again. Had taken most of his things and given her a thirty-day notice to remove herself from the premises.

I checked her over. Her knees were scrapped, the left one pretty bad. Dried blood was crusted on top. Her eyes were bloodshot with bags beneath. Looked like she hadn't slept for days. Her hair was unkempt. Her clothes completely disheveled.

"Have you been drinking?" I asked unnecessarily. I could smell it on her.

"He just took everything... almost everything. Took his laptop. Took his shoes."

"Day, how much have you been drinking?"

"Took his clothes, he took them, too. And his razor kit." She fidgeted incessantly. Sniffed. Scratched her scalp. Pulled her hair. Bit her nails.

I grabbed her wrists firmly and held her still. "Day, listen to me. Okay? What have you been drinking?"

"Vodka. Just Vodka."

"Straight?" She nodded. "You take anything with it? Any pills or anything?"

"Nooo, Z. Why would he leave me? Why can he do this to me?"

I pulled her into my chest and held her... rocked her while she cried a little longer. I had to remain rational. Couldn't think about my feelings about Marcus. I had to get Ayinde inside and cleaned up.

I guided her to her feet and kept her in my embrace as I entered the gate and the door and led her up to my apartment. I allowed her inside and locked up. I flipped a light switch. I turned to face her. By light she looked much worse than I'd realized.

Somehow she'd aged. She was dirty, and for the first time, I noticed the purple bruise on her upper arm. I rushed to her side and touched it softly, unintentionally causing her to flinch.

"Who did this to you?" I asked beyond angry. "Did Marcus do this? Did that bastard put his hands on you?"

"No."

"Who did then?"

"No one."

"Then how'd it happen?"

She glared at me then walked away dramatically, plopped onto my bed and yanked open my drawer. I glanced at my clean sheets, then to her and cringed.

Her voice snapped me back to attention. It was gruff... demanding. Her crying spell, no more.

"What the f'k is this?" she asked viciously while grabbing a handful of my stash... shuffling through the drawer. "Where's the f'king weed?"

"Gone."

"Why?"

"I got rid of it."

"Why would you do some dumb shit like that? What the hell is this?"

"Gum."

"Why is it here?"

"I put it there."

Venom was in her eyes as she stared at me. Nostrils flared, breathing strong. "You're happy he's gone."

I couldn't honestly deny it, but I wouldn't admit it either. Not now, not while she was being erratic.

"I'm not... I'm not happy he's gone."

"Where are the *f'king* trees?" she yelled, pointing an accusing finger at me.

I wanted to be calm, forceful, in charge, but she'd blindsided me. Had me off balance. I'd never before seen this side of her. She was beyond angry, and I was feeling afraid for her and for myself. I wondered if she was affected by more than alcohol but instantly shook it off.

"There are none, Day. None. I don't smoke them anymore."

Her eyes shot daggers through me. I fought to pull myself together. I couldn't be weak, now was not the time. I focused my energy. Deflected those daggers and sent them right back her way.

Ayinde threw the handful of gum to the floor with force.

"Bitch," she growled as she charged toward the door. She wanted to leave... was going to leave if I didn't stop her. I jumped in her path.

"Where are you going?"

"Move, bitch."

I hated to be called a bitch. Of all insults, that was the worst for me. But I gritted my teeth and withheld the urge to strike.

"I'm not letting you go, Day."

"Get out of my way."

"You gonna make me get out of your way?"

The poison in her eyes, anger in her face began to soften... slowly. Suddenly her lashes were again wet.

"Why doesn't anyone love me?"

My own anger evaporated. I wasn't sure if I could handle the emotional confusion much longer. "What? No... no. That isn't true. I love you, baby. I do. And Darwin loves you. Even Margot."

She stepped back from me as though I was contagious. "F'k Margot! That bitch betrayed me. Being friends with that rag-hoe-slut Kat. If she loved me, she wouldn't be friends with that cunt-whore."

I took a discreet deep breath and exhaled. I couldn't believe

my ears. "Forget Margot, okay. I love you. *I* love you. Come here...
come on." I pulled her into my arms and held her tight. "I love you,
Day, and I will always love you."

I continued to hold her. Let her tears catch in my shirt. Rocked
and promised a love that would be hers forever.

But then she whispered a request that nearly leveled me. "Make
love to me, Zella Dora."

"Wh-what?"

She stepped back from me, though not far. "Make love to me,
Zella. Please. Please."

"Wh – Day... no, I can't. I can't – I won't. I won't do that."

Her anger returned. "I knew you didn't love me. You're just a
liar like everyone else. Like my mom! Like Marcus! Like my pervert
of a father!"

"No, Day, no. It's not that. It's... listen Day, you're my friend.
You're my girl."

"So! You've done girls before, I know about it. You just don't
love me! No one does."

Guilt consumed me, though for the life of me, I could not
comprehend why. When would I learn to say no? When would I
learn to turn my back and worry about Zella f'king Dora? My best
girlfriend was asking me to make love to her. Unbeknownst to her,
I was already loving a woman I had no business loving. I wouldn't
sleep with Ayinde. I couldn't sleep with Ayinde. No got-damned
way.

Though still, I had the urge to prove I loved her... prove she
wasn't alone. There was this undeniable need to help her.

"Ayinde, listen to me," I grabbed her shoulders and held her in
front of me, looked into her eyes, "listen to me. I love you, okay. I do.
But I cannot make love to you. I can't... I just can't do that."

Her eyes fell away, and she wouldn't look at me. "You hate me."

I took a breath and tried to think. "Come with me."

"No, let me out."

"I'm not letting you out, you can forget that. Come with me."

I took her arm gently and led her to the bathroom. I pointed at the toilet and she reluctantly sat. I reached over into the tub... ran water. Adjusted the temperature and plugged the bottom with the stopper. I grabbed a small container of bath salts and sprinkled it across the water.

I reached under the sink and found a bottle of rose passion scented bubble bath and poured it beneath the spout. I left the bathroom and went to the closet. Left Ayinde sitting there silently with leaking, bloodshot eyes and a blank expression.

I returned with a couple small candles and lit them, placing them around the bathroom. I eased my hand into the water... the temp was perfect.

I went to Ayinde and pulled her black t-shirt over her head. I unsnapped her bra and let it fall to the floor. I took her hands in mine and pulled her to her feet. I unzipped her skirt and pushed it past her waist, then her black leggings and panties followed.

I encouraged her to step up and out and then proceeded to remove the sparse accessories she wore.

She stood before me naked and vulnerable.

"Are you going to make love to me?" she asked in a trembling whisper.

I bit down on my bottom lip, then took her arm... led her to the tub into the warm scented waters. I hurriedly turned the faucet off and guided her to a seated position. I took a hand towel, drenched it, and gently rubbed her hair over and over.

"Make love to me, Zella." Her voice was quiet, robotic. Emotionless.

"I am, Kid... I am."

This was how I made love to her... by showing her real love. I cleaned her, washed a few days' worth of dirt from her skin and hair. Cleared wax from her ears and sludge from beneath her nails. She cried softly as I cleaned her. When I was done, I took her from the tub and dried her, then wrapped her in my fluffy dark blue robe that

I rarely used.

I towel dried her hair then split it down the middle and made two thick braids. She sat silently on the toilet top, fresh and clean in my robe as I caressed her legs and feet with lotion.

"C'mon," I spoke. I guided her to my bed and laid her on the inside. I kicked my shoes off and climbed in bed, lay beside her and wrapped my arms around her waist. I kissed the back of her head gently and prayed silently. Prayed for my friend for whom I feared the worst. And for the very first time, prayed for the sins I'd committed against others yet hadn't the strength to cease.

"Please don't leave me, Zella," Ayinde whispered weakly.

"I'm not gonna leave you, Kid."

"You promise you'll always love me?"

"I promise. I promise."

I lay in bed silently and held her until we fell fast asleep.

I tossed and turned all night.

Ayinde slept as though she hadn't gotten any rest in months. She hardly moved at all. Her snoring sent vibrations rippling through my frame. I wasn't used to sharing my bed, nor did I enjoy it.

I awoke for good somewhere around the middle of sunrise and found myself unable to return to any sort of slumber. Ayinde took up most of the space in the bed. I lay on my back on the edge, staring up at the ceiling, connecting the brown dots.

I glanced her.

At peace.

I wondered what was going on with her, wondered what had gone down during the weeks that she'd avoided me. I wondered if she...I wondered if she was on some sort of hard drug.

Her behavior the night before, it had been unprecedented. She'd been unpredictable... irrational. Vodka didn't do that to people. No doubt enough alcohol would have a profound effect on one's mental state, but I couldn't imagine it would go that far.

I rolled my head away and focused my eyes back onto the ceiling.

Tried to figure out what should be done, what could be done… if anything. I pondered whether or not I should involve Darwin. If it were true, I should tell him. But I was speculating, and I didn't want to worry him for nothing.

Drug use and abuse was not my area of expertise. As far as I was aware, Jacob and Zahrah hadn't ever touched an illegal or illicit drug a day in their life. As for myself and those around me, none of us had ever graduated from the mesmeric power of cannabis. My education on hardcore drugs use was limited to what was shown on television and movies.

I was in the process of pondering how a potential confrontation with Marcus would go should I address the issue with him when a knock on the door rattled my thoughts. I glanced at Ayinde. She exhaled heavily and readjusted, but she didn't awaken.

I slipped out of the bed and crept toward the door. I didn't want my unwelcome intruder to wake my slumbering troubled guest. I needed more time to figure things out and plot my course of action.

There was another rap. I glanced back and moved faster.

"I'm coming, I'm coming," I spoke through gritted teeth.

I peeped through the hole. A smile broke out across my face. I unlocked and opened my door. No words could escape my lips before Lola's mouth was locked onto mine. I stumbled backward into my apartment having been caught off guard.

When I realized what was happening, I attempted to reverse our motions and move out into the hall.

"Zella, come on. Sean's gone, and I've been longing for you all night," she breathed the words into my mouth.

I tried to push her back gently but firmly, forcing an end to our contact.

"Lola. Lola," I whispered. "I need you to step outside."

"But why? I - "

"Shh. Please, step outside."

She stopped. Stood in my doorway, eyeing me suspiciously while refusing to budge.

"Is someone here?" she asked.

"Yes, and I need you to keep your voice down before you wake her up."

"Her? Someone is a her?"

"Lola," I whispered with force. "Keep your voice down and step out. Now."

I grabbed Lola's forearms, guiding her backwards as she looked around me trying to steal a peek at Ayinde. I glanced back before stepping into the hall and breathed a sigh of relief as she still appeared to be sleep.

I turned the knob and made sure the automatic lock was off before easing the door shut behind me.

Lola's arms were folded, and her lips tight and turned down when I faced her. Her anger was cute to me. I couldn't help but laugh.

"So, who is she?" Lola asked seeming not to find the humor in the situation.

I gasped playfully. "You're jealous."

"I am certainly not jealous. I'd just like to know who she is."

"Mrs. I-have-a-husband-at-home is jealous at the thought of me sharing my bed with someone else." I giggled.

"Not jealous, Zella, and I do kindly ask that you stop laughing at me. You're embarrassing me," she whined.

"You're embarrassing me," I mocked and laughed a little harder. "It's only me and you out here, how am I embarrassing you?"

She chuckled at first... then laughed louder. "Stop laughing. Look, I'm sorry okay. I'm a little jealous. Are you happy now? Now, who is the woman in your bed?"

"Her name is Ayinde Phelan."

"Well... who is she to you? Is it... is it serious?"

I smiled and looked away coyly. "Yeah, I guess you could say that. It's pretty serious."

Lola's eyes dropped to her feet. "Oh. So… what does that mean – ahem – what does that mean for us?"

I watched Lola. Didn't say anything for a moment. This woman who'd leave after making passion with me to be with a man who happened to be her husband, was questioning whom I shared my bed with when she wasn't around. It was funny to me.

"L. L, look at me. She's just my friend, okay? She's the one I told you tried to… tried to kill herself a while back. Remember?"

Lola blushed. "Oh. She's the one."

"Yes, she's the one."

"Sorry."

"It's okay. I think your being jealous is kinda cute. Now what are you doing here so early anyway?"

Lola took my hand in hers, began massaging my fingers. "Heard you come in last night, and I wanted to come to you. Of course I couldn't. Heard you arguing with someone… her I suppose, so I knew you were upset. Besides, Sean was home anyhow. Hoped to have some um, quality time before I left for work."

I found myself doing kegels involuntarily when those highly suggestive words escaped her lips. I gripped her hand tighter… pulled her to me. My mouth went to hers, sharing my morning breath with her Aqua Fresh. My tongue tangled around hers as my free hand traveled the length of her body southbound, stopping and clutching between her thighs.

My pulse accelerated, burning calories before breakfast. Lola's hand grabbed my breast, squeezed. I wanted to strip her right there in the hall. Didn't want to waste time picking an apartment to enter.

We could go into hers, but we wouldn't want to run the risk of leaving some evidence of our surreptitious affair behind.

My door opened, reminding me of exactly why we couldn't go into mine. Lola snatched herself away from me before I could react. The look in her eyes… it was as though she'd seen a ghost. That, or been caught in the midst of an adulterous, lesbian love affair.

I didn't immediately react to Ayinde. I was all too fascinated by the look of shame washing over Lola's face. She took another step back and wiped her lips discreetly as she glanced away from the eyes of my friend.

I couldn't help but feel like crap. Not for having been caught in the act but for being the source of such embarrassment.

I turned to face Ayinde. She stood in the doorway, dressed in my robe. The look of a true killer in her eyes as she stared unblinking at Lola.

"I'm going to uh… I'm going to…" Lola struggled to finish her statement. Finally, she focused on me. "I'm going to uh… I'll call you…"

She turned quickly on her heels and entered her apartment.

I watched her walk away, then felt the wind on my back a moment before I heard my door slam shut. I jumped from the unexpected noise. I turned and calmly entered my home.

"Don't do that," I stated.

"Don't do what?"

"Slam my damn door. You don't live here, you're a guest. I don't know what you were on last night, but it's a brand new day, and you know better."

"Who was she?"

I shrugged. "Nobody."

"You sure weren't acting like she was nobody when you were out there slobbing her down."

"She's my neighbor."

"You tongue down all your neighbors? That your way of saying welcome to the building?"

I growled quietly and opened my drawer. Gum. Nothing but f'king gum. I slammed it shut. Stood there, eyes closed, scratching my forehead.

"What's your point, Day?"

"She your girlfriend?"

"No, she's not my girlfriend."

"You were kissing her in your hallway at barely seven in the morning. She must be your girlfriend."

"She's not my girlfriend."

"Then what is she if she's not your girlfriend?"

I turned quickly to face her. "She's *not* my girlfriend. She's married. She's my neighbor. Just my neighbor."

Ayinde sat on the bed, played with her nails. "Hmpf. Well isn't that just neighborly of you."

At that moment, I heard Lola's door close. Heard the jingling of her keys, then listened as she rushed by my door and to the steps. Moved quickly like she wouldn't want to be caught dead loitering near my residence.

"What's your point, Ayinde, what exactly is your point? What's it matter to you who I kiss, when, where, or how? What business is it of yours?"

"You told me you love *me*. *Me*. You said you love *me*. Why did you lie?"

"I didn't lie to you. What is wrong with you? Are you on some kinda drugs or something?"

"Are you sleeping with that bitch?"

"Why is this your business?" I screamed the words as my fist pounded hard against my hand. I was fed up. Tired. Confused. "What makes you think I have to explain anything to you? You're my friend, not my mother or my lover. I don't owe you any got-damned explanations about *my* life! Do you get that? Can you understand that?"

Her eyes challenged me but not with nearly the same aggression as she had Lola.

"You don't care what happens to me. I thought you did, but you're no different than the rest of them. I should just leave. Obviously you don't need me around."

"You're gonna leave?" I laughed. Hearty and mightily. I laughed. "You're gonna leave?"

I looked at her sitting there, on *my* bed, threatening me in *my* fluffy blue housecoat. I looked down at myself, at what I was wearing and for the first time realized I was dressed in the same gear from last night. I hadn't changed. Hadn't even found time to pull my worn clothes off.

I recalled the candles in the bathroom and those ridiculously priced bath salts I wanted so much when I was in Macy's a few months back. I hadn't used them but once. Each mineral represented dollars that hadn't come very easy to me. I considered them a treat which I used sparingly.

I laughed harder... laughed louder.

"You wanna leave? Leave. Bye. Peace out."

She was suddenly timid. All that aggression, gone.

"Wait, Z, listen -"

"Get out."

"Zella, hold on. Seriously, just listen to me."

I moved across the apartment to the closet. There was a bag with clean clothes. One's I'd borrowed from her sometime back but forgot to return. I flung it at her.

"Go! You wanna leave? Was that supposed to be some kind of threat? Get out of my house, now!"

"Z -"

"Get out of my house, you selfish, ungrateful, little bitch!"

My breathing was labored, my nostrils flared wide. I looked away when I saw the water glinting in her eyes. Wasn't going to feel sorry for her.

I went to my kitchen and grabbed a cold bottle of H_2O from the fridge. Turned my back to her and drank as she dressed, softly calling for my attention through her tears. I refused to acknowledge her. Wasn't going to cave to her. Not this time.

The floor creaked beneath her feet as she walked my way. I heard her stop. Could feel her contemplation. I continued to look away.

She called my name.

I didn't answer.

She called to me again. Begging. The sound of thick tears weighing down her words.

I wouldn't answer.

I continued standing with my back pressed against the counter and my foot tapping against the linoleum. I remained in that position until I heard the door open, then click shut.

I flicked a tear from beneath my eye and worked hard at shutting down all of my emotions. I locked the door behind her. Used my anger to bury my concern for her as I started my day.

I called Darwin after my shower that evening. I didn't know what to do about Ayinde. Didn't know how to help her, or if I even cared to try. But if I did, I'd need Darwin's assistance. Unfortunately, as usual since he'd begun seeing Miko, he was too busy to talk. Greeted me pleasant enough, though I was certain I detected some residual hostility left over from our last meeting.

I certainly couldn't blame him if there was. I'd been the jerk on this most recent occasion, not him.

Our conversation was brief, and I never got around to discussing Ayinde. He allowed the minimal required amount of time for cordial conversation before he clued me in about plans he and Miko had and worked his way off the phone.

I let him go without a fight. Hung up and just sat there thinking… telling myself to be happy for him.

Be happy for him.

Be happy for Darwin.

The sound of my neighbor's door closing jarred me. I guessed it was Lola returning home. It was still a little early for it to be Sean. I held my breath, hoping that she'd knock on my door but somehow knowing she wouldn't. Not today at least.

She'd been shamed. Being seen with me intimately had terribly embarrassed her. The idea sickened me, and I was hopeful that she'd be able to move past it. The irony. She wasn't afraid for me to love her just barely out of view of the nosey eyes of society, where she risked being caught, yet *this* bothered her.

I decided I wouldn't think about it. Deana, Jannessa's colleague, had come by earlier and picked up her finished piece. She loved it so much she commissioned me to do another painting for her of her children. We agreed to meet to discuss the details over lunch in a week. I'd earned a significant wage for this piece and greatly looked forward to doing more work for her. There was good news in my life. I should focus on good news.

But my mind drifted back to Ayinde and her behavior. Something was wrong with her.

"She's not my responsibility," I said aloud. "Not my responsibility."

I pulled a large sketchbook from beneath my bed and contemplated ideas. I grabbed a charcoal pencil from my nightstand and hovered above the clean sheet of paper, trying to decide where it should land. I attempted to use drawing as a means of mental escape except... it wasn't working.

My thoughts continued to shift aimlessly between Darwin and Miko and their future union... to Ayinde and whether or not putting her out had been such a good idea. And ultimately to Lola and the reaction she had to being seen with me.

I needed a hit.

I needed a joint.

No, I was beyond that. I was craving a blunt.

But courtesy of a nosey know-it-all landlady, I'd foolishly ended my habit cold turkey. One that made me happy. A habit that wasn't hurting anyone and helped me to relax.

I dropped my sketchbook and pencil to the floor and grabbed a piece of gum from my drawer. I unwrapped it and popped it in my mouth. I glared at the open drawer. Took another piece. Shoved it in with the first one and slammed the drawer closed.

I sighed and stood. Grabbed my keys and walked to the front door. I'd go downstairs. Maybe Ms. Thea had the answers to whatever the questions were. She seemed to be chock-full of suggestions, comments, thoughts on every subject, and she wasn't scared to share.

She was the stereotypical mother. Butting in, offering unsolicited advice, trying to resolve matters that weren't her business. Had to admit, I rather appreciated it. A consequence of not having a mother around I supposed. Maybe she could help me out of the funk I was in.

I stepped into the hall. Wasn't in any hurry. Took my time, hoping that Lola would hear me… would have the courage to come out and face me. I took my time, giving her the opportunity to be the brave person it seemed that she only pretended to be. I shook my head in disappointment as I made my way to the steps and jogged down.

I approached Ms. Thea's door but didn't knock. I simply stood there, poised, and contemplating. Ms. Thea indeed was the proverbial Mother Hen, but she was my landlady… my neighbor, not *my* mother. Maybe… maybe it was inappropriate for me to go running to her with my issues.

How well did I really know this Theadore Thompson? Who was to say whether she wouldn't share my information and concerns with some of the other tenants? I wasn't sure I wanted to chance that.

But maybe it was paranoia that silenced me, or guilt. Never once had she exposed any info to me about anyone other than herself and her suspicions about me.

I changed my mind, turned to walk away. I heard a lock click and a door open behind me.

"Zella?"

I hesitated, then put on a happy face. I turned her way. "Ms. Thea. Hi."

"What's going on, why didn't you knock?"

"I... well, I..."

"Come here, child. Come on in here."

I obeyed.

I stepped inside, waited as Ms. Thea closed and locked her door. She turned to face me with both hands on her hips.

"Now, you care to explain to me why you're out there hanging around my front door?"

"I wasn't exactly hanging out by your door."

"Sure ain't what it look like to me. What's wrong?"

I shrugged. "Nothing."

Ms. Thea rolled her eyes and walked toward her sofa. "Don't lie to me, little girl. If there's one thing I can't stand, that's being lied to. Have a seat."

I shuffled over to her floral patterned couch and plopped into the corner. Ms. Thea stood over me with her balled up fists pressed into her waistline.

"I got some tea brewing," she continued. "Would you like a cup?"

I sniffed. "Plum Monkey?"

"Peppermint"

I nodded. Ms. Thea retreated to the kitchen to prepare drinks.

"So? This is your cue, y'know. Catch up."

I sighed. I didn't know where to begin. Didn't know what to share... what to keep private.

"I'm worried about one of my best friends. Well, two... I'm worried about two – both... of my best friends. And me. I'm worried about me, too."

Ms. Thea took a deep breath and sat the teapot purposefully on the oven mitt.

"Now that's a whole lotta worrying. I'm already old, now you just tryna kill me. One concern at a time please." She went back to fixing up our drinks. "First things first, why are you concerned about your friends?"

"Well I got one who might be on some kind of drugs, that or she's turned into a serious alcoholic which honestly isn't too farfetched. The other, well the other is marrying some scratchy toe broad that he's completely settling for because frankly he thinks he's getting old."

"Wow."

"Wow. Wow what?"

Ms. Thea walked over and handed me a mug of tea and took a seat beside me, moving her ridiculously long hair out of the way before she sat on it.

"I think I know which friend bothers you more."

"That would be Ayinde, naturally."

"Aya-who? These names, Lawd. That the alchy or the fiancé? 'Cause see, here's what I believe. The alchy friend troubles you as it should. But with that, what can you do but wait? You can't fight her battles, can't *make* her get help. Lessen she admits she got a problem, ain't a damn thing you can do but wait.

"But see, that's not the friend that bothers you most 'cause it doesn't surprise you. You pretty much just said it. You expected it. It disappoints you but it doesn't surprise you. Now this other friend, the one that's *settling* as you call it, that's the one. The question is, is that really what he's doing? Or, could it be now that he's found someone that makes him happy, you're realizing just what he means to you?"

I shook my head no. "Of course not. He's my friend. He was there for me when my mom died, been there for Dad and me ever since. We're like family."

"Honey, like family ain't family."

"Okay, now that's creepy. Now you sound exactly like my father."

"Your father's a wise man. Can't wait to meet him."

I chuckled. "Yeah."

I sat my half empty mug on the coffee table and stood to leave.

"Hey, Ms. Thea, thanks for the tea and the ear, but I think I'm gonna head back home. I just need to sort things through in my mind."

"Well, hold on now, that covers your friends, but what about you?"

I half-smiled. "I'm not ready yet."

Ms. Thea nodded her understanding. "Well if you change your mind, you know where to find me. Just make sure you knock next time. I don't like people just hanging around my door."

"Yes, ma'am," I said as I walked out. I headed to the stairs to make my way back to the third floor.

"Oh, and Zella," Ms. Thea called to me. I paused and turned to face her. "Just... just do yourself a favor okay. Follow your instincts. If you do what you know is right, everything will work out fine."

I stood there at the bottom step feeling stunned. Wondering whether she knew something, or if her words of warning were merely a coincidence. I shook it off, didn't want my guilt to be apparent on my face or read in my eyes. I nodded my acknowledgment and returned to my floor. I paused outside of my apartment... waited for a moment, watching the Brown's door and thinking about the much deeper meaning behind Ms. Thea's words.

Follow your instincts, Zella.

Follow your instincts.

These had become the sounds of my existence.

Panting.

Deep breathing.

Cooing and sighing.

Moaning and crying.

Exhales.

Giggling.

Gasping.

Stifled screams and explicit lyrics.

I didn't shake her, couldn't seem to shake her. I suppose that made me soft, a punk, a wuss. In love? No, no. That would be going much too far. In lust. In need. Possibly even – infatuated.

When she was here, I wished she weren't. And when she was gone, I craved her nearness. But it wasn't *her* that I wanted any longer. It was her touch that I wanted. I wanted to close my eyes and be lost in an erotic world of fantasy and libidinous fascination.

An enchanted land of hedonism.

I desired a satisfaction that I knew she could never provide, yet allowed myself to give in and settle for her version of love making… settled for what was tangible. Same as I'd done for the last six years of my so-called life.

She was Olufemilola Sahlemariam-Brown, a beautiful accented queen from the Motherland and my neighbor's wife, and here she was – yet again – in my bed.

Purring obscenities and touching me with gentility. Sucking my neck strong. Leaving beauty marks as evidence of indiscretion. She loved my breasts because they were bigger than hers. Referred to them as her down pillows. Suckled them like a newborn baby having its first meal. Did so for as long as I could stand.

Catered to me, she did, as we recycled pornographic moves that we witnessed in her rented flicks. Verbalizing her physical pleasure in accent marks and foreign tongue as she performed "cunning linguistics" for my carnal pleasure… or maybe for her own.

A woman with more wealth than me, better educated, physically greater than me but loved to be submissive. Dominated by a female, her ultimate secret suppressed fantasy come true.

I liked to use force… she loved when I did.

Whenever my hand grasped her neck and applied just a little too much pressure as we kissed, she died in my arms and was resuscitated by my passion. When I tugged at her thick dreds and carefully sank my teeth into her neck as I stroked that most sensitive spot, she was in sinner's paradise.

She'd taken to a new manner of sex play recently as she was turned out by a secret stash of erotic novels, exotic flicks, and dirty girl-on-girl websites that she hoped her tech savvy husband wasn't inquisitive enough to find poorly hidden in her browser's history.

She'd stopped in one of those naughty adult shops with XXX emblazoned on the marquee late one evening after closing shop. Found a bullet, a battery, and a whip and wanted to be tied to my bedposts as she rode the vibrator while I left unexplained marks across her bare bottom.

She was stretched across my bed, vulnerable. Each wrist tied to a post by a pair of her pantyhose. The bullet, powered on and pressed firmly against her clitoris, causing her to jerk and move in Turrets-like spasms.

I straddled her waist backwards, smacking her buttocks firmly with the newly purchased whip. Restricted her movements as she struggled to withhold her urge for orgasm for as long as I commanded.

"Oh... oh... sh... shit... Zella. Harder. Hit... harder."

"Don't cum. I'm not ready for you to cum."

"Y-yes... yes... oh... f'k yes... love."

She wanted me to tell her what to do... what not to do. Wanted me to take charge. Each demand made her wetter... increased her heat and intensity.

Her head jerked from side-to-side, sending her locs flying in all directions, their wind against my damp back. I watched as her ass moved and rotated, the sight increasing the intensity of my own desire. My own clitoris, swollen and ready. My own explosion on the verge. I swallowed hard... remained in control.

She wouldn't ever completely satisfy me, not any longer. I lost a little bit of respect, lost a little bit of passion for her specifically when that shade of shame passed over and masked her face.

She'd certainly make me cum. When she was done, when her juices were all over my sheets, she'd do what she loved to do most... spread my thighs wide and shove her tongue deep inside. And I'd cum hard, but in the midst of it, I'd wish her husband were there with us. Or better yet... someone else. Someone very specific.

"Oh love! Oh... oh... may I... cum, please... may I?"

"No. Not yet," I replied, slapping her with my hand as opposed to the whip. "Hold it. I want you to hold it."

"Shit... shit..."

I smiled devilishly at my own naughtiness.

A sound separate from the one's Lola and I were making caught me off guard and stole my attention. I glanced up disinterested.

There was a shadow, an ill placed one. I slowed my movements... tried to make out what created it. It was sunset, the apartment was darkening. It could have been anything.

The shadow moved... eased closer, I was certain of it. I stopped with the whip, arm raised, poised to swing but frozen by my nerves and a mounting fear. Lola spoke to me, but I couldn't make out her words. Heard her voice but didn't know what she was saying.

The shadow was that of a figure, that much I could tell but of whom? It was closer now, moving faster across the apartment, barreling down on me.

I saw the bat before I could make out a face. A steel bat, gleaming in the fading sunlight. My heart caught in my throat, and I began to hyperventilate as it rushed toward the top of my head. And in the split second before it landed, Sean's face appeared from behind the cover of the shadow.

"Ah!" I awoke with a start. My heart beating so fast I thought it would explode from my chest. Beads of sweat were grouped along my forehead. I looked desperately around the room. It was darkening from the setting of the sun, but no one was there, no unexplained shadows.

The sound of light snoring caught my attention. I looked to my left and saw Lola sleeping peacefully beside me. I was in a fog... trying to think, adjust to the land of the living.

"Oh crap."

I looked around for my cell phone. Found Lola's on the floor lying beside the bed and cracked it open, the time illuminated by the backlight.

"Oh shit, Lola," I exclaimed. I began to shake her. "Lola, wake up. Lola... wake up."

"Hm?"

"No hm. Up, up! Sean's due home in like five minutes. He could be here any second now."

Lola struggled to sit upright. "What?"

I thrust her open phone before he half-open eyes. "Sean."

"Bloody hell," she cried out. She scrambled to climb across me. Instinctively, she ran to the bathroom.

"There's no time for that," I said bitterly.

She ran out and grabbed her clothes... struggled to step into them. "Got-dammit!"

I scooted over in the bed to the window, looking down into the courtyard. I saw him enter. Sat in my bed, nude, wrapped in a sheet with his wife's scent still fresh on every patch of flesh, yet not saying anything to her.

He was on his cell phone having a conversation. Twirling his keys around on his finger. He glanced up casually, almost thoughtlessly. Saw me watching him and stopped twirling. Shame consumed me. He paused... stared up at me while continuing to talk.

For a moment, I was sure Lola and I were caught, but then a smile emerged on his face as he stood there watching me watching him. I smiled in return. We kept our eyes locked on one another for an inappropriate length of time before he finally continued forth into the building and I finally opened my mouth to say, "He's coming."

She swore loudly. Blurted out that she'd see me later as she rushed out into the hall and quickly into the apartment next door. The balance of that sentence left on the winds.

Mere moments later, I heard rustling in the hallway. Sean had made his way to the third floor. His call had maybe ended or had been put on hold as I could hear no words coming from the other side of my door. Only footsteps and keys that paused right outside of my apartment.

My eyes closed. I pictured him standing there in my hall contemplating knocking on my door. A full six seconds passed before I heard him continue on to the residence beside me.

Follow your instincts, Zella. **Words of wisdom from a wise** woman, acknowledged by me... yet ignored nonetheless. And now I was in deeper than ever before.

I pulled my drawer open. Grabbed a Ziploc bag that held five gutted and reloaded cherry flavored Swisher Sweets. No more effin' gum. I wasn't any closer to being a better person today than when I first tried. As a matter of fact, I was further away. So why give a f'k?

I lit it and walked in my birthday suit to the bathroom and ran a shower. I was soothed. I inhaled deep, holding the sweet smoke in my mouth. Holding the cigar between my thumb and finger, I held it up so that I could admire it. It was as though an old long lost buddy had finally returned, and I couldn't imagine ever letting him get away again.

I'd tried to quit, sincerely tried. But one day not long ago I was served an all too important legal document at my place of business. One that could alter the dynamics of my entire life. One I didn't want to think about nor speak about. Before the end of my workday, I was on the phone with my connect ordering a much belated refill. It helped me cope with the pending legal battle I had on my hands.

Lola and I were tearing her marriage apart. Helped me to cope with that too. All they seemed to do these days was argue and fight. The tap-tapping against my wall was all but non-existent unless it was coming from my side. If she screwed him anymore at all, it was missionary and it was brief.

Sitting in my apartment painting golden haired children on a colorful backdrop, hearing the muffled sounds of a marriage in trouble competing with my music... smoking a blunt helped me to no longer care.

I stood in the bathroom before my mirror, listening to the sounds of the running water slapping against the cast iron, beating like a drum. Like a field of congas being played in the jungles of Angola. I faced the steamy mirror, used the broadside of my fist to stroke clear a path to my reflection. Saw my mother's face staring back.

I glanced down and looked away from her accusing eyes... or

were they mine? Saw the remixed cigar sending smoke signals from between my fingers. Turned my back to my consciousness and put the sticky green back to my lips and took another drag before smashing it against the sink and jumping into the shower.

"When's the last time you actually talked to her?" Darwin asked me.

This was somewhat of a treat these days, Darwin on my phone. Typically whenever I called him, he was either busy with work, future wife, or maybe just avoiding me. And to be perfectly honest, there'd be times when he called me that envy wouldn't allow me to be available to him, encouraging me to put up a front and pretend to be busier than I was.

"I haven't actually had a conversation with her in well over a week, a week and a half maybe. Last time was when she pissed me off, and I put her out my house."

"So because of that one incident you've decided she's a crackhead?"

"Dawg, you didn't see her."

"But still, Z, you think she's on crack? Seriously?"

"Well, I don't know. Something. What do I know about hardcore drugs?"

Darwin exhaled. "Sis... man, that's a wild accusation. Why don't you just tell me exactly everything that went down?"

"Because how we got there isn't relevant. She was already being weird when I found her passed out in front of my building, come on. Then she called me a couple days after I made her leave, but she was blubbering, and I couldn't understand what the crap she was talking about. Suddenly, she just hangs up. And today when I called, some guy answered the phone sounding shady and I could hear Day in the background. Then the phone disconnects. She didn't sound right, D... she just didn't sound right."

There was a contemplative pause from his end before he said anything further. He sighed. "I don't know, Z. Crack? I'm saying,

Day has historically been a drama queen, this isn't brand new. And we know she's a borderline alcoholic. Maybe... maybe she's graduated to lacing the weed. Combo could make her a little nuttier than normal. I'd be hesitant to label her a full-on crack-head."

My sigh was guttural. "I don't know. I hope you're right."

"I'll tell you what, I'll try calling her okay. Maybe she's just mad at you right now so she's trying to give you a hard time. She's notorious for stunts like that."

"Please do, and make sure to let me know as soon as you do and what you think or find out."

"My word."

My heart rate accelerated and its beat ascended up my throat. I'd told myself prior that the next time I had an opportunity for one-on-one time with Darwin, be it live or via technology, I would broach the subject of us and what I *may* have been feeling for him.

"Darwin, I need to talk to you... about something else. It's kinda important. It is... it is important."

"Shoot."

I swallowed air and exhaled heavily. I battled internally with myself, trying to find the right words and manner in which to express what I needed to say.

"D, I... Darwin, I just-"

A knock at the door halted my thoughts. I asked Darwin to hold as I stood from Dad's old recliner and went to see who it was. I peered through the small hole in the door and was surprised to see Sean standing there, hands in pocket, looking at his feet. I quickly stepped back, my heart racing even faster than before.

"What the hell is he doing here?" I asked aloud, fighting against a new mounting discomfort. I unlocked the door and eased it open. I stood in the doorway trying to steady my breathing, holding the phone with Darwin on one end, and looking up into the eyes of my secret lover's other half.

I opened my mouth to greet him but no words formed.

"Hey, Zell." He looked as uncomfortable as I was feeling. "I'm sorry to bother you. Did I catch you at a bad time?"

"Uh no. No," I lied. I looked at the receiver held in my grip. "This... I was just wrapping this up. Come in."

Sean stepped inside, swathed in nervous energy. He stood to the side as I locked up behind him. I reluctantly told Darwin that I would speak to him about my matter later, then hung up the phone, cursing myself and cursing Sean for my missed opportunity.

With my eyes closed and back to my guest, I telepathically stated a quick prayer before turning to face him.

Sean stood near the counter. Stood there turning his hands over and over each other. He glanced up and spotted the new painting I was doing of Deana's children. He did a double take before facing it completely.

He pointed at it. "This your work?"

I nodded. "Yeah, it's a piece I'm working on."

"Wow. Lo told me you were talented."

I cringed at the sound of Lola's name being spoken from his lips. "Yeah, something I inherited from my mother. I'm sorry, can I help you with something, Sean?"

He moved his focus from the canvas... returned it to me.

"Um, I don't know how to say what I need to say. I probably shouldn't even be here about this when my wife isn't around. She's off to some book conference. Be gone overnight, but she should be back home tomorrow evening." He hesitated. "This is inappropriate. I'm sorry, I should really leave."

My tension eased, being replaced by curiosity. "No, you don't have to leave. Please, have a seat."

Sean slowly lowered himself on the edge of the recliner. His elbows on his knees, hands clasped near his mouth.

"How've you been?" he asked. "I haven't seen you in... ages. Funny how we live right next to people for so long yet rarely ever see them."

"Yeah, that is funny. I'm um, pretty okay. Thanks for asking."

He nodded. "That's good. I saw you sitting in that window. I thought you looked so beautiful. Looked like an angel, up high, wrapped in that sheet. Made me get to thinking about how much I miss you... how much I miss you being with us."

I blushed. Looked away. Wondered where this talk was heading and was as frightened as I was intrigued to find out.

He continued, "Zell, I know you hear us fighting over there, you must. If we bother you, I'm sorry, but I don't know what's happened to us... what's happening to my wife. She won't talk about it, refuses to. It's like... everything was all good between us and then when you showed up, I mean damn. It was killing me that you wouldn't let me... do everything I wanted, and I had mad respect for you for that 'cause I think I got why.

"But even though you wouldn't... y'know... it was no less an off the chain experience. No doubt. I was so shook when you left but at the same time, I appreciated why you did it. Lo had a hard time with it for a minute after and things between us... well it wasn't as it had been, I'll say that much.

"But then we got it back. I don't know what happened, I guess she started missing me as much as I was missing her. She was like this untamed animal. I'd come home from work and she'd be waiting in nothing but a – I'm sorry. Too much information. I'm getting carried away."

Sean stopped speaking for a moment, dropped his head... looked as though he might cry. I certainly wanted to cry, but I battled fiercely against the guilty impulse. I was made sick to my stomach. Literally ill.

I had contributed to this man's pain. I'd been raised better, was raised to be better. My heart bled for him, but I couldn't ease his pain particularly since he was unaware that I was partly to blame for it. I thought to offer him one of my dolled up Swisher's but he didn't smoke nor would that have resolved anything.

"I'm sorry." The words tumbled softly from my lips.

He shook his head. "You're cool, Zell. It isn't your fault. I don't know, maybe I'm just not man enough for her... or maybe I'm working too many hours. But I just love Lo, man, and I wanna give her the best of everything. She was used to really nice things, and she sacrificed that to be with me.

"I'm rambling but my point for being here is this. I just thought... maybe, y'know... if you'd consider being with us again, maybe it would make her happy. I know she wanted to believe you were there as a gift to me, but you fulfilled fantasies she hadn't realized existed within her. She loved having you there – I mean, loved it. And I admit, I'd get a little jealous of the attention that she was giving you, but she was just so happy. I just want my wife to be happy again."

I coughed, discreetly swiped a tear from beneath my eye. I was a co-conspirator in the slow dissolution of his marriage, and here he was coming to me to fix it. Little did he know. There would be no joining them as a couple, not ever again because that wasn't what his wife wanted. Lola had her way, had exactly what she wanted.

Anger swelled within me. She had *me* exactly where she wanted.

"I can't do that," I said, my eyes unable to connect with his but rather locking on the wall behind him. "It's not anything I should have ever done to begin with. For as great as it may have been for all of us, it's a dangerous game the three of us played, and there were bound to be some casualties.

"I can't be involved, Sean. I'm sorry, but I can't, not any longer. You two, you love each other. You'll work it out. She'll come around, I promise you. She'll come around."

Sean's palms ran down his face, smearing wetness along the way. They smacked hard against his thighs before he stood. He nodded repeatedly as he headed to the door.

Slowly, I rose and walked across the apartment to join him. We stood there, face to face, eyes connected. I felt self-conscious, but I was afraid looking away would cry guilt. I hoped he wouldn't interpret my shame.

His strong hand grazed my cheek. He licked his lips as he

watched me. "Like an angel." He whispered the words before leaning over and pressing his soft lips to mine.

Memories of our times together flooded my mind and the space between my thighs clenched tight. I withheld the desire to press my body to his and offer more passion than the borderline innocence we were dabbling in presently.

He stepped back and excused himself from my home. My fingers involuntarily moved to my lips as I listened to him reenter the residence he shared with Lola.

I ditched my crib shortly after Sean returned to his. I'd messed up. I'd so messed up. I was pissed at myself, angry at Lola. She had a good man – a great man at home. Women would give their right leg, left kidney, and eye-teeth for such a man. A man that loved with passion and vigor and whose greatest desire in life was her happiness. So much so that he would sacrifice his own.

I'd known a few of these women myself, and here she was, the recipient of such inviolable love, yet she was willing to piss it all away over an effin' fling.

Follow your instincts, Zella. That was what Ms. Thea had advised, just follow your got-damned instincts. My instincts, as usual, were dead on yet overruled by my heart which lacked common sense. My heart led most of my actions which screwed me almost every time.

It wasn't too late to make a change… was it? No. No, it was never too late to make things right.

I ran downstairs. Lola was away from the city. I could call her, but I wasn't exactly prepared to deal with her just yet. I needed to escape the emotional baggage left behind in my apartment by Sean Brown. I needed someone to talk to. I wouldn't be able to be direct with Ms. Thea, but possibly I'd be able to clear off some of what was on my chest with roundabout disclosure.

I knocked on her door and waited. I listened. All was quiet. I heard no stirring inside. I waited another moment and knocked again. It had been about a week since I'd last seen her on the premises and I was beginning to be a bit concerned.

I thought to knock again but instead walked to her nearest neighbor's door and tapped lightly. A female voice called out. I heard steps become louder as they came nearer, then locks turning. The door opened, and the face of an older Hispanic woman poked out.

"Yes?" she said in accented English.

"Hi. I apologize, my name is Zella Dora. I live in the apartment above Ms. The – Ms. Thompson's. I was wondering if you'd seen her around lately. I um… I need something fixed in my apartment, but I haven't been able to catch up with her."

The suspicion that was evident in her face when the door was opened diminished, and suddenly she was eager to share. The door opened wider, and the smell of tamales wafted to my nostrils, causing my mouth to salivate and instantly I wanted to befriend her.

"No, I have not seen Señora Thompson as a matter of fact. I think something might have been wrong. I see Señora's daughter come last week and take her away, but she no come back. She was crying and crying."

"Her daughter was crying?"

"No, Señora."

"I hope everything is okay. Thanks for your help. If she comes back, please tell her Zella Dora needs her."

"Si, si."

My eyes passed over Ms. Thea's door as I walked to the stairwell. I was now officially concerned. I hoped she was okay, but all I could do was wait. But I wouldn't wait here, not with my demons haunting me from next door.

I had time to remember Zella Dora during my tour of Chicago's North Side to South Side neighborhoods courtesy of the CTA's train and bus system. I had time to remember education. I'd been notified that everything was set in place for me, all I'd needed to do was show up to my first class.

That had been all I wanted, all I'd needed not too long ago. A life of my own, to do something for me, for Zella. To do something that would better me. But class wouldn't begin soon enough. I'd used my summer break to dig my hole and bury myself deeper than when the season began.

I sat in my window seat on the back of the bus, my head resting against the plate glass window. My eyes looking out into the darkening sky. A soft rain began to fall and crash against the pavement.

I rocked in time with the bus's movements while glancing across at the other passengers, painting mental pictures of my visions of their destinations. The woman reading the novel in the seat before me. The young man that sat across from her, nodding his head in time to the beat of the music pouring from his headphones. The teenage girls that sat nearby, giggling to each other as they checked him out.

Margot was expecting me. She was home entertaining Kat and a nameless girlfriend while Shane ran the streets. I planned to hide there, far from Lola's husband... further from the memory of Lola until she returned and I could settle things with her live and direct.

I pulled the cord just in time to not miss my stop. I jumped from my seat and rushed to the back doors. I pushed them open and stepped off and into the warm wetness. My cell phone vibrated in my back pocket.

I snatched it out as I quickly ducked through the rain and beneath an awning. I looked at the caller ID. Ayinde.

"Hello? Hello?" I answered frantically.

"Zella..."

"Day, where are you at? Is everything okay? Why are you just now calling me back? I've been worried. Did Darwin call you?"

I had a mouthful of questions. I hadn't realized just how many I'd shot at her before I recognized that she'd not had any opportunity to respond. I hushed myself and waited for her to pick a question and answer.

"Zella..." It sounded as though she was crying.

"Day, what's wrong?" I made my move through the elements, two doors down, and ran up the steps to the door of Margot's building. I rapidly pushed the buzzer. "Talk to me, please."

"I love you, Zella."

"I love you, too, Kid." The buzz sounded that informed me that I was being invited inside. I used my bodyweight to push the heavy door open.

"I... I *love* you."

I paused mid-stride as I ran up the steps that led to Margot's place. "I... what are you... Day, you're my sister and I love you... like a sister."

"But, Zella..."

Margot's voice rang out from above. "Girl, what took you so long? We were starting to worry. Come on up here!"

"I'm coming," I replied. "Day, listen to me-"

"Who was that?" Ayinde asked forcefully.

"Day, you do understand you're like a baby sister to me. Right? You get that, don't you?"

She ignored my statements. "It's that bitch, isn't it? That foreign bitch. That's why you don't love me 'cause you love that black bitch!"

"Seriously, Day? Seriously? You're gonna take it there?"

"F'k that ugly black bitch! F'k her!"

She hung up the phone.

Tears streamed from my eyes, tears I tried to quickly rid of before Margot saw them and asked too many questions. Something was wrong with Ayinde. I didn't care what Darwin thought – something was wrong. I felt it in my spirit.

I couldn't wait to see Lola.

But not for the same reasons that I'd previously been anxious for her company. This arrangement was ending, and I couldn't wait to get it over with. The things in my life had become too intense... too chaotic, and it was time for some belated spring cleaning.

She was back from her short trip, but I had yet to see her. Had to wait until she could break free... wait until Sean wasn't around. She would come to me at the first available opportunity, I knew that. It would seem our relationship, like her marriage, was on her terms.

It would seem that way, but it would no longer be that way. I was going to take my life back. Not only from Lola Brown but from everyone else that I felt was holding my progress hostage.

I'd sang that song and done that dance not too long ago. I'd thought I was ready. Visions. Disturbing visions had me prepared to break-free and recapture the essence of who I was. I'd begun the journey but instead of staying diligently on the path, I allowed others to come along and muscle me off the road.

Daddy.

Aunt Leigh.

Ayinde.

Lola.

Sean.

Darwin... even Darwin.

I sat in the center of my bed staring out into the gray skies above, listening to the resplendent voice of Ms. Lena Horne mesh with the soothing acoustic of rain treading pavement.

It'd been coming down for the better part of two days. I related to that weather. The pouring drops of water mirrored the mood I was in. I connected with the rain, my heart mimicked that emotion.

But, I couldn't bring myself to cry anymore. Couldn't stand to shed through my own ducts. The fears of moving on, being alone, fears of failure... could no longer release that through a salty river flow. So I let the sky do it for me. Let the clouds part and pour out all my baggage, hesitation, and hurt.

And when the downpour ceased, I'd be cleansed as well. I'd be ready. I'd move forward, I promised myself. But for the time being... in that moment, I'd sit in my bed... Swisher between my lips... eyes cast upon the open sky and be freed.

The air was fresh and thickened by humidity. Summer rains had a tendency to have such an effect on the environment. It felt wonderful outdoors. It was evening. The sun was sinking down into its resting place and still, I'd yet to see Lola. Sean had apparently taken ill and skipped work for the day ruining her plans.

She'd called me from the store, babbling on about what a bore the conference had been and how she'd wished I were there. Told me about a new idea she had for us to try out, something she'd read about in a book she picked up at the event. Talked about how sexy it would be and how excited she was to be able to try something like it with someone like me.

It was to be a surprise however. No hints. Just be ready to be spoiled physically and allow my being to feel things it'd likely never experienced before. I was silent for the most part, let her speak. Waited for her to recognize the potential problem we had. She didn't. At least not until I inquired why she would not want to try this new technique on her husband. That was when she became curious as to what was wrong with me... wanted to understand why I'd ask such a question.

I didn't respond.

She moved on. Said she really wished to see me tonight but that she doubted she would. However, provided Sean returned to work the next day, she'd be the one crying 24-hour bug. A customer entered her shop, and she had to go. Patrice was on her lunch break.

I took a mid summer's eve stroll a couple blocks over to the Heartland Café. Thought it would be nice to sit outdoors and sip a glass of Shiraz and enjoy the clean night air.

I sat in my favorite Tranny's section, waiting for him to deliver my food. I pulled my cell from my bag and dialed Dad's number. He answered on the third ring.

"Hi Daddy. What'cha doin'?"

"Oh nothing. Watching the news and letting this big meal my sister delivered to me digest."

"Oh. Auntie was there today?"

"Yeah, she passed through to bring me a plate of leftovers from dinner she cooked yesterday. She couldn't stay though. Said she was having dinner with my sister Sybil."

My eyes rolled back, and I answered absentmindedly, "Dinner, huh."

Penelope placed a plate of roasted free range chicken and wild rice before me. "Do you need anything else, honey?" he mouthed.

I shook my head and returned my focus to my father.

He said, "I haven't seen you in a couple days, Sweet Pea. Is everything alright?"

I sighed. "Yeah Dad, everything is fine. I've just been, y'know, trying to sort things out in my mind, that's all. I'll come by in the morning."

"Okay Sweet Pea, we'd love that. I'll see you tomorrow."

"See you tomorrow, Dad."

I put the phone down and began to pick at my meal. I thought about Lola, intentionally rejecting the urge to dwell on what I wanted to believe this dinner date between Aunt Leigh and Aunt Sybil was about.

I hated to hold onto my emotions. When my mind was made up about something, I liked to take action right away. How would I broach the subject the next day with Lola showing up at my door in trench coat and red lace thong, a tantric sex manual in one hand and a tub of French vanilla Cool Whip in the other?

I picked up my phone, typed a two word text.

Heartland. Now.

I sat the phone down and waited. Moments later, I heard that telling beep. I opened the message.

15 min. ;)

Enough time to finish my meal and order another drink.

I spotted Lola rounding the corner. She appeared taller than usual. Her dreds were pulled back from her face, and silver hoop earrings dangled from her ears. She was dressed in a crisp white tank top that she'd likely snagged from her hubby's underwear drawer and a pair of dark denim cropped pants. A broad smile stretched across her face.

I smiled in return but not at her, rather at the irony. This was the very place I'd met Lola for the first time a couple months back. Inside Heartland's General Store. This would be the same place I ended it. Admittedly, there was some sort of twisted romanticism to such a thing.

She took long strides past me, outside of the short black gate and made her way to the opening. She walked through the tables of patrons to where I sat in front of my nearly empty plate. Greeted me like a casual friend rather than the clandestine lover I'd been.

But, we were in a public place amidst the greedy gazes of strangers who'd see her, a woman, being intimate with another woman.

Penelope approached our table quickly after Lola had taken a seat. "Hi, ma'am, I am your waitress Penny. Would you like me to get you a menu?"

"No thank you, I just ate actually. However you can bring me a glass of whatever she's having. What are you drinking?"

"Shiraz," I said as I returned the glass to my lips.

"Marvelous."

"I'll be right back with your drink order. Zella, let me know if you need anything else."

"Thanks, I'm good."

Lola's eyes watched Penelope as he walked away. She sat silent, shyly smiling until she received her drink and Penelope disappeared back inside of the establishment.

"Oh, thank God you sent for me. I missed you so much. Was utterly going insane over there thinking you were home and I couldn't be with you." Her voice was low when she spoke, deliberate. Conscious to not be overheard by the diners relatively close by.

"Lola, I asked you to meet me here because we need to talk. Well... I need to tell you something."

"Don't sound so serious, Zella, you're making me nervous."

I glanced up, watched the train pulling into the station overhead. Trying to think of what to say... how to say it.

Lola's voice interrupted my thought. "Okay, I'm getting the impression this is as serious as it sounds."

I knew the best way to handle a difficult situation was to be honest, forthcoming. "Lola, this is over."

"What? What do you-" she abruptly paused for a moment as the el train pulled away. Waited until she could be heard at her selected tone without needing to raise her voice. She glanced both ways... made sure no one was paying attention. "Why is it over all of a sudden? Have I done something to offend you? I mean... you're joking, right? This is some sort of game? See how serious Lola is about me?"

"You didn't do anything to me, not directly. It's what we're doing. It's the wrong we're doing. I've got enough crap without that bad karma coming to haunt me."

"Bad karma? What in bloody hell are you talking about?"

"You know what I'm talking about. Tell me something, when's the last time you f'kd your husband?"

"Shh. Would you please keep your voice down?"

I ignored her request. "And I don't mean laid on your back and let him climb up and do his thing... bust a nut to get off while you got off on plotting your next little sexscapade with me. I mean, *f'ked* your husband. When is the last time you screwed his brains out 'cause if I'm not mistaken, I haven't heard that kinda head banging against my wall since you started making my bed bang against yours."

Lola looked offended. "What business is it of yours what goes on in *my* bed... between me and *my* husband?"

"It is my business. You made it my business when you involved me."

"Do I not please you? I do things to you that I have *never* done with anyone else."

"That's the problem," I yelled. A couple near us glanced over uncomfortably. I turned and glared at them until their attention returned to the meal that had been delivered to their table.

"Will you please keep your damned voice down?" She sat fuming. Likely thinking up a response... something to bring me back to her side. "Listen, Zella, I appreciate your moral compass and all, but what goes on between Sean and I really is of no consequence to you.

This... what's between you and I is all that should matter."

"What do you want from me, L? You wanna be with me? What if that's what I want. Would you leave him to be with me exclusively if that's what I wanted from you?"

"Well, no, I-"

"So you're just using me. I'm your little plaything. Using me to live out all your "f'kn fantasies". So what happens when you're bored with *me*, L? What happens to *me* when you decide you want something different?"

"No. No, I'm not using you."

"Then what game *are* you playing?"

I watched her coolly, sipping my drink as Lola struggled to find some logic that would satiate me and keep her plans for tomorrow intact, but my attention strayed from her. Laughter and loud conversation that came from a group who'd exited the train station distracted me. A small group consisting of two guys, two girls – and Ayinde, were headed our way.

Ayinde spotted Lola at the very moment I noticed her. I stood quickly, making my way through the café and to the other side of the short barrier, running... cutting Day off as she attempted to lunge at the neighbor she'd caught me kissing not so long ago.

"This why you ain't got time for me no more? 'Cause of that black, ugly bitch?" Day screamed. "That bitch don't love you like me. She ain't nothing. She ain't better than me. She ain't nothing!"

"Bitch? I know this crazy bitch just did not call *me* a bitch," Lola shouted.

"Are you crazy?" I asked, addressing Ayinde. I held her tight, my fingers digging into her forearms. Her wild eyes were locked on Lola. I couldn't understand her, couldn't understand why she was behaving this way. I heard laughter coming from her associates. They found her behavior to be humorous. I found it disturbing. I jerked her body, forced her to move her eyes to mine. "What is your problem? Have you lost your damned mind? What are you doing over here anyway?"

"Nobody loves me, nobody," she said the words to herself as she looked through me as though I weren't there.

"You know that's not true. Look at me. You know I love you, why are you acting this way?"

"You don't love me. You love them bitches, not me. I'll kill them bitches! Then you'll have to love me, you won't have a choice."

"Are you threatening me? Zella, please handle her before I jump over this gate and knock this psychotic bitch on her arse," Lola exclaimed.

"Lola, shut up… please. I got this." My eyes went to Lola. She stood, arms crossed, fuming. The restaurant had silenced… all eyes were directed at us, directed at me waiting to see how I would remedy this situation without management needing to get the law involved. Heat permeated my face. I was seething. "Look at me, Day. Look at me. What are you on? What did you take?"

Her eyes were glazed over and her appearance, unkempt. Not quite as bad as the night I found her sleeping outside of the building but not far off. She was slimmer, she'd clearly lost weight. She reeked of alcohol though I doubted that was all that was in her system.

She squirmed out of my grasp. "Let me go. Get your f'kn hands off of me."

"What are you on, Day, that got you trippin' like this? 'Cause I swear 'fore every White person up in this piece, if I find out it ain't some drug that got you acting a damned fool and this is just you being you… I will beat the dog mess out of you, and you will wish you had been on drugs."

The people with her began "oohing" in unison, laughing harder than before. She rocked back and forth, her red eyes spilling fluid. She looked away.

"I have to go now," she said.

"With these people? Hell no. They're probably the ones that got you sprung out in the first place."

"F'k you, bitch, ain't nobody get her sprung on nothing," one of the women spat at me.

I stepped aside to get a better view of the big mouthed broad. "Is that right? Don't think I will hesitate to stomp a hole in your ass out here, too."

"Try it, hoe."

Ayinde swung around to face her. "Shut up, Nay before I smack the hell out of you. You don't talk to her like that, you don't know her."

Surprisingly the woman backed down without a fight.

I rolled my eyes away and refocused my attention on Ayinde. "Come on, Day, let me take you home. We'll figure it out in the morning. We'll get you some help, I promise."

She looked at me. "No, Zella. I gotta go."

I wiped away the tears that were spilling from her eyes. "Please Kid, I am begging you. Just… just at least tell me what you're on."

"I'm not on anything, you don't know what you're talking about. I gotta go."

Ayinde turned to walk away. I grabbed her but whatever she was using gave her a strength that I could not match. She pulled away forcefully, causing me to stumble backwards. She rushed away, her crew following close behind.

I tried to quickly think of what to do. I wanted to call out, maybe go after her. But I wouldn't catch her and she wouldn't come back. They'd already started to run. Laughing loudly, they turned a corner before I could get back to my table and gather my things.

I watched the distance that she'd disappeared into, my face drenched in sadness. I returned to my seat, ignoring the glares of annoyance and the stares of pity that were bestowed upon me. I reached into my back pocket and pulled some money forth. I felt a hand touch me gently on the back.

"You going to be okay?" Penelope asked.

"Yes… no. Here." I placed the bills in his hand, more than enough to cover mine and Lola's tab.

"Z, I know it isn't my business but… it may be crystal. What she's on. I've seen it too many times, and one of the girls she was with, I recognized her and she's definitely a user."

I faced Penelope. "What do I do?"

He caressed my back and shook his head sadly. "Honey, until she wants help, I don't know how much you can do."

I stood there absentmindedly as Penelope returned to his job.

"Zella. Zella, please... have a seat," Lola insisted.

"No, no I've gotta go. I gotta do... something."

"Love, you heard the waiter. Look, I'm sorry about what just happened, really I am. But clearly something is wrong with her. If your friend is on crystal meth, there isn't anything you can do until she's ready for some help. Now please. Let's just finish hashing things out-"

"Are you for real?"

"She threatened to kill me, hell yes I'm for real."

"Are you for real?"

"Zella, listen-"

"Seriously, are you for real? There's nothing to hash out. Nothing. We're done. Get it? Done."

"Zella, please." Lola eyed the other patrons nervously.

"Zella, please what? Zella, please keep your voice down? Zella, please don't do this? I just hear that one of my very best friends may be on meth, and you're concerned about what a bunch of folks who don't know you from Adam will think of you? Or are you just worried about what's to become of your *bloody* mistress? You're that horny, screw your husband. You need a bitch in your bed that bad, pick one." I waved my arms around the restaurant referring to the numerous sexually confused staff and customers. "You've come to the right place."

If Lola weren't so brown she'd have been beet red. I grabbed my phone and bag and turned away, leaving her behind to be accompanied by her shame without my interference.

She grabbed my wrist as I walked by. "Zella, please wait."

I eased away, did so like she was the contaminated one. Same as she'd done me in the past. "Don't call me. Don't show up around my job. Don't knock on my door again unless you need to borrow a cup of sugar or you accidentally got my mail."

I walked away. Crossed the street and headed in the direction of my father's house. I could stand to pay him an early visit.

That night I couldn't sleep. Nightmares plagued my mind. I'd left my old bed at Daddy's and walked home at about the hour that sunrise was stretching its rays and preparing to shine. I left a note behind so Dad wouldn't be concerned, promising to come by the house later. Laundering was necessary and he was running low on his favorite foods.

I took a warm, refreshing shower as soon as I arrived home. Let the water soak into my hair shafts, weighing it down... plastering it against my bare back. Hoped maybe the experience would quiet the thoughts and fears that had been tormenting me throughout the night. Erased visions of Ayinde being found dead by me in a grimy alley. Each time I closed my eyes, I'd see her opened ones staring at me from her lifeless body.

I exited the shower. Wrapped a thick bath towel around my frame, another around my hair and laid in bed trying hard to concentrate on slumber but could not keep my eyes closed.

I gave up. Rose from bed. Slipped on a pair of pink boy shorts and pulled a gray t-shirt over my head. It was one of Darwin's shirts. Since I was notorious for washing clothing that was left behind at my home, unfortunately it no longer carried his scent.

I looped an elastic band around my hair and tucked it all beneath a bandana. If I couldn't sleep, I would work. I slid in a bootleg CD loaded with illegally obtained tracks. Heavy bass rang through my small speakers as I approached my canvas and began my preparations.

I heard the neighbor's door close hard. I glanced at the time,

Sean was on his way to work. My body tensed and I wondered if Lola would heed my warning or if she would take her chances knocking on my door.

I didn't anticipate any attempt at contact from her, not this soon if at all. I'd been rather harsh with her the night before. Hadn't meant to be, but I was angry and hurt and just tired of everything around me. I was tired of my needs and my emotions being placed last and her selfish attitude had pushed me over the edge.

I realized she was put off by Ayinde. After all, my friend had aimed to attack her. Had I not spotted her when I had... moved as quickly as I did and intercepted her, she most certainly would have had a handful of dreadlocks in her grasp and maybe a hard fist against Lola's nose. I wondered how she would have explained that to her husband.

I would work until the local library was opened. I wanted to call Darwin and tell him about the suspicion that Ayinde was using crystal meth, but I hadn't figured out how I'd explain where the assumption was born out of. I had to get my story together first. Additionally, it was still speculative, no different than my suggestion that she may have been using crack.

I'd go to the library and rent a computer for forty-five minutes and look up the symptoms of methamphetamine use, determine if it were a reasonable assumption. Until then, I'd suppress such concerns and focus all of my restless energy on the golden haired angels on my canvas.

I'd gotten lost in my work, lost track of time. The click and rumble of next door being closed shook me from my trance. I was made aware of Lola's presence. My body tensed and I battled between conflicting emotions.

I tensed from that small part of me that wanted her to tap on my door, tensed from that much greater part that prayed she walked on by. My senses became incredibly keen. I could hear every sound in the hall outside of my residence, above the sound of my music. Every breath, every step, every heartbeat, every jingle of her keys.

I was frozen in position. Yellow paint from the brush that was being held upright began a laggard journey down my hand. I could hear her approach my door and my breath caught in my throat. She was out there... standing there, contemplating landing her fist against my entryway. I wondered if she was poised for the act.

My waist was turned... my eyes fixed on the door, waiting. I stood there watching for so long that I began to wonder if maybe she'd already passed by. Possibly she'd crept on quietly to prevent me from hearing her.

The keys jingled again as she proceeded forward. Her sounds faded into the background ambience that classic Hip Hop created in my apartment. I exhaled. My ego nudging me. Though I was grateful not to have to deal with her again, the fact that she'd considered defying my request said that control was back in my possession where it belonged.

I smiled and sat the brush down. I looked at my arm, I'd barely noticed that the paint had drained that far. I held it up high so it wouldn't drip onto my floor while I walked into the kitchen to grab and wet a paper towel.

I cleaned my hand and my arm then grabbed a bottle of water from the fridge, cracked it open, and hydrated my body. I stood in the kitchenette guzzling the fluid, purifying my kidneys.

A hard knock startled me, causing me to jump, nearly spilling my water onto the counter top. I got a hold of myself and slammed the bottle down. She'd come back. I couldn't believe she had come back.

Anger filled me up where water had left off. I had been very clear with Lola, quite specific. She hadn't even given me a day... respected my wishes for one damned day. This was done, we were done and there wasn't anything more I could have said to illustrate that point.

She knocked again. I shook my head and chewed the inside of my mouth. I took a deep breath. I had to deal with her, once and for all, and this time she'd swear the prior evening had been me playing nice.

I charged to the door. Unlocked and snatched it open, fixing my mouth to deliver the verbal assault she had coming.

"Did I not tell you last night not... to..."

"I guess you were expecting someone else. Wouldn't happen to be someone we both know, now would it?"

I swallowed hard and stepped back as he entered. I struggled to breathe normal, be normal but somehow I knew this wasn't a normal visit.

"Umm... wh – um..."

"At a loss for words? Would you like me to help you out?"

I'd been caught off guard. It didn't matter, it was truly over. No need to be shook up. I closed the door behind him. Steadied myself, walked to my recliner and had a seat.

I exhaled heavily. "How can help you... this time?"

"One question, Zell. Are you f'king my wife?"

Sean stood over me, fuming... awaiting an answer to his question. His eyes said he already knew the truth but how and how much was unclear. Either way, I wouldn't confess until I was sure.

"Who told you that?"

"You tell me. But first, let me tell you a little story. So last night, I'm laid up... getting over being sick when my wife suddenly has to make a run. While she's out, there's this frantic knock on my door. When I answer, I see some... some dopefiend looking broad out there. She starts telling me that she's your friend or girlfriend or whatever she is to you, and that she's pissed 'cause she already done caught you with *my* wife and that I should be pissed, too.

"I don't know this female or how the hell she even got in the building. For all I know she's some crazy stalker wanting you or Lo except she claims that you two are on a got-damned date right around the corner at Heartland. While I'm laying up in that piece sick from friggin' food poisoning, homegirl telling me my wife is out kicking it with you."

"Sean, listen-" I tried to intervene.

"Naw, naw wait. 'Cause see the story just gets better. So I'm still like, hell naw. My wife ain't a cheat, and Zella wouldn't do that. She don't get down like that, that's not her character. I closed the door, tried to dismiss it except my wife still wasn't home. I come knock on your door, and you ain't home. I let it go.

"An hour later Lo comes home and looks like she been crying. Won't talk about it, just hits the shower and goes to sleep. Something told me, just check the phone and lo and behold, what do I see? A text from you telling her to come to the Heartland and a reply sent fifteen minutes before she walked out the damned door with a got-damned smiling face and I ask you... *are you f'kn my wife?*'

I looked Sean in the eyes. This wasn't the time to be clever and play coy nor was it the time to show cowardice. It was over... we were over. But thanks to Ayinde, it wasn't over, not yet. She had played me. That bitch ratted me out.

I gulped heavily. "Yes." My answer was so low I doubted he'd heard it but he had.

"Why, Zell? Why would play me like that? What was this all some kinda set up?"

"No, it wasn't."

"You fronting like you cared about our marriage just so you could have my wife all to yourself. I mean... what the... damn, man. Got a brother over here crying his eyes out on some pussy shit, thinking I can confide in you... thinking you got my back and the whole time you looking at me like I'm a bitch and playing me?"

I jumped from the chair, rushed up to him. Grabbed his arms... tried to focus his attention. "We weren't... I wasn't playing you. Listen to me, I'm sorry. I am so sorry. She was upset last night because I ended it 'cause it wasn't right, I know it wasn't right."

"So is this the part where I'm supposed to say thank you?" Sean snatched out of my grip. Stepped back, one hand on his waist, the other over his mouth. His eyes were reddening. He was trying to not allow himself to cry in front of me again. "This shit been going on ever since you claimed you ain't wanna come between us?"

"No, no, it hasn't."

"Don't lie to me."

"I am not lying to you. It started when she-" I paused. Was disgusted with myself.

He laughed spitefully. "Don't hold back now. You can't hurt me no more than you already have."

"It started... when she... untamed animal..." My voice trailed off as I reminded him of his own example of his wife's behavior and for a moment I was fearful of the wild look in his eyes. I thought he might try to hit me. I braced myself as my eyes quickly scanned for potential weapons. He began to pace and instantly I feared for the safety of my artwork more than myself.

He came to an abrupt halt. "Whose idea?"

"Sean, why do you-"

"Whose idea?"

"Hers," I whispered.

"How did it happen?"

"She... she came to my job. Unannounced."

"So you could screw her or lick her or, or whatever the hell y'all lesbians do to one another."

I was highly offended. "I'm not a damn lesbian."

"You ain't a lesbian, but you wouldn't let me hit 'cause you rather be with my wife?"

"Your wife wanted to be with me," I yelled. My temperature was rising. He was making me out to be the sole bad guy, but I hadn't done this alone, and I was not taking all the weight. I refused. "Your wife came at me, many times before it even got to this point. I told her no, *every* time. Told her to go home to you, but she kept coming back... kept showing up at my door with her damn coochie on a platter 'til I ended it. Wouldn't see her anymore.

"But she saw me in the hallway one day, saw me outside the building another time and she wouldn't take no. Then she came to my job. I didn't invite her there, she just showed up."

"And you f'ked her."

"Yes."

"So why didn't you tell her no, then?"

He stumped me with that question. I'd approached him, been in his face by this point. Anger had added courage but this question knocked my bravado down a peg. I stepped back.

"I don't know why. Timing. I was going through so much... I was vulnerable."

"Did it ever occur to you to tell me she was doing this?"

"Hell no, that wasn't my place."

"Nor was it your place to f'k her, but you did it anyway!" The bass in his voice rumbled throughout my apartment.

I turned away from him, began to walk, but he grabbed my wrist... pulled me back. Made me face him. I didn't want to, I was too ashamed to, but he gave me no choice. He stared down into my moist eyes and my heart raced.

"I'm sorry," I mumbled for lack of anything better.

"Is it that good? How good could one woman's pussy be that it would make another leave her marriage bed cold to get at it? Too bad I never got to find out."

A chill ran over me. He pulled me closer until I was pressed against him, pressed against the growing stiffness behind his jeans. I cursed the sensation of arousal that had taken over me.

"Sean..." I placed my palm against his firm chest and made a weak effort to push him back but he didn't budge.

"You and Lo... hope you had a good laugh at my expense."

He released my wrist. That hand touching my thigh, caressing softly up beneath my tee-shirt. My love throbbed and moistened. My mouth became dry. I gasped loudly when his hand found my breast and his thumb grazed my hard nipple.

"We didn't-" I swallowed then continued, "we didn't play you."

"Really? 'Cause I think you did." Sean's mouth found mine. Wasn't innocent and sweet like before. It was passionate. Domineering.

I tried to will myself to fight him... to pull away. I repeated the command over and over and yet – I continued to give him my tongue while one of his hands squeezed my full breast and the other pushed down my boy shorts.

I gathered all my strength and pulled back from his kiss but not his embrace. "Sean. Sean, stop. I know... you're pissed, but this won't make it right." I recognized that there was absolutely no power in my voice when I uttered my so-called resistance.

He kept his eyes locked on mine as he continued to push my underwear down until they landed around my ankles. He smiled at me, a sinister one that aroused me much more than it frightened me. His eyes never left mine as he unbuckled, unzipped, and pulled his jeans and boxers from over his buttocks.

Sean took my limp arms and threw them around his neck, then grabbed my ass firmly, lifting me high and sliding me onto his stiffness.

"Sean we... can't... oh shh..."

My eyelids dropped low and I'd become his. Whatever lingering resistance that may have existed was lost. I cared not about what Lola would think. As a matter of fact, I didn't think about Lola. After all, wasn't this her handiwork to begin with? Hadn't I been her gift to him from the start? Had she not already given us permission to come together like this?

I was lost in revelry. A feeling I hadn't experienced in what seemed to be an eternity... the feel of a man's thickness inside of me had me reasoning the unreasonable. So lost that I hadn't noticed we'd moved until my back was pressed firm against the wall.

Pressed against "our" wall.

The wall that we'd all now officially shared.

"I'm sorry... I'm sorry..."

Sean was leaned into me, panting those sorrowful words into my ear and somehow I knew in that moment that apology was not meant for me. I couldn't speak nor settle on an emotion.

He'd pulled out of me, caught his children in his hand but he'd yet to back away. I sensed a sort of fear. Felt as though he were afraid to see me, afraid to look me in the eyes for then he'd have to be honest an admit his *I'm sorry* held no greater weight than mine had.

I moved my arms down from around his neck, placed my hands palms up between us and tried pushing him away. I squirmed and adjusted until both feet were touching the floor. We stood mere centimeters apart. His head was bowed in sorrow. I felt nothing. I only wanted him to leave.

"Sean, you need to go," I spoke softly.

He raised his head though only slightly. Finally connected his eyes to mine and I could see the pain etched beneath the tears on his face. I almost felt for him... almost allowed myself to feel for me, but instead I shut down.

"You really need to go," I said with greater force.

His eyes dropped and he stepped back from me. I moved from him... moved with attitude. Walked to my bathroom as he pulled his boxers and jeans back up to his waist. I stood inside of there with my back against the door, willing him to leave in peace.

I waited. Listened to the sound of his footsteps as they approached my hiding place. He stopped right outside. We waited, together in silence. A moment later his footsteps moved away from me. I listened as the door closed behind him, leaving me alone with only the sound of an R&B crooner looking for love over a hook.

"What time are you off?" I asked Margot frantically.

"I traded shifts so for not another five hours. Why, what's going on?"

I grunted. I couldn't bear to bring myself to say it aloud, not over the phone. But I had to tell someone... had to get it off my chest and she was the only someone I could tell for she was the only person who knew what I'd been doing with my free time over the past couple months.

I let out an exasperated sigh. "Never mind."

"No, something's up. Look, why don't you just come to my job. I'll take my lunch when you get here."

"Are you sure? I don't wanna intrude on you at work."

"Believe me, it's not a problem. I get an hour. We can talk over sandwiches."

"I'm on my way."

I quickly hung up and ran inside the train station I'd been loitering outside of for the past ten minutes, while contemplating a destination. My first choice... my reason for being at the Morse stop was to hop a train over to Uptown, find Ayinde and kick her ass.

I changed my mind however. Not that I didn't think she deserved it but I was being led by pure anger and as upset and as betrayed as I felt inside, I had to remind myself of the possibility of her being on hard drugs.

I passed through the turnstile and walked up the stairs to the platform. The air was unseasonably cool and even chillier at that altitude. Although I thought the breeze refreshing, I could have used a light jacket. I'd warm as soon as I began my trek from the subway and to the building Margot worked in.

I'd showered again before I left my place. Scrubbed myself clean. I still smelled Sean's scent on my skin. On a conscious level I knew it was all psychological yet it seemed so real and I couldn't determine whether it disgusted me or turned me on.

There was no denying the physical attraction Sean and I had for one another. I felt it the very first time we met. There'd be moments during my ménage days that my insistence upon remaining on the right side of wrong was less about preservation of their union but rather of ours as a group. I feared that if I ever submitted my being fully to Lola's husband she would no longer be necessary. I was afraid she'd become a third wheel in her own creation.

I didn't want Lola's husband, that much I knew. However, once he was inside of me everything was irrelevant. I was Lauryn to his D'Angelo, nothing even mattered. While we were connected, we were one. We were African drumbeats, classical music, guitar riffs, and sax tenors.

With my eyes shut tight he could be anyone I wanted him to be. I could feel his movements and see the face that I wished to see. I could and I did pretend and became flooded with a deep sensation sorta like love and like being in love.

As he stroked me deeper, squeezed my breasts, sunk his teeth into my flesh, I knew it was true. I did want him. I *was* in love. But... when he was done, when he separated from me and I again opened my eyes... it wasn't him. Not the him I'd imagined penetrating me deep... filling me with his power. Leaving passion marks to prove we'd existed, if only for a little while.

No, when I opened my eyes it was not *him* but rather Sean Brown,

Lola's husband and I realized what I'd done… what I'd been doing this entire time. I didn't know why or how but I hoped Margot could help me make it right.

I waited restlessly in the lobby for Margot to retrieve me. Ten minutes later, and I was still flipping through an eight month old Cosmo pretending to be interested. I looked up at every sound I heard, watching others go on with their happy little guilt free lives and I was stuck sitting there on that hard bench while security ogled me.

"Hey Z, you been waiting long?"

I turned around to see Margot standing behind me. I was certain the heat radiating from me would make that big ass plastic novelty ring she wore melt right off her finger.

"Where have you been? I've been down here for like fifteen minutes."

"I'm sorry hon, you got here faster than I anticipated. I was in the parking lot arguing with Shane. He seriously pisses me off. Now guess what he did," she paused when she caught the no-nonsense look I was giving her. "I'm sorry sweetie, this is serious. Come on."

I followed Margot. Said nothing as she handled getting me a visitor's pass. Was silent as she led me to her floor to clock out for lunch. Was quiet as a church mouse as she maneuvered us through the building and found us a seat far away from everyone else in the cafeteria.

I sat with pursed lips, chewing the inside of my mouth… waiting for my cue to speak.

"Okay Z, exactly what happened?"

"I just had sex with my neighbor's husband."

"You did what?"

There was no admiration this time. No smiles, no laughter. No envy in her green eyes. Confusion, maybe even disappointment. I couldn't bring myself to reiterate. My eyes went up as tears filled the brims and I bit down hard on my lip.

Margot jumped from her seat across from me and slid into a chair by my side. "Oh honey, don't cry. You just made a mistake, right. We all make mistakes."

"How could I have done this?" I whispered more to myself than to my friend.

"Look, you messed up. You made a mistake. I seriously doubt he'll tell his wife he cheated. You don't say anything and she'll never know."

I faced Margot. "I don't give a damn about her. She's over, I ended it with her last night. I'm talking about... I'm talking about Darwin."

Margot looked dazed. "Darwin? What about Darwin, what does he have to do with this?"

"I'm in love with Darwin."

"Well, Zella, that's great except-"

"Except he's getting married."

Margot nodded. "Well, yea but she's no one and that isn't what I was about to say. I was going to say that's great, except you have to tell him."

"And just how do you propose I do that? I told you he confessed to be in love with me and I rejected him. Vehemently rejected him. Now because I'm screwing up my freaking life, I'm supposed to what... screw up his?"

She grabbed my arm and pulled me to my feet. "Come on, let's go."

"What? Where are we going?"

"I got some 'dro in the car and I do my best scheming when I'm not sober. Your piss still clean?"

"Hell no," I answered as we hurried out to do illegal things on company property.

The ringing of the telephone vibrated inside my mind. In moments like this I wished at the very least there were an old school answering machine available to deliver the message that no one was home or just did not want to be bothered.

The ringing was persistent and for a moment I thought maybe it was all in my dreams. Maybe I was dreaming of school bells during recess or maybe someone had pulled the fire alarm. I eased my head up from the pillow, tried to focus on something vaguely familiar… figure out where I was.

My head was spinning. Felt like I'd just stumbled off a merry-go-round and landed in a ditch. The persistent ringing was not helping. I smeared my wet mouth with the back of my hand and used my now contaminated fist to scrape crusted sleep from my eyes.

"Would someone answer the damned phone?" I screeched in an awful morning voice. My blurred vision began to focus. The phone kept ringing. I blinked a few times.

"Oh crap," I said once I realized that where I was, was home. I peeled myself from the bed carefully and dragged my body across the floor and to the recliner. My landline's ringing became louder as I neared it. Felt as though my brain would drop out of my head.

I fumbled to grip the receiver. "Hello?"

"Sweet Pea? Sweet Pea?"

I tried to respond but a sound like that which comes from a frog's throat was what was released. I coughed a few times and tried again. "Dad, is everything alright?"

"I was worried. You didn't come by yesterday. Your mother told me not to worry, you're an adult. Something maybe came up. I'm sorry to bother you, I got concerned. Didn't want anything to… well I'd hoped nothing had happened."

"Dad," I tried clearing my throat again before attempting to speak. "Dad, I'm sorry. You're right, I'd said I'd come back yesterday. You, um, guys need food. I'm sorry, it was irresponsible of me."

"No, no don't worry 'bout us. Just needed to know that… well, we can't go having nothing happen to you now can we."

My hearing was sensitive. It sounded as though my father was screaming through the phone but I knew he wasn't speaking any louder than normal. I tried hard to recall what I'd done the night before that would explain this feeling but drew a blank.

"Hey, Dad, my bad. I'll be by there later this afternoon."

"Well, don't you have to work?"

I swore under my breath. "Yea, uhm... crap. I'll call in."

"No, no. Go to work, Zella Dora. As long as you're okay. Just come by later. I'm going to go fix me and your mother some breakfast. We'll see you later, okay?"

I nodded... then wished to God I hadn't. "Yes, Dad."

I placed the receiver on the base. Sat with my head leaned back, trying to ignore the pain. No such luck. I carefully moved from the chair and with eyelids nearly closed, started toward the bathroom.

"Ow," I exclaimed as I stepped onto a hard, cold object that I immediately recognized as a bottle. I reached down and picked it up and read the label. Alizé. Cheap and potent, just what I'd needed.

I sat the bottle on the countertop and continued to the bathroom, the memories of the day and night before flooding my mind. I recalled everything as I drained my bladder. Sex with Sean. Blazing one in Margot's car in the back of the lot at her job. The numerous threatening messages I'd left on Ayinde's phone that she'd refused to answer.

And then there was the little matter of that bottle I'd purchased on the way home to help take my mind off the two people I'd cheated with who lived together in the apartment right next door.

I flushed. Opened my medicine cabinet and pulled forth a bottle of Ibuprofen. Popped two 500 mg's. Held onto the edge of the sink to steady myself... keep the spinning room from causing me to topple over.

A distant knock caught my attention. I paused... wondered if it was real or just the sound of my thoughts banging around inside my head. I stood and waited until I heard the knock again. I left the bathroom, approached the door cautiously... suspiciously. Mindful. The last time I swung my door open thoughtlessly I wound up pinned to my wall having my brains banged out by my former lover's spouse.

I held my breath as I peeped through the hole. My forehead scrunched. It was a woman who I didn't recognize, though she looked vaguely familiar. She looked about nervously, uncomfortable... as though she might leave or maybe if she weren't sure if she had the right place.

I undid the locks and swung the door open. I must have looked dreadful, for a look of pure awe covered her face. Her mouth gaped open but no words formed. I was becoming more agitated by the second and all I wanted to do was guide this intruder away from my door so I could call in sick (despite assuring Daddy I would honor my commitment) and curl up in the fetal position and fall asleep.

I moved a hand to my hip and shifted my weight to one foot, the one that still wore a sock.

"May I help you?" I asked quite unkind.

"I... I'm sorry. Are you Zella Robeson?"

"Could be. What do you want?"

"I'm sorry, have I come at a bad time? I could-"

"Tell me who you are and I'll let you know."

"I'm-" she stopped and glanced at her hand. Looked as though she was weighing whether she should share it with me or not. "I'm Maria Thompson-"

"Ms. Thea's daughter," I finished as I shook the hand extended toward me. "Oh my. I'm sorry, I didn't mean to be... I'm sorry. Would you like to come in? I just... well I had a rough night and I kinda need to lie down."

She smirked uncomfortably but accepted my invite. I offered her a seat on the recliner as she walked over to my painting.

"This your work?" she asked. I nodded and blushed. "It's

gorgeous. You're very talented."

"Thanks."

I lay down on my bed, covering my legs with my sheet. Turned to my side. Watched Ms. Thea's daughter admire my piece. She was certainly her mother's daughter. Tall and shapely with full breasts though not to the degree as her mother. She was darker than Ms. Thea, maybe a quarter of a shade tanner than my own skin tone. Her long brown hair was perfectly styled appearing as though she'd just left the stylist's chair and landed on my doorstep.

Her thin heels clicked across my hardwood as she walked to the recliner. She sat, delicately crossing her legs and carefully placing her obviously expensive purse on her lap.

"Zella, I'm very sorry to intrude. My mother talks about you all the time, she speaks very highly of you. I just thought maybe... well, I just hoped you would look out for her, that's all. Just stop by and check on her... make sure she's okay."

I sat upright in the bed, immediately regretting having moved so fast. My hand shot to my forehead and I held it in an attempt to calm the spinning.

I struggled against the pain and disorientation. "Is Ms. Thea alright?"

"Well, not completely. Since my daughter died four years ago, mom hasn't been-"

"Whoa, whoa, whoa, wait, wait." I gritted my teeth and carefully turned to place my feet on the floor. "What was that? Your daughter... isn't Delaney your daughter?"

"Are *you* alright? You look sick. Can I do something... get you something?"

I waved her off. "I'll be fine. I deserve this, believe me. Much worse actually. It's what I get for using cheap liquor to mask my problems."

"Maybe this isn't a good time."

"Please... Maria. What is wrong with Ms. Thea? Who is

Delaney?"

Maria took a deep breath. "Yes, Delaney is my daughter but she's dead. She died four year ago. Brain tumor."

"Oh my God." Slowly, I fell back onto my mattress. My palm remained firmly against my forehead. Could it be possible? Was my landlady afflicted with the same mental issue as my father? How could this be possible?

Maria continued to explain, "Mother has had an extremely difficult time accepting that Delaney is gone. She was only ten when she lost her battle. Mom still behaves as though she's here. She knows she's gone but she adamantly refuses to admit it. She's never acknowledged it... didn't even come inside the funeral. Refused to leave the limo.

"She has her good and bad days but at times reality hits her and... well, let's just say it's overwhelming when it does. I wanted her to stay at my house again for good but she refuses. She made me bring her home this morning."

A tear ran from my eye... dampened my hair. I couldn't comprehend how it was possible for me to have two people with a similar problem in my life. I was certainly the right person for the job of looking out for Ms. Thea, I just didn't know if I could handle it emotionally.

Maria stood. "I'm sorry, I hope I haven't overstepped. She just thinks so highly of you. You remind her of Delaney and she told me that your mom died, so I know you kind of understand."

I willed myself from the bed. "Don't worry Maria, I'll look after your mom. It isn't a problem, none at all. And believe me, I understand way more than you think."

A beautiful smile that was a perfect replication of her mother's spread across her face. "Oh thank you, Zella, thank you. Words can't express how grateful I am. It's just, I live so far and with my crazy work schedule I... well, thank you."

I nodded. Maria turned toward the door, I followed. She reached into her purse and handed me an elegantly designed card that described her as attorney-at-law.

"Call me if anything happens. If there's anything I can do for you, let me know. Oh, and please don't tell Mom about our talk. Don't even tell her I was here. She hates for people to pry in her business, especially me."

I half-smiled. "I won't. Promise."

I opened the door. Maria walked out, her eyes glued to mine. Gratitude on her face. She mouthed another thank you, then grabbed me... pulled me into an awkward embrace before turning and rushing toward the stairwell and out of the building.

Five hours of uninterrupted sleep after Ms. Thea's daughter left, had me feeling well enough to shower and dress for the remainder of the day. It was early evening by the time I emerged from my cave, holding my breath for fear that I'd bump into Lola coming home from work. I didn't know what I'd say or how I'd react and didn't want to find out.

I stood outside of Ms. Thea's door waiting for her to open up. I now knew her secret. Couldn't believe she was dealing with the same issue as my father. Maria had made me promise not to say anything and I would honor that.

The door swung open and there she stood trying not to look as happy to see me as I knew she was.

"Well look at what the cat done dragged in," she said, her lips pursed... turned up into a smirk.

"Hey, I came by to see you but you weren't home."

She held me tightly against her healthy bosom. "Yea well, Ria can't accept me living my own life. Always buttin' in... trying to pressure me to move in that big ol' house of hers. It's too much space, who needs all that space? If I can get lost trying to go to the toilet, I don't need it. I'm too doggone old to be trying to hold onto my pee while I'm out looking for a bathroom."

Ms. Thea walked to the kitchen. "I got some new tea. Ria's best friend Soledad bought it for me. It's a peach oolong. Child black as the night is dark but as beautiful as she wanna be. Think she from Brazil or something or other."

I chuckled. I'd been missing those good laughs and random topics of conversation that Ms. Thea provided. "No thanks, next time. I have to go look in on my Dad. He's expecting me. I just wanted to take my chances and see if you were back."

She walked toward me again. Stopped at the sofa and placed a fist against her waist. "Well isn't that sweet of you. Well, gone and tend to your daddy. Make sure you come back and try some of this tea when you get some free time. It's delicious."

"I will. I promise."

I turned to head back out the door but Ms. Thea gently grabbed my wrist. "Zella, hold on. I want you to take care of yourself, okay."

I was puzzled. "I'm taking care of myself Ms. Thea. What do you mean?"

"Marriage. It's a special, divine union between woman and man. Wouldn't you agree?"

"Yes, I would."

"I sure wish me and my husband could have lasted. But, things don't always work out the way we want. This is the world we live in. We can't let the outside influence what we do inside."

I was shook up. I wanted to ask what the hell she was talking about but I kept quiet.

"I'm not married, Ms. Thea. I don't understand."

She smiled at me. Looked happy. "I know. But if you were, shole would be a shame if someone interfered, now wouldn't it? Be careful of karma, Zella Dora. Be careful."

I was winded. Taken aback by her words... by her use of both of my names. Only those closest to me called me by both names. I was frightened momentarily but for the life of me, I didn't know why. She couldn't have known about my involvement with the Brown's. Couldn't possibly have known.

She spoke again, shaking me from my trance. "Zella, what's

wrong with you? Go on chile, don't want to keep your daddy waiting."

"No, I don't," I answered absentmindedly. I was frozen in position, staring unblinking at Ms. Thea.

"What's wrong with you gal? Look like you done seen a ghost. Now gone. Get."

I nodded and turned, headed down the hall as she closed up behind me.

Darwin was on his way and I looked like rolled over crap. Dad and "mom" were in bed. He'd retired early. I'd spent the better part of my evening being domestic. I'd done the shopping and prepared my Dad the rare treat of a Zella Dora home cooked meal of sautéed tilapia and broccoli steamed in the microwave. Two slices of his favorite Wonder Bread on the side to top it off.

Once he was fed, I'd cleaned and started the laundry. By the time Darwin phoned saying he needed to speak to me face-to-face, I was a disaster.

I ran upstairs, rushed into the bathroom and looked at my reflection in the mirror. I grunted and moved to the tub, turned the faucet on. I dropped harder than intended to my knees. I ignored the pain as I stuck my head beneath the force of the running water.

Once I was thoroughly saturated, I turned the knobs, then squeezed my hair firmly. I felt around for a bath towel, catching the excess water before it dripped to the floor. I dried as much as possible then scrambled to pull a ponytail together. I used the towel to dry my face.

The doorbell chimed, steeling my attention away. I stomped and swore quietly. He'd gotten there quickly which indicated he was already in the area. I faced the mirror again. I looked a little better – but not much. I took a deep breath, then lowered the light switch.

I paused at the top of the stairs and tried to pull myself together. I closed my eyes and counted backwards from five. This was it, my opportunity to follow Margot's advice.

I jogged down the steps and to the door. Tiny butterflies formed in the pit of my stomach as I unlocked it. I suddenly felt terribly shy. I smiled broad as I pulled the door open and allowed Darwin inside.

Darwin did not smile in return. He entered my parent's home. Walked past me without a word and didn't stop until he was in the living room.

"Where's Pops?" he asked.

Nervousness swept over me. "In bed."

"Good. I need to talk to you. Can we step out back? I don't wanna risk waking him."

"Sure," I mumbled. I steadied my nerves and led him to the back door. I opened it and stood off to the side to let him pass me, then pulled the door to. "So what's the matter?"

"Did you sleep with Ayinde?"

"What? No. What? Why would you ask me something like that?"

"Who is Lola?"

I tensed. "She's my neighbor. Why?"

Darwin nodded. "The African."

"Yes, the African. What is this about?" My frazzled nerves were calming but exasperation was taking over.

"That's what I'd like you to tell me. I just spoke to Day. She says a couple weeks ago when you told me she was at your house, you two had sex."

"What?" I exclaimed.

"Says you bathed her, slept with her, told her you loved her, then dissed her for the African."

"Are you kidding me? I already told you she's on drugs."

"She sounded normal to me."

"Well she's not normal."

Darwin had been right to move us outdoors. My emotions were

taking me by storm which meant my vocals were rising along with my temp.

"What the hell is going on? So you telling me she just pulled these accusations out of thin air?"

"Well no, not exactly."

"Then what exactly?"

"I bathed her because she was filthy. I slept in bed with her no different than I have in the past. I told her I love her because I do."

Darwin paced across the back porch, digesting my version of what happened. I began to calm. This had proven to be easy. Crisis averted. Ayinde was another issue altogether. She'd have to face me eventually.

Darwin stopped moving. "And what about Lola?"

My legs weakened and my knees buckled. I didn't want to talk about her, especially didn't want him to know what I'd done with her. At the same time, I didn't want to lie to him. Where had lying gotten me? When you lied, you had to continue lying. Unless you were a pro, eventually you'd either get caught – or caught up.

I gripped the banister to steady myself. I opened my mouth to speak but no words came out.

"Zella Dora. What did you do?"

I eased to the ground and sat with my back against the wood slats. I wouldn't look at him, just picked nothing from beneath my fingernails.

"I slept with her," I mumbled. I glanced at him, then quickly looked away. "I had an… an affair with her."

I listened to the sound of Darwin taking a seat on the porch swing. "Zella, she's a married woman and you knew she was a married woman."

"Well, so did she."

"So that makes it right?"

"No, it didn't. But it's over. It's over."

We sat in silence. A lukewarm breeze passed by, ruffling my hair. I sat, looking intently at my nails and feeling bad all over again.

"Dar…" I closed my eyes, prayed to God for an ounce of courage to say what I needed to. "Darwin, I have to tell you something."

I looked over at him. He sat, leaned forward with his palms placed together. He didn't say anything but his eyes darted to me, signaling the go ahead.

"I really don't know how to say this so… I'm just gonna say it. I… I love you. I'm in love with you."

"Aww naw… don't."

"I know I made a big deal about your being like a brother but I guess I just hadn't realized it yet. I mean, it's nothing I'd thought about."

Darwin stood, shaking his head from side to side. "Don't do this. Don't you dare do this to me, Zella Dora."

"I'm sorry, D. Look, why don't you sit back down and let's just talk about it."

"Don't do this to me." Bass filled his voice. Anguish filled his eyes. "I moved on. I did what you basically asked me to do. I'm getting married. I'm getting married, Zella."

"In all due fairness that's almost a year away."

"That makes me no less committed. I love Miko. I love Tarik. You made it very clear – very clear - you didn't love me like that… didn't want me like that."

"I was wrong."

Darwin stood there pumping a fist back and forth in front of his face. Mind reeling but at a loss for words.

"You can't do this to me. I won't let you do this to me." Darwin moved for the door.

I jumped to my feet. Ran past him… blocked his exit. I looked at him beneath my wet lashes.

"Darwin just wait a minute. Listen."

"Move, Zella."

"No, just wait. I made a mistake alright. Everybody makes mistakes, right? I'm just saying, I didn't know. And I... and I think I deserve another chance."

"That's what you think?"

"Yes. Yes, that's what I think," I affirmed.

"Zella, you had many chances. Before I told you I was engaged, you had your chance. There are no more chances. I love you. I do. You're my sister and you'll always hold a special place in my heart, but my mind is made up, okay. Now I have to go. My family is waiting on me."

"Your family."

"My family."

I reluctantly stepped aside and allowed him past. I didn't follow. I'd taken Margot's advice and put my cards on the table. Unfortunately for me, Darwin folded, cashed in his chips, and left the game and it would seem that there wasn't a damned thing I could do about it.

23 Chapitre Vingt Trois

I just wanted to be still.

I didn't want to do anything, say anything… didn't want to be around anyone. I only wanted silence. Only wanted to still the voices and visions in my head. I was frustrated, out of balance. Art couldn't save me. Carlos Santana couldn't help me.

I'd gone to work. I had to. It was a distraction from my issues and was the healthiest thing I could have done for myself at the time.

I resided beside a married couple, both of whom I'd had a secret and adulterous affair with.

I hadn't seen them but the one time I met Lola at the Heartland General Store back before I officially knew of the couple's existence. Only bumped into her on the premises twice since then but given the nature of the crime I committed caused a need for me to be even more cognizant of their presence so that I could avoid bumping into them. That in itself added degrees of stress.

Bringing my fatigue full circle was the added strain to Darwin's and my friendship. I was angry with myself for having gone there, annoyed with Margot for even suggesting it. Now I played the part of the ass, and I didn't know how we'd recover. After all, I had suggested the man dump the one woman who really saw the value in him as a man to be with me, a woman who'd wholeheartedly rejected him and then added insult to injury by having flirted in his face only a short time after he'd confessed his feelings to me.

I was exhausted. My body was heavy, felt as though I were literally dragging myself across the courtyard. It hadn't been a difficult day by any means, but I was so mentally drained that I could have easily spent six hours doing manual labor and wouldn't have felt any worse off. I'd been worrying about my pending court date, had been worried about Ayinde and then angry with myself for caring so much. The girl had exposed my secret and attempted to slander my reputation. She hadn't returned any of my phone calls, and I'd given up trying.

I inhaled deeply as I entered the building and headed toward the steps, my bed heavy on my mind. I'd left work an hour early. Timed it so that I wouldn't risk accidentally bumping into Lola. I'd made it this far and felt secure about not hearing her footsteps rushing by for another hour.

I hadn't spoken to her since Heartland. She had ultimately respected my request, but I wondered if that would last. It'd only been a couple days. I really didn't want to face her, not with guilt and hypocrisy cloaking me. I knew not how I'd respond to her and really hoped I wouldn't find out.

I took weighted steps down the short corridor and to my apartment. I reached in and dug my keys from the bottom of my bag. The sound of Lola and Sean's lock clicking caught me off guard.

My eyes widened and I moved faster. I cursed myself for not having been prepared. Their door opened as my key fit into the slot. I glanced over in time to catch a blur of Lola emerging at full speed.

"You bitch." She spat the insult at me, sounding alarms in my head. Lola charged toward me, stopping inches away. She stood glaring with maroon cheeks, flared nostrils and hate-filled eyes that were bloodshot red from crying. "You bloody, f'king whore! How dare you... how dare you!"

I eased back, opening the space between us a bit more. Steadied my stance. I didn't say anything, just watched her eyes, gauged her fury. Made note of the position of her hands.

"How could you do it?" she questioned.

I wouldn't give her anything. I needed to be sure what we were talking about and what Lola thought she knew. Ayinde must have gotten to her, but she was out there when I'd confronted her. There was no way she would take her word. And what could she have told her?

"Don't play dumb with me. You f'ked my husband, you dirty bitch. How could you?"

My brow furrowed. How could she know that? How could Ayinde have known? "And where'd you hear something like that?"

"My husband told me so don't you dare try to deny it."

My heart paused. Sean told? I felt the blood rushing to my cheeks. Why would he tell? How could he have done that? Men weren't supposed to do that. Men cheated all the time; they weren't supposed to tell their wives about it. That was the rule, was it not?

Lola's fury cut into my thoughts. "Deny it, bitch."

I woke from my daze. Snapped into reality. I was seeing Lola as she stood before me with a tight fist on her hip, seething. And I realized I was on the verge of a war. She had every right to be bitter just as I had the authority to stand up for myself, right or wrong.

My bag slid off my arm and landed to the floor. In case she swung I had to be ready. "I'm not going to be too many more of your bitches."

"Oh, what? You don't like it? Am I pissing you off? Do you think I really give a shit about what you want? You slept with my husband, how could you?"

"It was an accident."

"An accident? An accident? You can do better than that, can't you? You don't accidentally screw somebody's husband. It just doesn't work like that." Lola stepped back, grabbed her loose dreads and tugged at them near the root. "How could you be so... so... hurtful? All of that bullshit about karma and the wrong we're doing, all so you could plant your raggedy pussy on my husband's dick."

I laughed. "So now it's raggedy. Seriously? Please, L. Tell me something, are you more pissed because I did your husband or because I stopped doing you?"

"You... bitch. I was doing you a favor. When was the last time you had a sex life as great as the one I'd given you? If you were getting some, you wouldn't have been getting your rocks off listening to me and my husband through the wall."

"So that's what you were doing? Thanks, L, I'm so glad you cleared that up. 'Cause see, I was clearly confused. I foolishly thought your ass was the one desperate for change. I mean, you were the one begging for it, right? Am I wrong? You wanted it, you wanted me, and the only reason you're pissed is because your husband beat you at your own game." I stepped closer to Lola. "Or, maybe you're just mad 'cause I did your job better than you."

I held my ground... challenging her with my eyes. Daring her to take it there. She'd conveniently forgotten that she'd been the desperate one, implied I needed her. Wanted to believe my world was empty without her all because she was angry and jealous.

Lola accepted the challenge. Stepped forward, bridging the gap and with a raised arm and an open palm she swung. Swung mightily. Had I not sensed it coming the sting may have scalded my face and the force would have knocked me to the floor. But I saw it coming, dodged out of the way.

The slap was a predictable reaction. Mine was not. I moved in fast, my hand grasping her throat much like it had once upon a short time ago when were intimately involved.

Fear replaced the hostility in her eyes as I used all of my might to force her backward, against my door.

"Don't ever put your hands on me, are we clear? Ever. My bad about what happened between me and your husband. For what it's worth, I'm sorry but let's not forget... you started this. You. And karma has come back and bit you in the ass no different than it's done me."

I loosened my grasp. I let her go and stepped away. Her hand went up to massage her neck. She looked at me as though she wanted to kill me or at least severely hurt me, but my reaction had her shook. She'd made the mistake of underestimating me and now had to ask herself what I may be capable of.

She wasn't prepared, but I knew it wasn't over. Her voice came out in a hoarse whisper. "How could you do this to me?"

"Don't be so naïve. This was your idea, all of it. What happened with me and Sean was a mistake. It shouldn't have happened. I can't explain why or how it happened that way, but it did...it happened and I - we, can't change it. What you did though... choosing me over him, you pushed him to me. May as well have hand delivered him. So you can be pissed off and self-righteous all you want, but when you climb down off your pedigreed high horse, let's not forget... you asked for this."

Lola broke down. Tears poured from her eyes, and I was again caught off guard. I didn't think she'd cry, had thought she'd go the route of verbally assaulting me again... maybe even threatening me but not this.

"I was wrong... I know now. I jeopardized my marriage by not being there for my husband. I did that. You're right I did. But that didn't give you the right. You had no right to sleep with him. You shouldn't have done that."

"I apologize."

"Damn your apology, Zella, you had no right! You had no right!"

"Really? Well, I beg to differ. When you invited me into your relationship, you gave me the right."

Lola approached me. "Go to hell." She charged away from me, rushed inside her doorway. "Stay away from me and stay away from my husband because I swear to God if you so much as daydream about sleeping with him again I will blow your f'king brains out."

Her door slammed hard against the frame, sending vibrations throughout the hallway. I stood, fuming, trying to pull myself together with Lola's very believable threat ringing in my mind. A click caught my attention. I looked up and found myself eye to eye with the only other person who lived on our floor. The old lady who hardly ever left her home and never saw visitors. I felt the shade of shame pouring over my face, and I quickly turned and entered my apartment.

I blamed Ayinde. It didn't matter that I'd done this to myself. I had agreed to the threesome. I'd given in to Lola's requests. It didn't matter that I hadn't told Sean no when he confronted me. All that made sense to me was that had Ayinde not opened her damn mouth to Sean, I would not be in this mess. I suppose in that sense, I was no better than Lola.

I called Margot. In the midst of all the drama somehow she'd stepped in and become my newest confidante. Who else was there for me to talk to? No one was speaking to me any longer unless one counted Ms. Thea, and she already had her suspicions. There was no way I could share something as disappointing as this. Not with a woman who'd become like a mother to me, or to a lesser degree a concerned aunt.

I spoke as soon as she picked up. Refused her first right of greeting. "He told her. Why would he tell her, Margot? Men aren't supposed to tell."

"What are you talking about?"

"You said he wouldn't tell. You said he wouldn't tell her and so long as I didn't say anything, she'd never know."

"Are we talking about the neighbor's husband?"

"Bingo."

"You're joking! He told?"

"Yes. He told."

"Hell. No. Oh my, God. How do you know?"

"Because I just damn near came to blows with his wife in the hall outside my crib."

"Hell no," she said slowly.

"Hell yes. Why would he… why… I mean, who does that? I have to live here, right next door to them. I have to share a building, a hallway, a walkway. What was he thinking?"

I tried to keep my voice low and steady, but it was becoming increasingly difficult. I paced the floor while my fingers dug craters into my scalp. I wanted to confront Sean, remind him of those unspoken rules of engagement… the rules that men everywhere followed since the beginning of time. *It didn't happen.* Admit nothing. Especially if you haven't been caught and even if you have.

I looked at the time, rushed toward the window but as expected, saw no one.

"Maybe… maybe this was his way of getting back at you. Or maybe it's his way of making certain you don't fool around with his wife again."

I walked to the drawer and pulled forth my last Swisher. I placed it between my lips and mumbled, "Yeah, maybe," before lighting it up.

I inhaled strong and rolled my eyes toward the ceiling, the smoke stinging my eyes… or maybe it was stray tears.

"Hey, maybe you can offer her another threesome to calm her down."

Margot laughed. I did not.

"You know what? I'll talk to you later."

"What? Why? Z, I'm sorry, it was just a joke."

"It wasn't funny. Look, I gotta go. I need time to think."

I disconnected the sound of her voice, attempting to halt my actions or apologize. I didn't want to hear it, wasn't in the mood for it. I stood and walked to the window again, overlooked the property below. I hoped to see Sean entering so that I could meet him halfway and cuss him out. Ask him just what the hell he meant by telling

Lola.

Tears of anger, shame, and disappointment spilled down my cheeks. I attempted to calm myself. I turned, grabbed my ashtray from the nightstand, and carried it with me to the kitchen. I opened the refrigerator and peered inside. I was out of bottled water.

I swore and slammed the door shut. I turned and leaned against the counter, spinning the ashtray around on the countertop... thinking too much while embracing my drug of choice and glaring at my tainted wall.

I couldn't stay there. Couldn't curl up in bed and flip on my television, pretending that nothing was wrong. Couldn't stand in front of a canvas with a dipped paintbrush in hand, acting as though I was going to achieve something. Couldn't just be there fronting as though nothing in my life had changed.

What did Sean's telling Lola mean for their marriage? Would it mean on-going fights that I'd contributed to... that I'd have to suffer through while I tried to sleep at night? Did it mean their working it out and my being subjected to the erogenous sounds of make up sex coming through the wall and echoing throughout my apartment?

I was supposed to have been bettering my life. I'd decided returning to school was just what I needed... a great way to get myself on track. But now I was at the bottom of a much deeper hole with dirt being piled on top of me, choking my life-force out of me.

I approached Daddy's house. I'd sit with him. Maybe these things were the penalty's for the sins I'd committed against my father. Was I not properly honoring him? Maybe since I'd moved out, I wasn't spending enough time with him.

I had an attorney. The same one as before, the one who represented me when Mom died and Dad didn't recover. She'd been a friend of Mom's when my mother was alive. But I didn't fully know what I was up against. She promised to fire with all guns but made me painfully aware that my family did have a strong case. My days home with my Dad could be numbered.

An unfamiliar car sat parked in the driveway. My pace quickened. I jogged up the steps and placed my key in the lock, but the door had been left open.

The sound of female voices traveled to my ears followed by the sound of Dad responding. I crossed the threshold, entering the living room. I saw Dad sitting in his recliner in front of the television, CNN playing. My eyes moved across the room and landed on Aunt Sybil who was seated on the sofa, her hands folded delicately on top of her purse.

Aunt Leigh stood behind Mom's chair, addressing her sister. She stopped abruptly and looked uncomfortably at me. Aunt Sybil turned, faced me, but neither spoke.

"What's going on here?" I asked.

No one answered. They looked suspiciously to one another, seemingly trying to convince the other to answer my question. I moved deeper into the room and looked again at Dad. I noticed he was holding something in his hands, looking it over.

Dad glanced up, sadness in his eyes which he tried to conceal behind a smile. "Hey there, Sweet Pea. What a pleasant surprise."

"What's that, Daddy?" I asked, pointing at the brochure he held. I walked closer to him. Still my aunts said nothing.

"Oh this? Just something your aunties want me to check out. A nice place for me and your mother to retire to."

I took it from his hand. Saw it was a brochure for a home outside of Chicago. The home they planned to put him in.

I looked to Aunt Leigh, holding the paper up in my hand so that she could see it. "What the hell is this?"

"Sweet Pea, you'd better watch your tongue talking to me like that," she scolded.

I ignored her reprimand. "What is this? Auntie Sybil, you're going to help her do this to him? You're really going to go through with this?" I asked facing my timid aunt.

Her eyes widened, and she opened her mouth to speak but said nothing.

Dad's voice cut in, "It's alright, Sweet Pea. Your aunts are just doing what they feel is best."

"Best for whom? No... no, Daddy, it's not alright. This is your home. This is where you belong."

Aunt Leigh walked to me, grabbed my arms gently, trying to coerce me to look into her eyes. "Sweet Pea, now be reasonable-"

I snatched my body from her grasp. "Don't touch me. Don't you dare touch me right now."

"Sweet Pea," Aunt Sybil called to me, saying my name as though she were amazed.

I turned to face my father. I had to stop this, had to convince him it was in his best interest to come around. "Dad, c'mon... please. They're trying to lock you away. Don't you see? They're going to take your house. Our home. Don't you get it?"

Dad smiled sadly at me. "They're only doing what's best for your mother and me."

I was livid. My chest heaved with every breath. "Stop it, Daddy! Please, just stop!"

"Sweet Pea, calm down," Daddy said.

"No! Mom's dead! She's dead! Stop pretending she's alive. They are not doing what's best for you and *Mom*, they're doing what's best for them. They're sending *you* away. *You!*"

Dad struggled to stand from his chair. "Zella Dora, don't you say such things."

"It's the truth. You know it's the truth, you gotta know it. Say it so they'll go away, Daddy. Just say it!"

Aunt Leigh grabbed my arm with much greater force than before. "Zella Dora, you stop it. What done got into you girl?"

"Don't touch me," I screamed as I jerked away. I stood heaving, daring Aunt Sybil to get involved with my eyes. I turned back to my father. "Mom is dead, say it."

Dad's eyes watered, a horrified look plastered across his face. His pleading voice wavered when he spoke, "Zella Dora, please."

"Mom is dead. Say it."

"Zella Dora, stop this now."

"Mom is dead! Say it!"

I felt the burning sting of my father's palm land hard against my cheek. Maybe it was the hot anger I was feeling or the weed I'd smoked just before I'd come to the house that encouraged me to raise my own arm and slap him back without shame or remorse.

I only yelled at him. "Wake up! She's dead... gone! Wake up!"

My breathing was sharp, quick, and labored. My eyes remained deadlocked on my father's. Sadness and disappointment entered his eyes. It was at that moment that the reality of what had just occurred hit me in waves.

I had slapped my father.

I had slapped my father.

I glanced at Aunt Sybil who still sat on the edge of the couch, a hand covering her mouth. I looked back at Aunt Leigh who appeared to be too shook up to react. I turned back to my father.

"Oh my, God," I whispered as I darted from the living room and out of the house. I abruptly stopped at the edge of the front porch. Shame and confusion washed over me like an ocean wave, knocking me from my feet.

I dropped low, kneeling down onto the concrete. Tears poured from my eyes, convulsions vibrating through my body. I cried hard, struggling to catch my breath.

I had slapped my father. What was becoming of me?

"Zella Dora Robeson," Aunt Leigh's voice was harsh, filled with anguish and disappointment. "How... could you? You put your hands on your father, how could you?"

"I'm... I'm... sorry," I struggled to speak, struggled to apologize for an action that was unforgivable. I tried to look at her through my blurry, drenched eyes. "I didn't mean... to... I'm sorry."

I felt my aunt's hand touch my back softly. She took a seat on the step, wrapped an arm around my shoulder, and pulled me to her. We were there maybe five minutes... maybe five hours, who could tell. She held me against her bosom, rocked me like she'd done when I was a small child, same as my mother had done.

"Shhh... it's gone be alright, chile. It's gone be alright."

I pulled away carefully. Wiped my eyes and smeared my leaking nose with the back of my hand. I looked at my aunt through tight, swollen eyes.

"Auntie, no. It isn't going to be alright. Don't you see? No, Dad's not altogether... he's in denial, I know but that's just it – denial. He's not insane. He's not a threat to himself. He's a lonely man that misses his wife.

"He's all I have left, and you're going to take him from me. I have no mother, no friends. Only skeletons to keep me company at night. I barely have a father now, but what's left of him I love nonetheless, and I don't want to lose him completely and that's what will happen if you send him away."

I looked away from her. I caught my remaining tears on the tips of my fingers and stared out into the street. I sniffed hard, struggling to breathe through a stopped up nose.

Aunt Leigh sat there beside me in silence. I didn't know what was going through her mind, nor did I care to speculate.

My aunt took my hand in hers, brought it to her lap, and embraced it. "Sweet Pea, look at me... look at me. I know you think I'm only doing this out of selfishness... 'cause I got something to gain – namely the house. But honey, that ain't it. That ain't it at all.

"Jacob is our baby brother, and he's sick. Understand that, he is sick, and we only wanna do what we feel is best to get him back right."

Fresh anger rose again. "But Auntie, this-"

"Chile, hush. Just stop talking and making accusations and just listen for a moment. Okay? We don't want to hurt Jacob, and we don't want to hurt you. We only want to help him get right." My aunt paused, took a deep breath before continuing, "We'll drop this case – for now. Maybe you're right, maybe sending him to a home will make the situation worse, but we can't keep sitting idly by doing nothing.

"So don't worry, Sweet Pea, we won't remove him from his home – not yet. Let's look into some treatment options. We'll figure it out. Okay?"

I looked at my aunt and nodded as fresh tears of relief streamed down my cheeks. I couldn't find my voice to thank her. I allowed her to hold me in her embrace, allowed myself to be loved.

And in my mind while repenting for my sin, I praised God for small miracles as my mother had taught me to do when I was a child.

24 *Chapitre Vingt Quatre*

The first day of classes was less than three weeks away.

I'd talked to my advisor and had my schedule worked out. She was excited about my decision. So was I. I only wished this were happening someplace else, somewhere far away from here.

I sat quietly amongst the jagged gray rocks, staring into the distance and... observing the horizon of the lake's invisible borders and imagining that I was beyond them.

It was early in the morning, and the unseasonably cool weather of the late summer was made chillier by the breeze off the water. My temperature was pleasantly balanced by the soft fleece jacket I wore, making the moment that much more relaxing, almost therapeutic.

This was one of my hiding spots. It took me out of my less-than-a-comfort zone... took me out of reach of the taunting grasp of my demons. It removed me from earshot of all the verbal conflict next door, that conflict for which I barred some brunt of responsibility.

In the time that passed since that awful day where I was nearly engaged in a physical confrontation with Lola, I hadn't heard much activity on the other side of that wall. It seemed as though either

Sean was rarely coming home or if so he'd come in late, maybe after Lola had already fallen asleep.

As for Lola, I didn't hear her leave to open shop at all in the days following our altercation. Eventually her routine continued but unless she left and returned only whenever I was away, it would appear that she only came and went for work.

On those rare occasions that they were home together, I was aware. The hostile sounds of their voices cut through the paper thin wall separating us, replacing the melodious *tap-taps* that I'd previously endured with the muffled sounds of betrayal. The occasional wave of vibrations preceded by the thunderous bang of the apartment's door would conclude some of the more heated discussions.

I never looked out the window when I heard the sound. I couldn't bear to see either again if I didn't have to. Besides, I always imagined one or the other standing in the middle of the walkway, taping a shiny steel bat against the palm of one hand while glaring up with bloody lust at my window.

Oddly Ms. Thea seemed to be especially bothered by the slow demise of the relationship next door. As far as I was concerned, she hardly knew Sean and Lola Brown outside of a landlord/tenant relationship; I didn't understand why she cared so.

Even stranger was the uncomfortable vibe I'd been receiving from her since everything fell apart. It was almost as though she knew something...like she blamed me. I'd promised Maria I would check in on her mother frequently, but I just couldn't honor my word. There was an odd sense of shame whenever I faced her despite my knowing there wasn't any way for her to know what I'd done. And so, I distanced myself from everyone and prayed for the best.

I wasn't speaking to Darwin...that, or he wasn't speaking to me. I couldn't tell which end was up. I was angry. I was disappointed. I'd maybe even go as far as to say I was envious.

He chose her over me... chose Miko over me. My ego declared him my nemesis; however, in those small private moments of solitude and honesty, I had to take accountability for my actions. I had to accept that this was no one's fault but my own. There was no shared responsibility here; the weight of this burden was mine to bear alone.

It was during those other times, the ones where I wanted to speak to him but my pride reminded me that he had yet to reach out to me, that I placed the blame solely upon him.

So I would sit on my bed, a mouthful of gum with my phone in hand, his name and number on display, and my finger hovering above the CALL button. And every time I would coward out.

I'd apologized to my father for my unbelievable outburst and shameful actions and been forgiven but that didn't make seeing him or speaking to him any easier. The most important childhood lesson I'd been taught, honor they mother and father, had gone forgotten in the midst of my rage.

The one thing that I hadn't been ashamed to do was call Ayinde. In that relationship she was the coward. A majority of my phone calls went unanswered; my voicemails were not responded to. There'd been one occasion where I'd actually gotten her on the line…gotten ready to let her have it – but I couldn't do it.

She cried at the sound of my voice, babbled on about how nobody loved her but me. She didn't acknowledge the crimes she'd committed against me, and in that moment I knew with certainty that had I mentioned it, my words would have gone ignored.

I inhaled the fresh water scent as I pulled my body to standing. It was a perfect morning and quite possibly were I Caucasian or at the very least some degree of athletic, I'd have likely gone for a run. But I wasn't. I was a Black woman who kept her shape as a consequence of living in a big city and not having a vehicle.

And so I turned to walk back toward the main street. My phone rang out vehemently demanding my attention. I fished it out of my bag, casually glancing at the face. I froze, becoming overwhelmed with suspicion. I answered cautiously.

"Yes?"

"Ay wassup, Zella?" Marcus asked from the opposite end of the line.

"I'm fine," I answered, then waited. Wasn't going to volunteer anymore than that.

"You still painting and shit?"

"Is this a social call or is there something that I can help you with?"

He hesitated a moment. "It's a call for solidarity."

That line shook me a bit. Marcus and I had no love lost between us for years. Whatever would have him calling for a truce definitely was not good.

I proceeded with my walk, though slowly... absentmindedly. "What's going on, Marcus?"

"Look man, I know you don't like me and I'll admit... I can't much stand yo' ass either, but this ain't about us." He paused and took a deep breath before continuing, "This about Snaps. You think you can come through here sometime this morning? The sooner, the better. She's here now, but I don't know how long I can keep her put."

I stopped and took a seat on a bench at the edge of the park, torn between love and hate, care and concern and a disturbing feeling of bitter anger.

The feeling of utter disappointment soaked into my pores, and I shook my head. "No... I don't think that's a good idea. I have a lot to do today. I've got errands and-"

"C'mon, Zella. She needs you, dawg."

"Yeah well, I already tried to help her and got paid back with slander and malice, and I got way too much to deal with without adding her shit to my pile."

"Damn, Zella. Can you please just put whatever it is aside? Man. I'm sure she did some foul shit, but you gotta know if I'm calling you, it's serious."

I grunted and stood, moved forward down the block. I knew she was in trouble, knew something was terribly wrong and like Marcus said, for him to call me in a manner of peace meant it had to be serious. Still, I wasn't convinced.

"Exactly what's the problem?"

"She shooting that white cross, dawg."

"Say what?"

"Crank. Speed. Crystal. She been really on one for a hot minute, then I find out she on that stuff. I thought I'd give her, y'know... some tough love to make her quit. So I told her she had to jump in thirty days. Nigga'll blaze them trees, but I ain't tootin' or shootin' up shit."

"You left her."

"I went to stay at my sis' crib to illustrate my point. It ain't a game, and I wasn't playin' around wit' her."

My blood pressure climbed. "But if you wasn't always playing games with her emotions-"

"Ay man, look... now ain't the time for all that. Seriously dawg, I know you don't think I care about her, but I do. Now ain't the time to be pointing fingers and worrying about who's to blame. I didn't fk her up, her peoples did that. I don't want her to get hurt out here or worse. I don't want her to get merc'd or OD or something.

"You supposed to be her friend, that means whatever she did while she on this shit ain't supposed to matter right now."

I thought about what Marcus was telling me. He was every bit an asshole, but he seemed truly concerned about the physical and mental health of Ayinde.

"I'm..." I blew frustrated air from my lungs and tried to clear my mind state. "I'm on my way. Stay with her."

Marcus breathed a sigh of relief. "I ain't going nowhere, just come on."

"Don't get your hopes up though. I don't know what help I can really offer. I've never dealt with anything like this before."

"She'll listen to you. Whatever you can do or say... just gotta try something."

I ended the call. Tried to think of what I could possibly do to help the situation. I'd agreed to come to her aid and offer what piece of myself I could now that it'd been confirmed that she was in fact using. That gave the situation a much greater sense of urgency and necessity. Except, I'd already attempted to get through to her, and she not only rejected me but repaid me with disloyalty.

I worked hard at suppressing my anger toward her as I headed to the nearest el stop and paid my fare.

A distressed look was ingrained on Marcus' face when he opened the door. He appeared to be relieved to see me. It was a momentous occasion, for it was the first time in years that he'd invited me into his home.

But despite the novelty of the moment, we didn't honor it with handshakes, hugs or pecks on the cheek... no significant acknowledgment of any kind. I was greeted with a simple head nod to which my response was a finger pointed in the direction of the bedroom and a questioning look. He nodded and I continued forward.

Music spilled into the hall. Aggressive music. The kind that shouldn't have been played so early in the morning. The kind best enjoyed during midday drive time and on weekends.

I tapped on the door as I pushed it open. My jaw dropped and my eyes bulged in awe as soon as my eyes landed on Ayinde. She'd cut her hair. Chopped off at least six inches. Literally chopped it. Left it mangled and uneven just past the tips of her earlobes.

She smiled when she saw me, dropped the pen she was writing with on top of a pile of scattered papers and ran to me. I was pensive... still plagued with stubborn rage but conflicted and shaken by the truth of what I was witnessing in her appearance.

She wrapped her arms around my neck and held tight. It was as though nothing negative had happened between us. She behaved as though she hadn't confessed my dirty little secret to my neighbor. It was as though she'd never gone to Darwin and lied.

I swallowed hard and prayed for the strength to forgive and the wisdom to cope. Slowly, I eased my arms around her body and hugged in return. The faint scent of alcohol stung my nostrils and dampness stung my eyes.

Satisfied, she pulled back and turned away smiling brightly. She seemed to bounce on her way back to her place on the bed where she'd been seated when I walked in.

She said nothing to me... proceeded to lift the pen from the stack and continue to write. I stood by the wall, leaning back against it with my arms folded across my breasts, trying hard to think of something to say.

I observed. She was focused intently on what she was doing. She looked almost child-like. Like a kindergartner creating a portrait of their family with a brand new set of crayons.

"What, umm....what are you working on?" I asked over the blaring music.

"Writing."

"Well, I can see that. What are you writing?"

"A book."

I stepped forward. "Writing a book about what?"

"An autobiography."

"Really?" I glanced around the room, my eyes landing on the battered silver phone sitting on the bedroom dresser. I walked slowly through the room, pacing myself. "What made you want to do that?"

Ayinde shrugged. "I don't know."

This was like pulling teeth having, this conversation. I didn't know if she was on something in that moment, but I would be more surprise if she were not. I didn't know what else to say... what to do. I eased past the dresser, casually lifting the phone and slipping it into my bag.

I stood there in the background of her fantasyland, called upon to be some sort of savior but needing to be saved from this situation myself.

Ayinde zoned out, nodding her head to the sounds of the unintelligible music and writing with fervor in illegible handwriting. She'd only moments ago been so happy that I was there, but now it seemed she was completely oblivious and indifferent to my presence.

"What... what happened to your hair?"

She merely shrugged. I squeezed my fist tight and counted backwards from ten to calm myself.

"I'm gonna... I'm gonna go to the bathroom," I advised, excusing myself unnecessarily. She didn't acknowledge me.

I turned and walked away, left the room and walked across to the facilities quickly before Marcus could stop and drill me. I twisted the door lock, then sat on the toilet top. I stuck my hand inside my bag searching around until my fingers bumped Ayinde's phone. I pulled it forth, immediately seeking out the contents of her address book and scrolling through until I found the numbers I wanted. Julie and Josiah, Ayinde's mom and brother.

I typed the digits into my own phone and saved them to the internal memory. I sat a moment longer, staring up at the blue bath towel folded neatly and hanging over the shower bar. Staring at the small white piece of lint left forgotten or unnoticed in the center of it.

Staring at nothing.

I couldn't help Ayinde, I knew I couldn't. My words wouldn't be enough. My love wasn't enough and neither was I. I would offer all that I could. That would have to be enough.

I stood, walked to the door and exited. I paused for a moment and considered re-entry into the bedroom, but it would only further break my heart and anger me simultaneously and she wouldn't benefit at all.

I turned away instead, back to the living room, heading directly to the front door. I caught a glimpse of the dazed look that crossed Marcus' face as he jumped from the sofa and rushed toward me.

"How you leaving already? You just got here, what could you

possibly have achieved in that short amount of time?"

"Nothing."

"Nothing? Why you bother to come here if you weren't gone do nothing?"

"I don't even know why I came here. Confirmation maybe. Or maybe I thought if I tried then possibly... I can't help her, Marcus, I already told you that. That's not even Day in there. I don't know who that person is, but that's not her. That's not the Day I know."

"No, it isn't, and so you just gone give up? C'mon dawg, I seriously thought you was bigger than that, for real though. That's Snaps in there. That's your homegirl. Strung out as she may be, that's still Snaps on the inside. You supposed to be ride or die, how you just gone bail now?"

"And you're supposed to be her man, but you been bailing on sis for years. I don't doubt for a second that you're the reason she's on this shit to begin with, so don't twist facts and make me the bad guy."

I was ready for a fight... ready for war. If Marcus wanted a battle, we could bang. At this point, no fear lived inside my heart and I dared him with a look to try to conjure some.

But instead, Marcus dropped his head and backed away. "I messed up. I ain't sayin' this shit my fault, but I know I gotta man up and face facts that I maybe, to a degree, contributed. But honestly, it is what it is. Can't no *I'm-sorry's* and self-reflection rewrite history.

"You know how I found my girl? I came back here today and found my girl roaming the alley in back of the building like a fkin' vagrant. Hair chopped to shreds, dirty as fk, and smelling like shit. I just don't want her to die, Z. That's it. I just don't want her to die. Not like this, man. Not like this."

Marcus turned and walked to the island. Visually disappointed. I surrendered. Waved a white flag of peace.

"Marcus, check it. I'm with you, I don't want that either, but I'm saying... I can't help her. I just can't." I held the phone toward him. "I got her mom's and little brother's numbers. I'll call them... talk to 'em and let 'em know what's going on. It's about time someone in her family stepped up and took responsibility for what they created."

Marcus staggered toward me and took the phone from my hand. Hope lit his eyes. "Call 'em, Z, please. Do what you gotta do, say what you gotta say. Just help me out, aiight. Just... just help me out."

I nodded and backed out of his apartment. I stopped short facing him. "Just keep working with her. She loves you so much. Maybe you can convince her to get help. You have more influence over her than you think. And call Kat. I think her brother or her cousin or someone was a meth addict. Maybe she can offer up some advice."

Marcus nodded. We stood for a moment... in peace, in solidarity. Feeling one another's anguish. United for a moment before I turned and walked away.

I'd rarely been so anxious to get home as I was when I left Marcus and Ayinde. I'd made an important life altering decision the moment I stepped from that building and into the morning sunshine.

I power walked from the el stop to my building. I'd made a couple phone calls on the ride home. I dialed both numbers that I'd swiped from Ayinde's phone. The first call to her mom proved a waste, and I held even greater sympathy for her. A man, who I presumed to be her stepfather, answered and in a not so polite tone insisted he had no clue who I was calling about and absolutely refused to put Ayinde's mother on the phone. He held no reservations about advising his wish that I not call there again.

I held out hope for the second call to her baby brother. I was dropped into the answering machine of Josiah and Ana Phelan who weren't home but pleasantly requested that I, the caller, leave a name, number, and a brief message that they'd promptly return later. I prayed that were true.

My third call was a very successful one to an aunt that I hadn't seen in many years yet missed terribly. An aunt who'd donned a wild, thick mane which was mostly gray and who bore eyes like mine.

I rushed into the building, landing on the second floor and knocked anxiously upon Ms. Thea's door, hoping against all hope that she was home. I could hear her inside, shuffling and fussing about how it better be the police, but I couldn't stop myself.

"Ms. Thea, it's Zella. Open up!"

Ms. Thea began scolding me before the door was fully opened. "What you want, knocking on my door like you the got-dang law. This had better be a dire emergency. 'Bout to get my blood pressure to shooting up. Last person could get that goin' like that was Greg. That old fool-"

"Ms. Thea."

"What chile?"

"I need to talk to you. It is an emergency."

"Well, what is it?"

"I need to break my lease."

"Whoa, now what was that?"

"I know, I know. It isn't ideal and on top of that you require like thirty days notice, but Ms. Thea, I need you to make an exception. I need to leave here and I need to leave here now."

Ms. Thea looked as though she'd been ambushed which in effect she had. She took my arm firmly, leading me inside and closing the door behind me. She faced me with a look of confusion meshed with concern.

"What's going on, Zella?"

I swallowed hard. I'd already determined I would do this, I would tell her everything but unfortunately as was always the case, it was much easier in theory than in reality. I walked over to her couch and took a seat. She didn't budge.

I told her. Told her everything. Told her about my part in Lola and Sean's damaged marriage.

Everything.

Told her about my *it-just-happened* occasion with Sean and near fist-to-cuffs in the hall with his bride as a result.

Everything.

Told her about my father and his refusal to accept that my mother was deceased and the riff it had caused between my family and me.

Everything, including my role in the destruction of my very best friendship. Told her about my bi-polar, meth addict girlfriend who was determined to die a slow and painful death just for the attention it got her.

Everything.

And when I was finally done, I actually felt fifty pounds lighter and more self assured than ever. Ms. Thea, on the other hand, said nothing. Only looked at me. I'd expected to see deep disappointment. Part of me anticipated seeing a smug look that said *I-knew-it-all-along*. But all I saw was shock and sadness.

"Where will you go?" she asked finally.

"Oklahoma. I have money saved, the earnings from the paintings I sold. Don't worry, I'd pay you for next month's rent of course."

Ms. Thea looked insulted at the suggestion as she waved me off. "Why Oklahoma?"

"My Aunt Claudia lives there. Mom's baby sister. I already spoke to her. She tells me to come as soon as I can. She'd be thrilled to have me. Sorta like having a little piece of her sisters back."

Ms. Thea nodded as she looked away, seemingly still digesting all she'd just learned about her tea partner. "I see."

"But Ms. Thea, I have to go now while I have the courage. My Aunt Leigh, my father's sister, is setting things up so that Dad can get some help and maybe once I'm gone... once my mother's face is gone, maybe he'll actually get better."

Ms. Thea chuckled and looked sadly back to me. "Boy, can I relate."

I feigned ignorance. "How's that?"

"Delaney, my grandbaby. Delaney's... she's um..." she stopped speaking and stood, walked to the kitchen. "I'd love to meet your father."

I shook my head vigorously. "No... no, I don't think that's such a good idea."

"Oh, I beg to differ." Ms. Thea returned. She took a seat beside me, holding in her hand a magnet framed photo of Delaney that she'd removed from the refrigerator door. "Sometimes two people share the same affliction... sometimes it can help to lean on one another."

Ms. Thea's head was down, eyes glued to the photo... her tears creating small puddles. Her hand landed on my knee as her wet eyes came to mine.

She continued to speak, "So when you plan on making this big move?"

"In a week."

"That soon, huh? Well, I'd like the opportunity to meet your daddy before you go."

"Yes, ma'am."

"I'm surely gone miss you. Why, who's gonna try out my new teas?"

"If you don't mind my saying, if you went ahead and moved back with your daughter, she could."

"Hmpf. Chile, please. Now you know don't no corporate type even mess around with nothin' but coffee. Always gotta be wired. Too many meetings, meeting planning, and meetings about the meetings they done planned. I say, too many damned meetings driving them fools crazy what got them runnin' 'round like they got a wire loose inside they head."

I laughed heartily as my hand found its way into my landlady's and squeezed.

25 *Chapitre Vingt Cinq*

I had a train to catch.

In two days I'd be leaving Chicago headed to Oklahoma City by way of Forth Worth, TX. I hadn't been there since I was a child, years before Zahrah died. Auntie Claudia much preferred to visit us in the "big city". Said she loved the opportunity to leave those "old backwoods country nigras behind." And besides, she liked that it made her neighbor Ms. Sara envious.

Ms. Thea had made me promise to take her to meet my father before I left. Said she'd help to look after him as a favor to me. Promised she'd keep Aunt Leigh from going back on her word and putting Daddy in a home. I was glad that she thought she could manage that, but she hadn't yet met my aunt, a woman who could be just as unyielding as she was.

I sat timidly in the backseat of Ria's Benz, fighting butterflies in the pit of my stomach. Nervous because I didn't know how well my father would receive two strange women in his home. Only family had been inside since Mom passed.

He knew we were coming. I'd told him my landlady wanted to meet him the day I phoned to break the news that I was moving to Oklahoma to live with Auntie Claudia for awhile. I'd also called earlier in the day to remind him. He welcomed the visit, but I was still uneasy.

That feeling being trumped by a complete anxiety about looking my father in the eye again after having had put my hands on him. It didn't matter that he'd readily accepted my profuse apology, that wasn't enough for me to shake the guilt.

Daddy was pleased that I was going away. He'd told me that he and my "mother" would miss me something awful, but they were thrilled that I would be out in the world living my own life again. He only hoped that I would eventually return to my studies in London or a university in the U.S.

Maria pulled the car into a spot in front of my parents' home and shifted gears to park. Ms. Thea bounded from her position in the front seat, her lengthy mane blowing in the breeze, green eyes sparkling, and a smile lighting her face as she moved toward the gate carrying a crock pot of her homemade seafood gumbo.

Maria and I hesitantly exited the vehicle, concerned for different reasons though united in our apprehension nonetheless. I grabbed the covered dish of lemon cake from the backseat and carried it with me, taking over the lead and heading to the door.

"Daddy!" I called out as I allowed Ms. Thea and her daughter into the home and locked up behind us.

I entered the living room as my dad walked shyly from his place in front of the television. I approached him, timidly kissing him on the cheek, quickly averting the guilt in my eyes.

"How you doing, Sweet Pea? I see you brought me company… beautiful company."

"I know you're not flirting, old man," I joked. "I'm fine, Dad. How are you feeling? Is everything okay?"

"Everything's fine, just dandy. So who are these two lovely young ladies?"

"This is who I told you about, my landlady Ms. Thea-"

Ms. Thea pushed forward, cutting me off as she stepped closer to my father. "Theodore Thompson, but you can call me Thea. And this here is my daughter, Ria–"

"Maria, sir. Maria Thompson. It's a pleasure to meet you," Maria said, extending her hand toward my father.

Daddy took Maria's hand into his. "Very nice to meet you, young lady. Thea, it's my pleasure to meet you as well. I've heard great things about you. I guess y'all already know who I am. This beautiful young woman's proud father, Jacob Robeson."

Ms. Thea blushed and adopted the appearance of a school girl. Maria's eyes rolled slightly, and I stifled a giggle.

"I'll go put this food in the kitchen," I said signaling for Maria to follow me. She took the crock pot from her mother and walked behind me.

Ms. Thea clasped her hands together loudly, startling us all. "Well, Mr. Robeson I surely hope you're hungry 'cause I done fixed up one of my finest pots of seafood gumbo, and it is quite delicious if I do say so myself, and I always do."

"Call me Jacob and I always got plenty room for good food made by a pretty lady."

My eyes met Maria's whose were just as wide and curious as my own. I knew full well Ms. Thea was flirting with my father but could he have been flirting in return?

Ms. Thea giggled. "Well Jacob, a big strong man like you needs a good home cooked meal to sustain those muscles. Come on now. Zella, show me where everything I need can be found so we can warm your daddy's belly."

I led Ms. Thea into my mother's kitchen and guided her through the use of Zahrah's things. Though she was a guest, she was still a mother and had been a wife for many years and had grown accustomed to being domestic. She insisted on the privilege of serving up our dishes, and I didn't waste my breath fighting her.

We ate the delicious meal, Ria and I observing as Ms. Thea found every opportunity to touch her hand to Daddy's arm. When lunch was done, Dad and Ria's mom retired with their slices of lemon cake to the swing on the back porch, leaving us children behind to clean the kitchen.

"So," Maria began, "Mother tells me that your father is dealing with the same thing she is."

I nodded and sighed. "Yeah... yeah, he does except his is a bit worse than hers. He actually sees my mom... thinks she's here."

"Why didn't you say anything? When I told you about my mother and Delaney...why didn't you tell me?"

I thought about the question as I dried the last dish and placed it in the rack. I turned to face Maria, tugging unconsciously at the towel in my hand.

"I don't know. It isn't something I like to share with anyone. Maybe I'm embarrassed by it, who knows. I was caught off guard by your confession... I just didn't think..." my voice trailed.

Maria smirked. "Want some cake?"

I nodded and took a seat at the table across from her.

She continued, "Mom also says you're moving away."

"Yep. Going to O.K. City to spend some time with my aunt and clear my head. Kinda nervous about it though."

"Why?"

"Scared to leave my Dad alone. My aunt – his sister – wants to put him in a home. She threatened to sue me for power of attorney over him because I refused to accept that as the only option for him. She dropped the suit though... we agreed to try getting him some counseling, but I'm afraid once I'm gone she'll renege.

"That's why your mom said she wanted to meet my Dad so urgently. Besides wanting to check him out and see if he was hot... she said maybe two people with the same affliction can help each other through."

Maria's fork paused before entering her mouth. She dropped the piece of cake back onto her plate. "She told you that? I mean, she admitted... about Delaney?"

"Well not in so many words but… yeah."

Maria's eyes watered. She leaned back into her seat, smiling and swiping at her tears. She whispered, "Praise God, praise God. Thank you Jesus, hallelujah. Praise you, Lord."

We were silent. I said nothing to interrupt Maria's moment with the Savior. Maria finally exhaled, then faced me. "Listen, Zella, I appreciate that you've been there for my mother, I do. And if there is anything you need – anything, even an attorney, do not hesitate to ask."

"Thanks, Maria."

She took my hand in hers and squeezed as we smiled at one another.

"Hey, let me get you guys home. I've got to go into the office. I have so much work to do."

"Sure thing. Let me just go pry these two apart."

Maria cleaned the crumbs from the table as I dealt with our parents. They were like old friends the way they chatted all the way from the back porch to the front door.

I hugged and kissed my Dad, told him I'd be by tomorrow to spend the day with him. He thanked me for the company and Ms. Thea for the food.

"You're very welcome, Jacob. I'm just glad you enjoyed it."

"I did, Thea. I shole did. Sure would be nice if you came by again sometime. Gets kinda lonely 'round here ever since my wife passed."

I froze. Stopped right where I was, tears springing from my eyes like wells. I swallowed hard, prayed I wasn't dreaming or hallucinating. In my mind, I begged God for this to be real.

I turned slowly to face my father. "What did you say?"

Dad exhaled. "She's dead, Zella Dora. Been six years now. Zahrah been dead for six years."

My legs nearly folded beneath me. Were Maria not by my side, I'd have certainly collapsed. Tears drenched my face. Dad pulled me up into his arms, held me close… allowing me to dry my joy on his shirt.

I felt Maria's hand gently touch my back before she spoke into my ear and asked if I wanted to stay behind. I turned my face toward hers and nodded. She smiled and walked from the porch. My eyes landed on Ms. Thea's smiling face.

"I'll be happy to come by and see you again, Jacob. No reason two people fine as us should ever hafta be alone," Ms. Thea said.

I mouthed the words, *thank you.*

Ms. Thea smiled at me and winked before waving goodbye and following her daughter to the car.

I'd completed my final transaction with Deanna. She cried at the sight of the painting I'd done of her children. The ultimate compliment. She wished me well but expressed her disappointment with seeing me go. I had a "helluva talent", her words, and she'd hoped to get me more work. She insisted she'd keep in contact with me.

I'd be boarding a train in about fourteen hours and I had yet to tell anyone besides Dad, Aunt Leigh, and Ms. Thea that I was going anywhere. I was on my way downtown to meet Darwin. I thought I should tell him in person. Fortunately, on this rare occasion, he wasn't with Miko. I couldn't take seeing her and I didn't want to have to tell him over the phone.

He was already downtown, out with friends from work… was heading home to his fiancée soon afterward. I convinced him to allow me to meet him there by saying it was urgent and ensuring I wouldn't take long. My phone rang as I emerged from the subway station. I opened it as I power-walked down the block.

"Where are you?" Darwin asked.

"I'm on my way, just give me a minute."

"Z, what's this about? I told you I wouldn't be down here all that much longer, and Miko's waiting on me to bring her something to eat."

My face warmed. "Miko, Miko, Miko! Dammit! I know you love her, I know you're marrying, her but for once, please. Can you just put me first tonight? Just tonight. Just for right now. This is important, and it won't take long. I told you, I'm on my way."

"Where are you?"

"I just exited at Chicago. I'll be down there in a minute."

"By the McDonalds?"

"Yes."

"Just stay there, I'm on my way."

"D, I'm coming."

"Zella Dora, wait there."

The line disconnected and I stopped where I was. I swiped a tear of anger and disappointment and pondered how good of an idea this was as I walked back to where I'd walked from.

My apartment was packed up. Ms. Thea and Maria assured me that they'd have the things I left behind placed in storage at Maria's house. I was ready to leave. The only loose end remaining was saying goodbye to my friend, and he was making it oh so difficult.

I sat patiently waiting on the bus stop outside the fast food restaurant, watching the cars drive by and not recognizing any. I looked over in time to see Darwin walking my way. Butterflies flitted through my stomach. He looked too handsome in his gray tailored suit. The jacket open and blowing in the wind, his tie loosened and the top button of his crisp white shirt undone. I hated myself in that moment for having lost him to another woman.

I stood and walked his way. I stopped short, Darwin continued forward and pulled me into a platonic embrace. I absorbed his scent, held it for awhile.

I was reluctant to let go, but Darwin stepped away from me. "Now what's so urgent that you couldn't tell me over the phone?"

"I'm leaving Chicago… tomorrow. I'm leaving here tomorrow."

"You're doing what?"

"I'm… I'm leaving."

"What does that mean? You're moving away?"

"Yeah."

"What are you doing that for?"

"I have to go. I need to go."

"Where are you going?"

"Oklahoma to my Aunt Claudia's."

Darwin frowned and a hand landed on his waist as the other scratched his head. He had words for me… or questions but couldn't seem to find a way to say them.

"What about Pops? Who's gonna take care of him?"

"He's fine. Better than fine, actually. He even admitted that Mom is dead… he acknowledged it. How awesome is that?"

"What? Seriously?"

I smiled and nodded. "Yeah, and he has a crush on my landlady."

"What?" Darwin laughed.

"Yep. She's promised to look in on him and her daughter who's an attorney, will help us fight Aunt Leigh if she decides to pursue her suit. So see, everything is fine."

The light left Darwin's eyes. "So much has changed, huh? Just tell me that it's not because of me that you're leaving."

"Homey, please, you ain't that fine," I lied.

I laughed. So did he.

"What happened between us, Z? Damn. How'd we let this happen to us?"

I shrugged. "We're human. Humans are stupid."

"Tomorrow, Z? Why so soon?"

"Because if I don't go now, I won't go and I need this."

Darwin nodded sadly. "I hate to see you go, but I understand you gotta do what you gotta do."

"Don't worry, I'll come back for your wedding. Just don't forget to send me an invitation to Dad's house."

"Yeah…"

"Hey, I gotta get going. I gotta stop at Dad's before I go home. I just wanted you to hear it from me… hear it in person."

"I'll drop you off."

"No, no, I'm okay. I wanna enjoy my last opportunity to ride the el… mingle with all my city folk."

"By the way, how's Ayinde handling this?"

"She doesn't know. I didn't tell her. Couldn't. Marcus called me, confirmed she's on crystal meth."

"Aww, naw."

"I'm trying to get in contact with her brother, see if her family will step up and help."

A pained look etched across Darwin's face. "Come here." He guided me into his arms and hugged me tight, his fingers digging into my scalp like old times. I closed my eyes and savored the moment before reluctantly prying away.

"I'll call you when I get to Oklahoma… let you know I made it."

Darwin nodded. "Okay. Yeah, I guess I'll get home. Miko… y'know, she's waiting for these leftovers. Can't keep her waiting too long, right?"

He chuckled.

I smiled and turned away. I jogged toward the station. "Nah, bad for business. I love you, D, and I'll hit you!" I called out as I disappeared into the subway stairwell, concealing my sadness.

I'd hardly made it halfway down when I heard my name being called. I stopped… looked back, saw Darwin standing at the top of the stairwell. He descended, coming toward me two steps at a time.

"Zella, don't go."

"D, I have to."

"I don't want you to go."

"What... why?"

"I love you, Zella Dora. I love you. I'll break off the engagement, just please stay. We can fix this... we can work this out."

"D, don't do this to me. Not now. I leave tomorrow. I *have* to leave tomorrow."

Darwin and I shared a step. He stood before me, staring into my eyes. My heart plunged into the pit of my stomach. This was what I'd wanted to hear... this was what I'd hoped for. Another chance to make things right.

In a dirty subway stairwell, littered with trash and commuters coming and going we stood staring into one another's eyes. Darwin's hand moved to my face, caressed my cheek, and I melted. He leaned into me, his lips pressing against mine and suddenly we were one... suddenly we were transformed, transported to a field of green blades of grass and warm sunshine. Colorful flowers and beautiful butterflies.

His tongue probed the inside of my mouth. His taste was sweet. His taste was love. His taste... perfection and so right. I didn't care about who would see us, didn't care about where we were. There was no talk of Miko and little Tarik and their needs. He wasn't too busy and I wasn't too afraid.

Pinned to the graffiti stained wall, I gripped him... held him close. My body was alive in a way it had never been before. I craved him... every pore of my being desired his touch. Darwin held my face in his large palms, held me firm, and gave me all of him in a kiss. My salty wetness stained his fingertips.

With his thumb, he smeared the tears from beneath my eyes. Whispered his declaration to me, "I don't want you to go, Zella Dora. I love you and I need you. I just want us to start again."

I gazed into his eyes. Found love there and tried with all within me to ignore it. "I love you, too, but I can't... I can't stay here."

"You don't have to leave. We can fix things. Whatever happened, whatever's gone wrong, it'll work out. I swear to you, baby girl. Just trust in me."

I smiled... caressed his cheek. "I have to go, D. I don't have a choice, I need this. I need some time with my mother's family to clear my head. I've made mistakes here... way too many mistakes, and I need to right things somehow and I can't do that here. Besides, you love Miko and she loves you-"

"I love you, Zella... *you*."

"I love you, too, and if it's indeed meant to be it will. I promise you, it will." I slipped from his grasp. He reached for me but stopped short of grabbing me. I moved quickly, running deeper beneath the city, escaping the sound of Darwin's pleading voice and the desires of my heart.

Ticket in hand, I boarded my train. Ayinde had no idea I was leaving her... no idea I'd broken my word to her. I couldn't tell her, didn't tell Marcus either. But I honored my word to him at least. Josiah had returned my call. He'd gotten the message moments after he and his wife returned from a short vacation away from home and he phoned me immediately.

The pair lived in Los Angeles. He told me their older sister Becca lived in the area as well. He would contact her right away, and they would make arrangements to come and pick up Jenny. That was who Ayinde really was, Jennifer Phelan.

I'd resigned from the print shop. Didn't bother to tell Chaz why. He didn't need to know all that. He just assumed it was to do art full time. He could believe that.

I hadn't the heart to tell Kat and Margot either. They'd pry... maybe even try to guilt me into sticking around for their own selfish reasons. Instead, I left a letter behind with the United States Postal Service addressed to Margot with an explanation and O.K., City contact info.

I ambled down the aisle, carrying my portfolio case filled with supplies to keep me occupied on the lengthy twenty-eight hour commute. I didn't mind the extended ride. It was an opportunity to... well, to look toward the future. Unless it involved memories of my mother and father during happier times, I was done reflecting.

I'd closed that door with the final closing of the door to my East Rogers Park apartment. I had my closure. As I packed those last stray items and prepared to leave, hearing the jingling of a woman's keys in the hall paused outside my door... I knew it was over. This would be my last time hearing those sounds, my last time holding my breath. This would be my last time fighting temptation.

She didn't knock, I knew she wouldn't. She continued on her way. But I did something that I'd avoided for some time. I went to the window, overlooked the courtyard. For reasons even I could not comprehend, I had to see her... one last time.

I stood, gazing below... watching those magnificent dreads bounce off her back. Dance along, lithe and lovely as the way I imagined she danced. As though she knew it, as though she sensed my presence, she stopped. Turned and looked up to my window, facing me – for one last time.

Our eyes met and held each other as we'd wrongfully done so many times in our recent past. Held one another until she let go. It was complete and the memory of her eyes moving from mine as my train pulled me free from the station and my bondage, let me know that I was once again... alive.

Épilogue

My father had it right all along.

Zahrah isn't dead. She lives through my brush and the fumes of acrylics. She lives in the riffs of Gillespie as he plays through my speakers. She lives in the eyes that stare back at me when I look at my reflection in the mirror.

It is over, I now know it. I loved her in life, and I know she'll forever be with me in death, for every time I speak a word or paint a picture, there she is. Every time I laugh or flash a smile, she is there.

My matriarch.

My mother.

And now after three long years, I had moved on. I was ready.

She lives through me, and I am living her dream. She must be smiling down upon my head. She must be proud.

I feel my mother's presence as I stand in the center of the gallery, preparing for my fourth showing. I am officially a professional artist. Most are only appreciated posthumously, but thanks to my connection to Deanna, I get to enjoy the fruits of my labor during my lifetime.

I stand, staring at the centerpiece for this showing. My most glorious work to date. It isn't that it is any better worked than pieces prior... no. The beauty of this piece is that it is special to me... it is a work dear to my heart. It is the completion of the final piece that my mother was working before she passed, done in her style. A portrait of her holding me in her arms when I was but six months old, expressed in yellow, red, and white only. My small face pressed to her cheek, puffed up from smiling.

I completed it a year ago. Admired the way it looked on the mantelpiece above the fireplace in my new Hyde Park home on the south side of Chicago. Now I feel it's time to let it go, time to move forward. Time to create my own legacy piece.

"You sure you want to do this?" Darwin asks as he wraps his arms around my waist as best he can, and kisses me softly on the back of my neck.

I nod. "Yeah. Yeah, I'm ready to take the bid on it. Not that I understand why someone would want a picture of me and my mom in their home. Besides, in eight months, I'll be able to paint my own version to pass down."

Darwin's hands lovingly caress my growing belly, seven months after conceiving his and my first child. Doctor's tell us it's a girl. We've agreed to name her Dahrah for my mom and Darwin's sister. Her middle name will be Simone simply because we agree it's pretty.

"I love you, Zella Dora Frazier," Darwin says, "and I'm very proud of you. You know that?"

I turn to face my husband of fifteen months, look up into his beautiful eyes. I smile because I am happy. I smile because he's mine 'til death do us part. "I love you, too."

We kiss softly before he steps away to depart. "I'm going to check on Pops and Ms. Thea. You going to be okay?"

"I'm great. Go ahead before Daddy eats all the hors d'oeuvres, and there's none left for the guests."

Darwin kisses my cheek and walks off in search of my father and his live-in girlfriend, my former landlady Ms. Theadore Thompson.

My new cell phone chimes, the new sleek, modern one that Darwin insisted I get the day we found out I was pregnant. It's a text message from Ria apologizing for running late but insisting she'll be here before it's over. I reply letting her know it's okay. I know she's working a big case and besides, she's been at every other gallery showing.

Kat and Margot will be here any minute. Now that she's divorced her dog husband, Margot's getting out a lot more. We've become really good friends, and I needed a good female friend now that Ayinde is gone.

True to his word, her brother Josiah and sister Becca indeed caught the first thing smoking from LAX to O'Hare. She went willingly… guess that was what she really needed. There is a facility at Josiah and Ana's church called The Dream Center. They have a wonderful program designed to help people like Ayinde – or rather people like Jennifer – find Christ, get their lives together, and get back on their feet.

This was three years ago and after committing two years to the program, she decided to stay on and help others in need as a drug counselor. She is well on her way to completing classes to receive her Bachelor's degree. I miss her something terrible, but she doesn't want to return to Chicago, and I can't say I blame her. It took my being with Auntie Claudia for a year in Oklahoma City to be strong enough to come back, and I wasn't nearly as damaged as she.

Once Dahrah is born, Darwin and I will go see her. I love the church that my family and I faithfully attend, but I have to experience a place that can take someone as broken as my friend Ayinde and make her whole again.

Sometimes I wonder whatever became of Lola and Sean… wonder if their marriage was able to sustain what the three of us had inflicted. At times I remember them and feel bad about what I'd done particularly now that I've found my own happiness. I can't imagine anything like what occurred in their marriage happening in mine.

I thought I saw Lola once at my second showing. There was

much more media hype surrounding it, attracting more guests than my first one. Our eyes connected and held on briefly before Darwin distracted my attention. When I looked again, she was gone.

I place my hand to my stomach and caress gently Dahrah's home as I walk closer to Mom's painting, my free hand landing on her cheek and I hope that she feels me.

I know now that Dad was right... he'd been right all along. Mom never left us and she never will.

She will forever live in me.

She will forever live through me.

She will forever live through her grandchildren.

I am Zella Dora Frazier... and this is my existence.

And I'm loving every minute of it!

Acknowledgements

From the top of the dome... The story you just read is a work of fiction.

I know some of you probably thought some aspects of this story were – dare I say... odd, from the prelude to maybe even the main characters name. Maybe you're wondering what the inspiration for this book is but I can't tell you that. It isn't that it's such a big secret... it's just that, well... I don't know.

I remember where I was when I started this tale a coule years ago. I was living in Chicago at the time. I'd gotten an apartment about a block over from my old building in East Rogers Park and was happily sharing it with my spiritual sis MJ and my niecey Ameena (aka The Beenie Baby). I think the spark was born after a dinner party I had that ended with my guests fawning over these old flicks of me taken during the days and months after my infamous 2004 Bikini Krunch Diet.

Originally this was meant to be an erotic tale. I'd only gotten as far as the prelude before I apparently got bored and ditched the idea. Two years later and two-thousand miles west of The Chi, while unpacking a bin in my new home in Los Angeles, I came across a legal pad and a prelude. I read it while sitting in the passenger's seat of my then husband's Firebird and thought it was the most beautifully written work I'd ever done and I didn't want to waste it.

I don't know if I exactly hit my mark but I enjoyed learning Zella Dora and spending those six months following with her. This was the first story I told without too much forethought and planning. I allowed the character to guide me through and I'm happy that I did.

My thanks have to first go up to God and Christ for all the blessings bestowed upon me, including the ones that I am not yet privy too... before they come down to pay respects to my girl and impromptu editor, Shon Bacon. We've never met nor ever heard the sound of each other's voice, but I have love and gratitude that will never die.

I extend thanks to Glorius L. Martin and my sunn Storm Ariane McKee, both of whom I am so proud of. My sis Trina and homegirl Lemetric for at least trying to proof this for me. Thanks MJ, Anjel, Shawn, Shon, and B-Love for the pre-screening. Thanks to the Johnson's, Martin's, Green's, Brown's, Mansfield's, Williams', Beasley's and Mr. Brewington, simply for being fam.

Special thanks to Mark Vukelich, Robin Hickman, and Kardel Arnett for looking out for us and going above what's expected and required.

And to all that like me, love me, support me, bought a book, referred the books, forwarded emails, wrote a review, mentioned my name, said a little prayer for me, gave encouragement, gave advice, opened their home, gave me honest criticism, and whatever else... thanks!!

Love always,
Miki Starr

www.ingramcontent.com/pod-product-compliance
Lightning Source LLC
Chambersburg PA
CBHW030400180626
46812CB00005B/1860